# Captive

# Captive

A NOVEL

Megan Lisa Jones

MLJ Publishing

All MLJ Publishing titles, imprints, and distributed lines are available at special quantity discounts for bulk purchases for sales promotion, premiums, fund-raising, educational, or institutional use.

Special book excerpts or customized printings can also be created to fit specific needs. For details, write or contact the office of MLJ Publishing at:

MLJ Publishing
Megan Lisa Jones
PO BOX 49336
Los Angeles, CA 90049
www.meganlisajones.com

2 3 4 5 6 7 8 9 10

Published by MLJ Publishing


ISBN-10: 0-968617-6-3
ISBN-13: 978-0-9768617-6-8

Printed in the United States

# Captive

## Megan Lisa Jones

Megan Lisa Jones is a lawyer and investment banker who works primarily with companies in high growth, evolving or disrupted industries. A child of immigrants, she grew up in California. Ms. Jones now lives near the beach in Santa Monica with her two children. An avid reader and traveler, she writes about issues which capture her attention and imagination.

To my two kids with love,

Lauren and Jason.

The children of Adam are limbs of one another, created from a single substance. When one limb suffers misfortune, the others cannot be at rest. You who do not suffer the pain of others do not deserve to be called human.

-- Sa'adi (Persian poet)

Stone Walls doe not a prison make, Nor Iron bars a Cage; Mindes innocent and quiet take That for a Hermitage; If I have freedome in my Love, And in my soule am free; Angels alone that sore above, Injoy such Liberty.

-- Richard Lovelace

# CHAPTER ONE - REBELLION

## LONDON

The hand didn't belong on his arm. Khalil squirmed, trying to wiggle free. The fingers just squeezed tighter until the knuckles bulged. Khalil turned and met the eyes of a man almost his own height. The man's lower lip was firm, and his round eyes protruded. He looked like the cook in a mural on an English manor wall. Khalil couldn't help feeling like the fish painted on a platter before him.

His eyes shifted back to the hand. It was ghostly white and softly sprinkled with light brown hair. The man was in uniform, a proper bobby complete with billy club and handcuffs.

Out of the corner of his eye Khalil noticed a rubbish bin. He lunged toward it, pulling himself free long enough to rest his hand on its metal edge. The contents of his fist slipped free and fell in with the crumpled newspapers and coffee cups. One lone Cadbury Flake lay discarded, half eaten and crumbling in its vibrant yellow and purple wrapper.

Khalil didn't run. No point. He hadn't done anything visibly wrong – the bobby couldn't arrest him for walking down a crowded street. His crimes were protected by the softer laws that allowed for freedom of speech, religion and the right to associate with whomever he chose. Had the police in his own country stopped him he would be bleeding by now. But he wasn't in his own country.

"ID?" The tone was clipped, the accent lower class British, making the words undecipherable. Khalil moved slowly; didn't want the guy to turn violent, while he scanned the area. Just off Piccadilly Circus, the street bustled with the morning rush. It was almost opening time for the stores, though a number of breakfast places were already turning a crowd. A short, lumpy man shifted against a wall, his back brushing up against the whitewashed, barely crumbling building. So the bobby had backup. Why was that? They couldn't have fingered him in advance, could they? He had only just arrived in London, and had been avoiding the country for the past two years. Since the last bomb went off. Nonetheless Khalil couldn't banish doubt – much as its appearance could potentially be a downfall.

He pulled his passport out of his pocket and handed it over. The impatient officer was now squinting in what passed for sun in this city. Khalil didn't need to even glance at it – he had already memorized the name, birthdate, country of issuance and immigration stamps. His eyes were better utilized in scoping out the area.

The bobby leafed slowly through the pages, fingering each one as he visibly struggled to read.

"When'd you arrive? Oh, here it is." The bobby spoke, then continued to page through the passport.

Khalil turned from him. The ice cream shop was still closed, though a clerk could be seen through the glass. She didn't seem to be in any hurry as she arranged things behind the counter. First, she stacked cups. Then she opened a box of cones and began to transfer them one by one onto a tower that seemed shaky at best. Four wire tables out front were still dripping from an earlier rain. The clerk would probably come outside to wipe them down – would she be working the day of the bomb?

"How long will this take?" Khalil was getting impatient. He wasn't supposed to be stopped like this. He had wanted to see the area himself and not just rely on his brothers. The bomb would have to go off at just the right spot, between the ice cream shop and the adjoining tube entrance. Khalil noticed that passersby were staring at him, as if a dark man in London was still an oddity.

The bobby ignored him.

Khalil watched a double-decker bus drive by. It was a distinctive red and full of tourists. Glancing at the sky, he wondered how long the inevitable rain would wait before falling on their expensive cameras and unsheltered heads. Western society in all of its absurdity personified yet to what matter?

"Excuse me, kind sir, I don't mean to be difficult. Can you please explain the problem? I am not from your country and do not understand what is happening." In Algeria, explanations were mute. The process was simple: kicks, punches, a lot of blood and then finally a bullet or a bribe to freedom.

The bobby ignored him. Again. He was now looking back and forth between the passport picture and Khalil. Of course they were identical.

"Look, I am in a hurry. If you have a reason for stopping me, fine. If not, I would like to go." Khalil held his voice firm, but kept it non-confrontational. He wouldn't win an argument since he wasn't the one with the key to a jail cell.

"I'm taking you to the station." The bobby didn't look him in the eye, his gaze fixed on the ground.

"Are you arresting me?" Khalil let his shock show.

"Not yet. I don't like you, all you people coming here and causing problems. This country used to be safe, you know?" The bobby's face had turned red. "I want to ask you some questions."

"Kind sir, please. I was just looking for the Virgin Megastore. I am not causing problems. I am a bit lost. Perhaps if you could just point me in the right way…." How could he get taken in for questioning when he had merely been walking down a crowded street? This type of thing didn't happen here. Khalil's panic grabbed him much as he tried to will it away. Captured.

"I said I want to take you in for questioning. Hands behind your back." The bobby had pulled out his handcuffs.

"I thought you weren't arresting me." By now a few teenage boys had clustered outside the tube station, drinking beer, the morning coffee of unemployed youth. The group would probably kick the crap out of him if the bobby didn't follow through with the arrest.

"I don't like you." With that the bobby reached out, silver handcuffs gleaming and open. The pasty fingers with their brown hairs touched Khalil for the second time. This time he wouldn't escape them.

Bombs were going off around the world almost daily now. Arresting him wouldn't be enough to stop this one. Still, a doubt lingered – British authorities turned a blind eye with predictable regularity – unless they had specific intelligence. Had someone betrayed him?

# || CHAPTER TWO - MIRRORS

## PALO ALTO

George Harris yawned as he tried to read the profile in front of him. The duties we assume in life get both easier and yet more burdensome as they become more familiar. Standard, and predictable. Suspected terrorist. Algerian. GSPC, or the Salafist Group for Preaching and Combat (the acronym matched the Frenchified version of the name, as befit a rebel group in a formerly French Colony), now part of Al Qaeda. A particularly brutal and fundamentalist Algerian group known for killing any one not Muslim, or not Muslim enough. Once the *Herald Tribune* began ignoring their routine massacres in Algeria the group had hitched itself onto on to the larger organization. A bomb in Africa was only sexy if it had an international brand attached.

Late-thirties. Male. Hostile, full of hatred, uncooperative and stupid. Yes...stupid, easily influenced, a moron. Student of the Koran. Living as if it were still the middle ages, when Islam ruled supreme.

Spent some time in an American University? That meant he could rant in English as well as Arabic.

The kids at Stanford channeled their youthful energy into start-ups. In the Muslim world, the boys turned to jihad and death instead. In both cases the indoctrination was the same – extreme – and otherwise known as brainwashing.

The dim lighting from his lamps was intimate and lent shadows to the room's corners. George couldn't bear the harsh intensity of overhead lights so had installed dimmers throughout the house. He perched on the edge of his ergonometric chair, papers littering his carved mahogany desk.

The file. George rubbed his tired eyes as he continued to read, searching for something that would set this man apart. Philosophy major. That was something unusual and arresting. Terrorists typically preferred rules based disciplines – such as engineering or math. Accordingly, they looked for answers to their life in rules-based Islamic fundamentalism. The teachings and thought process both adopted structure absolutely.

His glasses slipped, and he pushed them back up his nose.

The man's progression was predictable for his age group but starting to disappear. Terrorism wasn't conducive to a long life. Fighting in Afghanistan, Bosnia and even Iraq. Stays in the Sudan and Chechnya. Algiers, London, Paris. Then disappearing from the map until he appears again in London, after likely spending time in a training camp in a miserable and failing third world country. The sudden change signaled that something bad was about to happen – shaving off a beard, returning from a foreign land, increasing cell phone calls.

Which led to another clue – a number programmed into Khalil's cell phone, for a now cancelled cell phone in Los Angeles. Untraceable. Why Los Angeles? It seemed too obvious – since Khalil had attended college years ago in Southern California. Was it just a red herring; fake and distracting? Or, had it been a handoff – meant to pass the number from one person to the next?

George felt exhaustion in every bone of his not so young body. But he didn't have time for weakness because his work was too important – so he kept up the intensity. Since we herd our people into shopping malls and office buildings, or some version of both at the same time, we need brilliant but idealistic types willing to question suspected terrorists. Until some judge let the detainee out of jail on some 'rights' violation. The government should have kept this one overseas with the rest of them, where our laws couldn't protect him.

George sipped his water. It was lukewarm, the ice having melted hours ago. He could refresh it, but why bother? More pressing, the file before him was flimsy, and a bit too pat. It wasn't blacked out, or conspicuously short; tricks his superiors played. Information could be sparse in national security because each agency controlled its own information. All appeared proper, but it was hollow, containing only the echoes of the man he was to interrogate.

The days had become long, the nights longer. George looked around his study; it was both an office and a library. He was, after all, a professor, another idealistic profession and one he was eager to rejoin. But he'd written that paper on the psychology of the terrorist, and won an award for it. That had lead to a visit, interview and security check courtesy of the CIA. They thought he was some genius, so they gave him a job in secret interrogations (on leave from the Stanford – three years now). Best of all, he got the tough cases – thc guys who hadn't cracked even, sometimes, after torture. George also got the honor of serving his country.

It was late. The clock, nearly lost among a stack of books, showed a time of 2:13 A.M. Thank goodness Karen was sleeping. He could picture her lying in the bedroom nearby. Her wispy blonde hair spread on white sheets – she would only sleep on white sheets. She was smart, and had chosen to be a literature professor – Western literature.

George took off his glasses, rubbed his eyes, then put them back on. He was nothing if not a good soldier. Discipline, once learned, never leaves you.

But his mind continued to battle his will. These terrorists, no, suspected terrorists (let's not forget their rights), weren't interesting anymore, if they ever had been. He was hardened now, and worn down. Why shouldn't he be? He worked his ass off, did his research, wrote his reports, and nobody cared. Nobody.

George fingered a paperweight. It was more of a rock really, but it had been on his desk for many years, since his son – then very young – had painted it and presented it to him for Father's Day. A paperweight forever more.

At the end of the year he would tender his resignation - again. His long journey was ending and he would rejoin the real world. Doing good had once seemed achievable, desirable and noble. But the process of getting there ate you up. It was a slow rot that left you hardened and indifferent. All of the passion had left his body, oozing out of him each time he questioned someone who had no right to live, someone full of hatred and murderous intentions. Profiling these fundamentalist terrorists was ultimately a waste of his intellect – better left to men with more energy and stronger fists. The truth was that society only wanted the scum to disappear, perhaps onto an electric chair or, for the more liberally minded, into a cozy and humane jail cell somewhere.

He turned back to the file, and began to read. The sharp black letters seemed harsh against the white paper. He willed himself to concentrate, to force the rush of his old enthusiasm to fill his body with restlessness and desire. He had to create the feeling of a hunt. For what else is intelligence work but a hunt for information that seeks to allude?

George jumped, his head whipping around as he heard a noise. Instantly he relaxed, it was Karen. She looked annoyed, as she was most of the time these days. Well, annoyed or indifferent. Or, was George just over reacting? That, he knew, would be her never ending comment.

"George, please come to bed. It's so late. You aren't studying for a final." Her voice was just above a whisper. She never was good at being wakened – sleep deprivation didn't agree with her.

"In a few minutes, Honey." The words sounded awkward as he spoke them. Their emotional connection these days was as empty as his file. The words were there but the meaning was missing.

The light went off as Karen flipped the switch. "Now, George. Someone has to keep you healthy, even if you won't help."

People were dying and she wanted him to sleep. Suddenly he knew why he did it; thankless, frustrating and hard as the work was. His enemies' God brought death and destruction. George's God brought trials and tribulations – but also redemption. He couldn't fix the world, but he could save a person here and there.

George bit back his words. A fight this time of night would do no good. The file would have to sit unread. Even if people died as a result. He stood up, wincing as pain shot through his back. Then, George followed her to bed.

## LOS ANGELES

Omar watched the girl in front of him. Omar watched her because he wasn't really listening as she prattled on, content in her simple-minded monologue. She was typical of the campus girls. Lean, in an athletic way. Burnished brown hair and light hazel eyes – the irises speckled gently with mahogany. Her short skirt, composed of a few ruffles, showed off her legs and exposed her for the slut she was. Ah, Americana. Her t-shirt hugged her breasts, highlighting her erect nipples.

"Well, we spent yesterday at the beach and blew off our classes," came out of lips glistening with glitter.

For a second he imagined her naked in front of him – as he knew she would be shortly. Her legs sprawled open, the ever so ripe breasts exposed. Then his mind went back to where it started. If he attached a wire to a digital clock, would that be more precise than an old-fashioned dial clock? How did each timepiece click to the second that formed a new minute? Should he trust that a bomber would detonate the bomb on time or should he not disclose that a suicide mission was actually taking place? Now that Khalil had disappeared, Omar should assume leadership. He was smart enough. True, the plan was complex – hence Khalil's involvement - so much faith in the seasoned fighter. But at twenty-four Omar was ready to assume a leadership role. The basic details were already set anyway. Only the execution remained. That he could do.

Omar, of course, was fully conscious of the concerns within his organization. The plot was too important to trust a rookie. Surveillance was more sophisticated than it used to be. Everything was just that much harder. And on. But, all excuses aside, whom else did they really have? Eventually they may try to replace Khalil – but not until Omar had used the opportunity to step boldly into Khalil's shoes. After all, stripped down to its basic elements the plot was only a few bombs. Bombs laced with sarin. His own background was crucial. How many brilliant scientists could a terrorist organization sneak into the United States? And yet, sarin was only a few ingredients mixed so elegantly together. Deadly to the chemist if done incorrectly.

"So, then, I thought we could go to the party together on Saturday night."

Omar flashed his perfect smile. The celebrity dentist in Century City. He knew that his white teeth were dramatic, set off as they were by the deep richness of his dark skin. He looked down at himself, pleased at what he saw. The daily laps in his family's pool in Riyadh had formed a muscular physique. His ripped jeans and tailored t-shirt had been his uniform since college in Hamburg. No point in hiding any of his assets.

Completing his PhD. in chemical engineering would take years. Except he had no intention of finishing. Omar glanced around the broad expanse of UCLA's lawn, with its steep steps heading up the hill. The campus was a far cry from the Saudi desert of his youth.

Omar put his arm around the girl standing before him, glad that she had finally shut up. He caressed her stomach, feeling the downy hair that grew across it. She reminded him of horseflesh, warm and firm.

"Allah has sent you here to be my angel."

Life was so simple if you just followed the rules. Everything clicked into place. Mix methylphosphonyl difluoride with a blend of isopropyl alcohol and inosproplyl amine and you get sarin. Add gunpowder and 'boom'. Everything nearby was obliterated. And life was certainly no more complicated when dealing with a woman.

"You are so beautiful, my dear." Omar heard his voice lilting, wafting through the warm Southern California air. The scent of perfume mingled with healthy sweat as he drew her just a little bit closer, enjoying the heat of skin through his thin shirt.

Ah, the sins of the flesh. He loved the freedom he had here to indulge himself. His sins would all be washed away when he died a martyr's death.

## EGYPT

Would they make him eat dirt?

The footsteps hitting the cold concrete of the hallway were unmistakable in their direction and would clearly bring no good. The air burned around him, without the promise of escape. The shadowy cell didn't even have a window cut into one of its four flimsy plastered walls. He was alone, until they came to torture him again. Or, perhaps even worse, to talk.

Khalil felt sweat beading on his forehead. It dripped into the open cut still bleeding on his cheek. The resulting salty sting felt bitter. He shifted his body on the rags that served as a bed, feeling the dull ache. Rubbing his wrists he marveled at the thick scabs that optimistically sprouted after each successive set of ropes was cut free. At least the body could sometimes heal.

The footsteps continued their even pace. His feet were crusted with mud. The door was speckled with dried blood. Dirt clumped up in the room's corners, forming a breeding ground for beetles and worms. The filth of the cell was emblematic of their souls.

He concentrated, trying once again to focus his fragmented mind. He needed strength. Khalil pictured his brother and his cousin as they walked away from him for the last time. Only a few hours later their bodies would be twisted, mangled, dead. Their blood had pooled together, resting on top of a hot earth which refused to drink it in. His dead cousin's mouth had been covered with dirt, as he lay prone in the hot sands of their aching homeland. The image still sent shudders through him whenever he tried to sleep. Now, when they let him sleep.

He would avenge the deaths of Hassan and Josef. No matter what these infidels did to him. Pain was his friend. Besides, it wasn't the pain that got to him. That shooting sensation of loosing your mind. No, he was trained to resist this sort of ordeal. Rather, it was the desperate attempts to remember his prayers, so beloved and his only source of strength in this world. How could he forget something that was such a part of his soul? Sometimes, tired, beaten, he did. No, he almost did. They hadn't won such a victory yet. Nor would they. Allah was testing him, quite simply because he was chosen. And, he would continue doing Allah's work.

Still, the steps, getting ever closer. The hallway wasn't long enough.

Allahu Akbar, he repeated until he could almost taste the afterlife. Dates and honey. Meat, roasted and fragrant as it dissolved in his mouth. The soft flesh of women as they rubbed up against him. Allah had shown him little mercy in this world. That would have to come later.

The heavy door opened. Two Americans entered the room, moving quickly toward him. With these people it was always haste. They had no time for Allah. Theirs was an evil world, full of temptation and sin.

"We're back to chat, Khalil." The tall one had red hair, light skin, freckles and brown eyes. His voice had a harsh twang. He wore a military uniform – a generic interrogator and a standard southern hick. He sat down at the excuse for a table.

The shorter, heavier one gestured to Khalil. "Come on and sit." His tone was fierce, as always. Khalil tried to collect himself. The man's clunky black boot hit his right shin, sending him crashing to the floor. Khalil's elbow broke the fall but sliced open. He stared down at the blood. A fly landed in one of the crimson drops.

"You can't do that. You know you can't do that, you cocksucker," Big Red sounded indignant. He must have seen much worse than a simple kick to the shin. Did the Americans really believe that the good cop/bad strategy would work?

"Shut up, you pussy." The other one said. Khalil was still staring down as a beetle joined the fly. He felt the air move just before a hand yanked him up by shirt and hair, shoving him into a splintering chair.

Dimly, Khalil was aware of his tormentors as they questioned him. The room echoed as they spoke. Not a word registered. He tried to focus on a spider, as it crawled down a bleak wall. He was frightened. His interrogators no longer seemed real and present. They had worn him away, as they expected to do.

And he hated them, despised them. His feelings were so intense they almost dissipated the pain. But not quite. He cursed himself for his weakness. Allah is great, Allah is good, he chanted.

"Tell us why you were in London, Khalil." The short one's blue eyes were small, while his thin lips twisted up. The veins splintered in a web of blue.

He smelled their oppressive sweat and felt the heat coming off their bodies. They carried a pungent, revolting stench, in spite of their detergents, deodorants and frequent showers. No matter what they did, the odor of the damned couldn't be rinsed off.

He had long ago abandoned his body to the stifling heat that made his scabs itch. Or perhaps the itch came from the bugs, feeding from his wounds as he tried to sleep.

"I told you, just visiting friends. I lived there eight years ago." Khalil's voice was soft, non-threatening. The words were rote, the story created long ago and much repeated.

He took a small comfort in knowing that his eyes wouldn't focus.

He used to find a point upon which to center his gaze during the torture; an attempt to concentrate elsewhere. He no longer needed to. Lack of sleep, the omnipresent bright lights and constant barrages had worked their charms. He was disoriented, completely, irrevocably.

But their mistake was that he was no longer a part of this world. Nor did he desire to be. That wish had died with his brother. Didn't he deserve to suffer? Why hadn't he gone with Hassan and Josef that day? Perhaps had he done so they wouldn't have died. And he wouldn't have felt this need to redeem himself.

One of the holographic men said something to him, infringing into Khalil's memories. "Not good enough, Khalil. We told you before – you're on a watch list. We know you have a lot to hide. Help us. For your own good." Too many questions. He stared at Big Red, trying to concentrate on his face.

But Khalil could only see the spider. He stood, and limped away. He reached the wall, everything was so close together: his rags, the toilet hole, the table with the interrogators and three chairs.

He watched the spider for a minute and considered crushing it. He also thought about using the grime of the cell to wash himself before praying. But Khalil had no need for a grand gesture. No reason to anger his interrogators and make the mission personal.

Behind him the short, fat one was speaking again. "Look you fucker, get back over here, we're talking to you."

Khalil ignored him and walked to the sink. After washing himself, he faced Qiblah and began to pray. This time the familiar verses came. Khalil felt the surge of strength that comes when you've thrown an opponent off guard and gained control. If the Americans came during prayer time, they would have to wait.

He heard a movement behind him. The piss hit Khalil's hair as he touched his forehead to the ground. The warm liquid soaked into his jumpsuit, and he heard the interrogator zip up his pants. So much for Khalil's benediction.

## SAN FRANCISCO

George pulled up to the prison. It was a squat two-story building; predictably it had bars on its windows. All possible sources of grace had been ignored during its design and construction. The murky color of its walls seemed unnatural when contrasted with a few grand old trees that sheltered the building. The trees had likely been saved by the crazy environmentalists in government. Their branches swayed gently, as if warning George not to enter the building.

Inside this new jail were housed an indeterminate number of enemy combatants, as they were officially known, as well as a random terrorist or two. He was here for interrogation number one with the prisoner otherwise identified as detainee 182.

George parked his car in one of the few empty spots. The parking area wasn't small, but the prisoners inside had triggered a mass wave of interested visits – many people wanting to make a career out of tormenting the captives. As a result, George noted many cars lined up politely – most with either government plates or some sort of rental car identifier.

George eased himself out of his car – a recent model BMW sedan.

A Brahman among the untouchables. He looked warily at the building plopped before him – tired from not sleeping the night before. What could motivate a respected psychologist and tenured professor to become an expert on the terrorist mind? Insanity. He headed up the few clunky stairs leading to the prison. Ah, to spend each day in a room with a murderer. He could feel the apprehension, the tension in his body as he made his way up the stairs. Yet if he didn't own the responsibility of doing these interrogations–for which he had a real talent – who would?

The heavy wooden door creaked as he opened it. The sound splintered down his spine. He entered a waiting room. He saw a corridor behind a barred door slightly to his right. A few empty chairs and a desk were the only furniture. The lighting was murky.

Whose brilliant idea had it been to bring these men to the United States? How long before some lawyer caught wind of their presence – held like animals in a zoo? The newspapers couldn't seem to get enough of the related issues.

George felt dust settling on his hunter green polo shirt as he walked in the room. The place looked dirty. A musty old smell had already settled in, a concoction of sweat, stagnant air and mold. He imagined his shirt turning a swampy color by the time he left, as if a toxic atmosphere could leach all life and vitality out. Well, okay, he comforted himself, so the government wasn't wasting money on cleaning crews. George would do his job and leave. But he would do it well.

He walked up to the desk, behind which a soldier sat stiffly. He looked so young.

"Hello, sir." The boy sounded like a stereotypical soldier from a movie, with that overly enunciated formality. He had a standard issue buzz cut and a neatly pressed uniform. He was compact and swarthy, but still managed to look painfully clean cut. His only feature which seemed out of place was one crossed eye. Paranoid, George imagined that it gave the recruit a sinister air. George admitted that if he drove himself crazy he would have only himself to blame.

"George Harris, here to interrogate detainee 182."

The soldier busily started working; the formalities required for interrogating prisoners were a serious responsibility. George stared out the window, afraid to let his eyes wander too much around the sparsely furnished and gloomy interior. Attitude, attitude makes all the difference, he reminded himself.

"You the shrink?" A harsh voice echoed unexpectedly behind George, causing him to jump. He hadn't heard the guard coming from the hallway behind the barred door. Turning slightly, George studied the burly and spookily smiling prison guard. Man, he moved quietly for someone with such bulk. George felt like cringing, the whole reality of the man felt unpleasant but was probably just projection. Still, to be ambushed. Next, to be called a "shrink". He tried to smile. This man may have important information about his prisoner. George nodded.

"Come with me. I'm Sean." The man's booming voice was unnecessary for the size of the room. George didn't like men such as Sean: loud, brash and big. But it wasn't so much the outer appearance that made him uneasy. Having been a slight child who read too much George could instinctively recognize a bully. Years of psychological education and practical training had made him able to explain such men and to articulate their inner neurosis. He still didn't like them and that was his weakness.

So George meekly followed his new guide. In his experience, it was easier to let a prison guard dominate. Especially one like this. Their job created a need to control. Perhaps they chose the job from an obsessive yearning to do so. He eyed Sean's large, square hands, following them as they turned into brawny arms and solid shoulders.

"So why does this terrorist need a shrink?" Sean interrupted George's thoughts. "Lock'em up and throw away the key is what I say."

"Why does he need a lawyer?" George couldn't resist, years in academia had formed a strong habit of asking questions, even impertinent ones. He wasn't so different from the prison guard. We do become our work, he thought, only half pleased with his own over-intellectualism.

"Yeah, well, I never really understood that one myself" Sean said.

Of course not. The man had probably never even read a book in his life. Why read a book when you can read a Nascar magazine? Idiot.

The man persisted. "What you gonna do, make him feel bad for killing. I've known a lot of murderers. They don't care. I can promise you that."

"Where did they get you?" George asked. Was this the army or Leavenworth?

'I was a prison guard before I enlisted. I thought they were going to send me to Iraq to kill those Arabs. But I was a prison guard before they sent me here, so they sent me here."

"Indeed. Tough break." George kept his voice controlled and businesslike. Time to move on. "Tell me about detainee 182." George tried to shift his voice and convey camaraderie. It was a tough leap.

"You know, if they're violent, they're violent." Sean said. "What does he need a shrink for? My old man used to beat the crap out of me. He never stopped. Can't stop those like that. But, you know, I myself came out fine. It's inborn."

"Yes, look how well you turned out." George replied. Poor you, not allowed to kill Arabs. George felt remorse. Had he gone too far? You could never tell how a moron would handle abuse.

The man kept walking. George reassured himself. Physical abuse rarely happens without verbal abuse. And Sean had just admitted that his father used to beat him. This man was probably used to sarcasm, or worse. He decided to respond to the original question.

"I'm not here to provide therapy," George replied. "I'm mainly a psychologist. But I'm also an interrogator. I came up with some theories about how terrorists are made. Not all people from similar dysfunctional backgrounds become terrorists, gang members or criminals." George studied the man's face for a glimmer of interest. Sean's expression was somewhat vacant. George continued his explanation anyway. He slowed down his pace, convinced they would be at his prisoner's cell at any moment. The prison wasn't that big. If he could get this man on his side it might pay off with information in the long run.

George almost tripped as they turned a corner. Was the floor uneven?

"I wondered why some men from Islamic countries become terrorists while so many don't." George continued speaking. "I noticed some of the factors common to their societies. Fathers are often absent due to how patriarchical and traditional the societies are – children are the mothers' work. Indeed there is a lack of a strong father figure in the life of Islamists extending from Mohammed all the way to Osama Bin Laden."

The guard's face remained a blank slate. Perhaps he just didn't recognize the names. George almost tripped again. He decided to continue his explanation.

"There are a few societal influences such as little focus on education, lack of jobs and demographics which lead to a large number of frustrated young men. There is no fairness, even the authorities are corrupt." Now George could feel the excitement building in his body, the pressure from discussing a topic about which he felt so passionately. Yes, he reluctantly admitted, I do love some of this crazy stuff I do. The guard still didn't look interested. George continued anyway, perhaps more for himself than for any other reason. Besides, he was a professor and used to lecturing.

"Violence is prevalent within the family such as in honor killing. It's also very much a part of society due to the repressive tactics of most of the current governments in Islamic states. A man may beat his wife and children; a government kills a dissenter. Life doesn't have the sanctity it does here. Throw some of these men into our more open society and they can't cope." George paused, still hoping to note some interest.

Light glared in a flash, hitting George's eyes and blinding him. For the first time George noticed small windows periodically piercing the hallway walls.

"Stupid Ah-rabs." The man drawled. George noticed the sweat

stains developing under the guard's arms, the slow shuffle of his bulky walk. He felt disgust. You call them stupid, he felt like asking the moron, what about you? The dingy hallway felt claustrophobic and he could hear his own footsteps echoing on the cheap milk-colored linoleum floor.

Suddenly George felt ashamed. Who knew what kind of life this man had lived. Beaten by his father, probably grew up not so bright, not a lot of advantages. Now he chose a violent job dealing with the scum of our modern society. Thinking he was escaping that to go kill – but also to become a hero, to improve himself in his own feeble mind, only to end up right where he started. Poor jerk probably drank a six-pack a night after he got off from work. Had he escaped his violent childhood at all, was George wrong? Had he even tried? George couldn't resist.

"So, have you had to hit the prisoners often?" George asked and watched pain flash across Sean's face.

XXXXX

Footsteps. Again.

A new prison, a new cell. Khalil looked around him. The dirt was different, yet really still the same after all. He sighed deeply, and focused on a spot in the upper corner, near the ceiling. Best to find strength in a dot – helped his concentration. Hopefully, Allah would once again give him an opportunity to prove his worth. Didn't these people know that their humiliations, and even blows, were welcome? Each time they tormented him he was able to impress Allah, and his brother, with the strength of his faith. He fingered his Koran – well memorized but still a comforting presence.

Khalil suddenly felt angry. This ordeal had lasted long enough. He was on their turf now, which meant that he had rights. The horrid jailor, Sean, had told him where he was. California, just south of San Francisco. The United States of America. They couldn't hold him forever. He had the right to a lawyer, to be charged and tried. Perhaps even released. These morons had created the system – a weak system. Khalil hated it, and had never felt bound by any western governments' laws as evidenced by his willingness to break them. Still, he knew the system, had indeed been well educated in it. He had taken advantage of its weaknesses before. He was going to do that again. They had no right to keep him here, the infidel dogs.

How could this government preach human rights, dignity and freedom? Hypocrites. He had been subjected to being held hostage – to their war on terror. Tortured, neglected and left to rot. So typical of the kufrs, infidels. Then these people wondered at the hatred they engendered the world over. Khalil spat on the ground – his floor. He stared at the flecks of dirt which settled on top of his saliva. At least it proved he was still alive. One more day to feel. Another day to hate. *Allahu Akbar,* he whispered under his breath, fingering his Koran one more time. He had work to do.

The door opened and a man entered the cell. Physically unimpressive, tall, but very slim. Brownish hair. Charcoal blue circles under striking grey eyes. Dignified, but in an almost affected and conscious way. Solemn, and with no enthusiasm. Probably early fifties. Expensive clothes, Khalil guessed, based on the cut and fabric quality. Khalil felt the way he always felt about westerners – he hated him.

XXXXX

The dog began to twitch. In a mere few seconds its breathing went from smooth to labored and strained. Omar studied intently, watching each move the dog made. Saliva flowed from between its sharp, yellow teeth, rapidly followed by vomit. The twitching intensified. Its eyes bulged from the sockets as the dog began choking. Air had been cut off as the dog's muscles ceased helping it breath. After a few bucking convulsions, the dog was finally still.

Omar heard a laugh. Scott, his contact at the farm, had come up behind him. Omar had been so intent on watching the dog everything else had faded.

"How long? Did you get the amount right?" Scott shuffled his feet as he asked the question.

"Four and a half minutes, from start to finish. Stupid dog." He swatted at a fly.

Omar opened the sky roof by pressing a button on the panel in front of him. The building itself was spare. The control panel was more suited to an airplane's cockpit than the plain shed. Only Omar and a handful of others knew that the knobs and dials controlled the machinery of death – a spectrum of choices.

"The sarin worked perfectly. Next, I need to deliver it with a bomb, not these few jury-rigged showerheads. I haven't done it since I left the training camp eight months ago. The weather is different here. I need to observe the results." Omar squinted as he spoke.

Scott shook his head. A smile ran quickly across his features. Probably dreaming of getting to a training camp himself. The siren song of jihad, the west choking on its own mythology. Omar smoothed his now sticky shirt. The weather was blistering.

"It was beautiful, man. Just beautiful. I hated that piece of shit dog. Always barking. Do you need me to go to the shelter to get more?" Scott spoke expectantly.

"No, brother." Omar replied. "Not now. I have to focus on the bombs now that the sarin is perfect. You don't have to hang around here. I am going to wait a bit and then check the dog." He stared at Scott. Fucking imbecile. Scott had no insight into how finally nuanced Omar's work was. It seemed like everyone wanted to join the jihad these days.

Omar turned his back on Scott, looking instead at the dog, as it lay slumped beyond the glass. It had fallen on its side and was covered with vomit. Disgusting.

Omar waited until Scott was walking across the open field toward the farm itself.

He then left the building and stepped out into the barren land. Hot air hit him. The drive from Los Angeles had been only about an hour but this world was entirely foreign to crowded Westwood, where UCLA and his apartment were located. Most noticeable immediately was the blistering air, dry like that at his home. Southern California was a desert, but of a different sort from Saudi Arabia. Here, the gold- tinted dirt supported small mangy shrubs and a few knotted old trees. His homeland was much more minimalist – all sand with a few rocks thrown in for variety.

He would go inside and study the dog after the sarin had time to dissipate. Luckily, it was a poison that floated away quickly, especially in warm weather. But he wasn't taking any chances. The death he had just witnessed was not a noble death, more suited to dogs and women.

The owner of this property also grew lettuce, but those green, irrigated fields were only marginally within his sight. This part of the ranch housed only the structure he had been using for the jihad. It was situated far from the more traveled parts of the expansive property and received little care or attention. Omar could care less how filthy it was. It was his weekend laboratory and valued only for functionality. Life wasn't all organic chemistry and frat-parties. His time was too important not to use wisely.

Omar reached inside the front pocket of his jeans. They were the low cut version. All the better to highlight his chiseled abs. He was taking an abdominal class at his gym. A better place to meet girls couldn't be imagined. And the clothes they wore! Girls in Saudi Arabia only dressed so obscenely at home, alone or with other women. Here it was all on display.

Pulling out his iPod and white headphones, he turned the device on. The earpieces slipped familiarly into his ears. Losing himself in the music he sat on the ground and waited. Eminem's voice boomed.

*I've been to the motherfucking mountaintop*
*Heard motherfuckers talk, seen 'em drop*
*If I ain't got a weapon I'm goin' pick up a rock.*

He would go check the dog soon. Time was running out. His bombs had to be perfect.

XXXXX

The first thing George noticed was how much like the others Khalil looked. Neither tall nor short. Slim. And, of course, the olive skin, dark hair and brown eyes. He wore no long beard, as many Islamists do. But, as that group was fond of saying, they wouldn't wear their flowing beards or traditional dress to execute an attack – too obvious. And his head had been shaved. All prisoners' heads were shaved. Where did that custom originate? The guillotine, right – so much easier to get a clean cut when no hair obstructed it? Much of modern history seemed to flow directly out of the French Revolution.

What also caught George's interest, for the first time in a long while, was the energy emanating from the man's body. Men in captivity generally became unhinged – out of fear. Some were traumatized by what had already happened to them. The most deadly terror was the anticipation of what was still to come – hence the interrogation technique of implying death or torture. Illegal, yes, but only in some places.

This man was like a coiled snake, ready to strike. George had rarely seen such burning energy in detainees. This prisoner had been through torture, solitary confinement, sleep deprivation, constant light and who knew what else. Still, he didn't appear beaten. Arguably, he even looked strong. George sensed hatred. Some emotion was smoldering, but he couldn't yet classify it. Why wasn't this man too tired or whipped for such intensity?

Well, people were always ultimately simple. To withstand so much, he had to be stronger than most. Or more of a fanatic. Something to watch and analyze during the interrogation process. The answer would come – it always did.

Really though, this guy had already piqued George's interest before their meeting. Khalil was just a poor Algerian yet he had been sponsored – by a terrorist organization - at an American university years ago. That was strange, and things that didn't fit always meant something. According to how life normally worked, the poor guys were usually just shipped to a terrorist camp and taught to die. As was generally true, it was the affluent that ruled the roost – in this case the terrorist organizations.

Based on the progression of his years as a mujahadeen Khalil should be long dead. Practically speaking, he was either exceptionally lucky or had been identified as a leader. George was betting on the latter. Luck always ran out. Khalil had even made a terrorist watch list – so his arrest was probably not a mistake – some poor Arab guy unjustly targeted. Khalil had information in his bowed head, George was sure of that.

George's eyes scanned the room. He felt no rush to begin the interrogation. Controlling his mind was the most important constant. The pressure to move quickly, especially with a prisoner who brimmed with potential information, had to be avoided. With haste came harm, potentially ruining the prisoner. If someone wasn't broken in the first twenty-four hours, and most were, you had to step back and begin anew, this time at a snail's pace. Unfortunately, George had all the time in the world.

Except for that Los Angeles phone number, programmed into that damned cell phone Khalil had at capture. Years of experience weren't necessary to know that such clues were never a good sign.

"Hey, you, asshole, move to the table." George winced as Sean's voiced boomed through the room.

He watched Khalil walk over to the table and sit in one of the rickety chairs. The man's step was light, a sign of training in the jihadist camps in Afghanistan and Pakistan. The gait developed from running up rocky hill nightly in bare feet – all part of the training regime.

The cell was small, somewhat colorless; but weren't they always? Just like hospital rooms. Perhaps color didn't fit any institutions – as a psychiatrist he should probably consider that sometime. A plant would die here in a day – what must it do to a person? Khalil's vivid orange jumpsuit was the only spot of color – a distinctly pop-culture effect.

Well, this skinny and very nasty prisoner deserved no better, George reminded himself. At least the place was only moderately dirty, not like those prisons overseas with the bugs, rats and pools of urine. George's time abroad had hardened his sympathies to the creature comforts of the detained. They were the ones who controlled their release – all they had to do was talk.

The man glared at him with burning eyes. Predictable. The prisoners were typically either petrified or defiant. The latter were often arrogant too. At the beginning they seemed to believe that they could withstand whatever George intended to do to them. Yet they never did, ultimately, did they? The bluff was empty. George looked warily at the man sitting in the chair, huddled next to the table. You, my man, have no idea what is in store for you.

Sean interrupted his thoughts. "Do you want to take him to the interrogation room? I had orders to keep him in here until you arrived."

"No – keep him here."

"You sure? Would you like me to stay with you? This guy is strong." Sean scowled as his eyes hit Khalil – who didn't respond.

"No, that's okay. I'll be fine." What with the not so hidden cameras trained on this man's every action. It was like interviewing a reality show star on television. Millions might be watching. Well, he had no intention of smiling for the cameras.

George held out his hand to Khalil. He heard the door close behind Sean. A bolt clicked into place.

Khalil refused the outstretched hand. Having been educated in the United States he of course knew the gesture. Like a naughty little boy he was going to show George that he wouldn't cooperate.

George sat down in the other chair at the table. He gazed down at it. A small crack ran across the table, ending at Khalil's wrist where a scar continued the crack's line.

XXXXX

Khalil sat at the table in his prison cell, his hands clasped before him. He was completely motionless, as he had learned to be long ago while fighting, waiting for an opportune time to strike. Those who didn't learn were dead. It isn't hard to see a slight movement in the crystal clear light of the Afghan mountains. At that altitude everything stood out more distinctly. Even the colors seemed more vibrant, harsh in the ethereal light. This interrogation was just one more battle. And Khalil felt calm, as was his custom.

"So, tell me about your capture," the man said. It took him less than two seconds to move from the door to the table, his stride confident, very American. Khalil could feel the man's watery gray eyes as they bored into him, unafraid as any jailor's would be.

Khalil stared at the man. Get me talking, get me on a roll. I know how interrogation works. I read the American manuals. Moreover, I taught interrogation to men better than you. Well, it won't be so easy, you American dog.

The man looked calm. The room took on an almost meditative quality as the two sat in silence. Khalil knew that he himself didn't look defiant. He never looked anything much. Another thing that fighting does to a man. Anything short of death and it just doesn't matter. And even death wasn't so bad. Die for Allah, go to heaven.

"So, tell me about your capture." The man retained his calm tone and pleasant face as he asked the question again. At least he wasn't perky and loud like many Americans. The man leaned back, relaxed in his metal-framed chair.

Khalil continued to stare, so they sat silently for a minute. Then he shifted his glance around the dingy cell, so familiar even though he had arrived only a few days ago. Not much to get acquainted with. Walls, a bed, two tables, chairs, a toilet, a door and one window.

Once more the man tried. "Shall I rephrase the question? How did you get caught? A girlfriend betray you? Landlady thought you looked shifty? Caught with a bomb strapped around your waist?" His voice hadn't changed, even though his words had become antagonistic.

Khalil moved slowly, shifting in his chair. He did it out of boredom. How long would he have to sit here?

Suddenly, the man jerked up and banged his palm on the table. His eyes lost their placid look. Khalil was fascinated by their gray and how it could change. He had read about eyes like that.

"Look, you Paki bastard," the man shouted. "I don't get a pension here. I don't have the patience for your moronic games!"

Khalil stared at the man. Then he started to laugh. Humor had been a stranger for quite a while.

"Paki bastard? You know better than that," Khalil said. "Aren't you some specialist? Even an idiot would read my file and know I am Algerian. And, is that the best you can fake anger? Why bother doing it at all, you dog?"

The man smiled. "My name is George, not dog. And what else do you know about teaching interrogation technique?"

"Nothing at all." Khalil replied. It was a bad bluff and they both knew it. Still, Khalil wasn't going to admit anything. The man's eyes had returned to placid gray. They had registered little joy in catching Khalil's ill-conceived words. His emotions really weren't in the interrogation – he had that much self-control. And, the man had also obviously read the file. Khalil knew he had been pegged as an instructor of elite troops. His specialty - other than bombing missions and poisons - had been interrogations. That information was all available on the Internet.

Khalil recalculated. "Interrogators feign emotions. They never betray them."

"You decided to be honest?"

"I have nothing to hide."

"Then let's prove that so we can let you out of here. You do want to get out of here, don't you?"

Khalil smiled at the man again. He had been caught once more. The man had managed to keep the dialogue going. Only the insane wouldn't discuss getting out of this depressing excuse for a prison.

XXXXX

"Why were you in London?"

"Visiting friends," Khalil said.

Lying takes more time and effort than telling the truth. And, the expression often won't match the words. Interrogation was mastering inconsistencies.

"Who?" George asked. The lighting was bright enough for him to watch the nuances in Khalil's face. Each shifting muscle was clear.

"Ahmad…."

George ignored the list. The names were fake. No, he was asking the predictable questions. But he wasn't interested in the answers. Rather, he wanted to watch the man sitting across the table from him: watch him lie, watch him tell the truth, gauge his reactions. The real questions would come later, after he had learned about him.

"So you are GSPC." It was a statement. "Was your visit to the UK related to your fight against the Algerian government?" A joke of a question. Who gave a shit about Algeria, and why fight their government in London? But that wasn't the point.

George watched Khali, who looked comfortable with the question. It was an expected one. "GSPC. But the visit wasn't related. London is very far from Algeria." Khalil said, then continued on, his voice turning boastful. "But if I were, what of it? You fought for your independence, I'm fighting for Algeria's. Don't we all have a right to democracy? Why did your government...."

"Yeah, sure." George cut him off. He didn't need another lecture from an Algerian terrorist about their stolen election. That was the problem with democracy in a Muslim nation – the fundamentalists could win. Luckily for Algeria, the army had stepped in and prevented that outcome.

Of course, the Algerian people ended up paying anyway by being regularly slaughtered for being in the wrong place – Algeria- at the wrong time – the 20th century. Pretty much business as usual there. Or at least that was how George understood it. And GSPC was Al Qaeda now.

"Besides, you don't believe in democracy," George said. It was a throwaway comment – he needed to establish the upper hand now, otherwise the interrogation would get nowhere. Besides, what he said was true, the GSPC really didn't believe in democracy – they believed in Sharia and a fascist application of it.

"In Islam there is no separation between mosque and state. The people don't rule, your Imams do," George said. Well, God, or Allah. But the Imams enjoyed standing in for God – who showed his face so rarely.

Khalil's eyes darkened. George could see him about to jump at the bait. Instead he hesitated. Then he shrugged. Good impulse control for a terrorist, who were typically action oriented and aggressive. Just the sort of person to go crazy when confined. They were also frequently narcissistic. So, George would keep baiting Khalil.

He let the silence continue. Khalil remained quiet. Smart. Whatever you said always came back to bite you.

Finally Khalil spoke. "I'm not a political man. My jihad is for Allah – so the believers can live in a righteous world." Khalil waived his orange-sheathed arm like a prayer flag blowing in the wind.

George ignored his proselytizing. Some traditional terrorists sought a political end. Others wanted to create an Islamic world – religion posturing as politics. A bomb was a bomb. The ideology behind it wasn't interesting. "So, you fought in Afghanistan? Five years – that is a lot. Did you really fight or did you just hang out in the camps?" 'Fighting' was often just a punch card item for an Islamist – jihad, the hajj to Mecca, kill some poor westerner, steal a few identities.

"I fought." George detected a flash in Khalil's eyes from the insult.

"How did you stay alive?"

"With good weapons. I was trained by the CIA. You can't keep me in jail for fighting a war for which you paid three billion." Khalil blinked, unable to hold George's gaze.

A misstep. Who would know how much money the CIA had poured into the Afghan fight against the Soviet Union? Only a smart, well informed terrorist. Khalil's statement was also propaganda – the CIA never directly trained any Arab militants. Indirectly? Who could say? Everyone had their own theories.

"Why Afghanistan? Algeria wasn't enough for you? Not enough guns there these days?" Of course, Khalil would be killed if he entered the country. Not that anyone would want to go to Algeria. Sweltering country of too many war-weary and hostile people. Why risk getting your throat slashed?

Besides, in his experience, once an Islamist started to fight the west they never went back to fight in their own country. It was easier in more liberal societies – fewer death squads and less torture.

"I hate Algeria," Khalil said.

"I empathize – not my favorite place either. Why can't you enter Algeria?" George asked. Khalil was acting as if he was in a business meeting – not in a jail cell. Keep pushing, even when he knew the answer.

"The government will kill me." Khalil's eyes were steely – an easy reaction to teach.

"So they know you're a leader in the GSPC."

"It is not a crime to try and free my country from the unwanted yoke of a military government. It is what your revolutionaries did. The Algerian government lost a legitimate election but refused ...." George cut him off. "You didn't answer my question."

"It was a stupid question." Khalil glared across the table.

"You know that by not answering you actually have." George smiled as he spoke, watching Khalil's gaze shift. He looked bored now; not at all troubled that he may have given away information. Confident.

"Why should Algerians want Islamic rule? Why go back to the dark ages, as the Taliban did to Afghanistan, or Khomeni did to Iran?"

George asked, more interested in Khalil's body language than in the answer.

"Because it is Allah's will." Again, the waving arm. "Because it is a return to Allah and away from sin. What has the modern world brought people – AIDS, drugs, drunkenness, illegitimacy? There is a better way." George studied the crack in the table. How did that happen? One hard blow or a gradual weakening of a fault in the wood?

George rose. Another chosen one. All these guys were the same. He had enough information for today. George noted Khalil's surprise as he packed up his navy blue notebook. It was Khalil's first real emotion of the day. George was leaving well short of a true interrogation. Tomorrow the real fun would begin.

"Do you need anything?" he asked. Uncertainty clouded Khalil's features. Broken protocol was always disturbing. It made a smart man wonder.

"Cigarettes. A newspaper. Toothpaste." A man able to think quickly.

George smiled politely and walked out.

XXXXX

A new spider had moved into the cell. It moved with precision, weaving the fine gossamer thread into an intricate and confusing pattern. The long legs moved deliberately and with confidence. Its mission was well defined, and nothing hindered its mindless determination.

It dropped, extending the taut borders of its artistry. As it plunged down fearlessly a fine thread held it firmly. The burst of showiness elegantly metamorphosed into a moderated and patterned diligence. The web was slowly taking shape.

Khalil watched. The spider's daring reminded him of his own missions. How carefully he had planned them, using his expertise to lay perfect and infallible traps. Allah be praised, he was blessed with the same single-minded determination for perfection, patience and restraint. Unexpected variables always arose, so timing had to be flawless. And there was always luck. Who could board four commercial flights that all took off on time?

Khalil pictured the new interrogator. George had been watching Khalil as closely as he was now watching the spider.

George was perceptive, of that Khalil was already sure. But he was not a physical man. While his gestures portrayed neither nervousness nor a lack of confidence they also missed the bodily control that Khalil had mastered. Physical control was important for a fighter – any mistake, no matter how small, could lead to death. Fear in your eyes gave an opponent faith in his ability to kill you. The mujahadeen had an advantage when fighting infidels. Staring in the eyes of a man unafraid of dying could be unnerving – especially for the young and raw recruits, soft around the middle, that the superpowers like to send to war.

Khalil had seen the twitches in George's face as he sat across from him at the table. The tiny movement at the corners of the eyes. The slight tightening at the edges of his mouth. The smiles had been certain of power; after all, George was the jailer. But they had lacked conviction. George wasn't here out of passion or idealism. Could it be duty, or just expertise?

Outwardly, everything about George was conventional American. At least thus far. Yet while his physical movements could be loose, he also carried an inherent ease. Almost as if he belonged in a jail cell and couldn't imagine being anywhere else. He radiated none of the urgency or impatience which Khalil associated with Americans and their noisy world. Like the spider, George kept up a steady pace, had internalized it, and proceeded to do his job.

Khalil could break George's thin body with almost no effort. The man looked like he needed glasses with his long forehead and stern expression. With his furrowed brow and bottomless gray eyes, he had the air of a thinker. Time had worked its effect. George had the washed out look of age. The wrinkles deepened in his forehead, spreading almost to the edge of his face. He had a furrow around each eye. Too much time spent pondering impossibles was Khalil's best guess. As a result, his face sagged, weighed down by the passing of time.

Still, it managed to be a vibrant face. The energy of the mind was reflected in the glittering eyes and the firmness of the lips. George hadn't yet even begun to consider letting go of life. He might be tired, but he was still engaged. In that, Khalil knew he was an equal match with George – each was still fighting.

A smell had entered the cell. It permeated the thin walls, causing them to swell and take on a rosy hue. Then the light reflecting from the sky got darker, and the smell more intense. The heartiness of meat – Khalil guessed beef from the lack of refinement in its heaviness. He could also make out the rich sweetness of a vegetable. Probably beef stew again. The guards claimed the food was all halil, prepared according to Muslim custom. He doubted it. He had been given non-official status. To the public surrounding him he didn't exist.

Did anyone know what was going on with him? Had he disappeared to everyone but a few government officials, a hand full of guards and one interrogator? Certainly people must drive by and wonder what this heavily fortified building was.

How could he believe that anyone was actually worried about his dietary restrictions? They had forgotten his inherent human rights.

Khalil watched the spider again as it so methodically continued its graceful dance. A fly had already gotten entangled in the contradictory denseness of the feather-light web. He watched the hapless bug as it fought the sticky captor, enmeshing itself further with each effort.

Did Khalil have a choice? Could he fight the chains that had been placed around him? Or must he instead stay true to his nature and wait, patiently, as he figured out what actions would help him escape this unacceptable destiny – that of a prisoner.

Effortlessly, Khalil hopped up off his bed. The hard, wire framed cot was his favorite resting place in his limited room. He went to the wall. Slowly he tapped it, rubbing his fingers over the flat surface. Realizing that he couldn't reach the barred window he grabbed behind him, moved a chair and stood under the square of light. Swinging his body up he felt around the window, rattling the bars to see how firmly they held.

He saw another fly pass him by as it went through the bars and out into the cooling breeze. It had escaped the spider's lair.

XXXXX

George tried to focus on the list of coffees posted on the wall in front of him. He wasn't a Starbucks regular and felt awkward asking for most of the menu items. He abhorred few things in life as much as milk in coffee. Milk killed its smoky bitterness and harsh edge. The creamy richness softened the beverage and changed its character into a weak approximation of what it had been. The menu in front of him was not only silly, it contained too many things he wouldn't dream of ordering. Mochas, lattes, chais. They all had milk, and probably sugar too. What had happened to coffee? He had once thrived on variety and had prided himself on his willingness to try new things. Now he just wanted coffee, plain black, old fashioned American coffee.

The girl behind the counter looked like any number of his students. Thankfully, she had no piercings or odd streaks in her hair. Too much was always too much. Why didn't the young recognize that?

"A small black coffee, please."

"What's your name?" Luckily the girl hadn't asked him to clarify his order by using one of the company's silly terms. She probably went to Stanford. He didn't know her, mercifully, since didn't want to be recognized. Normally he wouldn't have chosen a Starbucks in downtown Palo Alto—too close to the university. Perhaps today it wouldn't matter. He hadn't been teaching much over the last few years so his chances of being recognized by a student were slim. And this coffee shop was conveniently close to his home.

"Your name, sir?"

Her voice caught his attention, which had started to drift, as it tended to do during an interrogation. Pondering Khalil and how he was going to solve the problem of getting the man to talk.

"George." He said. That was enough, right? She didn't expect his last name too? He noticed some large cookies. His eyes lingered there as he took his wallet out. He loved cookies. "I will take that chocolate chip cookie as well, please." Already he could anticipate the sweetness of the chocolate, a perfect counterpoint to his harsh coffee. And, hopefully the coffee would be served hot – not lukewarm to prevent potential liability lawsuits.

George stood awkwardly a few steps away from the counter. He clutched his oversized cookie in one hand and his briefcase in the other. The store was mostly empty – which made his awkwardness more bearable. A few young girls were giggling together as they drank their monstrous, sugary frozen drinks. A even more youthful man sat in the corner, all greasy hair and baggy clothes, typing manically on his computer.

"George." He heard his name.

Ambling over to get his coffee George decided to sit near the typist – who looked much quieter than the three frivolous girls with their miniskirts and bright lipstick. The boy was distracted not only by his computer but also by an iPod. Privacy, 21st century style.

Carefully, he set down his coffee and cookie and he took his notebook and a pencil case out of his well-worn dapple colored briefcase. He set them on the table and put the case on a chair. Opening the pencil box he removed a coal pencil. He chose a blank page in the notebook and wrote Khalil on the top.

Expertly the coal hit the paper and an image began to take shape. George first focused on the face, long with strong cheekbones. The well-defined, almost sharp outline that formed Khalil's features was a combination of his leanness, Arab ethnicity and genetics. He had a chin that tapered to a point rapidly in contrast with the breadth of his cheekbones. His eyes were small, very dark. They receded into his face in a way that men would label unattractive but women would call smoldering and probably even sexy. At least if George had figured out women's tastes by now. The nose was strong and slightly bridged. It flared a little too widely at the bottom for western tastes, but was probably standard issue in Algeria. The bottom lip was cut too full. George often thought of killers as being cruel physically – with some sort of outward manifestation of their actions showing in their face. His favorite indicator had always been thin lips – an identifier used culturally in myths, folklore and fairy tales – especially during the $19^{th}$ century. Khalil had a sensual lower lip, though it was topped by a thin upper lip that already George had seen twist in cruel or indifferent ways.

With fluttering movements he penciled in the delicate eyelashes. They were of the sort to be called feminine – thick and curled at the ends. Yet, such eyelashes never seemed to appear on girls, being reserved instead for men that had a touch of beauty about them. Khalil was anything but traditionally handsome. Yet he had a daring recklessness and perhaps even an idealistic glint in his cold eyes. Why are so many people drawn to the beauty in danger?

The curly hair sprouted easily on the head George had drawn. Its wiry coarseness and even the density of it were easy to portray. Yet how could he draw its tightness running up Khalil's hands and onto his arms? Then it almost seemed delicate, like a spider's web.

George continued to fill in his picture, adding deeper shadows under the cheekbones and fine lines on the forehead and around the eyes. He formed dark crescents under the eyes, handed out to all revolutionaries with their Kalashnikovs. George also added in the birdlike wrinkles around the mouth that identified a smoker. Smoking was still hugely popular in the Muslim word. Not only did it kill hunger pangs, it also had a long history as a social grace.

George looked at his picture staring deeply into its eyes. He studied the recesses of the face and lingered over each feature. The picture was a good approximation of the man – at least physically. George had once considered being an artist before the practical implication of making such a career choice deterred him.

He suddenly felt an urge to shift his body. Cramps from holding a tense position too long. The drawing drew his attention back.

What it lacked were the intangibles which make up a man. The barely contained energy, the careful and measured expressions. The vibrancy of the committed. The way Khalil's mouth formed words, deliberately and with caution as he spoke in a language not his own. George couldn't add in the cocked eyebrow or the withering brow when Khalil got angry. The laughter of the lips and how it tugged at the corners of his eyes. And these were only the expressions George had recognized at this early stage of the interrogation. There would be so many more.

Yet the picture was a key tool for him. As the pencil formed the man he was forced to identify each subtly in Khalil's face. Focusing on the details enabled George to start getting intimate with his prisoner. As many people linger over the vision of someone they are learning to love, George lingered over the faces of each man he had interrogated – getting to know them sometimes better than they knew themselves.

George took a sip of his coffee for the first time. It had been keeping company with the cookie as he ignored them both. It was lukewarm. But at least it had no milk.

XXXXX

"Omar was Mohammed's successor," Omar said. "When the great prophet and founder of Islam died a huge wave of infighting broke out over who was to succeed him. Omar became the head of what was to become the Sunni Muslims."

"And you were named after this Omar?" The recruit looked at Omar, in awe. It was late in the evening after a prayer session. Everyone lingered still, savoring the intoxication that the words shouted out earlier from the pulpit had engendered.

"We must defeat the Great Satan. We shall return to our state of glory that is our due…." The words were familiar. They were repeated in both small and large mosques throughout the world. Omar had taken to holding his own prayers sessions in his small apartment. The words would flow from his mouth and speak to the hearts of those he had gathered before him. Tonight he was at a more formal prayer session.

This mosque was a modest one, tucked in behind a mini-mall. The sounds of a coin-operated laundry permeated the building. The clink of coins, the muffle of voices, and the steady hum of machines in their endless spin cycles. A larger mosque in Culver City was too high profile for the more militant sermons he preferred. Muslims were always watched these days.

Lately, too distracted by girls, Omar had been neglecting part of his mission, searching for willing minds. What a victory to convert someone in the United States to his cause. Each able body in the country that was his biggest enemy and the greatest supporter of the Jews was one more hand to hold a gun. Or deliver a bomb. And his leaders were still saying that he couldn't blow himself up. Too valuable. After all, he had the ability to get an American visa – the benefits of being Saudi. The swines – as if he didn't know his own worth. He deserved martyrdom.

He looked once again at the young man seated before him. Twenties. A soft look in his eyes. His faces alight from the words ringing around his head. He fit perfectly in the small dimly lit room. He looked too American: not Arab at all. If he were still in Cairo, his birthplace, the hands wouldn't be so soft, the eyes wouldn't hesitate. He would know how to survive.

"Well, yes." Omar continued, trying to sound omniscient. "I was named for him, and I hope to do great things in his honor. Of course, not that any of us can take credit for doing anything – it is Allah himself who must be praised for allowing us to act." Sort of. Obviously under Islam all was due to the mercy and benevolence of Allah. But the mujahideen were Allah's worriers. A special section of heaven was set aside for them. For him.

"Allah the benevolent."

"Allah the kind." Omar continued to study the potential recruit. Was he ready for the reality of political Islam?

"The sweet smell of your blood would perfume your mother's hands." Like talking to a girl – the flowery phrases he had learned training at Khaldan, a camp in Pakistan - flowed from his lips like water. How he loved the art of seduction. He smiled, coldly. No sense in warming this poor soul too quickly.

"Blood?"

"You do want to die a martyr, fighting for Allah's cause, don't you? Don't we all?" Omar took a deep breath. "I was almost martyred once. I pray for the brother who took the bullet intended for me. Alas, it was Allah's will."

Blood had drained from the boy's face. The harsh fluorescent lighting cast a dramatic shadow across his left eye.

"Or don't you Americans do that?" Omar sneered.

"No, brother, I didn't mean that." Off to the right, Omar noticed a familiar man staring at him, contempt gracing his features. Coward. This very same conversation had taken place between them a few weeks ago. The man had been too frightened to die for Allah. Now, he sneered. Pig.

Omar looked back at the man now sweating before him – his potential recruit. His skin look strangely uneven, as if it were about to crumble into dust.

"Sorry, brother. I came here only to pray." With that Omar watched his potential bomber slink away. "Infidel," he muttered under his breath.

Omar felt a hand on his shoulder. He turned and saw a tall man he had never seen before. He hadn't heard a sound behind him.

"May Allah bless and protect you my friend." The man spoke softly, almost a whisper.

"Same to you brother, same to you." Omar mirrored the words, as was courteous. Had this man overheard his abruptly terminated conversation and responded to Allah's will? Was he a recruit?

"Quiet, brother. They come to us. We have more martyrs than we need. Never breathe a word of this again. You expose yourself too much." With that the man walked away and rejoined another group, becoming immediately engrossed in their conversation. A burning humiliation flooded Omar. He felt angry, wanting to strike out at someone or something. He was being watched, and judged. His group had seen his failure and had relieved him of his duty to recruit. Once again, he was being told that he wasn't good enough.

He would show them. And when he did his actions would light up the sky. Allah and the world would both witness his devotion in a way never before seen. Right now, briefly, time was still on his side.

XXXXX

"Good morning," George said, crossing over the cell's threshold. He carried his briefcase and a paper bag. Khalil, lying on his lumpy cot, turned a page in his book – *The Shining* - and kept reading. He would rather read about ghosts haunting a crazy, somewhat recovered alcoholic than talk to George.

He heard George drop his bag onto the table. The resulting bang hit

Khalil with the intensity of a dart. A pin prick from hell. There was no peace in this shattered world.

"Get up," George said. The voice was a bark, firm and crisp.

To ignore him or not? What to do. Khalil swung his body up, feeling the stiffness in his limbs. He had been reading for a while. Nothing else to do.

George, evidently satisfied that Khalil was following orders, was easing himself into a chair. Khalil walked over and sat down across from him. He really wasn't in the mood.

"Want to see what's in the bag?" George said, sounding uninterested.

"Sure, why not," Khalil replied. He then watched as George pulled out toothpaste and cigarettes. No newspaper. What a surprise.

"You don't expect me to thank you?" Khalil asked.

"No." Crisp, again. "Tell me about the GSPC in London."

"Why would I do that? For some cigarettes and toothpaste? Did you bring matches or a lighter?"

"Yes," George said. "You get them if you answer some of my question." A dry smile, and then a shrug. George could take his flames and shove them up his ass.

"The GSPC has splintered," Khalil said, more to kill time than for any other reason. "Part is Al Qaeda now. Or whatever they call it. Bunch of young thugs. Don't have much to do with the core of the movement." Disinformation.

"Is that who is blowing up the bombs in Algeria these days?"

"I thought you wanted to know about the GSPC in London, not Algeria?" Khalil said.

"I want real information, not crap. Young thugs, indeed." George sighed. What information was he trying to convey with the gesture? George continued speaking. "Who do you deal with?"

"A number here, a number there. The voices change." Khalil said.

"Write the numbers down," George said, and pushed a notebook in Khalil's direction.

"They call me," Khalil said. More disinformation. He leaned back in his chair. This was going to take a while.

XXXXX

The lights stung. Fluorescent. A curse on humanity. As if the light from the outside needed to be supplemented, even with only a small window to let it in. Khalil, likewise a curse, was being difficult. Again.

"They don't just call you, Khalil," George said.

"Is that a question?" Khalil's sneered. Too bad he hadn't yet realized how little George got affected by such treatment. Welcome to his world. He would drink later tonight to forget. For now, everything Khalil said would slide right off of him. As though he were made of glass.

"You look smug," George said. Call him on it. Don't put up with the crap. "I will sit here and hold your hand through each and every tantrum."

Khalil watched. Reptilian, not moving or blinking. No, he was evaluating, the bastard. Weighing his options. George broke the gaze and began to study his fingernails. They needed to be clipped.

"What do you want me to do here?" Khalil's voice broke the silence. “You are risking men’s lives here. So they are GSPC. Fighting the Algerian government is not a crime under your laws. So a few GSPC declared themselves Al Qaeda. Any one with a video camera can broadcast to the world via the Internet these days. Doesn’t mean a thing, and doesn’t reflect accurately on our entire organization. Now we are all at much greater risk because of a few crazies.”

“That’s why you should more carefully consider your associations,” George answered before realizing his mistake. Yeah, tell the guy to fry his friends. What was that about honor among thieves? So recover. Soften the message. “Look, if you give me names we’ll watch them. If they really are just fighting your government we won’t touch them.”

Khalil laughed. “Yes, of course,” he said.

“Write something down, Khalil. We already know about the GSPC involvement.” George noted that Khalil didn’t invoke a comparison with his own imprisonment. Of course not. Khalil, his friends, weren’t just fighting the Algerian government, were they?

“Friends, enemies, what do you want? I don’t have my address book here. I don’t remember any numbers.”

George pulled a file from his brief case. “Okay, let’s go through some names and pictures,” he said. Five hours at least. Maybe six. Then he could go home.

XXXXX

Khalil sat in his cell. The light was soft, as it was only twice a day, his favorite time. Late in the afternoon, before the jail’s fluorescent light came on the cell was lit with a fading light. Khalil loved its gentleness. He was able to be reflective, assimilating what had happened in his limited and confining world. Having that ten-minute period, marking the transition from day to evening allowed him to come to peace with his current plight in life and to refocus on the importance of his mission. The other part of the day he loved, early morning before the prison guards made their presence known, was also peaceful but unfortunately often included the burden of his thoughts, those that had filled a sleepless night. Why aren't we ever able to escape our own thoughts? Instead we are forced to live in a world of our own making.

He had been spending a lot of time alone. Too much time. What had happened to him as a result? He was lonely, that was certain. The deep aching loneliness of being completely shut off from the world. Being cut off from loved ones was hard enough. Khalil was used to that – he had been on the move so long. The list of those he loved had dwindled. This loneliness was different. It was absolute. He was used to the camaraderie of his brothers, the fellow mujadeed. The smelly safehouses, the dusty tents of Afghanistan and the grungy European group apartments all came back to him, crystal clear in the remnants of his memory. Whispered voices. Discussing the future with Tariq, a distant cousin, always in the dark, with a lone candle burning. Holding his cousin's hand as they dreamed of the future. All just pictures moving through his mind now. Yes, the jihad was all-absorbing. But while it was a life with few true roots, it was also a community.

This new loneliness was something entirely different. It was as if the world existed completely separate from him. He had disappeared, but life outside his jail cell continued. Khalil no longer really existed – all of those who knew him didn't know his whereabouts or whether he was alive. And he knew nothing about them, or even about the world itself. Was it still there, after he had left it?

Each day was made up of routines; it had to be made up of routines if he was to stay sane. He said his prayers five times a day. He ate three times a day. He wrote or sketched for two hours each day. He showered and dressed for fifteen minutes each day. Then he shaved. Three times a week he was allowed to walk in the gated back yard – he chose to run – for forty-five minutes. He divided the rest of his time between reading, writing and thinking. He did each activity at the same time, religiously, day after day.

The Koran. He read it, recited it. He found comfort in Allah's words. His God had tested the true believers before. During the Crusades Allah had rescued them and guided them as they smote their swords on the infidels' necks. The men then had not wavered. Khalil found strength in their forbearance and tried to imagine the hardships they had endured, much worse than his own. "Attacked by Mongols – the Tartars – in the east and by Franj in the west, the Muslims had never been in such a critical position. God alone could still rescue them." (Ibn Al-Athir). And Allah had.

His people had been humiliated for centuries, driven from their homes, murdered, raped and pillaged. History, the endless crusades as the west sought to destroy the umma. But they had not been beaten. Allah had prevailed. Their faith had grown, then spread. It now covered much of Asia, large parts of Africa and had begun to take control of Europe. All in due time.

Khalil would recite the Koran, saying the verses over and over again until he entered a trancelike state. The gloom of the jail cell would slowly fade away, the edges of the objects around him blurring until they ceased to exist at all. His mind would relax, all tensions melting into nothingness. Even his body would enter a vegetative state, present but not intruding on his visions of Allah and the world beyond this heartless one.

Khalil would imagine the battle cries of the soldiers who fought before him. Their arms held high as they went fearlessly running to attack the enemy before them. A fight to the death then as now. The Crusaders had spared no one as they uncoiled their forces eastward. He was aware of the blood as it coursed through his body as well as each nuance of his rhythmic breathing. He could hear the life in his body as he prayed. And he knew that Allah was with him, more real now than he had ever been.

Khalil had known many verses by heart before entering this jail. He had now memorized many more. Perhaps Allah had given him this cell to pull closer to his beliefs. Had he been veering too much off the righteous path before getting caught? Had he become arrogant and dismissive of the power of verse? Was he no longer motivated by a love for Allah but rather from an obsession with power?

He hadn't asked to be given time locked up in a nightmarish prison – alone and haunted by his own mind. Memories could be powerful things. No one would willingly be stuck alone with them and no distraction. But the Americans wouldn't destroy him. Rather he would use this time to get stronger. And since his cause was Islam he would turn in that direction to escape his internal prison cell. Many prisoners before him had done so in the past. When you are completely alone there is no one else – only your God.

XXXXX

George stared at Khalil. He was fascinated at how the man could sit so still, yet exude energy. It was a common physical state for seasoned soldiers or others who had been forced to live with constant life threatening surprise. In the United States it was rare – some soldiers, occasional gang members – the older ones who had survived their lifestyle, and men like Khalil – who shouldn't really be here. Like a coiled snake – an analogy Karen and her literature-oriented mind would love. Never come out and say anything directly, wasn't that what her prized writers practiced ever so gracefully?

"Have you been treated well so far?" George was struggling to keep a conversation going. He was turning to a bag of tricks developed over the years dealing with many men. His techniques helped with both terrorists and in his day-to-day real world encounters. Most people didn't really listen to or observe others. It was all part of being a psychologist – just finding a way to build a repartee with anyone.

"No." Khalil still didn't move as he answered the question. His voice was low, indifferent.

"Do you want to tell me about it?" George asked.

Khalil smiled, almost as if he enjoyed identifying each move in the game. "No." His tone hadn't changed. Still, he was refusing to bond with George. The strategy was the normal course for the early stage of an interrogation. What was slightly unusual was that Khalil had lost his antagonistic attitude. Most prisoners kept that up for a while – until George wore them down. Khalil had dropped it, almost immediately. That was a smarter way to go – pretend that you aren't the enemy. Why justify an interrogator's suspicion that you are by proving it with your actions? An innocent man, if he could control his emotions, would be rational – knowing that ultimately he had to be set free.

"I have spent a lot of time abroad over the past few years," George said. First, the story. Never stop trying to build closeness. Ever. Show that they share a common bond – that of having been in the same places, living less than idyllic lives. "Afghanistan, Iraq, Egypt. My trips weren't pleasant. I saw desperate men, frightened men. I saw the guilty and the innocent. Khalil, I learned one thing – the sooner a man talks the sooner he is released." The words sounded canned to George. Fake. Had he lost his golden touch? Don't panic, he reminded himself. In an interrogation it is better to be confident in a mistake than unsure in doing the right thing. Of course, most important was not to make a mistake. An alert man like Khalil would notice any weakness or uncertainty.

Stick to your strategy. When in doubt, retain at least that much discipline.

XXXXX

Khalil pretended that he wasn't listening to George. He watched one of the many now familiar spiders haunting his cell. Yet he did hear the words. Would he be here had he confessed earlier? Confessed to what? What did he need to say to satisfy them?

London. He had slept in a piss stained cell full of drug addicts and petty criminals. Many of them had spoken Arabic and they had joked together until late in the evenings. The place echoed Charles Dickens – had grand old England really progressed much? The class distinctions between jailor and jailed were no longer socioeconomic. Now they were race and religion. Perhaps the Irish could understand. He was there for only a short time.

Then, a plane ride to nowhere. Dark goggles had covered his eyes. Shackles had weighed his limbs. He arrived dazed and jet-lagged. His sense of disorientation had been amplified when the guard accompanying him hadn't let him sleep during the flight.

"Hey, you, lazy bones. You think you in charge 'ere?" With a swift kick every time Khalil started to doze off.

A long drive through the desert to a place otherwise known as hell. Not a hell as Allah had promised to the infidels. Rather a modern non-Islamic version created by the blasphemous Egyptian state. The prison had been stone with few windows and no fans. Bugs, rats, an occasional scorpion. The temperature during the day outside in the desert often reached 120 degrees. Khalil could only imagine how hot it had gotten inside. He had been placed in solitary confinement. Even there he could hear the other prisoners. The screams, begging for mercy, desperate choking of a man tortured too far. Nights were the worst, full of terrifying sounds and an almost complete darkness. The desert winds had blown sand in through the small windows. Khalil got used to waking up tasting the grit between his teeth. Initially, he had only visited interrogation rooms located a few miles away and run by Americans. When they didn't get the answers they wanted, they had left him to the Egyptians.

"No, I don't want to talk about it." Khalil repeated his answer. He stared back at the man sitting in front of him. He had heard the best reason to talk yet – to get released. No one had offered him that in Egypt. Not even the Americans he met along the way. What was that western saying? Possession is nine-tenths of the law? Thus far his jailors were keeping him.

"Maybe we could talk about something different." He heard a small tremor in his voice and willed it to disappear. He still hadn't moved, but he had decided to let the conversation do otherwise.

XXXXX

"Where you have been in the last few years."

"How many years?" Khalil replied.

"Why don't we say around ten or so."? George watched Khalil as he gauged what sort of answer to give. How much information did George have?

"The Sudan…." Khalil said.

"Doing what?" Not a hardass tone, but a brisk, business-like one. Keep up the pressure and see if Khalil can provide the answers – coherently and quickly. Time pressure and staccato questioning could be intimidating. Would Khalil break under it? George focused on Khalil exclusively, ignoring the room around them.

"Business." Khalil drew out the word, after waiting a few seconds. He attempted to slow the questioning to give himself more time. Familiar strategy. George would do his best to prevent it.

"Business, what sort of business?" Again brisk tone, short question and no comment beyond that.

"Cement. I imported cement. My company – not the one I ran but…."

"What company?" George interrupted.

"Allah cement! Who cares?" Khalil replied, visibly annoyed.

George's face didn't change. There was a time for jokes. This wasn't it.

"What company?" Not that George cared. He just wanted to know where Khalil had been.

"Al Tahib Cement."

"Based in?" George continued his badgering.

Khalil sighed. Tiredness was showing in the deep shadows taking hold under his eyes and the redness spreading through the white of his eyes. Don't shoot until you see the white of its eyes… an old hunter's rule.

Khalil wasn't supposed to be deprived of sleep. Hopefully the guards were honoring that law. Was it the natural insomnia that haunts those left alone too long with their thoughts? Khalil's life must hold numerous bad memories and moral lapses, enough to keep him awake for many nights to come.

"Khartoum. Based in Khartoum." Great, probably a Bin Laden owned company. How else does an Algerian end up working for a Saudi company in the Sudan? Why not, right? The borders in Africa are porous.

"Then?" George asked.

"Bosnia." Khalil replied.

"Fighting?"

"Yes, of course. Not a crime in this country."

"No. Then?" George kept up the pace.

"Europe, mainly. I was based in London for a while. Then I moved to Amsterdam."

George looked into his folder. It was tucked in his lap, under the desk and away from Khalil's eyes.

"Trips? I have here Pakistan, Afghanistan – long stays on many occasions. You seem to have disappeared. Then the Philippines. Where else?" That list contained what the authorities had been able to trace. Who knew the real itinerary of his life, what with fake passports and European laxness.

"Small trips throughout Europe. Paris, London, things like that." Khalil said.

"How did you support yourself?"

"Odd jobs. Bookstore. Construction company."

"This looks like a typical terrorist resume Khalil. An Al Qaeda resume. You have been hitting every Islamist war and training camp over the years. Sustenance jobs for a smart guy like you – what were you really doing? You want to know how you got on a terrorist watch list look at your travels. Forget the other stuff."

George shook his head. He had changed his tone, becoming scolding as if he were now talking to a child. Khalil had to learn that his attitude wasn't good enough. George had the upper hand – he alone possessed the key to the heavy door a few feet away.

"Look, I am a fighter." Khalil said. "I have never denied that. Fighting the wars I have fought is not a crime in your country. I fight for Allah, and try to spread his message. But I haven't broken your laws." Khalil's voice had become so soft, so non-threatening. Almost passive. Soft was a trick George had already seen Khalil pull. But why passive. Why now when George mentioned Al Qaeda?

George had a hunch that Khalil was Al Qaeda proper, not the GSPC version. Yet Khalil's base was in Europe. The higher ups in Al Qaeda rarely visited the West – too dangerous. Meanwhile, less senior guys grew like weeds. Distinctions were blurring these days regardless. What was Khalil's role, and how could George find out?

"Theoretically, why would Al Qaeda base a smart guy like you in Europe? And how could you stay uncategorized as Al Qaeda for so long?" George mused aloud. Not that we really have a clue, he said to himself.

"I told you, I'm a freedom fighter for Algeria. That's it." Khalil raised his hands in a gesture George always attributed to Turkish carpet sellers in the vast bazaars of Istanbul. It was typical of the Muslim east's melodrama. These gestures were too familiar.

"Go with me for a minute. Let us suppose. You are based in Europe yet you are planning an attack against the United States. You blend reasonably well into western society. But you haven't been to the United States recently. Where you have been is here, there and everywhere in

Europe. How would that work? Why Los Angeles?"

Khalil stared into George's eyes as if looking for something. Then his gaze shifted, as his eyes got milky.

"I don't know." Khalil spoke, yet the words barely escaped his lips. "Doesn't seem to make sense. So, perhaps you are wrong." He leaned back in his chair, looking expectant.

"No." George didn't expect cooperation. But Khalil's physical responses would ultimately betray him – the body hides nothing. His thoughtfulness was a signal that George's words weren't being discounted. Khalil looked uncomfortable, tension visible in the set of his shoulders.

"Is it fake passports? Pictures of your future targets? A strong American-based network? It could be any of them, couldn't it?" George said.

"It could be, I suppose." Khalil replied. "If any of it were true. Planting a bomb isn't nearly as difficult as one might think – if you have the mind for it. Luckily for you, I don't." The flash of white teeth that followed was unnecessary.

"Of course not." George said.

Khalil looked at George and shook his head. The word insanity seemed to emanate from his now rigid form. As if that was new to George – but he no longer cared about what people thought – he cared only for results. It was the subtle tics in the face he was searching for as he tried to guess Khalil's true identity, not the one detailed in the government files. How can you really track an intelligent man when so many other global networks exist to ensure that you don't?

So, George continued.

"You could be part of a sleeper cell awaiting orders to attack your semi-adopted country. But you haven't stayed put. You could be a recruiter – but your personality is all wrong. You are too quiet and probably too tactical."

See, there it was. Plain as day, as the expression goes. The twitch of an eye. The slight change in the mouth. Khalil had tremendous physical control – his limbs often barely moved. – not with discomfort and not with fear. Yet he was still human.

George knew he was on the right track. Brilliant! Even well trained men couldn't hide such shifts. Eyes darting up and to the left with a lie.

"My guess is that you control a number of cells. Sort coordinator of European/American operations for Al Qaeda." There it was. The nostrils had flared and Khalil's eyes had shifted. Damn, I'm right. George felt sure. Khalil was still quiet. George continued. He wasn't yet ready to ease the pressure.

"But if you are planning an American attack – why haven't you been here to scope out the target? Perhaps you don't do that – you study pictures. Would that work? It would have the advantage of keeping you further removed from police or whatever." George took a breath – he was excited. "But my guess is false passports."

Now he was done. Time to wait. Would Khalil respond? Not that it mattered – his body had spoken for him.

Khalil's smile was slow and lazy. "Why would I want to spend time in this country? How does that help me free Algeria from the yoke of a repressive government?"

XXXXX

George was right. Every word was true. Khalil tried to deaden his face, to take all emotion other than an artificial smile out of it. Had George guessed or had Khalil been betrayed?

Khalil was trained not to crack. Giving in just proved that you had information and made the enemy push harder. It didn't help buy freedom. The best outcome was to slowly filter disinformation. Ibn' al-Shaikh al-Libi was able to trigger the Iraq war by alleging that Al Qaeda had been trained in chemical warfare by Saddam. He later recanted his "confession".

XXXXX

Omar brushed himself up against the girl as she lay sleeping next to him in his bed. She was curled on her side, half entwined in a pillow. Her brown freckles, lightly flecked across her tan back, matched the color of her perfectly straight hair. She seemed too flawlessly matched for his taste – what with her candy pink toes and finger nails, her tonal hand bags and shoes and, worst of all, the make-up palates that belonged anywhere but near him.

What was her name again? Candy, Kelly, Monica? Not that it mattered anymore. He would ram himself into her one more time before breaking up with her and throwing her out of his apartment. For good. She would babble for a minute before leaving in a rage, reeking of sweat and semen. Woman always left in a huff when you insulted them. Didn't they understand that getting them to leave was the whole point?

He certainly didn't keep them around for debate.

Omar was bored. The phone was quiet now. He no longer lunged for it with every ring, hoping for the rich melodies of deep guttural Arabic. Now, more likely than anything else, if he bothered to answer he would hear some high pitched monologue on feelings. As if he cared. Worse, possibly, were the telemarketers or political recordings. None of them would help him achieve his apocalypse.

Omar turned the girl over to face him. She groaned, then sighed deeply. Her sleep continued. He caressed her stomach, running his hands along the canyon around her belly button and up to the sharp ridges of her hip bone.

He replayed his memories of his last call, savoring them as he did so. Had he missed any of its meaning?

"But where is Khalil?" Omar had asked, fearful that the mission would be aborted in Khalil's absence. He had clutched the cell phone tightly as he spoke.

"We don't know. Don't ask so many questions. His whereabouts don't concern you." The voice coming across the line was deliberate, but empty.

"Are things still going forward as planned? Who fills his role?" Again Omar searched, no, grasped. He heard desperation in his own voice. His concern outweighed shame. His mission must go forward.

"Don't ask, brother. Leave Khalil in Allah's hands." The voice was quiet enough that Omar could hear his own breathe.

"What do I do? Do I keep building the bombs?" Again, Omar pushed on.

"Brother, no more questions." The voice was loud and clear now as it spoke. "Why would anything change? Your role is the same. I will call you again."

"Wait! Am I in charge now? Do I take orders from you?" *And who are you?* Omar didn't want the voice to hang up the line. He needed more information.

"Allah be with you. I will call you again. Keep working until then." The voice was gone after the final word fell. The information was finished, until the phone rang again. It sat now on his night table, perched a few feet away from Omar's hands. Silent. He would just wait.

Omar now worked his fingers into the girl's pubic hairs. She moved only slightly in response as her sleep continued. He began to massage her open. Not much else to do. At least he could enjoy himself as he waited for the phone to ring.

XXXXX

The wall didn't move. Why should it move? It was, after all, a wall. Still, Khalil couldn't help but try to will it away. If only his God would dissolve matter into gas, making the barrier before him disappear in a puff of smoke.

But that wasn't going to happen. Allah was watching him – giving him the opportunity to prove his piety and devotion to the ummah. Khalil would have to find his own way out.

Yet behind that wall lay a world – in which he now didn't have a part. He was the one that had dissipated into thin air.

Worse, Khalil was bored. Just plain bored.

The malady was familiar. His life had been full of boredom and waiting. The life of a fighter was all about killing time. Attacks had to be flawless and so Khalil had mastered the art of counting perfected it until it took on the sanctity of his prayers, organic as his heartbeat.

Waiting on a hill for the Russians to reach the booby traps, rigged with explosives and lethal. The cadences of each movement, figuring out how long a man would take to reach the perfect spot. How Khalil loved the hills and valleys of Afghanistan. The sharp sun had cast dark shadows on the uneven landscape. It was the perfect place to fight and win a guerrilla war. The perfect starting place for his personal jihad.

Now there was no reason to count. He was just sitting – with no end in sight. Instead of counting he read. Figures had turned into words, flowing as he tried to immerse himself in fictional worlds to forget his miserable cell. We each choose the reality of our own creation.

After all, Khalil's daily existence contained little of interest – nothing like that created in a vibrant imagination. His influences were so limited here – how he longed for a computer. The books were falling flat – too inactive. At one point Khalil had yearned to be a scholar. That was long ago. He had chosen the life of a fighter instead. Mere pages of paper couldn't hold him anymore. He couldn't stop moving; like a shark, he would die if he did.

Khalil hadn't fought in the mountains for a long time. Small spaces no longer signified safety but rather stagnation. In battle you appreciate breathing even if your hiding place is no bigger than a coffin. Khalil didn't fight in gutters anymore. He had escaped to the safe pastures beyond the battlefield where older man plotted. He felt stifled in this cell with its lack of any breeze.

So he was stuck with books. Khalil had perused the prison's make-shift library. The list of reading material was hopeless. He wasn't searching for escape from the travails of day-to-day life in the west. He didn't care about aging or how the culture was changing. Nor did he want to read about dinosaurs being bio-engineered. No, he wanted real ideas, eternal ideas to ponder at night, when his eyes refused to shut. His life now was but empty time. An eternal space, expanding with each passing day. Had life stopped?

The room around him remained the same. Spare, rigid, dead. The metal of the furniture didn't even gleam in the harsh daylight sun.

With a sigh of disgust Khalil picked up a spy novel – juvenile in its lack of intrigue. The hero's life was less dangerous and exciting than his own. This was the best escape from his dungeon?

And why did the villains in these American books always seem to smile when they killed? Killing wasn't about passion or enjoyment. It was an act of war and a victory. With any kill came the risk of your own death. No kill was ever completely clean.

The emotions involved were more complex than simple enjoyment why else would some men get so addicted to it. First came the exhilaration of adrenaline as you won the battle and killed your adversary. That was always followed by more complex emotions, clouding your victory. Initially, perhaps apprehension or fear would set in. Questioning or shame was also a possibility. But ultimately man could justify anything – even a kill. For none of us is truly innocent, are we? Sometimes death is the only option. And for a man of faith death wasn't the important thing – rather what mattered was being aligned with Allah. Life on earth is short.

Khalil sighed deeply. He couldn't breath. Was it the lack of air in the stifling room or his emotions? But why would thinking of death bring the latter? Hadn't he gotten past such complications long ago?

What wouldn't he give for just one honest gust of wind?

XXXXX

Khalil and George had been discussing London in excruciating detail for two hours. George prided himself on his skill at relentless questioning – never pushing too hard, always searching for inconsistencies. It was a process that wore a prisoner down. Ultimately, the prisoners were adrift. The breakdown of resistance was inevitable. They were too alone, without any support system or exposure to reality. Anyone so isolated couldn't keep a mental grip.

Khalil was smarter and stronger than most. But even he could only take so many days of this – if it was done right. George always did it right. Well, not every day, of course, he was human. But overall.

"You crossed the street, then bent over to pick up a piece of paper. What did it say again?" George asked.

"I didn't read it. I threw it into the trash bin." Khalil replied.

"The bobby said he saw you reading it. That was why he stopped you." When would Khalil come clean?

"Maybe I glanced at it – to see if it was important and had some form of identification on it," Khalil said.

"I thought you didn't read it." George pushed. "What did it say? If you checked then you must know."

"I don't remember." Khalil didn't flinch.

"Think harder. I can't believe you because you lied about not reading it." George stayed on the offensive as he spoke.

Khalil raised his hands, in mock defeat. "I didn't lie. It was a stupid piece of paper. I just don't remember it."

"Well, it lead to your arrest. You didn't throw it away, you put it in your pocket."

"Where was it then? They arrested me and took everything." Khalil said.

"That's why it's doubly suspicious. The paper disappeared. You must have managed to drop it without being seen."

Khalil looked exasperated.

"George, I don't remember." Bluffing, still.

"It was some sort of organizational communication." George said. "It's why you turned up in London all of a sudden."

"This is ridiculous. I don't remember." Khalil replied. The sunlight streaming in the room was a muted pastel.

If Khalil really didn't answer his line of inquiry, then George knew his guess was right.

"A bomb, Khalil. Is that what it was about?" George put his pen down as he spoke.

"What do you know about bombs?" Khalil's voice had turned ugly. "How many times have bombs rained down on your shoulders? Why is a bomb worse than any other way of dying? How many did your government bomb in Afghanistan or Iraq? One million Iraqi children dead from your American sanctions. It is you who murder the world's innocents, not me. We have a proverb, 'She found comfort in accusing me of her own illness.'"

George shifted his weight as he prepared to hear another monologue.

"Still, some people do deserve to die," Khalil continued, his earnestness evident, his eyes round and wild. Better to let Khalil burn himself out. He might be more pliable tired. "I would rather cleanse the world of the impure with bombs than see them converted to your civilization's corrupt lifestyle. Allah be praised for the martyrs your government has created. Especially the children." Khalil stopped, watching for the effect of his words. George must have known it was just another typical terrorist rant. Fanatics all spoke like shamans when they didn't want to answer a question.

Yet it wasn't meaningless to George. The martyrs we have created.

He stared over Khalil's shoulder, not seeing the block of wall behind him. Iraq. George had been driving with some soldiers in Baghdad. The roads were notoriously dangerous – car bombs, suicide bombers, gunfire. But a helicopter could be worse. All just different ways to die. George was needed at a different facility and the soldiers were his escorts. The day was warm and dust settled around them. Heat permeated everything. No cooling mountains hovered in the distance – no place to run and hide. George had been petrified. He was no soldier, and questioned daily his decision to be a part of war, any war. The hostility was evident as he passed them by on the road. Burnt out buildings added to his unease, as did the knowledge that guns were pervasive – even if he didn't always see them.

They had stopped to use the toilets at a small store beside a cluster of date palms. The owner was friendly, and made his premises available to American soldiers. Not all merchants were so welcoming. As George was gulped a warm Coke, purchased at an exorbitant price, a small boy ambled up to him.

"American?" The boy smiled. He looked about five, when a slight lankiness starts to replace baby fat. He grasped a ball in one of his hands. Soft dark curls fell into his eyes. His shorts were tattered.

"Why, yes. What's your name?" George said.

The answer had been in Arabic, a language for which George had demonstrated no skill. He pointed to himself. "George." Then he pointed to the boy.

"Mustafa." The boy held out his hand to shake. "Nice to meet you." He pronounced the words slowly, enunciating each syllable. They had obviously been carefully memorized since his English seemed limited to a few basic phrases. So common among children in the third world.

As George shook the boys small hand he noticed wonder in the melting dark brown eyes. The boy broke away from George with a throaty chuckle and ran away to rejoin his friends. As he kicked his ball a car drove by and blew up. Debris flew everywhere. George was knocked to the ground. A large section of the car's body landed only a few feet away from him. The almost impossibly loud blast had been followed by silence. Then the screams started. The boy was gone.

George decided to leave Iraq. He probably should have seen a trauma counselor. He knew that better than anyone. The war was over for him.

XXXXX

Khalil saw the shift in George's face. The man's mind was no longer present. Emotional trauma – it looked the same anywhere. Khalil was unsure which of his words had so shaken his interrogator. He had spoken the standard rhetoric – stuff George must have heard many times before.

George had ceased conversation. Very bad protocol for an interrogator - unless that was his strategy. Some men found silence unnerving. Khalil wasn't one of them.

He continued to watch George. That was what he did – watch and wait.

Time to go in for the kill. Always go after the weak man; while you had the chance. Control, once established, wasn't relinquished so easily.

"Too many memories clouding your mind, George? The wounded and maimed, haunting you when you sleep?" Khalil smiled, slowly, watching for George's reaction. He didn't expect much, but that didn't matter a bit.

George smiled back, his face empty and hollow. In the fluorescent lighting each line on his face was visible and his complexion showed the sun spots around the lines. George didn't move. Wait, Khalil reminded himself. We are all vulnerable, somewhere. George had just opened up his own emptiness.

"No answer, George?" Khalil said, turning George's strategy of attack back on him. "You scared?"

"Don't try it, Khalil," George said, as he shifted. "I can leave." The last statement was little more than a whisper.

"Of course," Khalil replied, with a smile. He already knew his victory wouldn't be complete. George was smart enough to shut down and follow through on his threat to leave. But Khalil had gained something. And he wanted George to know it.

XXXXX

Blood. Sticky, red and seeping. The age old question from *Macbeth* – once you had blood on your hands could you ever wash it off?

George accelerated too fast onto 280. He ignored the trees and hills around him. They were all just more background noise at this point. He had driven this freeway too many times to see any of the surroundings.

Perhaps he should read *Macbeth*. Why hadn't he ever read it? His wife could probably recite lines from it. In her sleep. Except that she actually slept when her head hit the pillow. No blood on her hands.

Why can't we be good? George was killing himself trying to be good. He soldiered on, probing, pursuing, toughing it out. Nothing macho about his job. It was just a grind.

What was Karen teaching now? Every year her seminar classes would change. How come he never asked her about them? She was probably writing a paper on it. Or them. Perhaps even a book. Why hadn't she written a book yet? Didn't professors have to write books to keep their jobs?

Why didn't she ever tell him any of this?

A red Volvo barreled into his lane. He slammed on the brakes but decided not to swerve. "So much for Volvo drivers being concerned about safety." He said, but only his leather seats heard. Where was the guy headed in such a hurry? None of us really got anywhere anyway.

The red car accelerated. Its color was vivid against the grey road. George's eyes easily followed its path as it drove off into the distance. The color of blood.

Khalil had blood on his hands. Speckled throughout his soul as well. Just a guess – not that such a leap took much faith. What about himself? George had never hit a prisoner. He had never held a gun. Unless, of course, he counted the guns the guards around him had toted over the years.

A bomb here or there; that he had seen. But they were always the enemies' bombs. Well, not really. How to differentiate when he watched wounded men being wheeled into various camps? Was he guilty by association?

George turned onto his exit and slowed. The light at the bottom of the hill was red.

What kept him awake were memories of men he had known or merely questioned, now dead or missing. They didn't fade, forming a YouTube panoply of film clips playing eternally in his mind. The past could both protect and damn at the same time, couldn't it?

Much as George liked to pretend that his own hands were clean, he had shouldered his share of messes. Torture, threats, and the borderline behaviors in between. All had happened on his watch, hidden just below the surface.

The Iraqi boy had blown up. Had George's presence, drinking a warm Coke on a dusty Baghdad road, pulled that child onto the bombs path?

The light changed. George was free to pull away, to escape. But he wasn't having much luck doing so, was he? His car sped up as he pressed his foot onto the accelerator. His mind wasn't keeping pace. George turned onto Stanford Drive. It was little road, lined by the university on one side and modest homes on the other. It didn't fit the promise of the name.

Khalil had rattled him. The interrogation wasn't going anywhere. George wasn't living up to his own expectations. Adding one last prisoner was a joke. No matter how hard he tried to run George was stuck.

And the joke of it all was his own safety. He tormented the prisoners, just as he tortured himself, freeing no one in the process. They went to jail, he went home to bed. And Karen had to live with him. Except she had escaped into her lectures and books.

George turned onto his street. His house was there, white, at the end of the cul du sac. Where it had always been, and where it would be tomorrow. No bombs fell from the skies in Palo Alto. No car bombs drove up and exploded. At least not yet.

So how was he to escape?

XXXXX

Omar walked into the store. It was a normal convenience store: discordantly colored with too much bright light. The counter was to the left of the door. Right beyond the counter was an area with hot prepared food and cold drinks – for those really in a hurry. He ambled in slowly, whispering his prayers. For him, there was no hurry.

Omar felt hot, though the discomfort was self induced. He was shrouded in a baggy sweatshirt even though the late summer's sun beat down mercilessly in the clear blue sky.

A man walked up to the counter. As he did so he passed Omar and their gazes met. The man's eyes were a deep blue, tinged with purple. The color of flowers. Probably similar to the flowers that would shortly be placed on his grave.

"Allahu Akbar." Omar whispered. Then he pulled at the cord that detonated the bomb meticulously strapped to his waist.

Seemingly off in the distance he heard a loud bang. He could feel the muscles of his body being pulled from the bones supporting them. His flesh singed as it was ripped off. His head catapulted toward the ceiling.

Debris was flying everywhere. Something fell with a loud thud. The screams had not yet begun.

Omar thrashed in his bed. The woman next to him stirred.

"Omar, what are you doing? I am trying to sleep." He heard annoyance in her voice.

"Stupid whore, shut your mouth."

Omar yanked himself out of the bed and stormed through darkness into his living room. He hadn't given the woman time to respond, though he could hear her tearing through the bed covers in the room he had vacated. It had been just a dream. His time had not yet come.

He kneeled on the floor and began to pray. The words rolled off his tongue. The woman yelled at him and stormed out the door, but he didn't allow her to interfere with his concentration. When would he get the glory he so desired? The victory he so deserved?

XXXXX

Khalil washed his hands in the sink. The water came out at his bidding – preparing him for what was to come. It purified him, as commanded by the Koran. When water was not available a believer could use sand, or dirt. "Allah is benign and forgiving."

He smeared water on his forehead, then his temples. The water felt cleansing. Its coolness was purely symbolic, but he clung to that as any lonely man will cling to his familiar rituals.

He had no prayer beads. His fingers tingled at their lack, as they would for a missing limb long after it has been severed. "Allahu Akbar." He mouthed silently 34 times. Then, "Subhan il'aha, God is pure," followed 33 times. "Hamd-u-lilah, praise be to God," was last, muttered 33 times. His hands and forehead fell to the ground beneath him. They found a solid foundation upon which to rest his fears and worries.

Tension was being released from somewhere deep inside his limbs. All the stress in his body flowed out of him, as the water had flowed from its chrome fixtures.

He remained kneeling for many minutes. Since his incarceration memories had escaped from wherever he had trapped them. How much we forget. How much pain we deny, slipping instead into a state of invulnerability – both artificial and fragile. He was being carried back in time, as the desert winds blow the sand. Khalil always felt strong in the desert – as if the scorching sun could nourish him.

Khalil hesitated, loath to leave his trance. This ritual provided comfort, allowing him to set his fate squarely in Allah's hands. What a child-like wish, really. In a world of so little control how wonderful to have an eternal force safeguarding his passage.

When would the bomb go off? One, two, three, four, five… How many would die?

XXXXX

George put the pack of Marlboros on the cracked tabletop. Marlboro Reds, the third-world favorite. Islam condemned smoking but – as with suicide bombs – a great number of Muslims had managed to ignore the relevant and forbidding chapters of the Koran. Something about defiling the body, if he remembered correctly. George studied the slim, ever-guarded man in front of him. Was it his imagination or did he see Khalil's right eye twitch? Note that. That twitch could mean emotion, even desire.

"Cigarette?" George's tone was curious. But he knew Khalil craved cigarettes, when he could get them. Time for a refill.

"Yes." Khalil's chocolate eyes gazed directly back at him, almost unafraid, but with a slight question. This stage of the interrogation was still about building trust, bringing back the need all human beings have – to bond with another.

George held out the pack of cigarettes and watched as Khalil took one. He then took one himself. He had stopped smoking long ago, only to start again to create trust with his prisoners. Pulling out a lighter he lit both cigarettes. Khalil inhaled deeply as he took a puff.

"Tell me about the day your brother died."

The man's eyes immediately went to a spot of dirt on the ceiling. Yes, thought George, it is always the same spot, his defense mechanism. Then the man took another puff of his Marlboro and looked at George. He began to speak, his voice soft and strangely nuanced for someone so otherwise emotionless.

"It doesn't matter."

"I want to hear about it. Please, give me the details." George said as he inhaled, feeling smoke fill his chest. He enjoyed the rush... much to his chagrin.

Khalil shook his head. "It was too long ago."

"Khalil, I need your cooperation if I'm to help you get released. Please." George kept his voice non-threatening. Khalil must learn to trust him. He tried not to shift in his chair. The room had to be tranquil – more conducive to building trust.

Khalil watched George's face for a moment and then began speaking. "It was a hot day. Oppressively so. I woke early to the mezzuin's call. I went to the mosque for prayer during the early morning darkness.

I always said my prayers. It was the one thing I did for my mother, who was a pious woman then. My brother slept, as usual.

"Later, we shared a breakfast, some tea and bread. We were very poor, and seldom had much more."

Khalil stopped. His cigarette had been burning in his hand. His eyes lingered on it. Were they sad, or merely reflective? George just watched. He inhaled on his own cigarette again. How quickly he had developed a taste for the harsh and acrid smoke. The small room was already getting hazy.

"Go on. What happened next?" George asked.

"I was late coming from school. I had been discussing a Koranic passage with a teacher. We disagreed."

Khalil faltered. His eyes went to the ceiling. Like pulling nails, thought George. He suppressed his impatience.

"Go on." George's voice was soft, comforting. Khalil was bundled up in his orange.

"I let him down, I was supposed to be there. I should have died too. It was only my religious questioning that saved me. Allah saved me, but in being saved I let my brother down, he was murdered, and I held him as he died."

George breathed, almost. The smoky air had him imagining ghosts. Melancholy had settled in as oxygen became scarce. He spoke. "How did you feel when your brother, his name was…."

Khalil stood up, hastily, angrily, yet with a certain grace. He walked away, not getting far in the confining jail cell.

George looked down at the cracked table. His notepad was carelessly lying at an angle before him. The page was blank. Sometimes he hated this job. He visualized his own sibling, a younger sister. He recalled her smoldering smile and the sarcastic glint in her eyes. Could he imagine her lifeless in his arms? The pain of those who started out with so little yet lost so much. This cold and bitter man was just a person, nothing more. George could almost feel his pain. Almost, but not quite Indeed, George was no longer conscious of the cell. Indeed, he pictured his wife and children. Then he tried to imagine them dead and covered with blood. He couldn't do it – the image faltered before it formed.

Bringing himself back to the present, George told himself that Khalil was a murderer. His mission in life was to kill innocent people, loved people. A voice rang out. George lifted his eyes. Khalil's face was red.

"Don't mention his name. You have no right."

Taking a deep breath George asked his question. It had all been leading up to this. "Would you like a picture of your brother?"

As George could have predicted, Khalil's eyes shot up to the ceiling. That spot. He spoke, though his utterance was more of a choke, from somewhere deep inside his throat. "Yes."

Khalil turned away. George stubbed out his cigarette in the silver ashtray he had brought. He removed a photograph from his manila folder and left it next to the cigarettes and matches. The lighter stayed in his pocket.

George then stood up and headed for the door, without looking back. He was disgusted with himself – but his job was too important to allow for weakness. The weak get destroyed.

"Lock it up," he said to the guard as he headed home. He would get nothing more here today.

XXXXX

The boy in the picture, his best friend. Familiar, but also not so familiar anymore. Hassan, his older brother. A shattered dream of the future they could have had.

The boy was so young. A child. The picture had been taken four months before his body was riddled with bullets and left to bleed under a hot sun. Hassan had been alive when Khalil reached him – only moments after the soldiers had fired on the protesting boys. Khalil had cradled his body, still warm. Hassan's blood had flowed on to Khalil's legs, soaking his trousers. It was the first time Khalil had felt life leave someone's body. The heartbeat surrendering to silence. It hadn't been the last.

Hassan had lived only a few minutes after Khalil reached him; it could have been a lifetime. He had never spoken, staring instead into Khalil's face, never able to fully focus his own eyes. Khalil had willed Allah to save his beloved brother. In his youth and weakness had he believed that he could ask for such an intervention? Later his imam explained that Hassan was blessed for having died a martyr. The holy man had urged Khalil to tread the same path.

Eleven boys had died, some still grasping the rocks meant for the soldiers. Another boy had become an idiot, his brain having been irreparably damaged by his one immature mistake and a reckless bullet. Youthful rebellion was not tolerated in Algeria.

Khalil had left behind the body of his cousin, Josef.

Hassan he carried home, struggling under the great weight. Khalil had known then that Allah had helped bear the weight of his older brother's lifeless body. It had still been limp as he carried it through the oppressively hot streets, sweat pouring down his back. But the body's warmth dissipated rapidly, even under the burning sun. A sweltering breeze had blown sand into Khalil's eyes as he walked. But he hadn't bothered to clear his vision, stumbling instead on the familiar path home.

Upon his arrival at their small hut the horrible wails of his mother had greeted him. Such cries were common in their neighborhood. No matter how much misery someone faced, the loss of a child was always a crushing blow. For what else of value did these mothers have?

The boy in the picture continued to stare unblinking at Khalil. His lips were turned up at the corners, yet no teeth showed. Khalil had forgotten his brother's mischievous smile. Who would have believed such a fun-loving boy would have picked the path of Islam and jihad? Khalil had followed him, as he always had, from his own first toddling steps. Khalil had chosen jihad partly to avenge the death, a little bit out of faith, and mainly because it was what the other boys were doing.

How many of those boys were dead now? The life of an Islamist wasn't very long in Algeria during the years that followed. And the killing hadn't stopped yet. Presumably there must be fewer people to kill – especially when factoring the mass migration out of the desert to the various metropolises of Europe. Or did the high birth rate just provide a cattle farm to slake the bloodthirsty warriors?

Well, Khalil wasn't fighting that battle any longer. He had moved on to a bigger fight, as was Allah's will.

"Hassan, would you be dead now anyway?" Khalil whispered, talking only to himself. "You wouldn't have been smart or discreet enough to survive, would you?"

Khalil propped the picture up on the little table next to his bed. He used a murder mystery to support the delicate image. Blasphemous, of course. Islam didn't allow for human images such as this one. But Allah, in his mercy, had provided this picture so Khalil would treasure it, as he could no longer treasure his brother, the martyr.

XXXXX

Omar could hear the laughter ringing in his ears.

"Raghead." The snickers more than audible as a crowd took up the cry. They were all men, of course. Jealous of Omar. Jealous of his success with women. To feel the creamy flesh against you as you jammed your cock inside the willing body. Screaming in ecstasy. That he could do, and these boys were jealous.

Omar felt very much like the exotic. Pocahontas meeting the queen of England. He wasn't at home in this place, ever. And it was the men who made him realize how alien he was.

Switzerland had been the same. Boarding school had been a frigid place. The country itself had been cold, the people pale and insipid. Not at all welcoming to a boy who had never even left his hometown before. But the cries of "Raghead" or "Arab" had been the same as those called out in this warmer place. Only the language and accent had differed.

"Omar, scored lately?"

"Omar, what is the price of oil?"

"Raghead, got any bombs under that shirt?" Infidels. If only they knew. What else did a chemistry student understand if not science? And weren't bombs or poisons science, just simple science?

The classroom echoed with the voices of students. Young men and even women spoke in tones that projected excitement. And insolence. Who in that classroom had visited another world, where people starved to be heard? Their knowledge of other-world countries came from aid telethons with their pompous and parsimonious celebrities, full of drugs and decadence.

The teacher entered the classroom. Omar felt a rush. What would his lesson be? Would he learn a new concoction of chemicals? Would he unfold the combination that would create a bang to be heard around the world? His body trembled. This was why he had been sent here, Allah be praised. To learn how to serve, as Allah witnessed his devotion.

"Omar, you raghead, what sort of bomb can you build for us today?'

"If only they knew, he whispered it under his breath again. Someday they would lie mangled, their flesh ripped from its bones.

He saw a flash of red, an unnatural color that flowed in waves around its owner's shoulder. The girl. He didn't know her name, at least not yet. But he did know her hair and it fascinated him. What chemicals did she use to turn it that color? Certainly she wasn't born with hair that gleamed so brightly.

He gazed down at the seats pyramiding below. She was a sea of color in an otherwise drab world. Why did only the dullest of students in the United States choose to be chemists? Didn't these Americans understand the beauty of watching substances mix? Didn't they want to see what happened when you mixed water with oil?

"Omar, what futures should I be buying? Expect turmoil in the Gulf regions?"

Always they mocked him. The strength of being on top. How long did any one stay on top? Omar whispered his prayers as he imagined UCLA blowing up. Could he persuade his superiors to detonate on campus? Did he have to? If he planned a strike correctly could anyone stop him?

The red hair flashed in the light again. He could feel his cock run through the thickness of the strands. He would have to learn her name. Girls liked you to know their names.

XXXXX

George moved groggily toward his bathroom. At least he thought he was heading in the right direction. "Ouch." As his foot hit a table he knew that he was off course. Rubbing his eyes he questioned why he taken his contacts out the night before.

Reaching the bathroom George closed the door behind him. He was tempted to lock it, but if Karen came looking for him she would get suspicious. They never locked the door to the bathroom. He didn't want her to realize that he was avoiding her.

"Oh Jesus, I want a cigarette". The words escaped his lips before he realized what he was saying. Smoking, that disgusting addiction. The fog of sleep still hadn't lifted. One more night of sleeplessness. Would the rush of nicotine help? Would anything?

The boy. He could still see the boy's face in the picture, Khalil's brother. A child. He had been just a child when he was gunned down. Younger than George's own son. The thought made him sick.

The boy reminded him of a young man he had met while doing interrogations in Iraq. The boy had been picked up with his father, a farmer and accused gunrunner. As with Khalil's brother, the boy's smile had tilted precipitously, without showing a hint of teeth.

Initially, with his father in the room, the boy had been full of bluster and bravado. Yet, he had quickly deteriorated into tears and hysteria during his first interrogation – or so the interrogator had told George.

In the end, the father and son had been innocent. They had been released, free to return to their miserable farm, traumatized.

Boys pretending to be men. Not fully aware of the harm the world held for them.

George turned on the shower. Karen had exited it not long ago, so hot water burst out immediately. As the stream of water hit his body he imagined it rinsing away his thoughts, freeing him from a guilt and sadness he couldn't fully explain. He willed the boy's eyes to disappear.

George recalled the echoes of a conversation he had the night before with his boss, Tom Campbell.

"We are hearing chatter about Los Angeles again." Campbell said. "Remember, Khalil had only one number programmed into his cell phone when he was caught. It was a now defunct and frustratingly untraceable one in Los Angeles."

"What kind of chatter?" George replied.

"That information is classified." Campbell's tone was dead, cold as anything Khalil could probably muster. Heat had risen in George's chest at that moment. It was oddly similar to the feeling from the hot water – the sign of a generally heightened anxiety level.

"How am I supposed to probe about Los Angeles when all of the related information tying Khalil to whatever related chatter is classified?"

"Sorry. Really, I am. Shoot over a memo explaining why you need the data and I'll see what I can do. In the meantime, get what information you can."

Had there been a point to arguing? At that moment George couldn't think of one. The insanity of it all. Instead, he had concentrated his energy on not throwing the phone out the window. Now, he wished he could wash the day down the drain. It hadn't even really started yet. And, he wasn't going to talk about Los Angeles. He was going to do the interrogation his way. Especially if no one would give him access to classified information on his prisoner.

# || Chapter Three - Tears

"Tell me about your father." Khalil looked at the man sitting in front of him. He kept his surprise at the question out of his face, out of his eyes. Why would an interrogator want to know about his father – unless his father was a terrorist as well? And Khalil's father was anything but, the swine.

"Why do you want to know about my father?" And Khalil really was interested – he couldn't figure out the game. This was possibly the first time he was interested in anything going on around him since his arrest.

"I am a psychologist." George said this as if it were the most natural thing in the world. Which perhaps it was for a psychologist. But this was an interrogation, wasn't it? Was this some sort of crazy American rights related thing? "Cure" the terrorist of his cause? Make him into a model American? Insanity – and not Khalil's.

"Well, that is nice." Khalil said. An American phrase to address an American notion. Khalil looked down at his legs, fingering the orange material of his jumpsuit. It was similar in color to the saffron robes worn by Buddhist monks; an interesting choice.

Khalil let the pause continue a few seconds more – for effect. Then he continued, his voice harsh. "Why do I have to answer these types of questions? I do have places to be. I certainly didn't sign up for therapy as you Westerners are so prone to do." A bluff, of sorts. Khalil was curious. But, mostly he just tired and wanted out. George had offered release if he spoke. This grueling introspection hadn't been part of the deal.

As if reading his mind George responded. "If you want to be released — ever you should cooperate." George's voice betrayed no threat. Coming on strong, intimidating, was clearly not his interrogation style.

Still confused, but resigned nonetheless, Khalil started to speak. He watched George, noticing how the morning light fell across the man's hands casually clasped before him on the table. It was a familiar gesture – his own. Was George deliberately paralleling him to establish a comfort level between them? Immediately he refocused on his own words, hearing his voice fall lightly. If this was the game he may as well just play along. What harm was there in discussing his father? George could learn about how he handled questions by discussing any subject. This one at least was less threatening than most.

"My father is a horrible man." Khalil said. "He took us from a small village about two hundred miles from Algiers to the city itself when I was very young, about three. We left our family, my mother left her family. We were alone in the city – well, a suburb really. He got work as a mechanic. Then a few years later he moved out, divorcing my mother and us as well. He married another woman. I saw him rarely after that – which was better. Unfortunately, he left my mother with nothing, and she had to find work cleaning and sewing for other families." Khalil stopped. What else was there to say? He waited for George's response – not really registering what he himself had just said.

"How did you feel when you left the village?" George asked. Well, that was unexpected. Khalil wondered whether anyone had ever asked him that question before. At first he couldn't remember. When he did, he regretted even having the thought. Jennifer.

"I suppose I was sad. I had many cousins, many friends. I adored my grandfather, my mother's father." Khalil struggled as he spoke. How does one answer such a question? Then he felt angry. Why should he be forced to discuss his youth?

"Was your mother upset when your father divorced her? Were you?" George said.

Rage. Khalil felt rage as he stared at the earnest man sitting before him. Why was he in therapy? He was a foreign subject, and he wanted to leave. Not that Algeria cared. This was almost worse than the torture. It was so slow and boring.

"I am here against my will." Khalil could hear emotion in his voice. Ah, so this was the game. Provoke him so he would lose his cool. Right? What was the game?

The light was glaring now. Hitting George in a distracting way.

"Please, just try to work with me here." George said. "I know what I am doing. My style is just different from that of most interrogators. I am here to help you get out." George's voice was soft again.

Smug bastard. The guy was here for information and a conviction. Khalil didn't hide his annoyance as he glared at George – still sitting properly on his chair.

"No. My mother wasn't upset nor was I. The swine beat us both. His absence was a blessing from Allah. We were very poor but Allah provided, as is his will."

"I thought you said your mother provided — cleaning, sewing...." George said.

Rage. Again rage.

"Allah is merciful. He rewards the devout."

"By giving them an abusive father and a poor, uneducated mother?"

Khalil felt like wiping the smug look off of George's face. Really he should kill him for the insult to his mother. But he willed himself to let it all go. At least now he knew the game – get him upset by discussing his childhood, needling him until a blow hit. So, he didn't answer.

George sat before him. He began drawing shapes on a pad of paper he had brought with him. Not taking notes, just drawing shapes. Khalil waited.

"So he wasn't around much?" George spoke. "When he was around he was abusive – both verbally and physically I assume. You had no other family around, no other males. Uncles, grandparents. Of course your mother never remarried, how could she in an Islamic society? Poor woman wasn't even around much either, right? Too busy working."

The sentences kept coming – the placid man suddenly in control, making assertions. Until.

"Where in Algiers were you?"

Khalil internally threw up his hands. This was out of control.

"A village called Kheis el Khechna, near Boumerdes" Khalil said. "Thirty-five miles outside Algiers. Two hours by bus."

"Ah," George's voice was soft now. "A poor suburb. The mosque preachers in Boumerdes, they were quite militant, weren't they? Indeed, they ran schools, didn't they?"

"Yes, they educated me."

George sat there, looking satisfied. This interrogation had obviously meant something to George. But it had meant nothing to Khalil. This country was mad.

XXXXX

Omar saw the flash of orange. That now familiar blur of color in a world of drab. The girl was named Stacey, as he had learned when the instructor called on her a few days before. Stacey.

The color was as unnatural as it was beautiful. Shocking really, it seemingly bragged to be noticed for what it was – a statement. And he had noticed.

Standing up, Omar adjusted his sunglasses, pushing them tightly to his face. One must always be prepared. The orange burst was moving briskly to the classroom door. The woman beneath the color was purposeful, no subtlety to her aggressive gait. Most likely she believed that she was not a girl to be tinkered with. American women always projected strength. That was why they were so easy to seduce. No subtlety went unappreciated, and Omar was all about the details. No, a woman alone couldn't be as strong as these girls liked to think they were – hence the uncountable vulnerabilities. They crumbled like dust. Whores.

Slowly he ambled to the door. He was closer and managed – quite skillfully – to approach the door at the same time as Stacey. He looked past her. Then, he dropped his textbook at her feet, forcing her to stop. The bang was loud, it being a science textbook, not a lighter subject. Pun intended, he told himself.

Omar noted the startled look in her eyes. He stared back. Then dropped his gaze to the book. She hadn't moved to help him retrieve it but he sensed her staring down where it had fallen.

Nimbly he bent down and retrieved the book. As he rose from his squat he looked at her once again. His curiosity had been clamoring for a good long look into her eyes. Had she noticed him? Not just seeing – of course she had seen him. But had she seen more, something that interested her? Omar resisted the temptation, reminding himself of his long-term goal. Short-term highs were never worth it. The objective was to make her notice him – enough so that she could recognize him. Then, he would show her such a lack of interest she would be intrigued.

Seduction was simple. It was all about mixed signals – move too fast and your prey ran scared. But a simple dance of push and pull always worked. Always.

The look he gave her was uninterested. It held in it absolutely nothing.

"Excuse me, I didn't mean to block your way. Please forgive me." Classic. Polite. Too polite for Southern California. The girls here were starved for chivalry. Not that they deserved it – whores one and all. But as such, didn't they appreciate the difference from how they were normally treated?

Omar gestured for her to pass in front of him. He kept all warmth from his face. Too soon for that.

Stacey flushed. Perhaps she felt his indifference. Perhaps she was impressed by his courtesy, not like the rough boys surrounding them. The disrespectful ones who's poisonous tongues he himself had tasted many times. What must it feel like to be pursued by such cretins, hanging their penises out to be worshiped by women who hadn't even been properly seduced? That approach would only make a dog proud – all animal lust and carnal desire. Dogs, infidels, one and the same, really. Disgusting. Much better to respect the game itself.

"Thank you." Her voice held a slight quiver. Omar felt a surge of success, though he struggled hard to hide it from his prey. She could see the impact she had on him later, when he was ready. But first she had to learn how much she could want him.

"After you." He gestured again; this time he added a slight softness to the curve of his lips. He wanted to show some humanity, a recognition of her as a person but not as a woman.

Slowly she moved. Her seat was a few rows in front of his. He followed behind her as she began her ascent to the second row – her domain. Before she entered, Stacey turned her head and she looked at him, deep into his eyes. Mission accomplished! Small steps. Always small steps.

Omar gazed back, but only for a second. It was a truly beautiful gesture, one of his favorites. For a fleeting instant the woman believed that you were gazing into her soul. Any hint of a smile and the gesture was sleazy and weak. Total seriousness made it poetic, perhaps even spiritual. Omar turned away – hold the gaze too long and you became desperate. He headed up to his own seat and ignored her presence for the rest of class. He would move again, when it was time. Clarity of the goal, he reminded himself.

XXXXX

George walked into his house. His mind was ablaze, everything fit so well. His surroundings didn't register as he walked to the kitchen where he could hear Karen. His footsteps displayed no hesitation as he strode into the large and very well stocked room. Life had been good to them.

He gave Karen a kiss on the cheek. Sometimes he got the lips, but not tonight – she was too intent on the cookbook open on the counter. Pots hung from the ceiling. The proximity of steel in earthquake country always unnerved him.

"How was your day?" Did he really care, or did he just want to get through the pleasantries so he could discuss the success of his interrogation. Well, usually I care, George consoled himself.

Karen lifted her eyes from her cookbook. Her glance managed to be impatient, though George couldn't tell why. Her contradictory and confusing way of expressing herself was part of what had initially attracted him to her and had kept him enthralled all these years. He was, after all, a psychologist and a very good one. She puzzled him.

"Fine. Busy, a little bit trying, but fine." She chopped a carrot, barely glancing at him.

She still looked good. Her soft blonde hair felt just past her shoulders. It was always perfectly straight yet never seemed flat. Her eyes were a watery blue, but wasn't that always a perfect combination with such light hair? She dressed mostly in jeans, preferring to be thought of as a 'cool' teacher even as she had definitely started aging once she hit her forties. Yet her manner suited the image – she had that casual nonchalance he had long ago stopped attempting to cultivate.

"Why was your day trying?" Did he really care?

"The usual hassles about grade inflation. It is a literature class, for literature majors. A lot of them deserve a good grades – they're so talented."

George studied her. As if his students weren't equally talented. You still had to make decisions and give real grades. She just always wanted to be liked, didn't she?

"What an annoyance." He said. "If the administration actually stepped into a classroom they might be better able to judge who deserves what grade." Why start an argument. Better to support her.

"Georgc, you are patronizing me."

Caught. "What are you making for dinner? It smells delicious." He managed a slight smile - when in doubt a smile rarely hurt. Talking about his day was the objective, he reminded himself.

"A Hungarian beef stew." George looked at her, so trim in her jeans. Why did she keep trying new recipes? Each was as horrible as the last yet she stubbornly refused to give up. Her cooking kept him slim as well.

"Great." Weak, but sufficient. He paused to provide the conversation with a break. "I had a interesting interrogation today. It was just what I expected. Absent father – a real jerk, hated. Overwhelmed mother. Educated in a religious school…."

"Focus on the family or tribe not individual, affluent or relatively affluent family…." Karen finished his sentence for him. Was it his imagination or did she sound bored? He ignored his suspicion.

"No, not this time. This one has a characteristic that doesn't fit. He's from a poor family. More common from an Algerian, but nonetheless strange." The excitement, he always heard it when he discussed his theories. God, he loved his theories, and they always worked.

"So what does it mean?" Was that interest in her voice?

"That I don't know yet," he said. "Nor have I really probed the narcissistic or excitement driven aspects of his personality. I'm still softening him up. Confusing him a bit too, I don't say." George was ready to keep talking. But Karen interjected.

"You don't say?"

What was wrong with her? She had been spared hearing about most of his interrogations because he had done them overseas. Now she had a chance to learn about his work, his theories, and she couldn't be any less interested, could she? He did hear sarcasm in her voice. It was almost too nice in tone to be sarcasm – but he had learned by now that that was how she did it.

"You aren't interested?" He said. The words fell like lead on his soft sandstone counters.

"George, I'm trying to make dinner. Can we talk later? Please."

Karen's tone was clearly dismissive. She dropped some potatoes into boiling water.

George went to his study and sat down at his computer. Then he began to type, the words coming faster than his fingers could hit his computer keyboard. He started by describing the heavily fortified building he had just visited. The building itself so new that the paint had barely dried. The security clearance memo would have to wait. It wouldn't help anyway.

XXXXX

Khalil lay on his bed staring at the ceiling. The room was almost dark. In the prison there was always some light. Presumably, the prisoners couldn't be trusted in true darkness. He could visualize the stars he had so enjoyed gazing at with Hassan when they were both small boys, staring up into the horizons stretching out above. The twinkling lights had illuminated the sky's otherwise thick, milky darkness. They had named each of the glowing stars. Back then Khalil hadn't known that the stars already had names. Sometimes the names they thought up were silly, getting increasingly so, until the boys finally fell to the ground with laughter. They had rolled in the dirt, wrestling until Hassan pinned Khalil to the ground. Hassan had always had the advantage of age, which brought size.

Khalil's flashbacks continued. His mind had little else to keep it occupied. He heard a bang somewhere outside the prison and chose to ignore it. No war was going on in California, so it couldn't be important.

His scratchy blanket beneath him combined with the jutting springs of his mattress reminded him of his days on the move, when he had slept in a jumble of safe houses. Those days came back fuzzy and blurred, as did the nameless faceless men with whom he had shared quarters. They had all been passing through – young men excited about the training camps they were about the face and the wars they were about to fight. All brothers.

Khalil fought. He had also gotten tough and learned how to survive. How to read a man's face so as to not trust the wrong one and wind up dead. To pull the trigger in an enemy's face – immune to his humanity. And, when necessary, to win in hand to hand combat, thrusting your knife into an opponent's belly, feeling the warm blood tricking down your arm and then the sag of the body in your arms as it went limp.

He hadn't known then that he had been sent to learn and not to die. He hadn't known then that he was being groomed for better. Had he not survived he would have joined numerous comrades – part of a decades old blood feud – still unavenged. But he had emerged instead as a leader.

He had been sent to Afghanistan. The bitter cold had been a surprise. He had thought the desert nights of Algeria had been biting in their harshness. He had learned of frost, and even of snow, as he felt his fingers chill beyond usefulness. The country was untamed, the landscape no wilder than the people. He had been very young and had made many friends who carried him forward today. The bonds that were forged then in that raw and beautiful country proved to run as deep as its valleys.

Eventually, he had ended up in Europe, always moving. The continent had been good to him until now. He had moved across borders with little intervention or interest. He had sent men abroad to train and had helped them get established as revolutionaries back on their own soil. And always he knew that he could do as he liked – the laws allowed for his type of subversion.

Now, he was in a jail cell. His brilliant future on hold, hopefully just delayed. There was so much work to be done. His hands almost shook with the repressed tension of being held captive. Certainly they couldn't just keep him here forever? Allah, o merciful one, give me strength to survive. He whispered words from the Koran, "So lose no heart, nor fall into despair. For you must gain mastery if yea are true in faith." Tazkia, purification of the self as called for by Allah. This was his opportunity.

Khalil refocused on the sounds of the makeshift prison. Another prisoner, down the hall he guessed, would always start shouting at this time of day, demanding to be let out, pretending to be going insane with the confinement. As if faking insanity required much effort when you were caged up like a rat and given no date for the confinement's end. Right now he was just waiting to be released sometime in the deep abyss of forever.

He could hear guards rumbling slowly through the building or playing cards lazily near the front door. Occasionally Khalil would hear a phone ring. It was a simple routine here. Simple, but solitary. He had met no other prisoner, though he could hear the hum of them through the walls. At night he could hear the place shake with the coughs of men who had been taken from their homes. The poor souls who would haunt this country one day.

His mind continued its wandering. What a strange interrogation he had experienced earlier. Algeria, his father? Why?

Khalil pictured the vision of Algiers that he most loved. The magical side of the city as it sat nestled right on the deep blue of the Mediterranean. The white walls glowed next to the sea that gently lapped its shores. Some said the French heavily influenced the city. Having spent time in Paris, Khalil could understand the comparison. However, Algiers had retained the distinctive smells and feel of North Africa. He recalled the smell of exhaust mingled with lamb and fresh flowers. The rancidness of too many humans living under a vibrant and warm sun as it mixed with the pungency of the sea. Teashops dominated the social life of the city – or at least for the men. Boisterous groups spilled out onto the sidewalks, lively and full of bravado. Or so it had been before the killing had begun.

Khalil had wandered its narrow alleys as a young man, when he had been beginning his tenure as a revolutionary, a freedom fighter, a mujahadeen. He had visited the small shops for his meager needs – delighted to socialize and explore around the city. As a boy he had visited the city infrequently, consequently it had a hypnotic effect on him when he was finally able to live there. He had wandered to his hearts content, reading the bold signs printed in flowery Arabic.

His time then had been spent between the mosques and the teahouses. The French were long gone – or at least nominally. But revolution – a remaining European transplant - had still been in the air, intoxicating to the young men with so little future ahead of them. It had been an optimistic time – for doesn't the future always belong to the young? Yet, like so many youths before them, dreams had hardened into reality. The illusions they had chased were replaced with many different paths, each unique to the individual who followed it. Death had been the end result for too many.

Though he hadn't been back for years Khalil knew that Algiers would never be the same. Too many people had vanished. Allah, be praised. The winds which blew desert sand everywhere also blew with the rustling sound of aimless souls. The country needed its God – not much else was left.

Of course, Khalil hadn't grown up in Algiers proper but in a suburb – a poor Kasbah, full of cheap apartment building, even simple huts. Another world. Where Algiers was cosmopolitan and even somewhat sophisticated, Kheis el Khechna was where Khalil felt the more primal side of Algeria. It was hot, with little air flowing through it's over-crowded buildings. The desert, which formed so much of the country itself, had begun to seep in slowly, like the scorpions that hid quietly in dark corners. Poverty lead to a sense of desperation. The Frenchification of the country was less pervasive here and indeed had only occurred in its most outward manifestations. Some women had rebelliously thrown off their hijab, dressing instead like provincial Frenchwomen. But the calls to prayer came five times a day, ringing through each window, whether open or closed.

And, indeed, Khalil reminded himself, even Algiers itself didn't always live up to its geography. It was part of the fertile, vibrant strip of Algeria that bordered water. The rest of the country was desert. But, like all large African cities it had its slums, full of filth, smells and suffering. This jail cell was a palace in comparison. Extended families in

Algeria lived in much less.

Still, Algiers remained a blessed place in Khalil's mind. He would always associate the city with the dreams of his youth, before they had turned to sand.

Yet, his fight continued. The ummah, community of Muslims, would rule again. Blessed Allah, don't let them figure out who I really am, he prayed silently to himself.

He cursed himself again for getting caught. A fluke, a stupid fluke.

His mind drifted again, the tension in his body now searching for an outlet, trying to escape that trapped feeling, one he hadn't felt for a long time before his capture. The bed springs creaked as he shifted his weight.

His father, the swine. Swine – a word used for westerners. He and his brother had chosen this word for their father. It was the only one that was harsh enough – other than godless, which was another word they used often. After all, his father, Ali had chosen the path set forth by the French and had betrayed his family, his sons. Working for himself. Leaving his family for a new woman and a new family. Never attending mosque. Adopting western dress.

Khalil remembered the man as he sat in his favorite teashop. Ali was never physically imposing. He was actually quite small and weak. Khalil had learned young that looks were so often deceiving – a lesson that had served him well as both a soldier and as a leader. The swine was a bully. He always needed to find someone weaker to make him feel like the man he could never be. Ali threw his body into the frequent beatings he had directed at his wife and children until his two boys had mutually agreed to stop him – physically. Violence begat violence. Ali – a noble sounding name. The swine didn't have a noble quality about him. To this day Khalil could only picture him with his thin lips drawn up in an angry expression, opening to let ugly words spew out in his nasal voice.

"You want to do as you wish? Let me show you the reward of a child who does not properly respect his father."

Respect. Ali's eyes were like those of a dead man – they shone without light because the man had neither values nor interests. His only entertainment was drinking tea with his few equally contemptible friends in teahouses and beating the weak. He had left Allah and the righteous path. He would be judged when his time came.

Shortly after the 1990 elections, Khalil had visited his father – back then he had respected tradition and had upheld the image of a good son. Back then he still visited his father – he was only 24 at the time – not yet the man he would become.

"You lost, as I said you will always lose." His father had said, sitting amidst his circle of friends. "Why must I have a loser for a son? This country doesn't want to go back to its past, back to the Allah you so love. Praise be to the army for stopping the crazy lunatics, especially the crazy lunatic that is my son." His father had spit on the ground, and turned his back on Khalil.

Khalil had felt the burning sun upon him – as real as any emotion. His world stopped moving, if only for instant. He could feel each muscle in his body tighten. And he knew what course he would follow. Humiliation, from his own father. He was being humiliated as the French had humiliated Algeria herself so long ago. Yet, the people's hearts had spoken. First they had fought and broken the colonial yoke tight around their neck. Now they had voted for a return to religion and tradition. Ali's world was dead.

"You will die one day old man." Khalil said. "If I don't kill you first myself."

Khalil had walked away from that teahouse, never to return. As he left the laughter of his father's friends drifted to him. "Your son doesn't respect you?" "What sort of a man can you be to have such a disrespectful son?"

Men who loved only themselves and their own self-interest. Selfish man. For so long Khalil had bitten back the words that threatened to escape his lips. But now he was a mujahadeen. He had fought in Afghanistan. He had held the lives of men in his own hands. And he was serving Allah. He was a man now – he did not need to respect someone who mocked what should be held dear.

XXXXX

It was her – Stacey. The object of his desire. Today he would make another move. Omar had ignored her for two weeks – totally and absolutely. A beautiful girl like that had to wonder how she could turn so unimportant after their eyes had locked together for an immortal second. Had she imagined it? Had Omar not found her attractive? Thankfully, she hadn't come up to him. How he hated aggressive women. If he wanted a man in bed, he would find one. Omar preferred the softness of a woman yielding, fighting pleasure as her body overwhelmed her with lust. Such a sweet victory: watching a woman drop her inhibitions and give in to complete and overwhelming desire. The passion was always there; most men just didn't know how to find it. Omar had learned to make them wait an eternity for that orgasm. Letting tension build until they believed they would die if they didn't have it.

He stared at her. His eyes didn't waiver as they bored into her head.

"So, if we mix these two elements...." The teacher's monotone voice echoed against the walls of the cavernous classroom. He droned on. Omar ignored him. He had already read the chapter. With his brilliance, ignoring a lecture or two wouldn't harm his grade a bit.

To be fair, the teacher was usually quite riveting. Chemistry was fascinating; Omar would use it change the world. Mixing a few elements together, indeed. But chemistry of that sort wasn't his main objective right now.

A flash. Orange. And two eyes, staring back. His gaze was long and deep. Surprised – why was she being studied so intently? Or, so she must be asking.

Omar gazed at her. Again, not a hint of a smile. Just a deep gaze, penetrating but not threatening. His earlier reticence would prevent the label of obsessive stalker. No, he just stared deeply into two roundly perfect eyes, fringed with brown lashes. So beautiful.

She flushed, her milky skin suddenly hued a soft pink. American women so rarely saw pure sexual desire. Too often men were focused on being respectful or they projected simple animal lust. The key was to really want the woman in question, not just sex. And, let her know – blatantly. Why fear true desire?

But American women typically couldn't handle it. They ran away at first. Being genuinely noticed after having been ignored for too long was frightening, a worldview he could appreciate. But the women always came back. Who can resist being worshiped?

This time Omar let himself smile – to Stacey's back. His plan was moving forward beautifully. He could almost feel the pressure of her body.

XXXXX

The morning was cold. An out-of-season cold. A soft frost had settled on the expansive grass lawn like the most delicate carpeting. As George backed his car out of his garage he saw his breath each time he exhaled. His coat barely sheltered him from the cold and he impatiently willed the car to heat up.

Another interrogation. Inwardly he felt a groan rising.

His body sensed the presence of Stanford University, only a few familiar miles away. His beloved classroom was filled by a visiting professor that he would have to pry out of his semi-vacant spot (George had been gone way too long) and physically force back to the much colder eastern university he had so willingly abandoned. Life could really be a bitch. Tenure meant a lot, and there were always those professors who were just waiting for an opportunity to steal one of the few highly desired slots at a top university.

The car entered the freeway as if by its own volition. George tried to make the drive last – even though he knew logically how counterproductive procrastination was. Suddenly the jail, the ungainly and imposing and just plain horrible building rose up before him. His routine followed its normal course and before he knew it George was seated across from his prisoner in the increasingly grotesque cell.

"So how was your night? George asked. The grim dance would continue.

"Fine. No, not so fine." Khalil replied. "Why did you remind me of my father – the swine?" The man stared at him, into his eyes. Unusual for a detainee. Usually they wanted to avoid looking at you, especially if they had information. And George remained confident that this man did indeed have information. Perhaps it was only instincts which propelled his certainty, but they had worked well for him in the past.

"It is important for me to get a good understanding of you." George said. A hard question to answer so best to be somewhat honest but brief. That way the prisoner, Khalil, would not get too much information but would trust that he was being dealt with honestly and humanely – a far cry from how he was likely treated earlier while in detention. Swiftly, George put all ideas of torture and humiliation out of his head.

"Why? What are you looking for? I have been questioned, and then questioned again. I have no information. I am guilty of nothing. I was walking down a street in London. I hadn't been to London for a while, cursed place; I forgot the route I meant to take. Please, let me go. Or at least charge me with something and get me a lawyer. What your country is doing is illegal." Khalil's voice was not desperate. It was searching. Typical excitement oriented personality. Being confined was probably driving him crazy.

"Illegal is not a hard and fast rule. You are a terrorist, on a terrorist watch list." George said.

"One man's terrorist is another man's freedom fighter." Khalil replied. The man smiled slowly, seductively. Neither his mouth nor his eyes showed any warmth or joy. His tone was slightly patronizing, but it also exuded confidence and conviction. The effect was hypnotic. George watched, fascinated, as the words transformed a man who had looked normal and non-threatening into much more. This was how the man before him recruited people, talked them into dying. George let him talk, reminding himself that this man was more like a cobra than a religious leader.

"I have done nothing to harm your country. I have lived in your country, not far from here, when I was a young student in San Diego. Ah, those days...I learned about democracy, freedom, the right to life, surfing. The right to free and fair elections. All I ask is the same for my own people. They are downtrodden, so poor. If only you could see my country, feel the heart of the people. There tears sometimes providing the only water that feeds the soil." Khalil waved his orange-robed arm, a now familiar gesture.

"Liberte, egalite, fraternite." George spoke slowly, hesitant to break the mood. He was learning about this man and how he operated. But he couldn't give Khalil too much power. And Khalil was slowly showing him that he was used to grabbing power by trying to take over the interrogation.

George thought of an old trick he had once played in an interrogation. He believed that the man he was questioning, an Iraqi, was educated and knew a lot more than he was admitting. Yet the man adamantly kept protesting that he was just a poor, uneducated farmer. George had brought some documents into the interrogation room and asked the man if he would quickly take a look. The man agreed, trying to be helpful as he generally pretended to be. He reached for the glasses in his pocket. Except he had no glasses – they had been confiscated. But his pretense was over – only a man used to reviewing documents would reach for his glasses when asked to do so – not a poor, barely literate farmer such as he claimed to be.

Likewise, George could already tell with Khalil that he could not give up some semblance of control over the situation. Khalil was used to leading.

"You mock me." The man's voice, barely a whisper, choked slightly. George couldn't believe it. Khalil was willing to go with the drama of the mood. He was a cold-blooded killer, desensitized to death. He was part of an organization that hated all of what the west stood for. Yet he was willing to go with his bluff, after George's disrespectful reference to the French revolution – seeking what? Compassion. Empathy. Recognition of his humanity.

George spoke softly, mirroring the man's volume a moment ago. "I don't mock you, Khalil. I just don't believe you. Do you think we could get you extradited to the U.S. if your name was on a watch list only because of terrorist acts against Algeria, or even England? Why do you think you are here – your great love of this free and fair country"?

Khalil hesitated. So many directions to follow, George thought. Which one would he choose? The most obvious was to ask more about his extradition. He had no idea what evidence the U.S. government had but it must be concrete, right? Khalil must be driven to distraction not knowing what sort of bluffs to make. Based on Khalil's direction today he was going to go all the way and admit nothing. George would fix that.

"Ah, definitions," Khalil said. "A constantly changing thing. Your government kills a man, it is in pursuit of freedom. You kill a child and it doesn't matter. Do you think a mother cries any less because of her skin color? A man such as myself, with dreams of freeing my country from military rule and a murderous government – I alas am but a terrorist, a brute. Your millions who live on an intellectual diet of television and celebrity magazines are my superiors. They who vote for your murderous and blasphemous government. Yet I read philosophy and the Koran. What a world you have created – so free and fair I can't get either a lawyer or a judge. I sit here and wait." The lilting voice continued. Melodramatic, as middle-easterners or north Africans, liked to be. A typical emotional appeal – the type that never worked on George. However, the voice did hold a certain melody as it richly emphasized each word, as foreign speakers so often do.

George's mind wandered. Khalil wasn't going to admit that he yearned to know how he ended up here – yet he must. George knew. He had intended to use it against Khalil, a way to slowly call his bluffs. By dribbling a little bit of information at a time he would give Khalil an opportunity to tell the truth or to lie. By telling the truth he would incriminate himself. But by lying, he would incriminate himself more – because George did have enough information to catch him in some of those lies.

But for the technique to be effective Khalil should have started the dialogue. George wanted to see real want in him. That would be a show of weakness. Spouting off about his philosophies and oppression were mildly boring and very predictable. Each terrorist he had met always ranted about the twentieth century utopian vision of a bastardized French revolution. How he wished the French had stayed out of Algeria – they didn't know the canon they were setting off.

Besides, while the information he had was pretty good, he had very little of it. Khalil would have to supply the rest.

XXXXX

Khalil could see the man in front of him losing interest. Sure, his words were empty and predictable. Any half-wit Islamist could repeat the same rhetoric. Though they probably couldn't match his conviction and the unique intonations he had added to his soliloquies. These words contained his cover story. He would stick with them. The revolutionary, the freedom fighter, the noble descendent of the American revolutionary forces. And wasn't there some truth to it all? He did want a new vision for Algeria, indeed for the whole world – at the cost of blood when necessary. Islam would rule again and then he would be sitting on the other side of this absurd little table. Allah be praised.

So he stopped speaking. He had heard these words himself many times before. If the man in front of him wasn't listening there was no point in continuing. And he waited. Watching. What would his adversary do now?

"How do you define a good man?" George asked. "You said your father is not a good man. You read philosophy. What have you concluded?" George's face as he sat opposite Khalil was welcoming. Khalil laughed.

"This is a cocktail party, isn't it? Let us enjoy a light conversation on the meaning of life. I wish I had crimes to confess so I could end this excruciating waste of my time." Deflect, deflect, always deflect Khalil reminded himself. Did this stupid man want him to admit that he thought Osama Bin Laden was the ideal man? Did he really expect him to disclose the plot that was unfolding on American soil as the two of them sparred? Well, hopefully it was unfolding.

XXXXX

"Tell me about Jennifer."

Khalil felt the world around him recede. He certainly hadn't anticipated this move from George. It was as if he had been punched – hard – in the stomach. He struggled for his bearings but instead heard only a roaring in his head. The white noise was replaced by the name, repeated again, 'Jennifer'.

Khalil heard a husky laugh ringing in his ears. It filled his head but was accompanied by no pictures. Strange how sometimes a person's voice returns, yet you can't remember what they look like.

Khalil's old apartment unfolded in his thoughts. It had been a small, dingy place – not really much different from the cell he was living in now. Then he had been very poor – his education paid for by his brothers in the movement of which back then he was barely a part. The room always had a faint odor and the wallpaper had started to peel. It was a palace compared to the hut in which he had grown up. He adored it because it was his.

Jennifer was intimately tied up with his memories of this apartment. Even now he remembered the early dawn shadows that fell on her face as she slept next to him. He would wake up early then so he could stare at her – the milky skin, the smooth expanse of her firm body and the ever so light blonde hair which spread across his pillows.

Jennifer loved to play music for him. Her passion was reggae and he still knew every Bob Marley song by heart. Somehow the lesser-known reggae stars she favored never managed to catch his fancy. Still, every time he heard the familiar rolling beats, which wasn't so often, his body would ache for her and the warm and alive feel of her in his arms. Bob Marley was global.

*I don't want to wait in vain for your love....*

Slowly his surroundings began coming back – as they always would. He saw an older and all too familiar man sitting on the other side of his cracked table. George's white shirt was too stark for the room.

Disorientation was replaced by anger. Why wasn't this man asking about bombs? Why wasn't he probing about fighting or Afghanistan, Algeria, Iraq? Khalil had prepared answers for those questions. He had a story, backed by an ideology, reinforced by a goal. Yet George wasn't playing by the rules. Why was he asking about Khalil's father? Why was he asking about Jennifer?

He faced the man sitting before him and started to speak.

XXXXX

"Who is Jennifer?" Khalil didn't budge, a pillar of bright orange.

George suppressed his smile. He had seen Khalil's face when he initially asked the question. Panic. A repressed topic. No longer painful because it was so deeply hidden and completely sanitized. George knew what that meant. He so loved to find the weak spots. It made his job much easier. Of course he wouldn't press the topic now. He would let it fester a while. The shock value in a hardened man like Khalil had already worn off. He would shut down the whole topic within his mind. But slowly it would burn. George would bring it up again, later.

"Your ex-fiancé." Not that George wouldn't play around a little bit first. He wanted it to really start stinging. A quick return to the files of the repressed wasn't going to be good enough.

"I've never been engaged." Khalil said.

"Really, not even in Algeria." George replied. "Your overbearing father never tried to betroth you?" A double whammy – bring the father back in.

Khalil visibly winced. "No, that was only for my poor sisters."

The pain. That was the part of the job George hated the most. He stared over Khalil's hunched shoulder, willing himself to continue. Nothing like kicking a man when he was down. Far from home, not that many of these men even had a home anymore. No, repressive governments and oppressive poverty had robbed them of that. Oh, and of course the lure of rebellion, or jihad. Murder. Whichever.

But sometimes you had to break a man completely to get the information you wanted. Los Angeles, his only real clue.

George focused again on the man before him, weakened yes, but not even close to being broken. He forced himself to forget about compassion. His objective was too important.

"You love your sisters." George said.

"Yes." The response was simple, as dignity always is.

"Tell me what happened to them." George continued probing.

"I don't want to talk about my sisters."

Khalil looked defiant. His eyes glowed, his body was tense. George always got exasperated when his interogees were defiant. Defiance was a child's game. Petty rebellion. It was the sign of a low-level recruit. A smarter man would worry about survival, and most importantly, release. It was the impulsive and unwise who got defiant and rebelled.

"Why not?" George kept his tone measured. His disgust was masked, absolutely.

"Allah be praised, they are happily married and have been blessed with many children. There is nothing to discuss – they are women."

Marvelous recovery, George thought to himself. Not fully believable, but okay.

"Jennifer is divorced now." George said. "But you knew that didn't you?" Hit him again, while he was still weak.

Khalil sat in his chair – not moving again. His shoulders were slightly hunched and looked small in his baggy jumpsuit.

George stood up.

"Good night, Khalil. I must leave now."

Khalil nodded his head in acknowledgement. His eyes no longer went to his safe spot on the wall. Instead they stayed completely still, staring at George.

XXXXX

Omar's stride was unhurried and confident. He had worked hard to perfect it. Cool, calm and in control. Life was a game, as he had learned from his teacher, Ms.. Haas, years ago. And the game must be won.

Stacey was heading his way, once again toward the classroom door. It was easy to run into her on the way into class – everyone was supposed to arrive by a specific time. Only the geeks and nerds, about half the class, got there more than five minutes early. Only the truly irresponsible, a rarity in a graduate level science class, got there late. So, the timing was easy to master. Class ran on a clock, and clicked with absolute predictability. Just like the bombs he was busily working on at home.

Today she was wearing a short skirt, denim with a fringed hem. She had paired it with cowboy boots and a thin white t-shirt. The outline of her breasts was clear in the sunlight. Who was she trying to impress? Or was she just a slut?

He moved with as little deliberation as he could muster, his movements smooth and rhythmic. So much practice.

He hadn't known when he went to Switzerland how to walk like this. Of course, his years of swimming had probably left him with a certain grace. But he guessed that his movements then had combined that fluidity with youthful awkwardness. All of those hormones making finesse a true test of discipline. Or, so Ms. Hass had told him.

Ms. Haas, he never thought of her as Ana – her given name. Indeed, he never much thought of her anymore. She had been his teacher at the

Swiss boarding school, a hellhole. Walking into his first class in the cold and miserable mountain town sheltering the small school, he had seen two blue eyes gazing at him. Blue eyes, could anything be more revolting? Her eyes had been watery and they had simmered. Back then he hadn't understood what her look meant.

"Omar. Please sit in that desk, there." The statement came out clearly, though her heavy Austrian accent should have distorted the words more.

Omar stumbled to the desk, dead center of the room. At that point he only felt awkward. The sexual tension would come later. At that instant the idea of being attracted to the woman would have seemed absurd. She was too wrong in every way: too old, too curvy, too garishly dressed, too made-up. Her blond hair had too much air in it and an artificial tint that lacked the sophisticated artistry of hair like Stacey's. She just looked cheap, even to a hopelessly homesick and lost boy who had left Saudi Arabia for the first time.

She had been the teacher, he had become the master. From her he had learned that being too obvious only worked on the truly innocent – as he had been then, at fourteen. Only the most naïve are incapable of recognizing a threat.

Stacey wasn't like that. He watched the slight swagger in her step. Her legs moved seamlessly as if she were making love while she walked across the broad, green lawn. This girl had been used repeatedly, as had most attractive American women in their early twenties.

They arrived at the classroom door together. He looked at her, feigning disinterest. Slowly, a naughty smile lit up her face; she had recognized him. Stacey probably expected him to talk to her, to show some interest. Hadn't his eyes been fixed on her for the past few weeks? A trick picked up from Ms. Haas, then perfected. He stared through her. Much as he tried not to look, he also noticed her confusion. Her eyes were a soft brown, and hinted at just a touch of green. The green lawn behind her almost seemed to pull new colors out of the irises. And they were gentle, bordering on sweet. Her smile had turned vulnerable. That was exactly how she should feel. Totally confused. That is what mixed messages did – they made you doubt your own perceptions. She had to wonder why her admirer had lost interest. So let her wonder. Seduction was more interesting than chemistry any day.

"After you." Omar gestured for her to pass. It was an obvious mimicry of their early interaction. A knowing look crossed her face before she passed in front of him. Let her wonder. He knew she would.

XXXXX

Karen. George dialed his cell phone again, trying her number. He listened for the familiar noises. Nothing. Dead, just dead. Was it the telephone? His phone or hers? How did that work exactly – if he placed a call and her phone was in an area without service? Did it just go to voicemail? Presumably. So it must be his phone that wasn't working.

He keyed in the numbers one more time only to hear the annoying failed call signal. Then, he slowed to avoid hitting a truck. Did the truck driver think he would get somewhere faster by acting as if he owned the road? Such an attitude had to be unwise in a world where most other drivers were struggling with technology as they drove. Like George.

Well, the failed calls neatly summed up the current stage of their relationship. He didn't seem to reach her a lot these days. In many ways. Except when they fought, as they had the night before. And, they both went to sleep mad. How many people actually followed that miserable advice about making up before bed anyway? What if you just continued the fight in bed?

Of course, he had been physically gone too much over the past few years – leaving her for the next round of interrogations in whatever God-awful place a voice on the telephone directed him to. How could he not chastise himself for that? And, he hadn't wanted her to visit. Every single country had been dangerous. Moreover, he hadn't wanted her to see the prison camps surrounded by barbed wire – there to keep people both in and out (that is, if he could even get clearance for her to visit). Why risk her life as well as his own?

But, in his own defense, he had tried hard to stay in touch. When there was access to telephone service he called her. When calling hadn't been possible he had sent letters. Each letter had been a masterpiece in its own way. Of course, he hadn't been able to tell her much of what he was doing – classified. And, he hadn't always been able to tell her where he was – classified, as well. But he had told her what was going on inside his own head – the conflicts, fears, triumphs and failures. And he had always told her how much he loved her. But it was all just paper, no matter how much time he dedicated to writing on it.

It is hard to feel intimate when you don't have access to a loved one. The telephone communicated thoughts at the instant you had them. But being with someone added a physical aspect to the dialogue – a heat that can't be felt when alone.

So the space had crept into their relationship. She called him less often now than she did before he had left. She didn't seem to need him much. Indeed, she could no longer find him on campus or meet him for lunch – had she even wanted to. George was no longer the presence he had been to his wife.

He pictured her face from the night before and reached for his phone again – to make one more attempt. Her hair had been pulled straight back off her face, leaving the smooth skin and delicate features fully exposed. At one point tears had dotted her eyes until she decided to call him insensitive and storm out of the room.

The call failure sound again. What was wrong with Silicon Valley? Why couldn't you make a local call in the hub of the technology industry?

If she already thought he was insensitive, what would she think if she watched him mentally pummel Khalil all day?

Well, things had changed for him. Perhaps he was more guarded now, even at home. He felt a new somberness in his daily life. He was a soldier in a way. Scared. How do you tell the woman you love that most of the time you are just plain scared? Aren't men supposed to be strong? George didn't feel strong anymore. He had seen too much of the real world. More than anything he wanted his life to be the way that it had been before. Instead, pictures of twisted metal and body parts haunted him, replaying in a virtual loop inside his mind.

The cell phone was useless in his hands. The buttons worked, but the phone itself had decided not to. In about twenty minutes he would arrive home.

XXXXX

The morning officially began as it always did. Khalil's first set of prayers was done by the time breakfast arrived at 7:00, brought by a nameless faceless guard. Was it the same man as yesterday? They all looked the same.

The food was uninspiring – a crescent-shaped pastry, cream cheese, an under-ripe banana, a bottle of water and a huge blueberry muffin. And coffee, always coffee. Khalil hated coffee and had requested an end to its inclusion in the meal. He was still waiting for it not to arrive. The distinctive smell contaminated his cell within seconds of arriving each morning. Luckily, bacon hadn't been served. If it had, he would have been stuck with that smell for an indeterminate time period as well. Muslims don't eat pork.

Like clockwork, the guards were always on time. Americans were very good at the functional parts of life. They just lacked passion. And soul. Hence the very mundane and tasteless food. During his imprison ment in Egypt the food had arrived haphazardly and sometimes not at all. But the Egyptians took jail very seriously and provided food meant to punish – rice with bugs, stale bread, and no luxuries such as meat.

After breakfast Khalil would be escorted to the showers, an armed guard behind him. He could see the cameras stationed in the hallways as he walked the familiar path. Most guards never spoke to him beyond the bare minimum of orders and the quick answer to a question. One guard, Joe, was very different. He loved to talk about his mountain bike rides and tell jokes. Khalil found him the most of annoying of a very bad bunch. They were all women, pansies. The only thing about any of them which carried any authority was the gun strapped around their waists.

The shower was always warm, but never hot. The jets would send cascades of water over his body. The steam was a welcome bit of variety – his sensual pleasures were so limited that even such a small thing could matter. Khalil's senses were ailing – who could survive on so little stimulation? After the shower Khalil would be led back to his room, the tray always having disappeared in the interim.

The rest of the day would grind on in a similarly predictable and dull manner. It was a limited existence. It wore on Khalil like an open sore.

XXXXX

Five bombs. Omar had to make five bombs. He had enough time to make them; that wasn't an issue. He had a supplier for the explosives and for the chemicals he needed to make sarin. Another non-issue. His expertise was beyond question thanks to five months spent training in Northern Pakistan. And Allah had blessed his mission.

So what was the problem?

Omar fingered a battery. He considered, very briefly, wrapping it delicately with the wire that he had sitting on the coffee table. Then, his mind wandered back to the hair, so thick and full of color. He was getting obsessed. Ah, but why not? Life got boring quickly. Going to class, working out, going to hear the imams speak. He had heard enough imams. It was time for action!

He felt his cock swelling up. How long would it take before he possessed that woman? He reminded himself as he always did when lust took control that the direct approach never worked, especially with the pretty ones. They would just look you in the eye, smile sweetly and say "No".

Ms. Haas had never approached him directly. Omar could still picture the hair between her legs. Light brown and coarse. With the slightest hint of a curl. He had loved licking it and tasting her sweat. Even the memory of that slightly pungent smell had the power to arouse him almost to an orgasm, his whole body alive with sensation.

Nothing about sex with her had been natural, yet he had always believed otherwise when trapped so deeply in her web. She had created an illusion.

"Omar, please wait one minute after class. I need to speak with you. It won't take but an instant." Her look had been innocuous, almost not even a look at all. The class had snickered. But then hadn't they always snickered when he was involved. To them, European aristocracy, otherwise known as Euro-trash, he was a rough Arab boy. Who cared if his father had money? Omar could feel the contempt. He had prayed that his cheeks wouldn't burn, at least not visibly.

"Yes, ma'am." More giggles. How was he supposed to say it?

As he had approached her desk he could feel the nervous energy in his body. The placid cow of a woman was looking at him intently, not hiding her interest.

"Omar, I am a bit concerned," she said. Not worried, no. Why completely frighten an adolescent boy? Better to wound him mildly.

"Yes, ma'am." Now she smiled too. Omar could feel himself turn red. He had waited, standing there before her like a sacrificial lamb.

"You seem to be having a rough time getting used to … well, I guess there is no delicate way of saying it…."

Omar could feel sweat breaking out on the back of his neck. He stared past her, avoiding the round, slightly reddish face and insipid eyes. Instead he stared at the map of Western Europe which she had left covering the chalkboard. Who knew Great Britain was so alone?

"…the ways of the school. We have a very sophisticated and cosmopolitan student body. A fast crowd if you will. Let me intercede to speed up your integration."

He had been forced to look at her then. Her whole face shone with earnestness and concern. Quickly he nodded ascent. If only he could have escaped then.

Suddenly, her movements were brusque. She picked up a pen and wrote out something on a piece of paper in front of him. She handed it to him.

"Please, come to my apartment this evening. 7:00 P.M. Don't be late. I will teach you about fitting in." With that she had waived him away, suddenly impatient. He had walked out of the classroom. Could she really make him be less alone? Why couldn't he just go home instead?

XXXXX

Stepping through the doorway George noted the boy sitting behind the desk. The same guard always seemed to get desk duty. He was so young it was probably better that he was kept away from the prisoners.

He didn't look tough enough to handle them. Not like Sean, with his linebacker shoulders and quick fists.

The boy's nametag said Joe. GI Joe?

"Good morning, sir." The tone of the greeting was brisk but the boy couldn't carry it off. He was too soft. Though with that wandering, half-crossed eye he certainly must have toughened over the years. Kids could be mean and undoubtedly they had teased him mercilessly. Who knew what kinds of emotional scars had resulted. Men were shot for such slurs in some parts of the world. Probably not in this boy's neighborhood.

"Where are you from, private?" George refocused on the boy, ignoring the eye. The soldier was all good will, with a touching innocence in his eyes, even the crossed one. The eyes were a deep, dark brown, like Khalil's, but they couldn't be any more different.

"San Diego, sir." Khalil went to school in San Diego. That was long ago but the boy would have been alive at the time. Although maybe just barely.

"Detainee 182 went to college there. Did you know that?" George said.

"No, sir." The boys eyes darted away, or at least his one good eye did.

George sat down on the corner of the desk. His back was half turned to the boy, but he was still able to gaze at his face. He tried not to stare as he studied the boy's features, evaluating each angle and plane. How features settle into a person's face reveal the underlying personality - always. Most people don't really look at others. The boy was clean cut, but dark. His skin was that milky coffee color which George always found slightly off-putting – if only he could come up with another image. The soldier was probably of middle eastern descent – not that all middle easterners were fanatical Islamic militants nor were all terrorists, even Muslim ones, from a middle eastern background.

The nose lost definition in the bridge. The eyes were a mess. But the lips were surprisingly strong and firm, especially when contrasted by the round chin. Interesting.

George just wondered – could this boy be part of a terrorist cell? Could he have infiltrated the army? What could be a better posting for such a militant? Were George's conspiracy theories going completely off the deep end? He really needed to give interrogation a rest for a while, didn't he? How far away from a serious personality disorder was he at this point?

"Do you like it here?" George asked, persisting, and knowing full well that he was probably crossing over into a new realm of psychosis.

"It's alright, sir." The boy looked frightened, as if no one had ever spoken to him as he sat at the jail's entryway.

"Please, no more 'sir.'" George used his comforting voice, the one that soothed tearful patients and calmed overzealous students. "Tell me how you ended up here?" Do you like it?"

"It's okay." The boy hesitated, and George could almost hear his silent 'sir'. The accent was flat – strictly Southern California. "When I volunteered I asked for something in intelligence and they sent me here. Not as exciting as I expected, I guess." The boy managed a slight smile and George noticed how his eyes came alight. Probably just a nice kid. Or at least one with a sense of humor. Still, he couldn't help but wonder.

How could a kid like that – who clearly had had to defend himself from teasing - be so pure? The kid was off, and no, it wasn't just his eye. George's paranoia was a valuable tool – he just had to keep his thoughts private. And, his instincts matched – spot on too often. This picture didn't work.

"You speak Arabic?"

"A little bit." The boy studied him. It was a cool appraisal – disengaged. His eyes had taken on the look of a snake – all killer. The transformation had been shockingly quick – like that of a psychopath. Or, was George imagining things?

"I would have expected them to send you abroad. Use that Arabic."

"Six months," Joe said. "Well, that's the promise. I was supposed to fill in on interrogations here as a translator first. But no one has needed me much. Seems like the shortage of Arabic speakers is all overseas." The boy was still wary, but his eyes had softened. Smart move.

"You were born in San Diego?"

"No, Cairo. You sure ask a lot of questions, sir." The boy attempted another smile but couldn't complete it. He just couldn't pull off the casual Southern California boy. Blame the eyes. The boy didn't fit. He switched back and forth between naïve and hard. Like a chameleon.

"Yes. I do ask a lot of questions," George said. "I am an interrogator, and you might be able to help me. You can talk to the prisoners in their own language, as you just said. You can befriend them. Do you ever leave this desk?"

"Every morning and evening, to help out. But I don't think the prisoners would be interested in befriending me. I am a guard, sir." The boy leaned back in his chair and crossed his arms over his chest, using his body language to shut George out.

"I think they might." George persisted. His job didn't allow for quitting. "These men are lonely. They could use a friend. Especially a compatriot. Tell me, do you think of them as terrorists or as freedom fighters? Are they like George Washington fighting the tyranny of the colonizers or are they no good criminals. What do you think?"

"How like George Washington?" George noted that the boy didn't look at all confused. He was bluffing. He knew exactly what George meant.

"The United States, as you know, was a colony of England," George said. "We were repressed and overtaxed. Controlled by a government not of our making. Brave men stood up to the Brits. Some have compared the Islamists to the patriotic freedom fighters who freed our own country from tyranny. The men we call terrorists object to the control the United States has over their lands and governments. They think we steal the wealth that is their due – oil and whatever industry they have. We support their corrupt governments. What do you think?"

"Man, that is way to much for me," Joe replied. "I joined the army because I didn't want to go to college." The boy looked bored. His bad eye seemed even less focused than it was before – if that was possible. Someone else who didn't want to listen to George. You would think he would get used to it.

*I'll be watching you.* George turned away from the boy. It was his job to be paranoid, to think of everything. Imagine if this G.I. helped

Khalil – or any other prisoner - get away and George let it happen because he never bothered to pay attention. Just one more private – a pawn. But, if something didn't fit you had to question your assumptions – and trust your instincts.

San Diego was also close to Los Angeles.

XXXXX

Omar had shown up promptly at 7:00, as instructed. Ms. Haas' apartment had been in a respectable, if inexpensive, neighborhood. A world of grey. Now he knew the world was full of places like that – they disappeared into the scenery even as they were the scenery. He had walked up to the drab building and rung the bell. After diligently locating her name on the directory first. Wasn't that what a respectful student should do?

In the lobby he had walked straight to the elevator. Marble floors, chipped here and there. Fear clung to him as he made his way to her apartment. This wasn't done in Saudi Arabia. He heard the bell chime as he pushed the small button. How he wished time could move faster so he could make his escape.

The door opened. Ms. Haas was wearing some sort of dress. It seemed to be a kaleidoscope of colors, all of them blurring ultimately into one. He had been momentarily blinded. Even today that sensation of being totally overcome with confusion could strike out of nowhere.

"Please, do come in, Omar." He had followed, obedient. A scent lingered behind her as she walked. He couldn't decide if he liked it or not.

The apartment had been simply furnished. Flowers, from the sofa print to the curtains, had taken over. Brimming vases cluttered tables and even a bookshelf, adding an even more dizzying smell to his already reeling perceptions.

Ms. Haas had gestured to the sofa. She herself sat down gently, as if conscious of her every movement.

"Would you like something to drink?" She had smiled. Had he been so innocent then that he had believed she was sincere? That, at least, Omar could remember.

"No, no thank you." Of course there had been a stammer in his voice. He had been but a boy, so far away from home. And alone.

"Oh, Omar, please feel at home here. I will help you. There is so much for you to learn. The children at the school are nice children. But, they're just not used to you yet. Omar, you must learn to get along with them and don't expect others to make the effort. Many of them have known each other for years."

Omar could still remember her smiling again. That first evening she had smiled a lot. They had been seated on her floral garden of a couch. Her hand had reached out and squeezed his knee, a small green and gold ring poising momentarily above its target before striking. He jumped. Other than his family, no woman had ever before touched him. No smile had been on her lips then. Her face had been serious and her gaze direct. Now he would recognize it as lust. The actual seduction had happened quickly.

"You must learn how to handle girls. As friends. Do you have girls as friends in your country?"

"No, ma'am."

"I told you to stop calling me ma'am, Omar." The look had been strict – a parent scolding a child, a teacher instructing a pupil. "You are a very interesting boy, Omar. So handsome, and so young."

The hand returned as she caressed his shoulder, the touch somehow both light and firm at the same time. He had only stared. Not sure what to say. Or do. She had been breathing slightly harder then, and a slight flush had illuminated her face. The smell of roses perfumed the air. Somehow her body made its way closer to him, and he could see the curve of her breasts stretching against the thin cotton of her dress. A blue dress covered with daisies. How could he remember such details even today?

Suddenly, her hand, firm and sure, was between his legs. From that point on he had been driven by hormones, his body unable to stop the torrent of control from between his legs. Her hand had probed, reaching inside his clothes.

Omar felt a glorious squeeze as she found his penis. A shiver ran up his spine.

Roughly she used her other hand to remove his pants and underwear. For a brief moment he felt her hand disappear as she removed her own clothes. Never had he wanted anything more than to have that hand back, grasping his cock. His wish was granted and she began to stoke him. She guided his hands to her breasts. He found himself cradling them, which somehow translated to a surge in his groin area.

His cock was fully engorged as she lowered herself moaning on top of it. He felt a warm engulfment as he entered her and his hips began to rock uncontrollably.

Ms. Haas was moving on top of him, her breath coming in great gasps. He remembered the great surge of tension that had exited his body. Then she lay prostate on top of him. Her sobs had moved him strangely; though he hadn't been able to identify the precise emotion they stirred. Nothing excited him more to this day than to get that depth of emotion out of a woman during sex or after. That moment when all inhibitions have broken down. The wet, stickiness of bodily fluids mixing together.

XXXXX

The old woman shivered. Her hut was bitingly cold. She couldn't afford enough wood to fight the harsh desert night.

Tenderly, she lifted her glass of tea to her lips – all anticipation. The hot liquid warmed her body, comforting in its acrid bitterness, the sweetness reminiscent of her favored candy as a child – so rarely tasted and savored. Setting down the clear, small glass she pulled her blanket around her. The flickering light from her candle lent an odd intimacy.

A brusque knock on the door surprised her. Company, especially at night, was rare. Slowly hauling her body to the door she opened it. No fear was left in her with respect to who could be on the other side.

"Leila," a voice whispered softly, Ama, her neighbor and a dear friend. "Sorry to bother you so late. My husband had a visitor. He heard that the Americans have captured Khalil. My apologies to you for the news, but I had to pass it on. Praise be to Allah." With that Ama turned, pulling her shawl tightly against her to ward off the wind. She disappeared quickly into the night, no doubt fearing her husband would notice her absence.

Leila closed the door, almost not feeling her movement. A new wave of grief and terror overwhelmed her. Her body knew the emotions well.

She was alone, no one to comfort her. Long ago, her husband had abandoned her for a newer and younger wife. While she didn't miss his harsh blows and even harsher words she did miss the dinars he had provided. Luckily Khalil had been a loyal son and had sent her what he could over the years.

Khalil, her younger son. His brother long dead. She remembered all of her children, as she often did. How she had cradled their small bodies while nursing them as babies. Their small faces had changed expressions, first staring at her with curiosity, then adoration. When they started walking their eyes had always returned to her for assurance and comfort, especially when they fell or tried something particularly daring.

But the looks had changed over the years. Her three daughters had been sold to her husband's favored suitors as soon as they turned seventeen. She remembered her middle daughter, Fatma, as she had clung to her mother's skirts crying, hysterical, begging to be saved from the old man she was being forced to marry. Fatma's gentle eyes, though red and tear soaked, had been all Leila could see of her through her hijab. But Leila had let Fatma down, as she had let them all down. As her mother had let her down.

Hassan, her older boy, who had loved life and never stopped laughing. A deep throaty laugh that always brought a smile to her face. She remembered his lifeless body as she cradled it in her arms until all of its warmth was gone. The body had slowly stiffened, becoming more like a statue than a person. She hadn't let go until the next day, again helpless as another of her children was ripped from her arms. This one had to be buried within twenty-four hours of death, as was Allah's will. The tears had rolled down her face as dirt hit his coffin with a thud.

Now Khalil was a prisoner. Who knew what they would do to him. Would they torture him? Was he in pain now, as she lay helpless in this miserable hut? Khalil who had adored her the most of her children when he was small. The sound of her voice had always made him stop whatever he was doing, his eyes focused on pinpointing her location, and, when old enough, running to her. That precious and familiar little body which she could still remember cradling. The gentle caresses, whispered endearments and soft kisses. Had they all been in vain? She couldn't remember the last time she had seen his face. If he came back to Algeria, he would be killed.

Leila lay down on the pile of blankets that made up her bed. She slowly pulled another blanket over her. Deep sobs shook her frail body. She didn't pray to Allah. She had no prayers left for him. Her husband had rejected her. She hadn't pleased him. Therefore her destiny was sealed – Leila would rot in hell, a sentence she had already started serving.

XXXXX

Khalil felt himself slowly waking. He saw the soft pink light of dawn, mingled with perhaps a bit of purple. The hue was hazy as he began to open his eyes. His dream lingered, warmth permeating his consciousness. Slowly focusing he saw the familiar jail cell and closed his eyes once again, falling back into the comforting memory of his dream.

He had been lying in his mother's arms. Her body, fleshy and full, had held him gently. He could feel her tender hands caress his small back, for he was still a boy in the dream. It was a familiar scene, replayed many times during his childhood. His mother had been the one to comfort him after his father's beatings. Only in her arms had Khalil been able to release his pain, the hurt and the betrayal caused by his father's brutality. Only there could he cry, listening to her lilting voice as she soothed him. With his mother he had felt safe, though even then she hadn't been able to protect him from the world.

Yet his mother had been a pillar in his early life. He loved her still.

During his first battle he had not cried, though he had wanted to. Years of resisting weakness, not rewarding his father with tears, the swine, had paid off then. Those years had hardened something within him. However, he had never been able to discuss that battle with his mother. When he tried, he could feel the tears crushing up inside him. But he had no longer been a child then.

Khalil visualized his mother's broad face in which her soft eyes were the highlight. The warmth of his dream was beginning to wear off, and he could feel a harsh blanket against his skin. The cover it provided couldn't approximate the warmth of his mother's body. He tried picturing her again, treasuring the image and trying to return to the dream. Of course, in reality only her face and hands could ever be seen; the rest was always covered. Still, he savored his memories of her full lips, her warn hands and the richness of her laugh. He could never go back.

Khalil's father was so different. He had the thin lips and harsh voice of the villain from a Hollywood movie. Almost a caricature of one. Character was reflected in a person's face, wasn't it?

"What does my own face look like now?" speaking only to the bare walls around him. Was it blank, devoid of all feeling or emotion? Was that why he didn't care about death? Perhaps he didn't care about death because he was no longer among the living. Early on he had believed in martyrdom. Now he didn't believe in anything other than winning. His lifestyle allowed for little else. Had he gone from extremism to nihilism?

And he had disappointed his mother. He could have stayed at home, gotten a job, had children. Protected her. But he had chosen instead to step into his dead brother's shoes.

The warmth. Khalil missed his mother's warmth. He felt it so rarely now. The only other place he had found that sort of warmth, and that feeling of belonging, had been with Jennifer. But, as with his mother, he had told Jennifer little, and had left her with even less. But he wasn't going to think about Jennifer, was he?

Khalil heard the leaden footsteps which signaled the imminent arrival of Sean, the sadistic brute. Sean was destined to be a prison guard, adding to the misery of many a prisoner's experience, including Khalil's own. One day Khalil would crush Sean's skull between his hands. It was only a matter of time.

The wind whistled outside the jail. Khalil could almost hear a woman crying.

XXXXX

The letdown, when it came, happened quickly. It was absolute. Snow had fallen. The world had seemingly gone from green to white overnight. When he had seen the first snowflakes Omar had grabbed at them greedily, marveling at their fragility. Their intricacy was so unlike the heavier desert sands of his home. Yet how completely they covered the landscape and transformed it into a new world.

The novelty had faded fast. What one day had the softness of frosting on a cake turned into a new burden forced by his father. The winter was cold – crushingly, overwhelmingly cold. Omar had never been so frozen in his life and the chill refused to lift. He begged his father to bring him home. The telephone line had echoed with the emptiness of his pleas.

"You're being educated. You should thank Allah one thousand times for this opportunity," his father said. I never expected that I could afford a school like this for you."

It could have been any parent speaking to any child. Yet it was he, Omar. Stuck alone in a frigid and hostile place.

Ms. Haas had tutored him in the ways of the west. She had spent hours explaining what normal teenagers were like and how they should behave.

"Just try, Omar. They're spoiled, but they are not bad kids."

But they were bad kids, and Omar couldn't fit in.

"They all take drugs," he had argued. "They drink and say things that are not respectful."

"Teenagers do that. More so at boarding school, where their parents can't watch them. But they don't all do that – not even here." Ms. Haas was lying naked on her bed. Her flesh was a pale and pasty color. Omar's slimmer and darker limbs were wrapped up tightly with hers as he sought a way to fight the cold. The profusion of flowers that surrounded them – the bed sheets, the curtains, the full vases – seemed oddly out of place, given the season. She seemed lost without her elaborate garden-like cocoon.

"They mock me. They hate me." Omar said.

"Get over yourself. They barely notice you. You don't try."

He stared at her. "I'm trying," he said. What did this whore really know? All she knew how to use was her body. And the best man she could get was a mere homesick boy. Could there be a worse place than a boarding school in a small Swiss town?

"No, you aren't." She dismissed his concern coldly.

"Shut up, you cunt." He slapped her; his palm rang hollow as it hit her face. The red rose from under the paleness of her cheek. Omar braced himself. He expected her to yell or somehow fight him.

Slowly, Ms. Haas began to move, getting closer as she did so. Omar pulled back from her. Immediately, he felt ashamed of his own cowardice. She caressed his inner thighs. He was too shocked to feel anything. What was wrong with her?

"Hit me, Omar. Hit me again. Hard, very hard. Just not my face." Her lips turned up in a grin. "See, you have learned something – you have learned to swear – which turns me on." Her breathing was heavy and the redness from his palm was no longer visible in the flush of her whole face. Her tongue stuck out ever so slightly. She looked grotesque.

Ms. Haas' hands probed his body, but they no longer felt sensual, not even to a fourteen-year-old boy brimming with hormones. She was grasping everywhere, her palms turning sweaty, leaving a wet trail like that of a snail.

For the first time since she had seduced him, Omar felt violated. He couldn't escape those hands and the flesh that swelled up behind them. Had he ever consented to this? Still, the fingers kept probing, pressing into his body's crevices. They crawled across his flesh seemingly not noticing that they were passing across a human being.

"Omar, I said hit me." The voice was a command. No, more a demand, uttered from the lips of one who told him what to do daily. She was his only companion. He could not refuse her. So, he hit her. Hard. His open palm slammed against her hip. He heard her yelp. Was it with pleasure or with pain?

"Again." He hit her once more, this time his hand crashed into her thigh. She leapt onto him. Her wet mouth was crushing his, her tongue probing everywhere. She straddled him yet he couldn't respond. The horror was too great. This woman was really raping him. And was he really alone with just her in this God-forsaken country? What sort of debauched world had he entered, courtesy of his father?

He pushed her off and looked at her, breathing hard against her flowery sheet. Her eyes glowered.

"Get out. Now!" Ms. Haas shrieked at him, quivering.

Omar almost tripped as he struggled out of the bed. A sheet had somehow wrapped itself around one of his legs. The bright colors and elaborate pattern made it harder for him to discern where one part began and another ended. He struggled, feeling her glare.

From then on, she taunted him more than the other students did.

XXXXX

"So, do you saw off people's heads? George kept his voice cheery. He was going to start the conversation today. And he was going to control it.

Khalil smiled, looking cool and slightly superior. His thin shoulders were visible under the shocking orange cotton coveralls. He looked slightly emaciated, as most revolutionaries manage to do.

"No. That was Abu Musab al' Zarquiwi, a Jordanian," he said. "Dead now. I am an Algerian. In Algeria we prefer the 'Kabyle smile'." He stared at George, clearly watching for the effect of his words. George reflected nothing, only returning the stare. "We slit their throats." Khalil said, as if an afterthought.

"Do you rape?"

"Not personally. I would not do that in front of my men."

George watched Khalil's face, a slight twitch in the left eye. Khalil shouldn't have said 'my men', and George had realized his mistake. Khalil continued on, pretending that he hadn't slipped.

"Others rape. Sexual defilement prevents entry to paradise. It is a very effective tool in jihad."

George rolled his eyes, choosing an obvious gesture to make a point. The boast of a waste of time – he had heard it all before. Khalil shook his head, acknowledging George's gesture.

"You want pretty pictures of war?" Khalil asked. "You must be kidding. My country has been at war for decades. Against the imperialist French. Civil war. Car bombings, massacres, torture. The government itself is now the biggest murderer of all.

"Do you know what the police do if they capture someone like me?" Khalil continued. He was animated, and he'd picked up his recruiter persona, with its smooth voice and deep conviction. "*Chalumeau.* A blowtorch is used to burn off a man's skin. *Gegene*, an electroshock to a man's genitals. The *chiffon*, a man is tied up and his mouth stuffed with a cloth and then dirty water mixed with detergents or chemicals. Beatings, hand drills and mock executions."

George began to get annoyed. More repetitive crap. Still, George had to admit, if only to himself, that he didn't like to face the reality of it. He crossed one knee over the other. No other defenses in the squat cell.

"I know what your country and countrymen have suffered," George said. The conversation was veering too far off course. "That doesn't justify attacks on America. We haven't done anything to you." Weak retort.

Khalil smiled. "Ah, but you have." His voice was soft, almost seductive. "But I have done nothing against your country. Indeed, it is America that has harmed me by holding me captive." The voice was harsh now, strong in its direction. George looked directly at the slight man. His neatly trimmed beard, which he had grown over the last week, made him look more sinister.

"Look, I couldn't keep you here if you hadn't been tied to a U.S. related terrorist act, could I?" His voice mirrored as best he could Khalil's more strident and confident tone. And George did have a link. A recent detainee, Mohammed Doha, had been plotting a car bomb in San Diego. He had recently been captured and identified Khalil as having trained him in Pakistan a year before. But Khalil didn't know that Doha had been caught. Or did he?

"Have you heard of the Geneva Convention? Have you heard of lawyers? Of being charged with a crime and not held indefinitely? Have you heard of sleep deprivations, threats of a return to Algeria, electric shots and a few kicks here and there? What about being stripped naked and forced to crouch for hours on end? That is the great United States." Khalil opened his hands.

"I don't care what happened to you before you got here," George said. He felt the spittle leave his mouth as he began speaking too fast. Tough shit. He was staying in control today. And for this discussion that meant hardass, though he usually didn't like that style. Khalil enjoyed pushing people around. That much had become obvious. And George wasn't going to allow it. He may not have grown up in a war zone but there were other ways of being tough than behind the barrel of a gun. He continued, his tone severe. It was the tone he had used when his son, then fifteen, had come home late and drunk.

"I didn't cause any of this mess. Sure I vote. So what. We are all doing the best we can and that includes me. I haven't laid a hand on you and if I see anyone do so I personally will get them court martialed.

"The choice is yours Khalil." George continued. "We can debate all day. We can discuss each and every tragedy. Or, you can cooperate. Give me information, and perhaps you can set yourself free. We have enough information to convict you. And we will. Or, you can help, and get yourself a deal."

Khalil shrugged his shoulders. "What else do you want to know about my father?" Wily bastard, George thought. He will continue playing games, no matter how often I exert control.

XXXXX

"I don't want to talk about your father. I got enough about your father." George made a squiggly doodle on his notepad while Khalil waited. What a game.

They just sat. It was a simple technique, but remarkably potent. He who speaks first looses. The instigator eventually had to give up if he wanted to restart the interrogation. Although, sometimes he didn't. Khalil had used that tactic before. Sitting, sometimes days on end, staring at the face of a man you didn't trust. It was unnerving.

Well, he had nothing to say. George could carry the burden. Khalil breathed deeply and closed his eyes. That was an effective counter tactic – remove yourself, any way you could. The removal would be more complete if he could utter his prayers. But that would be speaking.

"The itsy, bitsy spider climbed up the garden spout." George was singing. It sounded like a children's song. Khalil didn't know what he should do – open his eyes, keep them closed? The man was ridiculous. And so Khalil started to laugh. This wasn't a serious interrogation was it? They were just playing with him.

He opened his eyes and saw George smiling. He had pulled a magazine out of his ever-present briefcase. *The Economist.* Had Khalil any idea of the date he would have checked to see if it was a current issue.

He gazed in bewilderment at George, who seemed to be enjoying himself. Totally out of place behavior in a decrepit jail cell.

"I thought you might like to catch up on some news. No, I won't tell you how current it is."

He stacked two Twix bars, more cigarettes and a collection of poems. Great. Khalil hated poetry. Who had the patience to read words that had been pretentiously strung together in an attempt to create a meaning? At least the rest was welcome.

George couldn't really believe that presents would soften him up, could he? Nothing could be more ridiculous. He was fighting to the death. Khalil would welcome death. What did this world hold for him but pain?

Until then, he would try to stay strong. Nothing would break him. Not ever. And the chocolate would help soothe him a little.

If only he could figure out George's game.

XXXXX

Props. Distractions. Interrogation wasn't all that different from dealing with toddlers – something George could only vaguely remember since his kids were now in college. Any time a toddler misbehaved you just redirected their attention elsewhere. Indeed, interrogation wasn't all that different from therapy. Most people never grew up. And the ones that did, never grew up completely. Hence therapy's never ending discussion of events that happened during childhood. Well, perhaps he was oversimplifying. Perhaps.

To be fair to Khalil, these prisoners were reduced to mental children.

Totally out of control and dependent. No escape. No one to bond with other than their captors. Like an abused child, they had no source of comfort other than their abuser – the jailor. George would be a fool not to capitalize on it. Hence, he had brought presents. Then, after Santa's gifts were handed out the conversation would resume.

Even humor – these men were dying to laugh. Tough freedom fighters and all, they were still just men.

"Tell me about the scar on your wrist." George said.

Khalil's eyes were on the Twix. He hesitated for a moment before deciding to take it. He unwrapped the candy and took a bite. His eyes were fixed on George and had an intentness that would be funny in any other context. But not this one. He seemed to be willing George away from his candy, as if silently commanding him, while also begging him not to take it away. God, we reduce them to so little, don't we? George permitted himself to think before redirecting his attention back to the interrogation, not the person being interrogated. Pitiful.

Khalil started to speak, his mouth still containing candy. The bar's remains were clasped in his fist. "I was in Amsterdam." He smiled wryly. George could see dark stains on his teeth from chocolate. The delicate smell had already perfumed the cell – it was so small. "I was late at a prayer meeting."

"Read terrorist planning session." George smiled, trying to keep the mood light. No need for another standoff today.

"Whatever you want to believe is up to you. Anyway, I was at a prayer session late. I was walking back to my hotel. It was very close. Two guys jumped me. They had knives. The story is a familiar one.

Demands for cash. Racist statements. Threats to kill me."

He paused, taking another bite of the Twix.

"So, what happened? Why did they cut you?"

"They surprised me. I hadn't liked the look of them as they were walking toward me, but I hadn't expected them to jump me. As I knocked one down, the other got in a jab with his knife."

"How did you get away?" George was startled thus far by the answer. The great warrior scared by a few thugs.

"I killed them."

"Yes, yes, of course. That would be a way to solve the problem." George tried to keep sarcasm out of his voice. It was one of his defenses, and one that he couldn't fully control – unfortunately. He just could never treat murder, even in self-defense, so naturally. As if it just happened. Then again, it didn't just happen in his world. But it did in Khalil's.

"It worked." The voice had an undertone of danger in it.

"So, what did you think of Amsterdam?"

Khalil stared at him hard. Then he took another bite of candy. Once again the smile flashed across his face. "When will you let me out of here?"

"When will you give me good information?" George asked.

"Could you recognize it if you heard it?" Khalil replied.

George thought for a minute. He stared into the still eyes before him. They were thoughtful, yet betrayed little else from the depths of their darkness. It was an interesting question, and one he had never considered.

"Try me."

XXXXX

"Some things are senseless." Khalil waited for George's response.

"That is useful information." The sarcasm again. "Much of life is senseless, Khalil. Certainly you have realized that by now." George looked suddenly older, but not more mature. His shoulders had deflated a bit. Khalil wasn't sure what to make of this unexpected response. He would wait as George continued.

"All the death and destruction you have seen. All of that which you created. What did any of it achieve?"

"America pulled troops out of Saudi Arabia. The Soviets, a great power, were defeated by the backward Afghanis. Spain pulled out of Iraq. A lot of good things have come out of the jihad, George. You are just too corrupted to see them." Or, perhaps it was just a lack of visibility. Night was falling and the cell's fluorescent lights hadn't come on yet. Something about conserving energy by turning the lights off for four hours each afternoon.

"So you support Al Qaeda?" The eyes staring at him were dead but Khalil could see the trap already. They would battle on, George pointing out the inconsistencies in what he said.

And Khalil was tired. He wanted to be left alone. Perhaps he wanted to nap or just stare at the ceiling. But he had no autonomy whatsoever, did he?

"Just leave."

"So you support Al Qaeda and what they do?" George persisted.

"Sure I do. That doesn't make me Al Qaeda? Most of the Islamic world supports what Al Qaeda does." Khalil said.

"That point is debatable. Give me some names. Then I will leave. George said, still pushing.

So, the best defense is a good offense. Okay.

XXXXX

"The idea of evil – you paint me as such." Khalil said. "Isn't that always the best way to dehumanize someone, to dehumanize a whole group of someones? Just classify us as evil and ignore that some of what we say is true? How many dead children have you seen personally?"

Always the children. Khalil kept bringing them up. And, truth be told, the image worked on George everytime. It upset him and threw him off ever so slightly – which was the best advantage Khalil could hope for, wasn't it? George was annoyed with himself for so consistently falling for such a cheap trick.

"I didn't use the word evil. I would like to get away from using such words." George's voice was measured. His tone was the same reassuring one he used with his psychology patients when they uttered those words, the tone he used to steer them in a new direction. Psychologists all knew – extremes never amounted to anything constructive. Did he think Khalil was evil? No, he mustn't think that way – to even ask. He needed information, not to condemn Khalil for his lack of humanity. George continued. "We both used 'senseless'. The tragedy of the World Trade Center was senseless. What good came out of it? I want you to help me prevent more bloodshed, Khalil. Increasingly, I believe that you can."

George's own ploy wasn't much better than Khalil's. But it was an old interrogation technique. Appeal to their better side, rewarding them heavily for it. Admiration, flattery, all of that would soon follow. Hopefully Khalil would take the bait.

"Yes, the World Trade Center. I wondered when you would bring that up." Khalil said.

George didn't like Khalil's tone. It was too something. Reflective, controlled, restrained?

"Well, your group is now part of Al Qaeda." George waited. He knew Khalil would hit him with something soon – it was hanging over him in the dollhouse-sized room – almost crushing him. Luckily, it wouldn't be about dead children. Khalil only pulled that once each session.

"Such organizations only very loosely exist." Khalil sounded dismissive. With his next words his voice softened. His cobra tone, as George now called it, hypnotically lulling people gently into his lair. "I saw pictures of the World Trade Center after the strike. You know what it reminded me of?"

The pause was dramatic, for effect. Here it comes, George told himself.

"Kabul. Have you been to Afghanistan, George? The twisted metal, the debris, laying so thick no man could ever walk through it. Buildings flattened. What had once housed families now serving as tombs. The stench of rotting flesh. Twisted limbs lying useless on the grounds. The smoke of dying fires. The eerie silence that settles when no life exists to break it. Rubble, and more rubble – and all of it dusted with ash. The edges of everything blurred so that the landscape no longer looks as if it belongs in this world. And it doesn't, it is a playground for ghosts. Ghosts and small children who have nowhere else to play.

"The pictures of the World Trade Center reminded me of Kabul as it is today." Khalil continued. "It is no longer the beautiful and graceful city I saw years ago. Nothing much is left. A wasteland.

Khalil paused, bright in his orange. Then he began his diatribe anew. His body swayed with his words, a gesture more artificial than hypnotic. George tried to listen. Another monologue from a self-righteous extremist.

"And, George, what if Bin Laden is right?" Khalil babbled on. "What if it's just his means you don't like? What if the Muslim holy land shouldn't be under American troops? What if our children shouldn't be used as cannon fodder? What if Afghanistan deserves better than to be annihilated because it is strategically located next to Russia, your Cold War enemy? Why should America be allowed to send its corruption around the world? Historically, Arabs have settled things through the use of blood feuds. We had no other means of justice. We still have no other means of ensuring fairness. Bin Laden's army can't match you weapon wise. But they can defeat you with strategy, conviction and the blessing of Allah's will. What is wrong with fighting for equal rights for the billions of Muslims in the world? Maybe you Americans just can't accept the truth." Khalil was shaking as he spoke. Was the emotion real?

"Are you done?" George used the coldest tone he could muster. "What if, indeed. Bin Laden may be right about some things. Why do you call it 'his army' when you know that it's yours as well. By the way, you are right about Kabul. I have been there, and I have seen for myself how little is left. I have seen the desperation and pain of the people. We are trying to help those people. Kabul is rebuilding now." George saw Khalil roll his eyes. He continued, ignoring the gesture.

"But Khalil, how is your network of terrorists helping anyone, except for the people at the top of your organization? Where is your swell of popular support? What have you really accomplished? You are as useless as the communists you replaced. It is all just an ideological basis for imposing your views on the rest of the world. And, to add insult to injury, your leaders often live like kings." The chair squeaked as George shifted his foot, which had fallen asleep.

"Bin Laden doesn't," Khalil said. "He is a pious and unassuming man. Why should you and your countrymen have the right to define terrorism? I reject your definition. We are fighting for the right to live our own way – in Algeria. Allah be blessed, each man will find his salvation. Many of those you label terrorists are searching for salvation. They are following Allah's words. What gives you the right to judge?" Khalil waived his hand in the air, as if in dismissal.

"By killing innocents deliberately. By targeting them." George held firm.

"See, you don't get it." Khalil's tone was patronizing. George couldn't help feeling that Khalil was once again starting on a well-practiced speech. At least he had opened up, right? "Al Qaeda wasn't targeting civilians on September 11. They target landmarks. They were after the World Trade Center, not the people in it."

"So they crashed two planes during morning rush hour. What about Bali? That nightclub was also a landmark? Discos, restaurants and trains?" George heard the sarcasm dripping as he spoke. Then he changed the tone back to flattering. "Khalil, you are too smart for this life. Get a deal for yourself. Call Jennifer."

Again the look. Jennifer continued to strike a chord inside Khalil. Good, get him rattled.

"Strike a deal and go where? Do what with my life? Go back to Algeria? Didn't we discuss that already – what happens to me if I go back?" No mention of Jennifer.

"Get a U.S. passport. Call Jennifer." George said.

"Enough of Jennifer. Stop. She was a girl I fucked long ago – that's it. What kind of a dog interrogator are you anyway?" Khalil shook his head. He looked disgusted.

"Tell me more about Bin Laden? Have you met him?" Bait and switch.

The exasperated look again. "I am GSPC, not Al Qaeda."

"GSPC is affiliated with Al Qaeda."

"Only certain branches. Not mine."

"Do you know Hassan Hattab?"

"A leader of the GSPC – of course I know of him, but not personally."

"Hasn't he spent some time in London – as you have- where the real brains behind terrorism have historically been located?"

"You are getting boorish." Khalil said. "What sort of insinuations are you making? I stick with Algerian related issues."

"Which is why you spend time in Pakistan?" George smiled coldly.

"Pakistan?" Khalil asked.

"And, more importantly, who were you calling in Los Angeles?"

"Why would I call anyone in Los Angeles?"

"Why would your cell phone have a number in Los Angeles programmed in if you weren't calling it?" George pushed.

"It wasn't my phone." Khalil sighed. George could tell that Khalil knew what to expect. It was going to be a long night. That was always the best way to get your answers in an interrogation. Learn your guy; find his weak spots, his escapes and memorized responses. Then sit in a room for ten, twelve or more hours. Asking the same questions, over and over.

# CHAPTER FOUR - ILLUSIONS

Alone. Omar was totally and completely alone. He hid in the library, often even skipping meals. He had nowhere else to go. No one sat with him in the dining hall; no one spoke to him during the lull between the start of one class and the next.

Tears flowed. By himself he could give in to the desolation which had taken hold. He belonged at home, with the friends he had known since before he could remember. He felt like his heart had been ripped from him and was being tossed about like an old soccer ball. His body almost couldn't move but yet it did. How was he supposed to survive the years of this school ahead of him? Should he kill himself?

"Omar, you did terrible on this test." The whole class watched. Ms. Haas was humiliating him again. As if he needed to be singled out and embarrassed in front of a hostile audience once more. He stayed silent, willing Allah to come and strike him dead. There must be some deliverance.

"Omar, why do you keep failing my tests?" She was breathing hard and had turned red – looking exactly as she had on that horrible night when she had kicked him out of her apartment. The flowers on her too-tight dress reminded him of the sheet that had refused to let him go. He began to feel angry. Rage clouded the picture of her in front of him until all he saw was her naked body – fleshy and sweaty, as she looked now. Whore.

"Look, you cunt." He chose the word he had used before, which had presumably prompted her to command him to hit her. Her rheumy blue eyes bored into him. Nausea. He thought he saw hatred in them, but the burning inside him was so overwhelming he couldn't be bothered to figure it out. Instead, he knew he had to release the tensions before they drove him insane. She was an infidel. "Don't you dare bother me anymore. I fucked you but I'm not going to hit you – even if doing so helps me pass your tests. You will rot in hell, infidel."

Omar stood up. He felt eleven pairs of eyes on him. The whole class was silent. He couldn't feel much worse. He was already an outcast. Now this. He hadn't even humiliated her properly. His line was pathetic at best. He had been such a star at home, so popular and witty. Here, he was less than nothing. A worm. But at least he was better than this woman. He knew that. She would rot for eternity. He would rot here, until his soulless father brought him home. Hanging his head and avoiding all eyes, Omar headed for the door. He still could taste the salt of his tears as his last bit of self-control died within him. Who could live like this forever, alone and in a hostile place?

A peal of laughter surprised him. It started small then turned into a chorus of great chortling gasps of pleasure. He stopped in his tracks, shocked. At that moment, he had been so unsure of what could possibly happen next.

Looking around him he saw the students. They seemed thrilled by their teacher's humiliation. Or, was it his humiliation they were enjoying so much? Their eyes glowed with a light that he had never before seen. Vaguely, he noticed that Ms. Haas was rooted in the same spot she had been moments before.

Suddenly curious, he stepped out of himself. It was his first memory of doing so. Had he become a man at that moment? What would happen? Would he be sent home? Could Allah be so merciful? His heart pounded. The rest of his body had fallen away.

Her pale skin shined with the burning redness of a humiliation he also felt. A harsh emotion, it left little room for subtleties. She was so still, yet he could feel the animal heat of her trapped body. The sum total of his schooling in Switzerland was this body standing exposed before him. Sweat was beading on her forehead. She had always been wet, too wet really. Her whole being had overwhelmed him with its fleshiness and human yearning.

The students were riveted. They were talking. Some had even risen from their standard issue desks – a clear violation of the schools rules.

"Is it true?"

"You mean that he fucked her?"

"Where did he learn that language? I thought he only spoke Arabic."

"I wouldn't fuck her."

"I would fuck anything that would stay still long enough."

The rough talk, the laughter, the sheer joy of rebellion that can come from adolescents. Omar cringed. He didn't feel ashamed of having had sex with her. That was what women did to a man – they took over his reason and made it impossible for him to resist using her for his carnal needs. She had been a release for him, an escape. Now she had to find her own escape. Her students were waiting.

Slowly, a smile formed on her face. It was as artificial as the pink lipstick she favored. The blue of her eyes had become opaque. Omar couldn't care less why. He was now as curious as his classmates with respect to what she would do. Indeed, he was more focused on her response at that moment than on his own punishment.

"What a ridiculous thing to say Omar. I shouldn't even dignify that statement by responding. Class dismissed." With that statement completed she strode out of the classroom, head held high. He never saw her again. When the principal asked him to verify his claims Omar had simply smiled and walked out of the room. If she could do it, so could he. Let them pester him – he would make the affair public knowledge. The wealthy parents would love to hear that the teachers in their convenient boarding school raped fourteen-year-old boys.

XXXXX

George entered his house as quietly as he could. Of course the alarm warning went off when he opened the door, "Disarm system now." Hopefully Karen hadn't heard the noise. It was close to 4:00 A.M. He was definitely too old for the intensity of a real interrogation. Khalil hadn't cracked much – a real frustration. Some, but not much.

Karen had left the hallway light on. Now that was a surprise. Usually she was too passive/aggressive to do so. George gazed at his stairs warily. Oak, or faked maple? They looked impossibly steep tonight. He began his ascent, annoyed at a pulled muscle in the back of his thigh. Stupid hamstring. Damn treadmill. He knew he shouldn't have added an extra two miles to his run this morning. He had just immaturely tried to delay his interrogation.

At the top of the stairs George didn't head to his bedroom. Feeling very tired, he nonetheless wanted a few minutes in his office before bed. He flicked on the light switch, the one for the desk lamp, then entered the room. Still trying to stay quiet, George walked to his desk, sitting down in his familiar chair. He began sorting through Khalil's meticulously ordered file.

He found the picture. A preschool in San Diego with a little girl running to the camera. The girl was about four and wore a light pink dress with a skirt composed of ruffles. She looked like the angel she almost was. It was this preschool that Mohammed Doha, Khalil's associate, had been planning to blow up before he was caught and thrown in jail. He hadn't been tough to crack – implicating many people, including Khalil. Before he had been murdered in jail, that is – rendering much of his testimony useless for prosecution purposes. Well, the fact that he had been denied a lawyer hadn't helped either.

Much as Khalil liked to talk about fairness and revolution, ultimately he was just a dirty manipulative terrorist. Blood not just on his hands, but dripping from his whole body.

Tears welled up in George's eyes. Sentimental jerk that he was. God, how he hated this. All of it. He was just so tired tonight. It was too hard. How do you make someone like Khalil crack? There were always the tough ones, who had survived torture and usually some very talented interrogators. How had he gotten himself into this position? Each of his charges stubborn and committed. Often hateful. He breathed deeply. Then he did it again. It was the advice he gave his children when they faced something tough. Breathe. But he wasn't a child, not that either of his kids were anymore either. He was capable. All of the prisoners talked eventually. He would just have to find the key to open this lock.

George shut the folder, reopening it to the beginning. He turned up the dimmer on his desk lamp, further illuminating the dancing black words. Then he began to reread the file, not sure exactly what he was looking for.

Targeting civilians was never all right. George focused on what he knew, which didn't always feel like much. The rest would come later.

XXXXX

"My name is Emine."

Omar stared at the girl. He wasn't capable of more. Still. She was softly pretty. Barely pretty. Her eyes, praise be to Allah, were not the sickly blue he had suddenly come to despise. Instead they were golden, hinting at brown. If he were to describe her now as he remembered her the word 'almost' would play the predominant role. She had been almost a lot of things, yet never really looked like anything. She was almost tall, almost thin. Her face was almost touching, her eyes almost beautiful. She was almost aggressive yet had the remnants of her years spent disappearing into the background so as not to bother her almost parents. Her hair had been an almost mix of red and brown. And, she had been almost funny.

He couldn't say anything. What was he supposed to say? Even now Omar could marvel at what a child he had been at that instant. Now, he felt no hesitation talking to girls – when it was in his best interest to do so. It was the men who caused him all the problems.

"What is your name? You know you haven't been too friendly since you got here." She stared back at him, very obviously. Nothing almost about her stares.

Omar had felt annoyed. Why couldn't he be left alone? How was he to know then that his real salvation had just arrived?

"Omar. My name is Omar." Simple. About as eloquent as most of what he said in English. Why couldn't he be somewhere where he could use his Arabic – the language he felt comfortable speaking?

"Well, Omar…." The voice was firm, and she elongated every syllable. Omar squirmed in his chair. He had come to the library so people would leave him alone, not so he would be chased down by a whisper of a girl who stared down at him, pinning him between his desk and chair. A fleck of paint was peeling off the wall before him. "You seem like a cool guy. Why are you hiding in the library?"

And still she stared. Kept staring as she talked. Her eyes almost didn't even blink. He had really been trapped, which made him even more conscious of how much he didn't fit in here. No, he hadn't been particularly friendly. But then again no one had been friendly to him either.

Oh, had she asked him a question? The walls of books moved in closer, cutting off all avenues.

"I wanted to study," Omar said.

"No." The eyes, lightly flecked, studied him. The look was long and clearly an appraisal. "No, you are not the studious type." She paused. "Did you really fuck Ms. Haas?"

"Do your parents know you use words like that?" Omar couldn't keep the edge out of his voice. What was this place? A modern day den of inequity? And was that why she was bothering him – she, like the entire faculty and perhaps the student body as well, wanted to know if he had had sex with a now gone teacher?

"Fuck, fuck, fuck," she replied. "Allah be praised. I left my Muslim country to escape that sort of repression. Don't pull that Saudi crap with me."

"Where are you from?" Was she really a fellow Muslim? Were there fellow Muslims here?

"From Turkey." He felt his hope fall; a half-hearted Muslim country if ever one existed. They didn't even speak Arabic.

"So, tell me, did you fuck her?" Emine persisted.

Her face was interested. The first real interest he had noticed while at school. Even Ms. Haas hadn't really cared about him – just his body. He looked down at himself. Young, but starting to take shape. He was growing and developing earlier than many of the boys around him. And, no one at the school had as perfect a face. He knew each inch of his own good looks. The long eyelashes that framed large, almost round eyes. The thick lips and dramatic cheekbones. The thick, wavy hair. Even here, in this hated place, the girls stared at him. And he himself had nothing to distract him from his mirror.

Suddenly he laughed. This girl was still standing before him, an expectant look on her face. She was bold, wasn't she? Her parents probably sent her here to keep her out of trouble. Or perhaps they had just wanted to send her far away from wherever they were. And she was the only student in the whole school brave enough to ask the question.

"Yes, I did."

The eyes flicked. Was that what they did? How else could he describe the expression that passed across her face? Back then when he was still just a boy. He had been lucky to notice anything at all. No. Not lucky. Smart.

"How was it?" Again, the stare. So intense, yet no longer intimidating. She looked riveted, like a child studying a piece of candy and trying to figure out how to get it. Her strangely fragile hands were grasped together in a clasp in front of her. Her rumpled white uniform blouse was so unlike his own, which he kept purposefully pressed. Yet from her he felt the attention he had been missing in this cold place.

"The sex itself was amazing. I have never felt anything like it before." He could feel himself opening up – it felt so natural talking to this girl who really seemed interested. "The woman was wet, sweaty and too squishy for me."

Emine smiled. Her grin took over her face and lit her from within.

"Will you have sex with me too? Please."

Omar ran. He left his books and just ran. Panic took hold. Something about the exchange was too intimate for him, in a way sex with his teacher had never been.

XXXXX

Khalil was on his bed once more. Not much else to do. He yearned for something, anything, to end the boredom.

He hadn't breathed a word, no matter how bad things got. He had to be the picture of innocence. But instead he had ended up here. And he knew why. Mohammed Doha, the fellow Algerian he had trained and instructed on bombing the preschool. The man had talked and one day he would die for what he had put Khalil through.

Until then Khalil had to figure out how to get out of his prison.

XXXXX

Dear Mother:

May Allah watch over you and keep you well. As Saladan, the great prince who battled the Crusaders, had his times of trial I am facing one now as well. Like him, I don't doubt that I will emerge victorious. The will of Allah always prevails.

You will hear many things about me and my situation. Do not let the whispers of serpents lead you astray. I am alive and as well as one can be. The trials I am facing have only brought me closer to my mission. Allah has provided me with the strength to emerge from this time of solitude refreshed and ready to follow his path.

I am nowhere. But you should not worry about that – it is of no consequence. As I have faced down greater enemies I fear the one that causes me irritation not a bit. The true believers are emerging victorious around the world as I write these words.

Each day as the sun rises I hope that I shall once again gaze upon you. However, I am confident that if nothing else holds true we shall meet again in paradise and then I shall tell you more of my travels and travails.

I wish for many things. To hear your sweet voice and gaze once more on the face I love more than any other. I wish to taste your kebab and drink deeply of the fresh juices you squeeze. I wish to sleep on the floor of your hut by the fire and know that the breathing I hear is yours, in the next room as you sleep. I wish to tell you where I am and to let you see for yourself that I am safe. Alas, that is not to be. The details would endanger both of us. I apologize for the life we both must live. It is Allah's will and we will be rewarded for our piety.

Please do not renounce Allah as you have threatened to do. It is he who brought you two sons, not he who has taken them. We will all be rejoined in paradise.

Please give my love to my sisters, my nieces and my nephews. One day I will gaze upon their faces. I have arranged for money to continue flowing to you even in my absence – but not enough to arouse suspicion.

If people ask of me say nothing. Not even that I am alive. Trust me on this, it is for the best.

Love always,

Khalil

XXXXX

The letter was ridiculous. Florid, stilted language. Treackly and artificial. Typical Islamist crap. The wrote as if they still lived during the Crusades. Did they teach it in some hidden training camp tucked up behind a mountain?

George threw the letter down in disgust. "Each day as the sun rises…" was still ringing in his head. And the joke of it was that he was being forced to read the truly stupid thing because the guards were afraid it might contain some code. Had these people ever been to a place like Algeria? Had they even read about a third-world Muslim country? Khalil's mother was poor. She was a woman! Khalil wasn't sending her some coded message. How many elderly, illiterate, Muslim women had ever been identified as terrorists? He could answer that question. One, and she had been a Palestinian.

It was half the battle: how can you fight an enemy that you don't understand – at all?

George had watched the news shows and read the books. Mostly they broadcast the viewpoints of people living in the west. How often were books written by Muslim-world authors best sellers in the Unites States? How often did such authorities do *Meet the Press*?

He recalled a debate, no, altercation, he had had once after a psychology conference. George had given a speech outlining some of his theories on what created a terrorist. During an intermission, an attendee found George in a hallway.

"Nice speech, professor." Something in the man's tone warned George of an impending attack. Perhaps it was the slight edge of barely concealed hostility which men's voices can carry. Perhaps it was the sheer frequency with which people blamed him for the government's foreign policy after they heard what he did.

"Glad you enjoyed it. This audience is sophisticated, so I hope I provided appropriate insight." He kept his tone neutral and non-threatening. Terrorism was controversial and everyone, it seemed, had strong opinions. Over the years, he had found that merely raising the topic shut peoples' ears and directed all their energy to their mouths. He would then be forced to listen to their crazy, generally misguided, theories. Quite honestly he didn't care what they thought.

The man was not to be deterred.

"You know that you're wrong, don't you?" His eyes bulged. Perhaps it was from the bright hotel lights. "These men aren't slightly confused and a natural outgrowth of their environment. Terrorism knows no borders, doctor." The sarcasm in the tone was perhaps exaggerated for effect. Still, George was in no mood for an argument. After all, he was the expert.

George studied the man before answering. He was only about an inch taller than George himself was. Yet he filled the room better, spilling over his clothes. His face was pasty. Probably an academic; pale from too much time reading books. His beady eyes disappeared behind his hawk nose.

"Sorry you feel that way, sir." George gave his voice the best cheery California spin he could muster. He had learned it from the highway patrolmen in his glorious state as they happily wrote him ticket after ticket.

The man glared. "How can you not blame the religion? What other terrorists blow themselves up? Islam has a long history of suicide attacks. The Assassins in the 12$^{th}$ century perfected it."

"I am sorry if I offended you in any way," seemed like the safest thing to say. But then George just could never back down. "The Assassins were an anomaly," he said. They were the only suicide killers until modern times. Suicide attacks were reintroduced into the modern world by the Kamikazes during World War 2. Suicide bombs only became a tool of Islamic groups in the 80s in Lebanon, and was condemned by many Imams."

A woman bumped into George, spilling his bottle of water. She walked away without apologizing.

"Bullshit." George's new companion said. "It is cultural. You're just adding a politically correct spin. 'Dislocated youth, patriarchic societies….'"

"I'm entitled to my theories." George replied, reminding himself not to get defensive. So he had a theory, so it seemed to work. He wouldn't be the first academic to have one. If people took it the wrong way that was their own problem.

"I just wish you wouldn't be an apologist for murderers," the man said.

"But I'm trying to understand why." George replied. "I think it includes haphazard assimilation into a western society which does nothing to embrace these men. They can't adapt to our freedoms."

"Islam calls for murdering those who don't convert." The man said. He could have been foaming at the mouth. George noted the wrinkles in his shirt – white with red stripes.

"That's contested by serious Islamic scholars." George replied.

"History would agree with me. Look at the Crusades."

"Yes, when the Christians massacred, raped and enslaved," George said. "No one wants to return to that. Not even the Vatican." George was losing his patience. The next speaker was scheduled to start in two minutes.

"The Taliban do." The man refused to be quieted.

"The Taliban are ignorant extremists consisting largely of war orphans, like the Khmer Rouge and the Revolutionary United Front. Collectively, they are some of the most brutal fighters in modern times."

"Who were also funded by the Saudis – the bearer of Islam in the modern world." The man smiled, as if he had scored a point.

"The Saudis spread Wahhabism. It's not mainstream Islam," George replied.

"The Iranians sent boys to clear out mines." The man continued, still undeterred.

"Not related to Islam," George said.

"Both Turkey and Iraq massacred Kurds."

"Not related to Islam."

"The Palestinians blow up any Israeli they can find."

"Not related to Islam. That's political – it all comes down to land."

"Al Qaeda blew up the World Trade Center." The man wasn't slowing down.

"Not related to Islam!" George was exasperated. At a certain point it all just became hate speech, didn't it? No matter who said it. The hallway was empty now. Words were coming from the conference room.

"What if you convince your bosses that it isn't the religion and you are wrong. Mohamed was both a warrior and a holy man." The man glanced at the door to the meeting room as it closed.

"Yes, the land of peace, and the land of war." George whispered, paying attention to him for the first time. What if George was wrong? The Koran did call for jihad against all nonbelievers. The problem was interpreting that pillar of Islam – did it justify World War Three?

"A good friend of mine died in the World Trade Center," the man said. "Are you excusing that too?" With that he stopped. Finally.

George watched him walk away. How could anyone say he forgave these murderers, let alone serve as an apologist for them? He despised them. But you still must understand your enemy. Religion was just an excuse. No God could sanction murder.

And, even if the religion itself was a contributing factor it could never be the entire answer. Life wasn't that simple. Ideologies didn't kill – people did.

Throughout history revolutionaries had always used words to justify blood. The terminology changed – God, communism, democracy, socialism, tribal conflict, Sunni versus Shiite, no taxation without representation – yet the resulting violence had a numbing predictability. For some reason most men needed a battle cry before they felt justified in murdering another. Islam was just the latest fad.

George couldn't afford to be wrong about that.

XXXXX

George walked the same path to Khalil – his constant companion. He watched his feet in their black tassel loafers as they hit the horrid linoleum floors. The walk wasn't long.

George had a surprise for Khalil today. He had spent some time on Amazon.com choosing books. If Khalil liked fiction – like the stupid letter – he would give him fiction. The prison had a library but it was small and limited. George rarely read bestsellers so he had declared the library bereft of books. How could you limit a reading list to one genre?

What could be worse than sitting in a cell with nothing to do all day? He would soften Khalil, making him dependent on his only companion and savior, by bringing him an escape. George had never understood the tough approach. Prisoners would say anything when tortured – including what you wanted to hear, irrespective of truth. They could also play all kinds of nasty games if they hated you. And most of them hated you – something about being locked up in a cage.

As George walked into the cell he nodded to Sean, letting the guard close the door and lock it behind him. Luckily George managed to escape conversation. The guard had been even more surly than usual and seemed to be nursing a hangover. Still, always good to be polite. Friendly was overkill. After all, if Khalil attacked, George wanted the guard to respond quickly.

Khalil was lying on his bed – motionless, like the reptile he was. A light bulb had gone out in the cell.

"Christmas time. I have presents," George said. A cheap jab, but they were the best: your less than pure intent was evident.

George noisily put the stack of books on Khalil's table. *The Failure of Political Islam*, for obvious reasons. *Being and Nothingness*, by Sartre – a boring read but a much less direct message. Sartre said that man decides his own fate. Khalil liked philosophy, and he was in a position to choose his fate – Allah willing. *Gone With the Wind*, for the romance and all that went with it. George hadn't been able to think of a less appropriate book for Khalil, except perhaps for *Don Quixote* which was also in the bag. Maybe somehow he could get the message through that Khalil's dream was the impossible dream. Last, George had brought a biography of Abraham Lincoln – time to show Khalil what a truly great man was.

The grin on his face was met by sullen silence from Khalil who was studying *Gone With the Wind.* Let him stare at a wall if he doesn't like my choices, George thought.

"I figured you had read everything by Sayyid Qutb." Khalil could probably quote Qutb's unwieldy Islamist prose.

"Thank you." Khalil's voice was polite, deferential. That was a surprise. Perhaps he was finally starting to become more malleable.

"Let's talk about Jennifer." May as well jump right in. That was the best way to get the interrogation finished. The books suddenly seemed just another impediment, like the driver who cut him off as he entered the freeway driving over. Yet again.

"You are going to just keep bringing Jennifer up until I discuss her, aren't you?" Khalil sounded resigned. His earlier interest in the books was seemingly forgotten.

"Yes, Khalil, I am."

"Well, then let's discuss her."

George had won. He didn't really cared about discussing Jennifer. He just suspected that Khalil wouldn't want to, so George scored a point.

Finally.

XXXXX

Khalil started to talk. Pretending to cooperate seemed like his best chance of getting out of hell. He had no obligation to be honest. With each word that came out he could feel rust disintegrating in his brain. He never discussed Jennifer. Indeed, only rarely did he even think about her.

George was just poking him, trying to find his weak spots, making him vulnerable. But if he didn't cooperate, George wouldn't help him escape this hellhole. How did George even know to ask about Jennifer? How much about him did they really know?

"Jennifer was a girl I dated briefly while I was at the University of San Diego," Khalil said. "We were friends for a while first. I ended it after we had been dating for less than a year."

"Why?" George sounded interested, though his eyes were wandering ever so slightly, looking over Khalil's shoulders. A gesture Khalil had noticed before. What could it mean? Not much to see here. Just four dirty walls and a half-baked attempt at furniture.

"I had to leave the country soon. There was no point in prolonging the relationship and making the breakup worse. I couldn't stay."

"She could've converted, and you could have married her."

Khalil pondered the point, but only for a second. An internal vision of her arose. He saw her smile, with its fragment of a downturn at the edges of her lips. Then he willed the picture away.

They had been so young, and he had desperately loved her. But he had chosen not to risk her life as he had risked his own. Better to have her safe and alive. He was owned by an organization and didn't get to make his own choices. Then again, who did?

Khalil rubbed the scar that ran across the palm of his hand. He studied it for an instant. Then he answered George.

"Perhaps she would have converted – hard to guess now. But she never would have belonged. I would have begun to hate her, as she became an increasingly greater burden. Who knows? All I know is that I have no regrets."

"She is pretty." George pulled two pictures from his briefcase, both of Jennifer. The first was taken around the time Khalil had known her. The other was obviously a more recent photograph. She had remained beautiful. The blonde hair was still long, brushing well past her shoulders. Her large blue eyes still gave her the same doll-like appearance. She had always reminded him of the stereotypical California blonde – a Hollywood type seen in movie theatres across the world. He would fall for a woman like that, wouldn't he? As opposite as possible from the girls he had known growing up, before they had started wearing the hajib and staying indoors.

George pushed the pictures across the table toward Khalil, who didn't move to pick them up. He waited for George's next question, deliberately taking his eyes off the pictures. He didn't want to be reminded of Jennifer.

"So the books should help ease your boredom. I can't help in any other way until you start…" George had dropped the topic of Jennifer. Thank goodness. "… cooperating. However, I think you will enjoy these.

George picked up the first book, “Don Quixote”, and began to describe it. Khalil watched his lips move but couldn’t hear what he was saying.

Why had George stopped asking questions?

XXXXX

George sat at his desk. He had brought the bottle of wine from dinner and was in the process of finishing it. He could hear Karen downstairs washing up after dinner. Thank God she wasn’t the type of woman who expected him to help clean up.

As George savored the dark, nectar-like red wine he methodically made his way through departmental memos and mail forwarded from his office at Stanford. Tonight he had to write his course descriptions for the winter session. What a relief to start teaching again. He was, for a change, doing nothing related to his interrogation. Another relief.

The phone rang, interrupting George’s calm, but not his good mood.

“Hello.” George beat Karen to the phone.

“Hello, George, this is Tom Campbell.” Ah, George’s current boss, or at least the man he reported to since he was a consultant. George had never actually met Campbell, nor was he happy dealing with him. Overseas he had reported to a range of people, some in Washington D.C., but most locally. The local guys had a feel for the interrogations and the prisoners themselves. The ones out of D.C. spent too much time hounding their minions. As if you could just walk into the room and get the information you wanted!

Campbell was D.C.-based, of course, and mostly pretended George didn't exist – which suited George just fine. To call so late at night, Campbell must have received his own call from a higher-up – probably only moments before. Another nice thing about academia – no one bothered you at all hours with unreasonable demands.

"Well, hello Tom. To what do I owe this honor?" George was at least polite.

Campbell kept his tone brisk and firm, as befit his post.

"I was calling to check up on your new guy, the Syrian."

"The Algerian?"

"Yes, that's right. Have you gotten anything of interest yet?"

"So far things are going well," George said. "He has been opening up, though very slowly. I am still trying to soften him, getting to know his personality, and how he reacts. He is fitting some of my expectations but not others – always a complication since it makes me identify why the quirks...."

"Look, you have had him now for over a week," Campbell interrupted. "Isn't the best information supposed to come in the first twenty-four hours?" Campbell sounded impatient. Asshole.

"That is an interrogation theory," George said. "And in this case that twenty-four hour period would have been right after his capture. Months have passed since then, and he's been harassed and tortured. I need to get into his mind and use his weakness to get him attached...."

"We don't torture prisoners George, you should know that." Tom's voice was crisp. George took a sip of his wine before answering.

"No, of course not. But we send them to countries that do." George wasn't backing down. He didn't care who Campbell was. George was one of the best worldwide at what he did, and he was doing it his way. Or they could fire him. Please.

"Well, if we had more Americans who spoke Arabic we wouldn't have to, now would we?" Angry. So what. George dropped his memo.

"Hence Khalil, with his near perfect English, spent some time in Egypt where he was likely tortured. All courtesy of the U.S. government."

"What are we debating?" Campbell asked. Well, at least Campbell didn't like wasting time on senseless denials. George knew what really happened overseas. He had been there.

"Listen, my process takes some time." George kept his voice patient. "I identify personality traits that I believe occur often, though not always, in terrorists. Next, I use an old interrogators' trick which is to use their vulnerability to assume a parental role. I don't do the harsh stuff. In my experience it rarely works for me. If I were 6'4, burly and had a loud voice I would already be intimidating and that approach might work."

"Fascinating." Tom barely responded. George ignored the lack of interest. Tom was just going to have to learn something. The next time someone bothered him, he would be able to answer without bugging George.

"Some authorities don't agree with my theories on personalities but they work for me. Usually there is a heavy dependence on a group. Often is some sort of disruption – a new school or country, difficulty assimilating into a different society or imprisonment. The religious belief provides an answer to dislocation and resulting confusion. Anyway, the terrorism works like group think." Was he being clear enough? George stared into his wine. The soft lighting made it look black.

"Their friends make them kill?" Tom sounded generally confused.

"Not exactly, but close," George said. At least some interest, right? "Becoming a religious extremist requires a real commitment to a way of life. They live differently, dress differently and are typically separated from general society as a result of the weird extremist habits. Freaks, essentially, they form closer bonds within their group. And, remember, their originating societies are often tribe-based historically – so they are used to valuing the group." George fingered the stem of his wine glass.

"Sounds like you're over intellectualizing the problem, professor," Tom said. "I want you to focus on the lives at stake here, American lives. I don't really give a fuck if your Tunisian feels alienated. I want to know what he knows, not how he feels."

George felt like snapping the delicate glass stem. Instead, he answered. "Well then you have to wait. This is my method. I figure my guy out first. Right now, Khalil isn't fitting my patterns. That disconnect makes the interrogation process slower. For example, educated terrorists are rarely philosophy, literature or other humanities majors. They typically prefer rule-oriented areas such as engineering. They tend to prefer finding answers in structured and logical ways – including the well-defined rules of religion. Yet Khalil was a philosophy major, and he loves literature."

"Enough! Good God, you are not writing a dissertation on this guy!" Tom sounded exasperated. Not that he really could get George fired. If only… George leaned back in his chair.

"That is how I work. Sure it is slow. But what answers has anyone else gotten out of Khalil? And they all had lots of time."

"Look, I don't give a rat's ass about your guy – his motivation or whatever. A killer is a killer." Campbell paused. His tone changed, becoming disinterested again. Probably focusing on the next harassing call in his cue. "I don't mean to be an asshole. It isn't your fault no one has gotten much from this guy. But we need answers, professor. I don't want any fucking bombs going off...."

"Well, keep me posted." Campbell continued. "A lot of guys are watching you."

Which means they're watching you too, George felt like adding. Instead he hung up the telephone receiver. Tom had already dropped his.

George felt that old familiar sinking feeling. No one cared. This stuff was important, even fascinating. But Tom didn't care. Understanding terrorists was not his department. But when a group of people was willing to die destroying you didn't understanding their motivation make sense? Apparently Tom didn't agree. George would discuss only intelligence information during the next call. He wasn't long for this assignment anyway.

XXXXX

Emine came back. It was four days after their first conversation. Omar recognized the outline of her body and the peculiarities of her firm walk even before she got close enough for him to identify her facial features. He had moved his location from before, and had indeed never returned to the other desk (except to retrieve his books), though at it had been his favorite, his refuge. This time she seemed not to notice him as she sat down in the next chair. She placed her red backpack on her desk and opened it. Quickly she removed a biology textbook and yellow highlighter and began to read.

Omar pretended not to notice her. Certainly she must have chosen that desk because it was next to his? Why else would she pick it? Why then did she not speak to him or at least say hello?

He was tense and felt watched, but wasn't sure. A heightened sense of his own body, indeed his own presence, filled him. Yet Emine just sat there, ignoring him and appearing focused only on her book. His mind refused to concentrate, instead allowing thoughts to run wild, no order or reason to them.

They both sat in silence. And the next day events replayed themselves. Exactly the same. Omar couldn't decide if he should change his routine and stop going to the library. When Emine showed up every day that week Omar found himself starting to relax – very slowly – as he became increasingly comfortable with her presence. He found his mind once again concentrating on his homework – English was first, his least favorite subject, except perhaps for French. However, his body retained a trace of tension; after all there was a girl sitting next to him, close enough that sometimes their elbows almost touched.

"Will you have sex with me?" The question again. Omar was jolted out of his textbook, shocked.

"Do your parents realize you say things like this?" he said.

"My parents could care less. My older brother dared me to say it."

Their eyes met.

"Ah, so you don't mean it?" Omar felt strangely deserted, as if his closest friend really wasn't so fond of him after all. Yet she wasn't his friend. He knew nothing about her at all. And there was that stare again. She never tempered it. The bright glare of the library was inappropriate for the intimate conversation. Sex shouldn't be held up under a spotlight.

"I mean it. I don't want to be a virgin any more. I want to have sex. I discussed it with my brother – who is sixteen, and goes here as well. Oh, and he is not a virgin. We discussed it and he agrees. He recommended that I have sex for the first time with someone with experience. So I decided on you. And you are adorable, did I mention that?" She gave him what must have been her best attempt at a seductive look. A stray lock of hair dropped into her eye.

"What? Are you crazy?" Omar said. "What kind of a brother is that, who recommends that his younger sister lose her virginity to someone she doesn't even know? You're a Muslim girl; you're supposed to stay a virgin until you are married. You're crazy." Omar shook his head. He was getting heated. The library felt even more aggresively hot than normal – heaters were always blowing balmy air to make the students forget the ice and snow outside. The bookshelves created an unnerving labyrinth.

Yet he felt a bit unsure. Was he getting hot out of disapproval or was it the thought of ramming himself into her tight body.

Surprisingly, she didn't back down.

"Save your moralizing for someone else. My brother looks out for me – he got me birth control. He says sex is fun. Why can't I enjoy it too? Other kids here pair up. You did – and with a teacher."

Well, she had a point. And sex really was fun. He certainly had nothing better to do with his time in this prison of privilege. Omar returned her stare. Brave girl. Rebellious girl. Her blouse had fallen open slightly, betraying the curve of her firm, small breast. Perhaps she had opened the blouse herself, before he had fully noticed her. Her hair had fallen further into her face, covering one eye completely now. And he could feel her hunger. Even then he was beginning to recognize desire. Ms. Haas had taught him that much. Her lips, so small and red. Well, it worked for him.

"Okay. When?" He smiled at her. Already the game, an easy one, was getting fun.

"Now. Come to my room with me. My roommate won't be there." She returned his smile, looking happy. Someone had just handed her a candy and she knew she was about to eat it. Who could deny a girl her sweet? Certainly not him.

XXXXX

Sean pushed Khalil at the bottom of the curve that was his spine. Khalil felt a quick shooting pain. He began to count. At the count of three he could turn to Sean behind him, disarm him and kill him. At which point, another not so bright guard would probably notice what had happened and come after him with a gun. Khalil, holding Sean's gun, would kill him. Then many guards would come; all bearing guns, and they would shoot him dead, littering his body with an excess number of bullets.

Khalil put his foot down in front of him. The linoleum floor had its normal muddied cast, slightly tinged with the surging red of the rage inside him. To be subject to this, from such an animal.

"Allahu Akbar." Khalil whispered under his breath.

"Whadju say, you raghead?" Sean spit out the words.

Khalil felt the guard's heavy hand on his shoulder as it yanked him around. He was now facing Sean and only about 9 inches away. How easily he could crush the man's windpipe. But not now, not here.

The guard's hand crashed into his face. The sting was real, but it didn't leave much of a lasting mark. Sean wasn't even capable of a proper slap. Khalil stared off in the distance. This was just a repeat of his childhood. A slap here, a kick there. Blows delivered by an inferior man who had no other way of exerting himself. Physical force required little finesse. Not like the complicated bombs he himself preferred. One day Sean would die. And it would hurt.

"I said, whadju say?" This time Sean's words slurred together.

"I think you said 'whadju say, raghead?'" Of course, Khalil knew better. But it was worth the price of one more slap. The guard couldn't kill him – he would see to that. The errant palm came once again.

Khalil turned back to the direction he had been heading before Sean's rampage – the showers. He began to walk. Behind him he could hear the guard's nasally voice. "Hey, you, don't walk away from me. Who do you think you are?"

He could imagine sweat breaking out on the big man's forehead. So typical of the west, wasn't it? They thought they could push you around because they were bigger and carried the guns. He knew the drill – but right now he wasn't in the mood. Didn't they recognize that the long-term victory would go to the one with patience and the ability to execute a superior plan?

"Someday I will kill you, Sean. I will break your neck between my hands." Khalil continued his walk down the monochrome hallway.

"You bastard. You really are a funny bastard. Don't you realize where you are? I could kick your ass from here to the Persian Gulf and no one would give a shit, you Commie bastard." The rampage continued.

"Allahu Akbar." Khalil whispered again, gentle enough so that he knew only the wind could hear.

"What the fuck you saying?" So predictable. So easy to bait. It was like playing with a child. A child with big guns and no ability to restrain himself from shooting them.

His mother's eyes popped, a vision from Allah, into his head. Khalil had been about six and he had similarly been baiting his father, the swine. Ali had come home between work and his hours at the teahouse. The daily household routine didn't include this stopover – he normally came home late, after everyone was asleep. Perhaps he had come home only to slap his wife a few times. Perhaps his purpose had been larger. Khalil hadn't cared to venture a guess then, and he didn't care now.

"Worthless whore." The open palm struck his mother's cheek.

She had stayed silent, staring at the ground. She had always advised her children to do the same. Khalil had a hard time staying quiet. He resented mindless authority then, and he wasn't too fond of it now.

"Swine. Kufr. Infidel. Mindless dog." The insults from a child's mouth were never sophisticated. But they were always spoken with conviction.

His father had turned to him. In Khalil's memory his father's eyes glowed red and spit dripped out the side of his mouth. Now, farther removed and more mature, he doubted that his memory was completely accurate. But the slap as it hit his chin had burned with real pain. He remembered the horror on his mother's face as she saw the blow land. Her eyes had begged him to stop. But he hadn't.

"Infidel pig." The hand hit again. But even at six he would have preferred its cruel sting to just watching his mother get beaten again.

Today the dance continued.

"Bought you a lot of allies in Europe, didn't it Sean?" Khalil could feel the arm sailing through in the air behind him. But he had entered the shower now. He walked past a jet then turned it on. Sean's flying hand met only the resistance of the water as it completed its arc.

"Watch out, Sean. The water's hot."

XXXXX

Emine held his attention. With Ms. Haas, it had been all ramming and cramming – totally acceptable to a fourteen year old boy learning about sex. Emine couldn't be more different. For her sex was a game, perhaps even a sport. She drank it in, every aspect of it. Her curiosity surprised Omar, and benefited him as well. Who else could have conceptualized so many different things to try?

Her brother, Salim, approved. He even brainstormed with Omar and

Emine, helping them devise new games – a completely unwanted and bizarre turn of events. At least for Omar.

"So look at this diagram. You two could twist into that position. Put Emine's head here and …."

"No, we put Omar's head here." Emine's voice lilted on while Omar's mind lingered. The whole thing had turned too competitive and twisted. Was Emine doing this to prove to her brother that she could match him in every way?

"No, I have done this one. The girl must put her head there." Salim's face was belligerent. He half rose from Emine's bed, perhaps to emphasize his point.

"You have no imagination, no romance." Emine seemed firm as she spoke. Her eyes had turned amber, littered with dark streaky fossils. Perhaps it was her mustard sweater that softened their usually browner tone. Salim's harsh laughter broke the intensity of the mood and brought Omar's attention back into the conversation.

"Romance. What romance? You and Omar love each other?" Salim's mouth twisted into a nasty grin. "I dare you to each fuck five other people in the next month. The one who does can come hear about jihad with me in London. My treat." Salim's eyes were round and unblinking, daring them to back down – a true nihilist. And one with an unlimited allowance. Omar had just studied nihilists in history class and could still remember feeling proud then to actually know one. A man who held nothing sacred – not even his own sister.

Omar could still see Salim picking up a cigarette and sticking a match. The sulfur smell had added drama. Salim's eyes were flickering behind the flame he held burning between his fingertips. Then he had gently placed the cigarette between his lips and inhaled as the fire hit the tip.

Omar remembered turning to Emine, sitting as frozen as the snow visible through the window behind her. Her face had lost something, though he hadn't been able to grasp exactly what. Perhaps her eyes didn't sparkle any longer or the color had darkened. Her hands were shaking; that much was clear.

Salim was still grinning, as he continued puffing on his cigarette. After each inhale he exhaled slowly, blowing the smoke directly into his sister's eyes.

"Scared." Salim hadn't blinked. He drew out each syllable of the word. It hadn't sounded like a question. Emine seemed to wake up upon hearing that word; had it meant something special?

"I am not scared, not scared at all." The bravado was back in her voice, though she still seemed to be less of the person she had been moments ago. "I will do it. But only if you are one of those five people."

Salim's grin only widened. Omar's stomach churned. What was wrong with these people? Omar felt an urge to run. Yet where could he run? They were his best friends, and his only link to his other friends at the school. Without them would he have anything at all? Or just the crushing loneliness from before? Had he but been able to fade away, disappearing into the stark white dormitory wall. But no, he was stuck alone on a snowy hill with a group of over-privileged and abandoned aristocrats working hard at becoming as jaded and dead as their parents.

"Only if Omar watches." Salim rasped the words. Emine winced.

Omar backed himself slightly closer to the wall.

Salim's eyes shifted to him. Omar never remembered actually agreeing to the horrible plan, but he seemingly did. Emine and Omar were both on a plane to London – Salim's treat – at spring break. And they both went to hear the mullah at the Finsbury Street mosque speak about jihad and the obligations of all good Muslims.

Omar had done as he was dared to do. He had watched as Salim and Emine had sex. He found one partner, and then another. It was then he first began to understand how his good looks and smile could seduce a woman. So many of them were willing. Now it was Stacey's turn.

And, while Emine had faded quickly away, jihad had taken over his life.

XXXXX

Of course, George was excited. Today was his birthday and his two children would be arriving soon, flying in from their shared college. George studied a picture of them as he waited. Lily, with her wispy blonde hair – just like her mother's, only longer. Justin with gray eyes, like his own. He remembered the instant he had snapped it, memories of colors and feelings swirling together.

He had visited them in Manhattan last winter. Christmas had been a week away, and the city was adorned for the holiday season. Lily thought of herself as a sophisticated New Yorker now that she was a Columbia undergrad. At the time, George had been shocked at how all traces of California had disappeared. She had rejected everything about her parents' lifestyle, choosing her school not for its Ivy League standing and challenging intellectual experience. No, the daughter of two professors had chosen it as a stepping-stone to investment banking and money. Moments before he had taken the picture she had argued that smiling for the picture would look fake. Her image was now frozen into sternness.

And the expression was a truer representation than a smile. Lily was emotionally distant – which George treasured. She had inherited that quality from him and used it as he did – to analyze things. Her wit was equally concise.

George leaned back in his chair. He put his feet on the desk, knocking over a stack of mail in the process. He ignored its cascading fall.

Justin was the opposite. In the picture he wore a large grin and made two-fingered bunny ears behind Lily's head. Justin was warm and open – the kind of person who made friends with everyone. He was genuinely interested in people's words. His depth of compassion couldn't be found anywhere on the family tree. Justin was athletic and popular – two other completely foreign traits.

Justin had followed Lily to Columbia. Born only sixteen months apart, neither child could imagine life without the other. Their bond was similar to twins. Or so it seemed to George. Karen didn't agree – pointing out that the two kids had argued continuously growing up and shared few interests. As if she was entitled to her own opinion. George wished she would focus her insight on her fictional characters and leave psychology to him.

Justin shunned the real world as much as Lily embraced it. He was studying literature, as his mother had done before him. He was also pairing it with philosophy and Latin. Go figure. Now in his sophomore year, he had yet to even consider a real summer job.

George couldn't focus on his newspaper. He sat alone in his study trying to read a book of Arabic comic strips. Karen was downstairs making some of her specialty – truly horrible chocolate chip cookies.

The kids were taking a cab from the airport. George checked his watch again, impatient. Surely they should be here by now? The idea, or so Karen had admitted, was to surprise their father. No chance. Who got the bill for their credit cards? Who noticed airline tickets on those bills?

George heard the doorbell ring and sprang from his chair. He headed for the stairs, not attempting to hide his smile.

"Hi, mom. Wow, did you make cookies?" Justin's voice, deep timbered, but with a slight nasally edge, echoed up the staircase. Tears came to George's eyes. He was getting old and sentimental. Wasn't forgetfulness the next stage?

George walked toward the stairs and looked down. His eyes hit Lily first. She was shaking her head. Probably declining the truly terrible cookies. Her cornflower sweater was brilliant against the honey-colored wood floor. Beside her was a strange man. A young man. Another surprise. Thank God he hadn't been on George's credit card.

The young man looked like most of George's students. Or as much as he could remember, a gloomy thought. The boy was fairly tall, the height necessary to top George's willowy daughter. His hair was sandy, neither fully blonde nor brown. His eyes were blue, but not distinctively so. He wore a simple white button down shirt and jeans that were a size or two too big. A nice mix of east-coast prep with gangsta rap. Very contemporary. Perhaps. George was no longer up on campus trends.

Well, the relationship must be serious if Lily dragged this young man across the country for a family event. She could have mentioned him earlier. George decided to be civil as he made his way down the stairs. Reaching the last step he finally saw Justin. Did he seem taller? George gave each of his kids a hug, enjoying the feel of them in his arms. Then he turned to the stranger.

"Well, this is all such a surprise. I'm George, the birthday boy." George held out his hand for a shake and consciously put on a harmless smile. He taught kids like this. He knew better than anyone the threat to his daughter could be. No need to reveal that fact now.

"Eric. Nice to meet you, sir." The return smile was warm, fairly genuine. Eric was, after all, quite young and only had had so much time to develop his deceptiveness. Hopefully, Lily would be married by her thirtieth birthday. The men could get really tricky after that.

XXXXX

The mattress was better than sleeping on rocks. Khalil could remember sleeping on rocks. His stomach let out a loud grumble, its discomfort evident. Whoever was in charge of the prison food still hadn't figured out that north African food wasn't the same as Indian, with its rich spices and ghee. Dinner had been hopelessly over-seasoned. Khalil guessed he wasn't the only prisoner unable to sleep from its effects. The last Indian restaurant he visited had left him similarly ill, but for a different reason.

Mustafa's eyes hadn't been the least bit gentle. Khalil had hoped that Mustafa also had no compassion. His expression was a bit dull. A good indication that he wasn't the brightest, and wouldn't ask too many questions. Mustafa didn't have to be smart – just willing to die.

"Allahu Akbar." Mustafa's voice had the guttural harshness of the Arab Gulf states.

"Allahu Akbar." Khalil softly mimicked the young man's words.

They sat in the back room of an Indian restaurant that was run by two Pakistani brothers. The air was thick with heavy spices. Cardamom mingled with the rancid scent of too much ghee. They sat in overstuffed chairs. A small coffee table held cups of Turkish coffee and a copper bowl of dates. Everything was dirty, most especially the one small window looking out onto an alley.

Khalil could hear the clipped tones of the diners in the other room – almost exclusively native British. The restaurant catered to that crowd, being sufficiently dingy to fill the desired expectations of authenticity.

"So you want to serve Allah's cause?" Khalil had asked. The words sounded too familiar. Of course Mustafa did. Khalil wouldn't be wasting his time if his contacts at the mosque hadn't identified the youth as being willing, no - eager - to die. Khalil would have preferred shipping someone into the country. Someone well trained in the camps of Iraq, and not as soft as the homegrown version. But he was being told to look domestically – bringing someone in to die had gotten harder. So, Khalil was interviewing. Just as he would interview to fill any other job.

"Yes. Yes, I do. I want to fight, brother."

"Ah, but are you ready for this mission?" Khalil said. "Are you brave enough to become a martyr?" Khalil watched him. "I don't see it in your eyes, my brother." His voice even was soft, skeptical. He had a huge pool of candidates. Could this one sell himself? Did he have the guts, or would he back out?

"Oh, I am. Really, I am.." The boy's voice was eager. "I am brave, sir. I am a good fighter. Allah, the merciful one has granted me the duty to follow his path, and that path has lead me to you."

"Allah be praised." The standard response. "How old are you?" Khalil could feel a yawn building up. The air was stifling, too hot and too heavy. He was getting bored.

"I am nineteen, sir," Mustafa said.

"Aren't you too young?"

"No, no." The boy stuttered. Sweat beaded above his mouth as his dreams of greatness receded slightly. "I am a man. I study hard during the school year, and I work during the school breaks. I am a man."

"What do you study?" Khalil asked.

"Computer science." Good, rules based discipline. Give him a program to write, and he did it: could be simplified: *give him instructions, and he would follow them.*

"Do you pray, go to mosque?"

"Sir, I am most devout." The boy stared at Khalil. His eyes were almost the same, they had simply added desperation. Khalil could ask this boy why death was so compelling. Did it matter? He had to choose one. Over the next week Khalil would watch all of his candidates. At the mosque and in prayer meetings. He was looking for something specific and he hadn't identified it in any of them yet. An ordinariness, a lack of specialness. Those were the ones who most wanted to die – the ones with nothing but faith to distinguish themselves. The ones who had been ignored for too long. Only they knew for sure how much they didn't fit in.

And so Khalil had felt ill – the responsibility of deciding who would die.

Now he was ill for many reasons. Bad food. No fresh air or enough exercise. Too much solitude. He now fully understood that desperate grasping to break free from a life that was so crushingly constraining it drove you mad.

XXXXX

Omar saw her off in the distance again. Predictability in a schedule made seduction much easier. He studied her as she walked toward him. She might wonder at why he was standing outside the classroom and leaning on the wall. She might question if it had something to do with her. Yet his position was ambiguous, ensuring that she couldn't know for sure, but awkward enough for her to believe it could be.

Most women would want to believe that he was waiting for them. After all, they would have the upper hand then, wouldn't they? This man is chasing me. I can either give him what he wants or deny him. I have the power. And don't we all like power? Wasn't power the reason that the United States, up until now, had been able to enslave and impoverish the rest of the world. Until now.

Her legs were encased yet again in blue jeans that seemed shrunk-wrapped around her trim thighs. Denim was a mainstay of her wardrobe, as it was of his own. He could imagine the firm flesh, outlined, thereby removing any subtleties of shape. It was only a matter of time before he was parting those strong thighs. Just like the rest of his life, waiting, plotting, bidding time and looking for the signals that the next step was to proceed.

Right now his mission was dead. The plot still existed, as did the functionaries such as himself. He had bomb materials, a testing lab and the ingredients for sarin. He had contacts and diagrams, dates and telephone numbers. A calendar, five targets and enough money to set up some serious blasts. What he lacked was a ringleader. Khalil had stopped calling. Everyone had stopped calling. What did that mean? A whispered voice on a cell phone had told him someone new would eventually call him, to fill the void. Omar wanted to fill it himself. He may not be seasoned like Khalil but he was probably a whole lot smarter. Instead, he was spending his time plotting a girl's seduction.

The plots weren't dissimilar. Not really. A direct approach never worked. Never. You had to go for maximum surprise. Rework the details. And so on.

Stacey was only about ten feet away now. Omar watched her smile as her eyes caught his. Such an American response. She continued walking toward him. Indeed, how could she not, she had to pass him to get into the classroom. So easy.

He saw her nipples arising slightly from the protrusion of her breasts. How did women walk around unembarrassed in such flimsy t-shirts? The pale yellow color beckoned him, begging him to suck those nipples as he would suck a lemon drop.

Stacey's smile widened as she got closer. He stared at her, into her eyes. He looked past the irises and deep into whatever lay beyond.

"Hello." Such confidence as she uttered the word. He continued to stare at her, turning away just as she passed by. He had noticed the sudden hesitation in her, once she realized her warm gesture was being rebuked. Let her wonder. Most people would avoid someone they had deliberately wronged –out of shame and an unwillingness to face their cruel side. Wronging someone by mistake often led to the same response or to an urgent need to right the wrong by behaving with nauseating niceness.

In seduction, everything was different. You cut someone on purpose and then confused them by responding unpredictably – as if they had imagined the slight. You got them doubting their own perceptions.

Allah be praised, he was good.

XXXXX

Karen was clearing dinner alone. She had insisted George enjoy their guests on his birthday. Only he realized that she actually preferred using this time to escape. Who knew what she did in the kitchen after she finished the dishes. Most likely she was reading a hidden stash of *People* magazines.

"Dad, Eric and I are going up to my room. I want to show him my old pictures." With that simple statement, his daughter elegantly pirouetted around and led her boyfriend up the stairs. George saw her executing the same move years before in a tiny pink tutu before the image faded away. Then he noticed Justin's look of amusement. All these years of specializing in psychology and he still couldn't hide his emotions in a personal setting. Not that anyone really could.

"Sentimental gesture for your sister, don't you think? I didn't even know she kept old pictures." He lamely tried to address his son. Eric seemed okay, but nothing George had yet noticed warranted so much attention from his coldly ambitious child.

"She's a girl, dad. Girls keep pictures in their rooms.." Justin looked so innocent as he reassured his dad. But he had also kept Eric's existence a secret – hence he was a co-conspirator. Who knew what other information he had. Interrogating a college student was easier than wringing information from an older, hardened killer. Should George go for it?

"Why don't we sit in the family room? You can update me." George gestured for his son to lead. He fell in behind, and watched his son's broad, athletic shoulders as they moved. What other family genes were appearing for the first time in this anomaly of a child?

They both settled into the deep plush of Karen's earth-toned sofa. Not a speck of real color in the entire house. Tasteful by way of safety. She was, if nothing else, consistent. George studied his son's features. 'He who speaks first loses,' he couldn't help thinking. Deeply ashamed, this was his own child, he decided to lose.

"So, what do you think of Eric?" At that instant George vowed to drop the topic without getting enough information. He wouldn't exploit his child's mind. George wrung enough people dry during the day.

"You lose." Justin flashed a broad grin, as his eyes got crafty. The expression hadn't changed since first appearing at around three.

"Eric is fine. He's pretty cool." Justin didn't just pause, he came to a full stop.

"Attending an Ivy League school, and studying English literature and that's the best description you can provide?" George knew he sounded annoyed. Well, this was his birthday!

"Dad, don't worry about Eric. He is an okay guy. Lily knows what she is doing."

"Is it serious?" George asked. Just one more question. He sounded so old, didn't he?

Justin flashed his grin again. "Of course it's serious. She wouldn't bring him here on your birthday if it wasn't." The expression metamorphosized back into the craftier version. "Have you thought about where he's going to sleep tonight?"

No, George hadn't considered it. But Justin had a good point.

"Right here. On this very couch." He returned Justin's smile and moved on.

"So what have you been up to?"

"Same old, same old." The eloquence of youth, round two. "How is your interrogation going?" As if George needed more introduction. Maybe Justin would be interested. No one else was.

"It has been an interesting interrogation. I think he is Al Qaeda, old school classic. There is a core group who formed deep bonds while fighting the Soviets in Afghanistan. We don't really know all of them; we just say we do. This group tends to be involved over and over again in the Al Qaeda plots." George studied Justin. People typically began ranting about the Iraq war at this point.

"How big is Al Qaeda?" Justin asked. George was pleased to see that Justin was engaged and interested. The boy hadn't moved, and seemed to be sitting comfortably. Bless his son. We all need to unload sometimes, don't we? He himself often felt like an extremist – just like his prisoners - when discussing interrogations.

"We don't know. Al Qaeda may not even exist. It means "The base". Initially, the organization worked like a venture capital firm – terrorist groups would approach them with an idea and they would decide whether or not to fund it. Most sleeper cells are not Al Qaeda. They just carry out strikes – like being hired as a consultant."

"Except they are willing to die." Justin was still paying attention, or was the dim light deceiving? George reached out for his wine, perched on the coffee table.

"Yes. But sometimes the bombers don't know they are on a suicide mission." George put his glass down.

Justin stared back. His eyes were round.

"Why would someone want to die?" Justin asked.

George felt a surge. The eggshell white walls faded. This was such a great conversation. Why indeed?

"The short answer is that these men, and they're still mostly men, are persuaded to die for God." George said. "But the long answer is more complicated. These men are marginalized in their societies. Opportunities exist only for the well connected, yet education is widespread – which leads to discontentment. Their worlds are insular and extremist religion is the only political outlet. Mosques provide a social structure – the only meeting places allowed."

George took another sip of his wine, sipping compulsively now. He was getting tipsy. Justin mirrored him – Karen and George had both agreed to serve wine to everyone at family dinner.

"Interesting." Justin paused, brushing lint off the couch. "But to die, dad." He wasn't yet displaying any outward manifestations of boredom.

"Think of drugs. Objectively, no one should ever experiment with them, right?" George saw that Justin felt no discomfort with the analogy. Good. "You can become an addict and wreck your life. You can die from an overdose. Yet people do. It might be peer pressure, a self-destructive streak, fostered by an abusive home environment or insecurity. There is always a reason – it just might not be easily discernable. But if we study patterns we can begin to see trends, consistencies."

"Which is what psychologists do." Justin looked triumphant in his ability to follow his father, whose conversations always ended up in psychology.

George empathized with Justin. He was even more triumphant than his son. Not only had he found a willing audience, he had found an able one too.

"There are stages." George reached over and turned on a ceramic lamp. Dim had turned to dark. "A terrorist isn't created out of nothing. First, is a belief that something is wrong and must be righted. Next, the person perceives that the wrongs can't be fixed through existing political or legal framework. In the last stage, the individual goes from being an activist to a terrorist. At this point the worldview changes, allowing powerful social barriers against violence to be overcome."

Justin still seemed interested. His eyes were wide open and focused.

"Which is why I am doing interrogations," George said. "I can understand these men. They aren't monsters. To kill. Think about that concept. Sometimes they look right into the faces of those they murder as they do it."

Discomfort flashed across Justin's face. Yes, none of us like to face death's realities. Yet these men plotted it. Death was their victory.

"Much of this is rooted in the politics of the 20th century," George said. "The idea of utopia, and the willingness to exterminate vast numbers of people to achieve it. Early Islamists were often former communists who took the basic concepts of liberal revolution and used it to bastardize Islam. Consider the 20th century willingness to murder anyone who disagrees with you."

George had gone too far. Justin's face shut down. The warm lighting and plush living room furniture did nothing to soften the harshness of George's words. They are murderers. They have a cause. Sometimes their cause is a just one. People shouldn't indiscriminately kill, yet they do. Often.

Justin sat for a moment, his face puckered.

"Well, I'm proud of you dad for trying to help," he said. "I can hear the toll it extracts when we speak. Your voice has lost its vibrancy. But, I am proud of you."

George hugged his son. Finally the boy had found his tongue. Perhaps if only one person understood that would be enough.

XXXXX

Anger lingered in the room, adding its own shadows.

"Hey you, Mecca." The guard had tried to kick Khalil when he had returned him to his miserable cell not even an hour before. Khalil had sensed the moving limb. Swinging awkwardly, it had missed him, but only because he had quickly moved his own shin out of its curving path.

Khalil had been allowed to watch some television with other prisoners earlier that day. They couldn't speak to each other as they sat knee to knee, shackled and chained. He had seen news, real news. Still killing each other in the Sudan. Floods, bombs, scandals and mergers. Not much had changed. He could smell the men's sweat; it permeated the air. The excitement of a link to the outside world had been enough to turn the group almost jovial. For a brief moment they had been men again, not caged dogs. Then the sea of orange jumpsuits had dissipated into the farther reaches of the jail. All was quiet now.

The Sudan.

The girl had been dark, her skin mottled with small scars. Were the scars from a long forgotten disease or were they poorly healed bug bites? Khalil didn't know and he didn't much care. He did ask himself the question sometimes when he awoke in the mornings and saw her lying in bed next to him.

"Lamia," she had whispered one morning, after she had been living with him for about a week. "I'm fifteen". He felt her slight breath, as she seemed to try and disappear into the well-worn folds of the bed sheets she had wrapped around her body. He could rip them off at any time and did just that, having already taken her repeatedly the night before.

In the Sudan, fifteen made her a woman with all the privileges, but mostly punishments, that womanhood entailed. Khalil had paid forty dollars for her. The sum was too high. But he had paid it because she was the girl he wanted. He liked her eyes. They were gentle and held the promise of a smile.

She was scared. Every time she looked at him her eyes held a trapped look, which conveyed worry and acceptance at the same time. Probably afraid that he would hit her. But her fears had been unfounded. Khalil had long ago vowed that he would never hit a woman. He wasn't going to be like his swine of a father.

Lamia was there to clean his small apartment. He had explained his expectations. "You are mine now. Cook, shop and wash clothes. You share my bed. Don't ask too many questions and don't get pregnant. Or, if you do get pregnant, fix it. Otherwise I will kill you. You are not my wife, nor my companion. I have no intention of staying in Khartoum."

Her large eyes, set off even more by the pinched and starved look of her face, had widened in fear as he mentioned killing her. Welcome to Khartoum, my dear...no safer than the hellhole you left in the southern part of the country. He felt like whispering those words to her, but he didn't. He certainly couldn't save her world, he could just acclimate her to the realities of his.

Instead he asked her questions, softening his earlier words with an endearment. "Where are you from, my dear?" Not that even a young, uneducated woman would misunderstand her precarious position. Like him, she had been forced to fight hard to stay alive. Only her instincts and a little bit of luck had saved her. In that respect they were both exactly the same. Almost.

"I'm a Dinka. My town is small, it has no name." She was sitting on the stone floor, her legs drawn tightly to her chest. Her translucent thobe lay in folds around her slight body. "But it is down near the church, the one next to the river." Deep in the south of the county. A world only touched by modernity through weapons and genocide.

She was a typical Dinka with her dainty limbs and a slight curve to her stomach. Her skin was a deep, dark brown. He could still see her moving slowly around the white apartment and diligently cleaning. She was always cleaning for she had little else to do. He let her spend time with a few neighborhood women, but only if they lived with his compatriots. Gossip could be deadly.

The only color in the apartment had been the profusion of flowers she brought in. How she found fresh flowers regularly in Khartoum he couldn't guess. She probably paid dearly for them. It was her only real pleasure, so he let her do it. What did the money matter when the currency was in a free fall?

Why not try to make life a little better if you are stuck in hell?

Khartoum lay at the confluence of the White and Blue Niles. The musky water lapped lazily on the filth along the shore. The air there had been menacing, reminding him of the guards eyes earlier this evening. The atmosphere of holding men against their will. In Khartoum the hostility was perhaps the hangover legacy from having hosted Africa's largest slave market. Was America creating its own bad karma – something to infuse its history going forward?

Amidst the brick buildings of the city hunger sat everywhere. Men like animals scrounging and foraging to stay alive. Ghostly shapes lined up across the wide boulevards, rarely stirring. Waiting with burning eyes for something to move so they could pounce.

How to describe a menacing feeling in the air? Having eyes never leave you, their hostility not veiled. The smelly crush of desperate bodies, yearning for what little you had. The lack of humanity that comes with utter desperation as men scrambled like rats to survive.

Khalil had tried once, in Amsterdam, talking to a group of potential recruits. Their eyes had brightened with each successive story Khalil told them, as if he was reading from *One Thousand and One Night,* not describing men's *Heart of Darkness*.

"You could hear the gunfire?" Spoken with saucer-like eyes.

"The air pressure changed as you felt the missile about to hit the earth?" Spit out between half rotten teeth, and in broken Dutch.

"How did you know there were land mines there?" As if such moron's could ever learn.

Menace just was. Your body could sense it. Khalil had never slept much in Khartoum. He had listened to Lamia breathe for hours each night. She had a kittenish snore that ended in a small growl. Like everything about her it was slight, almost disappearing. Probably how she had disappeared into the reeds the night the rest of her family had been killed, the machetes ripping through feeble flesh, sometimes not even stopping when hitting bone.

So his memories of Khartoum seemed centered around a broken old bed and the breath of a girl who was probably long dead. Yet he could still feel the heavy air, still hot as it blew through the noisy fan. Now menace had settled here, in a world that was not run by friends, in this jail. Khartoum had lost all pretense of humanity as its people fought to stay alive. He would have welcomed seeing Lamia on the television. Instead, the only Sudanese he saw were men. The darkness of their skin was like hers, but their faces held none of her gentleness. How he could have drawn strength from her breathe this evening.

A loud crash rang out. Khalil wondered, but only for an instant, what it could be. He knew his body was intact. What else mattered, inside the jail? Let it all fall down, the entire place. What did one more bang matter?

XXXXX

The door swung open. George imagined a clang, though he knew that it was a melodrama in his mind. This wasn't some medieval torture chamber. It was a simple and very shoddily constructed 21st century version of a medieval torture chamber. A Geneva Convention version, though what was the official status of an enemy combatant under that treaty? Not that it mattered. He was a functionary, and as much a prisoner as Khalil. Thank you Tom Campbell and comrades. *I love this job.*

Khalil sat at the table. Skinny as ever. The sky outside was overcast, and the small streak of light that came through the barred window just made the room gloomy.

Mood. It makes all the difference. George found his inner psychologist and tried to heed him.

"Heard you got some television privileges last night." His voice sounded creepily cheery, like some sixties sitcom.

"It was for good behavior." Khalil drew out each word, as George knew he liked to do.

"I didn't know you had a sense of humor." George gave him a smile, grateful that it felt more sincere than his oppressively cheerful tone of a moment before.

"How else could I survive here? There is a world beyond these walls," Khalil said.

"You mean the one you're trying to destroy," George said.

"Always a critic." Did George see a hint of amusement in Khalil's eyes?

"No, Khalil. I am here to save you. I don't care about that. I want to get you out of here. I'm doing this job only as long as it takes to get the information I know you have out of you. Then, you go back to your life, and I go back to mine. So, all jokes aside, the questions are about to start." George had already eased himself into a chair. The air had a rank and pungent feel to it. Up until today the weather had been hot, and ventilation had not been on the government's list of priorities.

"Was last night's television just a tantalizing whiff of freedom? Is that why we were allowed to watch – to tempt us?" Khalil answered.

"If only we were so organized." George said. "You think anyone actually thought that decision through? The guards were drunk and decided that television would make you easier to manage."

George could see the doubt in Khalil's eyes. Better he was unsure. Doubt would keep him pliable. And who really cared why the guards did it?

"Been to Indonesia?" George asked.

"No, I hate Asia." Khalil replied. A lie.

"Been to the Philippines?"

"I hate Asia." Another lie.

"Been to Thailand, specifically the south?"

"No." The lies continued. Khalil was fully aware that George knew these answers were all lies. The old *he knows, that I know, that he knows* game.

"Been to Malaysia?"

"No."

"Do you always lie?"

"Asshole."

"Where did you learn to swear so well in English?"

"San Diego. Remember, I went to school there."

"Who paid?"

"My father."

George laughed. The bastard really could be insolent. Khalil looked bored. He did it so well. George watched for those one second changes in expression that displayed true feelings.

"What group, Khalil? I have information. Right now I am just trying to establish how cooperative you're being." The room seemed darker than usual. Perhaps it was a mood thing. "Today isn't your day – at least not so far." George said, when Khalil hadn't replied.

A lazy smile crossed Khalil's lips. "If I had something to tell you, don't you think I would? It is quite a bluff – pretending not to be a terrorist if I am. My only passion is to fight the Algerian government, and that isn't a crime in your law ordered country."

"Have you been to the Sudan?"

"No, I hate Africa, too."

George threw down his pen. This was going nowhere, yet again. He couldn't even get Khalil to admit to what was written in his report – the cold, hard facts. Might as well backtrack for a while. He had many hours more to go.

"So, tell me what you watched on television."

XXXXX

Omar ran his hand along the briefcase. He caressed the leather, rubbing his hands across the bumps of stitching. The slightly too purplish burgundy betrayed its less than prestigious origins – like half of the merchandise sold in the United States it had been manufactured in China. The west had addicted China to opium. Now China was addicting the west to inexpensive consumer goods.

The case's size was standard. Very likely a compatriot was carrying an identical case back home. Yet Allah had blessed it.

The clasp moved easily as Omar pushed the lever and gently opened the lid. The case was hard-sided and quite light when empty. Only it wasn't, any longer. A nuclear bomb could now fit in a regular size suitcase. A briefcase provided more than ample space for a less hazardous, though still very deadly, standard bomb. There was even room for the two canisters that would eventually hold the chemicals to make sarin.

With an indrawn breath, Omar gazed at his work. His demo bomb. The first of five.

Ten cylinders sprouted white wires. They were all connected together, enabling them to detonate at exactly the same time. The wires were held in place by rubber stripping, carefully sized and then pierced by little silver screws which firmly grasped the backing. Another wire led to the center of the case where a cell phone was positioned – like a king surrounded by loyal subjects. The cell phone would provide the charge for the explosion. Two larger canisters were positioned at the top of the first canister, divided — but only temporarily. They would house the sarin ingredients, to be mixed when the final signal came.

Omar breathed deeply and filled his lungs with the acrid scent of explosives. Wasn't this what life was truly about? Power. All it took was training, a cell phone and a good hardware store.

The case closed with a slight thud, not even loud enough to serve as a precursor of things to come. Omar couldn't get enough of the bomb. It was so elegant. And unlike a woman, it didn't give him a headache. He could caress it to his heart's content without so much as a word ever being spoken.

XXXXX

"Somewhere in La Mancha, in a place whose name I do not care to remember…." Khalil began the opening page of *Don Quixote*. Next to him on the bed were his three pictures – that of his brother and the two of Jennifer – alongside a pack of cigarettes, a tin ashtray and a Bic lighter. He was beginning to amass a small mound of treasures thanks to George, and they provided a sense of home to his dismal cell. The small familiar comforts provide strength. Over the years Khalil had set up so many temporary homes. Long ago he had lost the luxury of a real home – too dangerous. No, Khalil's life was dominated by his role running his part of the jihad, a fact George thus far suspected but hadn't gotten out of him.

Khalil read a few pages, immersing himself in Cervantes description of chivalrous sixteenth-century Spain. Occasionally he glanced at his pictures. Two people he had loved and treasured. Now all he had was some cigarettes and a few books.

He also had the struggle – his 'brothers' involved in the movement. As the communists had comrades, he had brothers. They were loyal friends, up to a point. His community was devout, and they stuck tightly together. But their world wasn't one of permanence. And since Khalil made decisions and orchestrated plots he had to be prepared to send his friends to die.

At the end of the day each man is alone with his God.

Khalil's thoughts turned back to the book. Like Don Quixote, he had a distinctive viewpoint of the world. Unlike Don Quixote, many shared his vision. His brothers were paying a huge price to spread the ways of Allah. Allah be praised. He may be impotent now but these kufrs couldn't capture all of his compatriots. Victory was only a question of time. The filthy serpents of the west were weak. Men here had no conviction, caring only about shopping malls and other forms of debauchery.

But Khalil knew better than to chase false Gods and windmills. His brother, Hassan, had pointed the way. The answer was found in a book – the Koran. Mohammed was a warrior, as well as a religious leader. He used the sword to defeat his enemy, the non-believers. Don Quixote helplessly charged a windmill with his sword. Khalil used a proverbial sword: he preferred bombs. Hopefully his disappearance from the real world into one of fiction hadn't stopped the violent proselytizing of his reports.

Khalil looked at Hassan, still alive on a scrap of paper. "You would be so proud of your younger brother," he whispered. "Your dreams of glory for Islam didn't die with you. I know you watch me from your martyr's paradise." His brother's eyes gazed upon him, unblinking.

Khalil turned once more to *Don Quixote*. It really was a gripping book. If George was trying to send him a message by choosing this book it was falling on deaf ears.

"In short, our gentleman became so caught up in reading that he spent his nights reading from dusk till dawn and his days reading from sunrise to sunset, and so with too little sleep and too much reading his brains dried up, causing him to lose his mind."

"And so now I am perhaps Don Quixote," Khalil whispered once more – further evidence of his point still being developed. I shall go insane here, locked up with my books and the ghosts haunting me from pictures. My mind has been commandeered by those not living, in all their fictitious glory. Surely no good can come of it. Still, he picked up his book and began to read again. What else could he do? And who can say what's real and what isn't?

XXXXX

"What did you think of *Don Quixote*?" George heard echoes of past conversations. Tom Campbell and the pursuit of truth. Justin and the realities of the cold, hard world. The voices that filled his head. They came from another world. He shut them out. Intellectual discipline.

George watched Khalil's eyes as they shifted, focusing directly on his own. They turned hard and cold as they drained of emotion. Probably the same face he had when he killed. Or did that face contain a trace of passion, or perhaps primordial release? Why even bother imagining it?

The look shifted almost immediately, Khalil's whole face relaxed.

"I loved it."

And wasn't this what human relationships were like? We entered them guarded, trying to protect ourselves. As newness turns into familiarity we either recoil forever or begin to open up – letting our inner selves slowly come into the light. Doing it in an interrogation was a skill. George's patience was beginning to pay off.

"Me too. What did you like?" Bonding. I am just like you. Please, feel free to talk. I know that you feel you're seldom heard. Don't we all?

Khalil's face took on a softness George had never seen before. Perhaps because attention had been deflected from him and on to something of beauty. Even killers could love art.

"I loved the imagery, the description of a world that has long since ceased to be – if it ever truly existed."

"Is Don Quixote a realistic character?"

Khalil paused, a smile alighting his face ever so softly, as the dawn alights the world it caresses.

"No, of course not. And that is why he is so beautiful"

"Who can truly believe with such faith in a world devoid of chivalry?" George said.

"Yes. Of course," Khalil replied. "That is a problem. Yet he breaths, he lives and he dies. A world order is replaced with a new one."

"You get it. Did you know that Cervantes was captured in war and became a slave for a while? He died an impoverished and beaten man."

Khalil studied his palms. "Who can understand the hand of Allah? Cervantes' pain is my salvation." *As my pain will be the salvation of others*, George could hear the echoes resume.

"You are a poet at heart, Khalil."

The look in return was genuine. They were no longer prisoner and warden. They had now reached a new, albeit artificial, closeness. Who else did Khalil have but George? He was finding the warmth he lacked by being locked up alone. All it took was an idealistic knight and some flowery, though truly beautiful, language.

George smiled at Khalil. Yes, the camaraderie was genuine, not merely alive in his hopeful imagination. He was winning. Slowly, excruciatingly painful. But at the end of the day, men were men; textbook definitions rarely deviated from the truths.

His bosses could wait. This man would break.

A bird was chirping outside the window. It had to be close, though he couldn't see much of anything out the box window.

"The great question of the book is whether or not Don Quixote really believes what the world calls his insanity," George said. "What do you think? Do people like him really believe?"

Khalil appeared reflective. His face still also held onto the last traces of joy. The beauty of fiction, as George had learned from his wife, was how it took us out of ourselves while also highlighting who we really were.

"It doesn't matter. The beauty lies in the telling of the story," Khalil said.

George slowed his voice. "Khalil, do you really believe in what you are doing?"

Khalil studied George, half a smile lingering on his lips. Of course he wanted to answer, of course he wanted to continue the conversation. He must. Would he?

"It is a process. It is our faith," Khalil said. "We must set an example for our brothers so that they can join in their responsibility. It's art in its own way – as Don Quixote is art. We are spreading a message of faith and love."

"You are killing people." Again, slow, measured. Don't panic the man.

"Death. Why the focus on death?" Khalil replied. "Life is death. We are proclaiming our faith to the world, to Allah. The whole world knows our mission. Your focus is misplaced. You should be asking what happens to the infidels after they die. That includes you."

"You are trying to create a world – a utopia – that isn't possible on this planet," George said. "You cannot return to the better world that existed when a purer Islam ruled, just as Don Quixote can't return to the more perfect world of chivalry. They never existed, they are illusions."

"You are an illusion as well." Khalil spoke, and his tone was harsh. "And you live in a world of fantasy. Did you lock your car when you came in here today? Of course you did. This perfect society – democracy and freedom, which you try to force on the rest of the world is a corrupt and bitter lie." Khalil's face darkened. On his chin a few dark hairs sprouted. He must have missed them while shaving that morning. "We all delude ourselves. Where else can either of us go? We are stuck here discussing a book – yet neither of us has a life of beauty that can approximate it."

"Cervantes was a slave in Algeria." Let's see where that leads.

"I was a slave in Algeria, too. Now I am a slave here. Perhaps it was then that Cervantes recognized that we're all slaves. Our masters just change names."

"I need to think about that." George couldn't think of another response.

"No, I don't think you do." But Khalil sounded sure.

"Why stay a slave? What hold do they have on you?"

Khalil's face turned bitter. He hesitated before speaking. Sometimes, eventually, caution takes a back seat to the blinding desire to be heard and understood.

"They hold my life." Khalil said. "I can't change course now. I will be killed if I do."

"That isn't what keeps you bound." George was grasping, trying to find the answers. He shifted in his chair. "You have faced death many times. You are just too scared to admit you were wrong, that the decisions your younger self made led you on a doomed path. You are petrified to face your mistakes so you can't dare begin anew." George felt instinctively that he was right. The mind often knows what it can't see.

Meanwhile Khalil's face convulsed – for but an instant. Then, once again in control, he stopped moving. Preservation of energy, since emotions can be draining.

"What do you know, George? You are trying to find out about terrorism by bringing me books."

But George didn't need to celebrate his victories. Add ego to interrogation and a lot of people will die. Interrogators had to see beyond themselves. He was getting somewhere. Finally. Hopefully, he would get enough time. Why was he always so full of misgivings? Why wouldn't the bombs just stop for a while so he could catch up.

And Khalil was still sitting. So the interrogation must go on.

XXXXX

Escape. The conversation was escape. A world beyond these four walls. The hardness of men, softened only by what? We walk through the world and we don't see real people – instead we see the defenses they have built to hide the person trapped within. Khalil had no defenses left. He was raw and exposed. Forced to sit here day after day, discussing the topic of interest. But whose interest? He wasn't a person any more, just a number. Still, any escape was better than none at all.

"Who were you talking to in Los Angeles, Khalil?" The words rang out, too much for the small cell. Just as he was starting to relax, Khalil gave himself a second to think.

"Sancho Panza." Khalil said it for lack of a better answer. Then, he watched George's face become thoughtful.

"I believe you," George said. "Is a bomb going to blow there soon?"

Had his answer been a mistake? He had meant to be flippant. Had he perhaps instead admitted that he had a sidekick in Los Angeles?

"I was kidding."

"The greatest admission of guilt I have heard fall from your lips. You don't joke, Khalil."

"Well, perhaps you don't know me as well as you think you do," Khalil said.

George smiled. Perhaps he really was just another American.

XXXXX

When the time came to strike, you had to have the courage to follow through. Omar watched Stacey as she strode briskly to class. Her hair gleamed in the too warm sun. Late autumn hadn't yet begun to break through the endless summer weather. Stacey was wearing another mini-skirt, this one in cargo green. Her lime tank top was, as always, too tight and thin, even with the hot sun burning down. Why advertise like a cheap streetwalker? Wasn't it sexier to tease, alternately showing and then hiding your breasts? Still, he hadn't found many girls who knew how to titillate effectively. It was always either too little or too much. Mostly the latter.

Stacey was almost at the classroom. Whether he went to her or made her walk by him didn't matter. After six weeks of teasing her – getting closer then backing away – it was time to move. He loved this part. Cool, confident and a little bit distant.

"Stacey, hang on a minute." Slang, Omar had mastered a little bit of America. No please, too awkward in an impolite, informal country such as this one. Amazing how quickly a society could devolve back into the primitive.

Stacey slowed down and looked at him. A slight flush came to her face. Inwardly, Omar felt a surge of confidence. She was ready. Look at how she brushed her hair out of her eyes. Nerves. He smiled, directing as much warmth into his eyes as possible.

"Stacey, sorry to bother you," Omar said. "I missed last class. Do you mind if I get your notes?"

She continued to stare at him. He could see a questioning look in her eyes. Homework notes were a perfectly respectable request. Did he want more?

"Of course, if that isn't too much trouble." He let the smile fade and tried to look apologetic.

"No, not at all," she replied. "Do you want to take them now and photocopy them? Oh, no, wait, I don't have them with me."

"Can I get them tonight? Will you be at the library?" He looked at her, without a stare or threat.

"I don't go to the library at night", she said, something Omar knew – having staked out all of UCLA's libraries. "Why don't I give you my phone number, and you can call me when you want to pick them up."

Forcing her to offer her number – which she had been wanting to do. Lust is hard to hide. And, she had added an opportunity to come to her apartment at night. How long would it take him to fuck her, he wondered, if it took so little time to wear down her basic defenses?

"I would appreciate that." He smiled again, as Americans liked to do. Perhaps it made them feel less the murderous barbarians they were, killing innocent people and stuffing themselves down the world's throat as he would soon be stuffing his cock down hers. "I will call you tonight," he said. And he would. Her time had come.

"After you." As she turned he guided her, placing his hand in the hollow of her back. She didn't let on that she must have felt his closeness. He could almost touch the softness of her skin through the gauzy material. With her in front he allowed a small victory smile to cross his lips.

Stacey wore the same lime green tank top when she answered the door that evening. Omar could see the outline of her ribs underneath the cloth. The night had grown colder. A blast of cold air hit her when she opened the door, causing her nipples to protrude. He felt an urge to rip the shirt from her body and lick them right then. Soon enough. His women learned quickly that he didn't like to wait for sex. If they couldn't keep up then he didn't bother sticking around. After all, he could die a martyr's death at any moment. He had no time to waste.

"Do you want to take the notes and photocopy them? Would you like a drink first?" She turned to him, still standing. Her face looked expectant and impossibly beautiful.

"I'd love some water," he said. Untrue, but expected of him. This country was obsessed with water. "Can I just sit down and copy them myself? I find that I retain them much better that way. With the test coming up next week I want to make sure that I understand what I missed. You don't mind do you?"

"Not at all." Stacey smiled. Her features softened gently as her lips turned up. Omar sat slightly off the middle of her sofa. He glanced briefly around him then decided not to bother. The apartment was completely uninteresting. Not that it mattered. He wasn't here for the apartment. His eyes returned to Stacey. She stood in the kitchen and reached for a glass. Her shirt rose slightly as she lifted her arm, revealing her white skin. Like fresh cream, an expression he had read once and never forgotten. He loved women with that almost colorless skin, so different from his own.

Her kitchen looked rather bare. In that way she was typical of a science student – a dysfunctional group as a whole, who seemed barely able to navigate life outside a lab or a Petri dish. Not that he cared about her domestic abilities.

Stacey seemed comfortable with him by now, even when he stared at her. Perhaps she now found comfort in knowing that he was definitely interested in her as a woman. She smiled. His final cue.

In a minute she was back in the living room with his water and her notes. "Here, let me know if you can't read anything." She sat next to him, leaving a foot of space between them. She picked up a heavy science text. Omar didn't bother trying to see what she was reading, but noted how her body leaned slightly away from him, even as she had chosen to sit next to him and not one of her two worn looking chairs. An invitation, but not a confident one.

Women invite, and men possess, he reminded himself.

After letting silence sit for a few minutes he spoke up. "What does this say?"

Stacey leaned over the notes. Omar could feel her warmth. She looked up, right into his eyes.

"Mix the carbon…."

Omar reached out and brushed a strand of hair out of her face. His touch was deliberately light. He saw her flush.

"I'm sorry. I didn't mean to offend you." The respectful foreigner.

"No, no, you didn't offend me." She looked concerned.

"Are you sure?" He asked. Then she smiled.

He kissed her softly on the lips. It was a butterfly kiss, so soft their lips barely met. "How about that?' He looked at her and mirrored her earlier grin.

"It's okay, too." Her voice was barely a whisper and sounded slightly scratchy. "But I don't know you."

"My name is Omar. I want to get to know you." He was confident. He knew this part. Once a girl had decided she was interested he only had to wait for the right moment to take her. They all wanted to be conquered. He reached for her and drew her close to him, feeling her body as it melted into him. She wasn't ready for sex tonight, but she would definitely let him kiss her for a while.

Omar reached up her mini-skirt and caressed her firm thighs. He felt her breathe as she drew it in and shivered. At what point would she stop him?

XXXXX

As George pulled his car into the prison parking lot he noticed a familiar man getting out of a shocking blue car. The man's movements were distinctive as he rolled his weight onto his feet. Getting closer, George slowed down and peered closely to confirm the identity.

"Kevin, great to see you." He shouted out the window. Kevin turned around, and gave George a big smile. George returned it.

George parked his car and hurried to meet his colleague

Kevin hadn't changed. He had the formal bearing of a career military man. His warm demeanor and lively, green eyes belied his more upright body language. His dark brown hair, at least that was George's guess, had been almost completely shaved off, leaving only stubble. Kevin's muscular body was the type that George, an intellectual, had once envied when younger. The man trained for triathlons when his schedule permitted. His rippled arms, trim waist and broad shoulders could easily intimidate a less secure man.

They shook hands. "What are you doing here? No longer needed in Iraq?"

"Since you left not much has changed, George. There's so much work. I almost wish I hadn't entered the interrogation-training program years ago. Sleeping in my own bed would be a nice change." Kevin shook his head. "Everyone thought I was crazy to study Arabic then. Well they were all right, I was crazy. They were just wrong with respect to why. I can't get a break.

"Anyway, I finally got leave. Can you believe it took this long? We had to voluntarily waive our leave for a while. There just aren't enough translators to fill in."

Kevin paused, as he always did before a joke.

"So, a good buddy of mine says, 'While you're on leave …can you check up on a prisoner for me – in California! So, being an idiot, I said yes. Here I am." Kevin gestured at the trees, blinking as sunlight hit his eyes. “As far from my bed as I was in Iraq – well, almost as far. What about you? I thought you quit the interrogation game and went back to school.”

“Very funny,” George said. “Like you I said yes to one more request. Wait, slow down. Let’s talk for a minute before you go in. As you know, once you’re in getting out is hard.”

“Amen,” Kevin replied.

The two men paused at the bottom of the stairs. A slight breeze provided the only distraction, as the parking lot was unusually empty that day.

George resumed the conversation. “They keep giving me the tough cases. I have an Algerian fingered by a guy about to blow up a preschool here in the States. By a stroke of luck, he was picked up a few months ago and extradited here. I think he is some sort of organizational guy – a ringleader. He has made the rounds, you guys, the Egyptians, who knows where else. He is saying nothing, yet we seem to think the guy who fingered him is reliable. Well, as much as a crazy extremist with a bomb can be. Who can understand the logic anyway?” Kevin grimaced in response. “So, here I am.”

By now Kevin was frowning. He had the intent look of a man who loves his job – in this case, interrogation. George envied him. He had once looked that way. George could feel Kevin hanging on his every word.

“Is this prison legal?” Kevin asked. George shrugged. “You question it.” Kevin didn’t blink. Then he began speaking.

“So what are you going to do – other than withstand the frantic calls from Washington…?"

"…asking why I am so slow?" George finished Kevin's sentence. They had both faced similar frustrations. He continued, serious now. "Well, so far I have been bidding my time, getting to know my guy. But the easy questions are about to stop. I have two strategies in mind. First, I'll try 'futility'"

"Persuading him he has no hope." Kevin finished the thought.

"Yes. I have given him *Don Quixote* – all that impossible dream stuff. And, I'm about to tell him about our informant – hoping to create panic. That is actually today's agenda.

"Additionally, I have started building the foundations for 'fear down.'" George continued.

"Building a belief that you aren't so bad, maybe even likeable." Kevin finished the thought. "That's tough, George. It's difficult to turn those emotions into concrete help from a prisoner without losing respect. You sound desperate."

George nodded his head. "Like I said, I always get the difficult cases. I'm so limited on information here. Though we do have a tie to a cell phone number in Los Angeles." George watched Kevin's eyebrows shoot up. "Khalil almost seemed to pop up out of nowhere. Most of the incriminating intelligence relates to Algeria – years ago. This guy skated almost below the radar screen since – weird if he's a leader, as I believe. He just has that aura. And, he's very smart. I often get more information. So I can't try more reliable approaches like pretending we know everything already – I can't pull it off. I also can't try a more direct approach – just asking questions. Anyway, it never works with these Al

Qaeda types. They would rather die than talk."

"Hence the idea of suicide missions." Kevin grimaced again. It was a new expression he must have picked up recently. Like dysentery or head lice. George concentrated on Kevin's words as he spoke. "Yeah, well, some of them aren't so tough. Have you seen these home movies the Iraqis are showing with captured terrorists cowering. Great to show the man who murders someone for Al'Jazeera television crying like a baby." Kevin was all bravado now.

"Yes, but how much information do you get from them?" George kept a more serious tone."

"It is a problem." Kevin threw up his hands.

Just then a car pulled up. Sean, the prison guard. George suddenly felt uncomfortable.

"Are you free for dinner tonight?" He asked. "Can you come over."

"Absolutely. Love to." Kevin seemed to sense that the conversation was ending. Meanwhile Sean had stepped out of his car, banging the car door behind him. He started moving in their direction. Something is not right with that man, George told himself.

He quickly wrote out his house address and telephone number then handed it to Kevin. "Seven sounds good?" The paper flapped in the wind as he handed it over.

"Great."

Together they walked into the building with Sean.

XXXXX

"...idiot son. Wasteful, profligate, ungrateful pig." The voice droned on, the telephone receiver serving as his father's soapbox. Omar continued to caress the smooth alabaster leg sprawled across his body. He looked at the skin, marveling at how it was speckled with very fine brownish freckles.

"I send you there to study. Yet every month you call and ask for more money. Why don't you call to tell my about your grades. Do you even get grades or have you flunked out? Why do I have such a moron...."

Omar pressed harder, watching as a slight flush spread across the skin following the path his fingers had taken.

Stacey's eyes jerked up from her book. "Ouch. Don't press so hard." No reason for her not to study. He wasn't going to fuck her while he had his ranting father on the telephone. Not that he was listening to any of the words flying like bullets out of the swine.

"Father, are you done? Do you want to hear what I have to say?" Of course not, the man never did. Still, all he asked of Omar was that he take abuse. And for that he paid all the bills. Seemed a fair trade, especially sincc the old man was continents away.

"I am not done," his father said. "You are coming home. No more education for you, ungrateful louse. You are no better than a snake, waiting to bite my hand off as I struggle to take care of you. You are a man now, though you don't seem to have noticed."

The room disappeared. Omar felt an overwhelming rage filling him. He struggled to think. An image of his father loomed in his mind. Always loud, always speaking. The threats that didn't end. Kaleidoscopes of noise clouded his vision.

His father's house had never felt like his own, even though Omar had been born there. A fountain bubbled up in the center of the courtyard. The water flowed, never-ending. The threats also flowed, never-ending. Omar could still picture his father, his hand running through the water, silhouetted against the entryway's desert colored stone, as he spoke. His voice was always loud.

"You will do as I say. It is your duty. I will cast you out as I reject a scorpion that disobeys me. There is always the desert, my boy, for those who disobey their father."

His father's eyes were cold; they always were. But he lived in the sweltering heat of the desert. As he spoke now he was probably standing in his favorite spot, pacing around the fountain, cordless phone in hand. Only Omar wasn't there anymore. The words came through a telephone line. Still Omar heard the bubbling water thousands of miles away.

"I love you my father. I respect you my father. As Allah is my guide I bow down to your wisdom." Allah must protect him from this man standing between him and his destiny – that of a martyr.

"Father, oh blessed father, he I love next after the Allah to whom I pray, deliver me from this sinful and Godless society. Bring me home. Oh, please bring me home to the land from which the prophet spoke."

Omar could feel his cock start to well up. A whisper of a moment ago Stacey had taken him into her mouth. All it took was her lip's gentle pressure - or was it her tongue - to bring him to life. He struggled to stay present in the conversation. The edges of the room around him had already gotten blurry. Allah was testing him. Or was his father testing him? Did he care any longer?

"But papa, please just let me finish off the semester. I am learning so much." The white ceiling was spinning.

The industrious copper head moved beneath him. He felt a groan emerge deep from his belly.

"I have another call. We will address this later," his father said.

"Yes, father." Lucky break.

Omar heard the click. The telephone was dead. His cock wasn't. He groaned deeply and reached for Stacey's russet nipple. The night wouldn't be long, but it would help him forget his father.

For a moment the man once again popped up. His father always loomed larger in his memory than he did in real life. Perhaps that was because Omar had been so young when he had been banished from home to a parade of schools. The lush lips, the eyes just like his own with their butterfly's flutter of eyelashes, and the hatefulness and rotten breathe that spewed from the man. Cur.

Omar looked down across his smooth stomach with its clearly defined abs. So different from the flab that his father wore like armor.

Stacey's headed bobbed beneath him. Praise be to Allah that she had other uses for her mouth besides talking. Would paradise be better than this? It would have to be, wouldn't it?

He wasn't going home. Except perhaps in a coffin.

XXXXX

"Do we have to blow so many people up?"

Kevin's eyes widened, a deliberate effect. He would never let real emotions show; he was too skilled. "We aren't the ones blowing people up, George. You know that." His voice sounded empty, all emotion leached out. Not drained out, leached. Forcibly and violently extracted. The voice of men who spoke about an ugly war when trying to discuss their daily reality to those who lived in comfort and safety. Only, George had been there too.

"Well, they weren't getting blown up daily before we got there." George said.

"George!" Panic showed in Karen's eyes. Well, let her hear reality for once, instead of the fiction she read all day. "Kevin is your friend." She stared at him, as if willing him to behave. Or was she just embarrassed by his lack of manners? He watched incredulous, as she proceeded to smooth the embroidered tablecloth. White, with rainbow-colored flowers.

"George," Kevin's voice was soft and patient. Delicate even. Or at least as much so as a big, tough soldier like Kevin could carry off. "I'm the one who is supposed to be worn out and jaded. You escaped, remember? No more car bombs to worry about. No more guns everywhere you look. I am going back. Ignore what you read. That is what freedom of the press does – it highlights the 'crimes' of whoever is in power. Before, under Saddam, you got shot if you printed something about the massacres and executions. Even now, no one wants to read good news."

"Long live Saddam." George was annoyed. His voice didn't reflect it. Kevin was too good. He had to be on his best behavior. "Kevin, you must admit that there are benefits to a military dictatorship. The streets are safe. Things work – power, water, mass transit systems."

"Yeah, it's great for the people who aren't ripped out of their beds at night because they read the wrong newspaper. Or, maybe just for the crime of reading at night. Do you want to get shot because you read what you like, subversive though some of it may be?"

"That is it. I am leaving," Karen said. Probably in disgust. "I will not discuss politics like this, guys. You are on your own. Dessert will be plunked on the table, alone, in a minute." Karen stood up, a plate in each hand.

Both men watched her walk away. Karen looked lovely that evening. Her hair was pulled back from her face. A few tendrils escaped, softening the look. She was wearing some sort of caftan dress, lilac with a turquoise trim that brought some long lost deep blue colors into her eyes. The gentle light of the room – dimmed since they were in George's house – had erased her wrinkles, making her look much younger.

Part of George wanted to follow her. He rarely listened to that part these days. They were taking separate paths. She would go read Jane Austin, and he would discuss how many people would likely die over the next month in a dusty town halfway across the world. No one would mention that Kevin could be one of those who died.

"It isn't that, simply reading too much subversive literature," George said. "We can't just destabilize a region, then leave it to go to hell." George decided to escape back into the conversation.

"Because we aren't the Soviet Union? Because Cambodia and the millions dead there didn't happen when we withdrew from the region." Kevin's voice had risen a decibel. "Or, even closer, what about the Kurds that were massacred when we withdrew from the first Gulf War, deserting them. What's your point, George? We are the bad guys? War is never pretty. It is necessary, sometimes." Kevin just stared. Of course he did. His life was on the line daily. He had to believe the rhetoric or he was just a fool.

It was George's turn to smooth the tablecloth as he formulated a response. He felt the bumps of the embroidery.

"I am just as much in the middle as you, Kevin. Until a few months ago I was even there. They still won't let me escape. I keep going and torturing this guy- metaphysically, of course. I can't get away." George felt a pain shoot up his back. The room's lighting now seemed more somber than gentle.

Kevin smiled at him. Unexpected. He was still controlling himself. Like a soldier who recognizes battle fatigue in a colleague. Perhaps he just thought George was being silly and his words weren't worth serious consideration. George would never know – Kevin hid thoughts too well.

"George, listen. Please believe what I say. You are a good man, a strong man. This situation is testing us all. Each and every one of us will break; that is inevitable. But don't stay broken. Remember your goals – a decent life for everyone. All we can do is keep trying, no matter how many human shells are willing to die trying to stop us."

"I am being…." George started to respond then saw Karen walking back in. She held a plate piled high with brownies. Her last minute compromise for hosting a guest for dinner with no notice. Something about a one bowl thing. George paused, not wanting her to hear his words.

Kevin broke the mood. "My favorite." He beamed. "Have you ever tried to find homemade brownies in downtown Baghdad.? Not possible. Biggest crime of the war."

George watched Karen. She shot Kevin a skeptical look. His words made no sense, yet she couldn't really comment. Doing so would risk entangling her in the political discussion she wanted to avoid. Denial. Silently, he thanked Kevin for propelling her re-exit (she hadn't bothered to reply), which allowed George to finish his sentence in private.

"Silly. I am being silly aren't I?

"Not in the least," Kevin said. "I wish you were. There are no easy answers, George. We all try. In the end, we end up focusing on core beliefs and a hope that we are honoring them. We have become the sentimental men we accused our fathers of being."

"And we're as scared as when we were boys." George felt his own face soften. At his age he had to admit to little control over both the world and over himself.

"I'm more scared now that I know what death is. I'm not ready to die." Kevin shifted his bulk. George could sense the blood coursing through each vein and artery, feeding those muscles. How easily flesh could be torn from even the strongest body, spilling blood over everything nearby. Hopefully, he would never hear of Kevin's body so desecrated.

"Hey, you should try these brownies," George said, deliberately changing the subject. "If you thought the fish was bad wait until you try these." The verbal equivalent of a slap in the back.

"That was fish? I thought the mess hall food was bad," Kevin said.

"Yeah, she can't cook at all," George replied. "But don't say anything – she doesn't know."

George breathed deeply. Equilibrium was restored. All he could do was keep breathing. Everything else would have to take care of itself.

XXXXX

"But, I don't agree with the theory. It is just a theory. Even in science, we have theories that can't be proven. Moreover, we have theories that are eventually proven wrong." Stacey was arguing with the professor. Her milky skin was flushed, just as it got during sex. Omar could see her jaw line as she turned to the professor. Though Omar was seated a few rows behind her, he could sense her shortness of breath.

The late afternoon sun cast shadows across the generic lecture hall. The effect was dramatic because an unseasonable rain had struck the campus that day, darkening everything. Rain pounded down on the roof of the building, its rhythm constant until an occasional barrage of harder hitting drops.

"There exist many theories we know are correct but haven't yet proven." The professor sounded exasperated. Or was it annoyed? Perhaps just resigned, as he usually was, but more frustratingly so. Omar didn't care. He was enjoying his lover while she argued with a familiar passion. How had he not noticed before how sharply defined her jaw was? Like a knife, cutting through air.

"And, there are theories that we believe for years, only to have them refuted." Stacey looked furious. What was the big deal? She was arguing with the man who would give her a grade. Why couldn't she just back down, and let the class move on?

"Less so the case when dealing with chemical principals, young lady," the professor said.

Ouch. 'Young lady'. Omar grinned. Stacey considered herself a feminist. She would probably counter attack with some crack about how men, when their argument was weak, always attacked a woman for her sex. After all, that was what she always said to him. Most women used that line during an argument. Projection. Wasn't that what it was called? Well, he would consider looking it up if he ever cared enough to know. Not likely.

"Oh, come on, let's just move on. Who cares? Can't you just argue with the professor after class? We have a test on Friday and I am sure that the rest of the class would prefer to go over to what we need to know."

Omar turned around to see who was speaking. A short, nerdy guy in a watery-blue shirt – with stains. He looked completely washed out, as if all life had dripped out of his body, from the tips of his hair follicles to the end of his toenails. How could anyone living in Southern California so effectively avoid sunlight? Must have something to do with lab hours. Meanwhile, the boy's face darkened as the last of the light disappeared outside the window. The sun had surrendered to the clouds.

"Well, I don't agree with you, young man." Omar heard his own voice, strong and deep. A perfect contrast to the nerdy whine that had attacked Stacey. "I don't want to learn something for a test – even if the test is on Friday – that isn't true. I am not here to learn how to fake being a scientist. Please, professor, continue your conversation, and let the lady speak." Gallant, and simple. Also, deferential to the professor and his authority. Right?

Omar watched Stacey as he spoke, glancing only momentarily – out of courtesy – to the professor. Moments earlier her face had blackened, like the weather outside, at the geek's interruption. He had then watched as a hesitation was reflected in her eyes. The look was familiar, from the brief beginnings of their relationship, before he had taught her that a woman could unleash her passion. And, then, when Omar had spoken in her defense her eyes had brightened, also familiar, with that flash of gratitude. He then noted a surge of courage. How predictable women could be. Their emotions always on display.

The nerd, mumbling behind him in protest, Omar would address later. In his woman's eyes he had shone, if only for an instant.

But why did he care? Dimly he was aware of the professor and Stacey resuming their arguments. Chemical properties and theories were flying through the air. All he could see was the side of her head – the sharp jaw, the bright hair, the pale skin. Why did he feel so proud of her and that flush in her cheeks? He didn't care about her, did he? She was after all a girl and a slut at that. No, not possible. He just liked to watch her face, remembering the last time he straddled her and brought that same passion into her eyes. That must be it. No other possibilities could be allowed.

"Retrograde virus." The nerd continued to mumble. "Don't they all realize we have a test coming up?"

XXXXX

George felt the crush of the soft down pillow against his head. His body was lost in the smooth blandness of the bed sheets – high thread count of course, not at all like the hellish beds his mother had made him sleep on. His physical state contrasted starkly with the activity running rampant in his head. But then, aren't moods really just illusory?

Did a lack of empathy turn a man into a monster? How could you kill another man if you truly understood him and could picture yourself for a minute in his shoes? How could you dictate another man's, or woman's, life based on religious doctrine a thousand years old?

Did George himself understand the meaning of empathy? If he didn't understand it, could he teach it? Why must he keep asking himself such questions? Why couldn't he just sleep like Karen, next to him with her dreams of Henry James or the fictional murderer from *Crime and Punishment*? Why couldn't George empathize more with Karen, his own wife? Fiction versus fact. Yet did Khalil not live a life that was almost fictional? Unfortunately, he was all too real.

George tried for a moment to feel what Khalil must live, to hold a dying man you have killed and to feel his blood run through your fingers. What would such a horror do to a man?

George couldn't do it. Always his weakness as a psychologist, and he was a good psychologist, but still a frail and weak human being. George couldn't fully put himself in Khalil's shoes. And he knew it.

But Khalil was capable of so much more. He was smart, perceptive, knowing. He thought, and questioned. But still he chose to kill. The innocent, children, anyone. Usually George wasn't a big believer in redemption for a terrorist– the desensitization process of distancing people from their humanity was too powerful. Redemption could happen occasionally. But typically among the low level, less committed, recruits. Those who had found only the basest of meaning in a crazy organization. But Khalil wasn't that type. Khalil wasn't canon fodder. He was a formidable ally – a truly frightening man. Only a twist of fate had lead to his capture – he was too wily to get caught in a more obvious way. George snuggled more deeply into his covers, the only armor he had.

Back to his original question, the one that kept his mind churning. Could George do anything for a man with no empathy? Humanity so often came back to that amorphous, ambiguous emotion. And, to compound his problems this evening, the darkness had lost its normal comfort. Is there no escape? We turn our environment womb-like when we want to sleep. Yet, now, the night was simply blackness, and George felt disengaged from his bedroom.

He had hated most of his interrogates. They were rough, uneducated men – hopelessly biased and dogmatic. He had looked down upon them – sure that no redemption was possible for such merciless and misguided killers. But his views hadn't really evolved, had they? He distinguished Khalil from the rest because Khalil was better educated, albeit mostly self-educated, and could articulate reasoned and erudite opinions. The educated ones he had met had been scientists or engineers – practical with little imagination. Sometimes they were brilliant, especially, unfortunately, in planning. But they weren't like Khalil, who was more like him. And that was why George wanted to save him – to turn him from evil.

So, unfortunately, empathy was the last thing George could teach Khalil – empathy was entirely missing from the picture. George was hoping for the superiority of the educated and open-minded man over the savage. As if anything could save a man from himself. Was he any better, truly, than those he judged? Would he have chosen murder to remake the world had his pen proven impotent? How could he answer that question?

George continued to stare at the darkness. His body was tense, too tense. As it shifted, slowly but perceptively, he could feel Karen stir beside him.

"Why are you awake? It is so late." Karen's voice was groggy, not happy at her awakening. George didn't care. He was confronting earth-shattering issues – more important than her sleep.

"Karen, how am I different from them? I am as dogmatic, as judgmental, as unyielding. I hate them as much as they hate me." The words flowed. His agony was as subtle as a young child's. Not only couldn't he face himself alone, he couldn't face himself at all – at least not without a confessor – a desperate attempt to purge his sins.

"Have you killed?"

"No."

"Do you intend to kill?" Her head rested sideways, on the pillow nestled next to him. Her easy lines were visible in the darkness.

"No."

"Then you are different," Karen said. "Certain lines do exist. As long as you haven't crossed them you are morally distinct."

"But Karen, who sets those lines?" The certainty in her voice was reassuring – almost deceptively so.

"Go to sleep, George. Those lines are eternal. We see them in holy books, in literature and in philosophy. Stop being so hard on yourself. None of us is perfect. You mean well – unlike those with whom you consort. Sometimes the only difference between two men is in their intentions. But that distinction is important."

Empathy. From Karen. A woman. But what did she really know? Her world was all about fiction.

Where did these universal truths come from? Didn't he once know?

His sense of unease continued. Karen's warmth next to him likewise didn't have its normal comforting effect.

"Are we right to judge him?" George asked. "Don't we do the same things – we kill, support corrupt governments, allow for atrocities. Perhaps we are worse than these men who try to fight for justice, for equal rights."

"Liberté, and all of that." Ah, his line to Khalil, fed back to him. Karen continued. "You have been reading too much revolutionary literature, George. Men like Khalil are nihilists. Their aim is to destroy. Death to all non-believers, remember."

"They are still men." Even George heard weakness in his voice.

"By your definition. George, what defines a man?" Karen's tone was annoyed. George could understand – he wasn't generally open to philosophical debates in the middle of the night either. However, he was having a deep and painful crisis. He was questioning his world. And, Karen was, after all, his wife with all that the commitment entailed.

"You want to ask these kinds of questions…" Her voice droned on, unhappy but perhaps more willing than he gave her credit for being. "…then ask them. But try not to do it at night. I believe you mean well.

Don't lose that focus – what you believe in hasn't changed George. The nuances are just being further defined. Now start counting sheep, or whatever it is that works for you, and go to sleep."

Silence filled the shadow left by her voice. The room felt oppressive – still. Had her advice helped? Had her words soothed? George still felt the burden of his thoughts. He was getting old, wasn't he?

George sighed, realizing too late he was probably bothering Karen further. Yes, well....

He tried to count sheep. But that made him think of the men he had known who weren't much better than sheep. He glanced again at the clock, but did not sigh this time.

XXXXX

"Tell me about Los Angeles?" George said. "The familiar cell felt smaller today. Or maybe it always felt this way for a fleeting second whenever George returned.

"What do you want to know." Khalil sighed loudly.

"When were you last there?"

"Ten, or more, years ago." Now Khalil shrugged his shoulders, turning up his palms as he spoke. George couldn't help but be annoyed. Worse, he didn't know why he felt annoyed. Damn moods, so unpredictable. Remember, control.

"You sure?"

"Yes." Khalil held his voice firm.

"Date?" Use your annoyance and impatience. Push Khalil today.

"George, how would I know? I said ten or more years. Let me out of here, and I will try to find my old calendars." Now Khalil sounded exasperated. Good.

"In your house?" George's mood was definitely exaggerated now, for effect. Suddenly a spider dropped from the web it had been unraveling from the ceiling. They both stared at it as it scampered away.

"These spiders are everywhere in this jail. Don't they clean?" George's voice clearly remained annoyed.

"Look around you, the guards don't clean. That spider is my friend. He was trying to protect me." George didn't smile at Khalil's attempted joke.

"From my questions about Los Angeles?" George kept up a brisk pace, no silence. "Why was a Los Angeles number found on the cell phone you ditched in London."

"A mistake. Not my phone. I dumped a piece of paper into that trash bin. The police were just being overly zealous. I have told you this many times before."

"Rat's ass, Khalil. Your fingerprints were on it." George wasn't going to give Khalil time to lie. A lie takes more effort, hence people pause for a moment longer before responding. Khalil wasn't getting that second. "Come on, I need an answer."

"Okay, the phone was mine." Finally.

"Who?" George pressed on.

"A guy I barely know. A friend gave me the phone. I was supposed to call the guy in an hour. I got arrested instead." Khalil looked slightly off. So that was how his guilt looked.

"To discuss what?" George said.

"A bomb, is that what you want to hear?" Khalil stood up, as if to leave the table. Not that he could go anywhere.

"Sit down. Don't make me say it again. If you say a bomb you mean a bomb."

"Yeah, so what. Now what are you going to do?" Khalil's face was expressionless, his voice dead. George glanced at the bars on the lone window. The sun was bright outside today.

"Look." George gestured at the window. "Outside the sun is shining. You can decide yourself whether or not you ever want to be a part of that world or not. Is there something going on in Los Angeles?"

"There was going to be, but you arrested me before it got started. Who knows what happened with it afterwards." Khalil sat down again as he spoke.

"Give me details." Again, George kept up a brisk pace.

"I hadn't heard any yet," Khalil said. "That was what the call was for."

"You are lying." No outward clues, George sensed it. "You are a planner, not a functionary."

"I am not so high in any organization that I no longer take orders." Khalil held his eyes unwavering as he spoke.

"Give me names."

"I don't have any."

"Your friend." George said.

"Not really a friend."

"Don't make me ask again. You are lying." George felt stillness in his body. For him success never came with a rush.

"Okay, I will give you one. That is all I have." Khalil broke.

"Phone number or address, as well?" Khalil knew more, but George would settle for a name today. Once the resistance starts to break it is hard to slow the ensuing momentum. Doing something is only hard the first time.

"Yes, both."

"Go ahead." George picked up his pen and waited.

XXXXX

Khalil fingered the new books. He cracked one open and bent his head down. His nose lingered in the binding as he inhaled the scent. A mix of chemicals and paper – distinctive and familiar.

George had gone, praise be to Allah. He hated when George was in that mood. Good riddance. Almost as if rewarding Khalil for a name – a disclosure which one day might cost Khalil his life – George had left a package behind. Inside were books and more chocolate. Why did he always bring chocolate? A distinctly western thing to do. Or was it an effort to infantilize Khalil? Probably. More likely it was a cat and mouse game; designed to make him question his own mind. Drawing closer, only to pull away. Well, the simple pleasures would save him: they had to. Now, being alone with new books, was enough. George, with his endless questions, would one day be in his own purgatory. If he wasn't already.

Khalil knew the books would be inappropriate. George wasn't going to reward him with anything he himself might choose. That would spoil the purpose – controlling what went into his prisoner's mind. A biography of John Adams (a revolutionary freedom fighter – what an odd choice), *Journal of a Solitude* (by an 80 year old woman?), *Just So Stories, The Inferno* and *The Silence of the Lambs*. Such an eclectic mix. Yet Khalil knew George exerted considerable effort making these choices. George had absolute control over what information went into Khalil's head. This particular group seemed designed to keep him awake. Perfect. As if he needed more to go insane.

Khalil had felt fear before. Physical fear was one thing – possible to temper through will power and Allah's grace. The real fear came when controlling your own mind got harder and harder to do.

"Protect me, Allah be praised, protect me." Khalil let his head drop into his hands. The vision of another day, long ago, bloomed in his head.

The morning had been hot and dusty – but brilliantly radiant. Khalil had woken early, as always. He had left his flat – hoping to escape the oppressive heat for that brief instant before it permeated everything. Crouching down, he remembered staring at the rust-colored dirt beneath his feet. The color and texture were unlike that of his home village, though he was not even a hundred kilometers away. The square white buildings felt oppressive, like patrons in a coffee house clustering closer to catch each word of a story. In his experience, such were the feelings of being stranded, not allowed to return home.

Deliberately Khalil had struck a match then used it to light a cigarette, his first of the day. Cigarettes were often his substitute for food. His group, a motley band of impoverished young men and an Imam or two, had been poor then. Most groups founded to fight their government started that way. The money would pour in later when the young boys began to win. Only then will a government's enemies emerge from the woodwork, happy to fund death and destruction. On the first inhale, the cigarette smoke singed Khalil's lungs and jolted his mind awake.

The dust began to move, swirling ever so slightly above the ground. He had glanced up, reluctant to end his solitude. Only then had he seen them, marching in a ragtag and disorganized group. The mass was mostly women and young children, though he also distinguished a misshapen old man. They carried little with them, and seemed to be stumbling more than walking. The cluster was silent, deathly silent. How do you keep young children quiet?

As the group got closer Khalil began making out individual faces. He didn't recognize anyone. Indeed, they seemed too dirty and tired to be human. Their eyes gave him a momentary fright, causing him to wonder if he was seeing a mirage or a nightmare. The pupils were completely empty. They blazed with a vacancy he had never witnessed, as if eyes could become completely transparent. Yet a distant fire blazed behind the emptiness. Horror?

"Khalil!" A shapeless blob had spoken, directing her haunted eyes in his direction. Involuntarily he had winced, trying to draw himself back.

Then he recognized the soft timber of the voice. His cousin, Grace. She had been named after the actress turned princess of Monaco – a frequently mocked choice in not so Frenchified rural Algeria. Staring at her, not recognizing her, Khalil realized that only her voice betrayed her. She was so grimy, her clothes ripped and hanging limply from her body.

"Grace, what happened?" By now he was standing, his cigarette burning in the hot sand. Reaching for her, oblivious of the barely human creatures standing next to her, he reached out and rested his arm around her shoulder. Khalil expected to pull her tightly in an embrace. Instead she jerked away – as if stung.

"Grace, what happened?' He repeated the question, his voice softer now, soothing. She stared back at him, her eyes darting around to see if anyone else was nearby. He saw a movement and a small bundle darted out and grabbed Grace's legs. The matted hair was a deep black. He could see no face but suspected that the child was Daria, Grace's daughter. He didn't move, but instead waited for them. He had all day to hear an answer. Utter stillness, the only way to calm a wild animal or a shell-shocked person.

For about five minutes everyone stood there. Finally, a woman fell, worn out. Still, no one else stirred. Grace lifted her eyes and looked at him.

"Some men came. They pulled our men out of the houses and accused them of treason. They said that the men were all rebels, and they tied them up. Then they took most of the women and children and sat them in the middle of the town square." Her voice cracked, and she looked away. Moments later, speaking only to the ground, she resumed her story.

"We had escaped, into the bush. Our houses were farther north than the others." With this Grace waved her hands, gesturing to those behind her. "Our men were already at the coffee house so they weren't so lucky. But one boy, Ahmed had escaped and come to warn us we must flee." Khalil guessed that Ahmed must be among those present, but no head or hand volunteered itself for recognition.

"We were hiding and couldn't see clearly. We did hear the shots that rang out. When the smoke hit us we knew that our village was no more. We came here because we had nowhere else to go. And, our husbands' comrades are here. They must help us. Khalil, you must help us. Do you have water?"

How many were they? Twelve or so? Grace had shed not one tear as she recounted the banishment of their former life. Not one tear. They were too far beyond tears.

Khalil had still stayed quiet. He squatted down, and reached for little Daria. She must be close to three. He caressed her tiny shoulder and felt her small body yield to his. He held her tight. Still, not a sound. Nothing fell from her lips nor from the crowd. They had been walking how many days? Two, three?

"Yes, water, wait here," Khalil had said. "Or, follow if you feel safer."

Tragedy. So much had still been coming. Khalil fingered his new books. He didn't need horror stories to keep him awake at night. There was no solace in solitudes. Books were just books. Words were just words. And fear had been so deeply ingrained into little Daria's eyes it would never go away. He didn't need to see her now to know that much.

Vengeance was out there, waiting. And Khalil had no intention of giving in to fear. He fingered the book with John Adams' portrait staring up at him, arrogant in his legacy. A hero because his cause won their war – for that reason only. So many men. How many hold a potential to do great things? How many don't, out of fear, when they have never faced real fear?

XXXXX

When Omar got home from the mosque he saw a red light blinking on his answering machine. He averted his gaze, perhaps if he ignored it the light would disappear. His wandering eyes brushed over a stack of books, almost lost amidst the clutter of dirty clothes and newspapers. Did he have a test tomorrow?

His stomach rumbled. Fleetingly he questioned his decision to skip dinner with his friends from the mosque. But – unlike them – he didn't have time. He was a jihadist and on a mission. Plus, he did have that test. Right?

Better to hear the message. Otherwise the threat of it would distract his studies. Perhaps it wouldn't be what he expected. Omar walked over to the machine on the small black table next to the couch. He pushed the play button, brushing clothes off the couch and onto the floor so he could sit.

"Omar, this is your father." The hated voice rumbled. "Call me back so we can discuss you coming home. I am serious. Call me, or I will cut off your credit cards. You know I will do it."

Infidel. No, worse than an infidel. He had no right. Omar was on a mission. His pay from the movement was nominal. The foot soldiers of this war were expected to carry their own weight. It helped them not get caught – very few fund transfers going on. He needed his father's money. Even if only a bit longer. The old man shouldn't come between him and jihad. Indeed, he would rot in hell for doing so.

Omar bit his lip, pausing to think. Then he headed to the kitchen for something to eat. He would call the man when he was ready. If his father really did cut off his credit cards, Omar would call his mother and demand one from her. His father wouldn't dare fight her decision because doing so would force him to talk to her. That was one thing his father wouldn't do.

XXXXX

George cradled Karen under his arm. Her face was flushed, her breathing hadn't yet slowed to normal. Her translucent skin barely disguised her bones, which shifted only slightly as she leaned forward to kiss him. She settled against him and the white sheets under her scattered hair. He felt her breath against his chest.

"Be my friend again," he said and he heard huskiness in his muted tone. He'd been affected no less than her. "Please." A mere whisper.

She moved slightly, bird-like even in her 50s. Her slight frame would never thicken. After twenty-seven years of marriage he could predict that much. She could find nuance in obscure poetry but would never decipher a recipe.

"How can you ask me that, now?" Her voice almost broke as she spoke. But of course it didn't. She was too far away. Was this how marriages finally fell apart – when one partner refused to continue watching the disintegration? Should he beg or just let it collapse?

"Is there someone else?"

George could smell the remnants of her perfume as she pulled away from him.

"You left me, George. You left me physically. But even when your body came back, your mind never did." The softness in Karen's voice had vanished.

"You weren't here when I came back." He paused and she let him. Certainly other men would have noticed she was alone; Karen was so lovely. Silence descended over the dark room. He wouldn't speak next. That duty was hers; only she could tell him if he had been right about her emotional absence, and its consequences.

"Did you read *The Odyssey*?" Karen said. "Coming back isn't so easy. Life goes on without you." She seemed so strong, her tone inappropriate for the marital bed. Yet he was the one who raised the subject.

"Is that a yes? Was there someone else."

"Not really. Almost. You were gone a long time, George." Her voice wavered.

"Who? Do I know him?" He choked out the words. It was the best he could do.

"Nothing really happened." She stammered, too scared perhaps. He felt her body collapse. She had never been strong, much as she pretended otherwise.

Their talk could head in so many different directions. He felt guilt, hurt, fear, and anger. What did 'not really' mean in this context? And he had left her. For once he would have to put her first.

"I'm sorry. That I left." Or, maybe that I came back.

The light was low, so George felt little pressure from her eyes, which had turned to him again. What should he say? Why did he still have such a hard talking with his wife? As a psychologist shouldn't he be able to do better?

"Let's forget about the past, George. Otherwise we will get lost in it." Karen's whiteness glowed under the night that colored the room as she spoke.

He fingered her hair, feeling its softness as it fell through his fingers. "How did we grow so apart?" He was trying. Would it be enough, or was he too late? *I never meant to go quiet*, he told himself, *I just sometimes forget how to talk.*

"I'm back now," he said, firm now, agreeing with her. Better not to drown in what had already passed. "I won't leave again." George would have to live those words, now that he had spoken them. Hopefully, they wouldn't prove to be a lie.

"I hope so, George. I miss you."

George saw a few tears streaked across her cheeks. He tried to kiss them away. Behind her the windows had fogged up. Soft mist turned the panes opaque. A bead of water slid down the glass, cutting a path through the dew.

XXXXX

Khalil looked up just as she entered the room. Typically, he didn't look up when his door opened because there wasn't much of interest to see. Food, George, perhaps the glare from a guard. Why did they take this job anyway?

This time was different. As he heard the faint creak his eyes darted toward the sound without being aware of how or why. They just did, as they had to do. And he saw her.

Lean still, her legs braced by faded denim. Her hair was longer than when he knew her before. It fell in burnished yellow down to linger along the top of her breasts. Her gaze skimmed across the room, then focused only on him. Faint creases spread out from the vibrant blue of the eyes they fringed. Her shirt was a loose, off-white flowing thing that gave her the air of an angel.

She walked in, seemingly confident, but he knew her well enough to know that she was never really so sure of herself. And he sensed that she hadn't matured past that inner hesitation. He felt almost not conscious of her, as if he was dreaming her presence. It was a dream he had had often enough, long ago. Before she had faded away.

And what does one do when reuniting with an old lover, in his jail cell? What is the appropriate thing to say? Do you embrace, willing away the years and all of the changes they have brought?

Jennifer seemed to know what to do. She did what Americans do. She smiled at Khalil, her teeth sparkling an unnatural white, her eyes lighting up.

"Hi. How are you doing?" With that, the breeziness which had always marked her behavior – as if she never really cared about anything – time slipped away. It was really Jennifer. But, the world still hadn't returned to any version of normalcy. Khalil felt that he was in an alternate reality – just watching. Jennifer had been dealt with and expunged a long time ago. Only she hadn't, as he was now starting to realize. Slowly. He saw tears beginning to form at the edges of her eyes.

She walked over to him and Khalil felt her embrace him. But quickly. The gesture was adamant in its time limit. He saw two bright blue eyes stare into his own.

"Jennifer. It's nice to see you. Shall we sit?" His voice was strong because it wasn't his voice. These words came out on their own – he wasn't yet involved. Why had George brought her here? Did he think she could influence him?

Jennifer took a seat without hesitation. She had never been fussy, and now acted as if she regularly sat down in a jail cell for a conversation. Khalil thought about offering her a drink, what he would have done in his own home. Social graces don't disappear so easily; he almost laughed at himself. He visualized calling a guard and asking for a Coke. That wouldn't be graceful – it would only put him at the guards' mercy. Why show her exactly how weak he was now, stripped bare of everything, including his humanity. As useless as he had been as a student, when he had dated her.

"I didn't think you would ever turn up again." She smiled, her nervousness apparent once again. Afternoon had just settled. The tender sunlight was bright as it glinted through the small window. Jennifer's hair glowed golden.

"Neither did I." Khalil watched her visibly wince. The past desertion reinforced. "But at least now you know why I had to leave." A true explanation. So many years too late.

"It is true then?" Jennifer asked.

"What do you think?" Khalil watched her as she studied him. He was being cagey. But what was he supposed to say? Especially since the meeting was being recorded.

"I worked against the Algerian government for a long time." Khalil said. "Some of the people I knew back then migrated into Al Qaeda. Most of them are dead now. Still, I am being held here. What can I say?

The life I chose was neither safe, nor free of risk. Be grateful you never became a part of this. It wasn't right of whomever got you involved now to put you at such risk." Khalil internally winced at his own concern for her safety. He had recognized the emotion as he articulated it. One more weakness to destroy him. Allah be praised, the tests were intensifying.

"Why didn't you tell me before?" Jennifer asked. "Why did you feel you couldn't include me? I was capable of making my own decisions." Her voice wasn't strong. He could hear hurt lingering in each syllable. Women take everything so personally. He stared into her eyes, shocked that the blue color really was exactly as he remembered it. Other than his orange jumpsuit those eyes were the only color in his insipid cell.

"Jennifer." He began slowly, caressing the name as he had once touched her body. His voice held the echo of a tenderness he had forgotten. "You couldn't have understood. Even I didn't fully realize the decisions I was making. You would have been even more at a loss. I have committed everything to my cause. There is no going back." The words stung. '*There is no going back.*' He hadn't ever said that before, and somehow hearing the words hit him with an even greater force than seeing Jennifer had. Where could he go?

Where could he go indeed? Where wouldn't he be hunted? Now that he was on a terrorist watch list was there an escape left? He could go back to the Sudan, of course. Killing wasn't a crime there unless you were on the wrong side – and if you were, breathing was a crime as well. Should he try to melt into some European city again? How long would he last? If he tried to renounce his cause and begin his life anew he would do it with no protection at all. Would his colleagues ever let him go? Probably not. No, his network of allies would be gone, and he would be at anyone's and everyone's mercy.

Her eyes pooled with tears and a hint of mascara began to smudge, framing her eyes. He just stared. How could he pretend to comfort her? What solace was there really? This meeting was a farce. What did anyone hope to achieve?

"Khalil, I have missed you," Jennifer said. "I married. You may know. But I never forgot you. Perhaps it was a silly first love sort of fantasy but you meant so much to me. Even my husband, well ex-husband now, never managed to touch me the way you did. Did you miss me at all?"

"I did," Khalil replied. The words fell out, then hung in the air. Was he lying or did he mean it? Khalil had once desperately missed Jennifer, right? He searched his memory looking for an answer. He softened his tone. "That was so long ago. We can't question what happened then. It is done. But I did miss you." Why did he tell her that, when he himself was no longer sure? What was he hoping for? Did he want her back? Khalil felt confusion. He let himself feel it, wondering what direction he would take or even wanted to take. Did it really matter? What sort of options did he have – to be part of a government protection program until someone found him and shot him?

"Have you been all right?" He spoke, entranced by her eyes. Memories pulled him back. Her firm body as she pressed herself into him. The intoxication of hearing her breathy whisper. The crush of her lips as she kissed him deep in his soul.

"Yes. I've been through a lot, but I am fine. At least now I am. I just finished going through a nasty divorce. No kids, luckily. My mom died last year, and I am a lawyer now. Things are well enough. Really, they are." She now seemed uncomfortable, awkward as she summarized over a decade in a few sentences.

Khalil continued watching her, afraid she would disappear. Nothing could have forced his eyes off her. She was still so lovely. He tried to imagine her world. But he couldn't.

Suddenly, all he saw was the smudge left by mascara. He noticed a puffiness to her chin. Long ago she had loved nothing so much as a good margarita. Was she drinking in excess now, or was her face reflecting an unhealthy diet of bad food and laziness? Whatever spell had him mesmerized for a second lifted so quickly it almost hadn't existed at all.

Jennifer reached out her hand and placed it on his. Khalil felt its heat, as well as the clamminess from her sweaty palms. He jerked his hand away without thinking. Instincts that have been honed take few vacations.

He continued to sit there and study her. Whatever discomfort she felt when he pulled his hand away magnified under his gaze. The sunspots on her skin, the sag in her shoulders, the slightly harsh color of her lipstick. How could he have thought for even an instant that this was the same woman? The Jennifer he knew was as long dead as was the world they had inhabited together. Dream or memory, it didn't matter. Their lives were worlds apart now, and he couldn't waste his limited energy on some dried up Western whore. His future was at risk; he wasn't going to waste it on the approximation of a woman he once loved.

"Leave. Go." Khalil watched Jennifer's face fall. He felt a stab of compassion, almost tenderness as he saw the once treasured hesitation in her response. So he looked away.

"Go." He said it more harshly, and stood before heading to his cot in dismissal. He could sense her moving toward the door, and heard a throaty sob. Much as he willed himself otherwise, he turned to watch her back as she walked through the doorframe into the hallway and freedom. A guard had obviously been watching the whole exchange.

He felt a deep cry rise up as she turned, at the last instant before she disappeared out of view. The sapphire of her eyes flashed as they caught the light. And his eyes. For the second time he watched her walk out of his life forever. Hurt in a way she could not forgive.

XXXXX

A confession. There had been days when George would have been glad for one. Today wasn't one of them. Fuck convention – a nice little road map to a conviction. Data to save lives was George's only concern at this point. The man he was watching on the screen was his prisoner until he provided details and many of them. Khalil had been transformed into a shadow now — no better than a television character in a plot that had veered out of his control. Rights were an anachronism with only the west pretending otherwise.

"Why didn't you…," the woman spoke. Her voice through the sound system was soft and high pitched. She liked a little drama. Well she was getting it. Then again, had she picked her boyfriends better she wouldn't be here.

Still, George felt her emotion. She really was an easy read: poor thing. Still, Khalil's micro-expressions were the key — so George rarely let his gaze wander to the blonde – except to see the canvas off of which Khalil's expressions played. The camera was cruel and caught everything.

"Khalil, I've missed you," Jennifer said, as if it mattered.

There it was – the bastard flinched, and a slight light came into his eyes. Jackpot – George had been right – Khalil was still tender toward Jennifer. That's what happened when you never found someone else. A life of terror and crime made you so susceptible when you actually did finally form a bond. Men could be hopeless in relationships to begin with; but the more unconscious and in denial about their lives they became the more vulnerable they were to a woman's escape.

"Did you miss me at all…," Jennifer went on. She sensed the softening in Khalil as well and was brave enough to seek reassurance.

"I did," Khalil said and the bastard stared into her eyes. His psyche must be getting shattered. None of this vulnerability had existed before, even in the depths of a dependent captivity. Lord knows that George had worked to build that much. Suddenly George felt his leg cramp – he'd been hunched forward so intently he'd forgotten himself. He rearranged himself in the awkward swivel desk chair; shoved his way earlier by the tech expert. He looked down at a scuff on his shoes before refocusing on the screen.

"Go," Khalil repeated and turned from Jennifer, banishing her. She rose. George hopped to his feet knowing that he'd have to move fast to reach her on her way out the door. Events in life sometimes only took one second — how could he get distracted for even that long?

A last lingering look for all three of them – Khalil and Jennifer between themselves, and George as he lunged out the door and left his new age television behind. The interaction was too short. Khalil was smart or had good instincts to end it before he fell apart completely.

George saw Jennifer heading out the door of the jail. Daylight framed her silhouette as she headed out the door. Then, she must have caught sight of him from the corner of her eye.

"You bastard," Jennifer screamed. "You absolute, sadistic bastard. Why did you even bring me here? Are you trying to destroy me – as if I don't get enough of that already?"

"Jennifer, please," George kept his voice soft, aiming to temper her emotions. Don't ever excite those already upset (do no – more – harm). She wasn't his prey but rather his bait. He needed to protect her if at all possible.

Jennifer stopped, choking on tears she said something. Her mascara had taken over her eyes and her lipstick was smeared. She wiped her nose on the back of her hand.

"I'm sorry, I couldn't understand you," George said, again using a soft voice. He moved closer to her and willed her not to leave.

She was half turned now, with the sun from the outside illuminating one half of her face while the other was shaded. Her jeans were snug but her shirt looked ethereal in the sunshine.

"You didn't understand me, you jerk? Why did you bring me here?" Jennifer screamed the words. Two guards standing nearby turned upon hearing her, concern on their faces. George tried to ignore them.

"There, there, what happened?" he said. "It's okay; don't worry. If I had known how upset you were going to get, I never would have asked you to come." He reached over, attempting to put an arm around her shoulder. She knocked him away. A bit melodramatic, dear, he felt like saying, but restrained himself. No point playing with a powder keg. The girl had a temper.

"Sick son-of–a bitch," Jennifer continued her rant. "Don't touch me. I'm not playing your game, and I'm not helping you any more. You set me up, and you set Khalil up. You know it. Bastard." With that she headed for the door. She was moving so quickly. He needed to stop her. George wanted more of her help. Had she noticed anything he'd missed or could she add some insight having known Khalil once?

"Stop, please, stop. I am very sorry. I didn't think things would go so badly. Please." He found his last apology addressed to the door. He followed her anyway. She couldn't do this. He needed her help.

"Jennifer, please help me." He found himself shouting at her back as she turned the key in the door of her white rental car. As if in slow motion, he watched her head turn toward him. The tears were flowing more freely and her smudged mascara had turned even uglier.

"No." With that she slid into her car. He heard the lock slide into place, and watched her as she backed the car out of its parking space and drove out onto the road.

How could she leave? George had meant her no harm. He just needed her to weaken Khalil. Lives were at stake. He had to use any and every tool in his arsenal. Couldn't she understand? What was wrong with everyone? The world had gone mad, and he couldn't make sense of it. Not now, perhaps not ever.

George turned back to the building. He willed himself to go inside and face Khalil. Just how rattled was he? Time to strike quickly before Khalil recovered. George took one step, then stopped. Was he really a bastard for bringing that poor woman here? Did he no longer have any shame or humanity left? Terrible questions to be asking oneself before facing a strong and determined adversary. Khalil would leap on any weakness. And sometimes George was weak. What sort of a person was he becoming? His discipline had followed Jennifer as she drove away.

He sat down on the top step. He could run away. Just get in his car and drive. As Jennifer had done. But he wasn't going to. No, he may not like himself much anymore. But he wasn't going to escape to avoid facing the consequences of his decisions.

George would go back into the jail. He would face Khalil. But he would take a minute to clarify his goals and reflect on his strategy. Besides, in the four minute exchange Jennifer may have given him exactly what he needed. Now how best to capitalize on it? George leaned back into the door frame and crossed his legs. Time was ticking.

XXXXX

Khalil willed the room to be still. Or was he trying to exert control over the pandemonium in his mind? He couldn't afford distractions or a loosening of control. He needed every ability to save himself. Getting rattled was out of the question. "No, no, no. Not now, and not here. No." The words echoed.

He fell to his knees and bent his body to the floor. Koranic verses rolled from his tongue as he tried to induce the transcendent state of his prayers. But the mood never materialized, corrupted as it was by lingering perfume and a blonde-headed ghost.

Allah was testing him? No, it was the blasted infidel, dangling corruption and temptation before his eyes.

His Koran was sitting on the table by his bed. Black leather. Familiar words printed on the cover. He could read the familiar passages. He knew them all by heart; why bother. Propped next to the Koran was *Gone With The Wind*. So he stood. Walking with new purpose he strode to the latter book and grasped it. The cheap paperback edition already looked frayed, worn in with a tenderness that normally took much longer. But typically the book was not one of its owner's few comforts. Though perhaps even that wasn't true. Didn't literature fill a void in many lonely or lost lives, creating characters that were more alive than the cold and detached people inhabiting the real world?

So many writers felt compelled to describe hell. Was that an attempt to understand, or just to describe the worlds they observed around them?

Khalil lay on his bed, ignoring the pounding in his head. He began reading. Let the whirlwind blow between his ears. He was strong, and would ignore it. What did he care for Jennifer, anyway? He had made the right choices for her. Life was always better than death. Too many people around him had died already.

Suddenly, Khalil looked up. He could still see Jennifer sitting on his chair. She was a mirage. Yet she had really been there, only moments ago. Before he had driven her away. He had driven her away, hadn't he? Strangely, he couldn't remember. His mind desperately sought to recollect their short meeting, yet he could only grasp its shattered fragments. Had she really been there at all?

It was all just a dream. Hadn't it been just a dream? His book was heavy in his hands. Escape wasn't always so easy.

Too much to bear. He was tired of being strong. Laboring on, unhindered by the death or suffering around him. Frost settling as he nearly froze to death. Immune. Always he kept moving forward, in the name of Allah. For what else could be cherished when nothing else lasted?

Now words had lost all meaning. The brief attempt to remember created an overwhelming need to go beyond forgetting. A total obliteration. Just utter blackness and an abyss, that was what Khalil needed. Yearning had dissipated. He couldn't care about anything, even survival, anymore.

The bed didn't move, and neither did he. The possibility of movement was gone too. Things, he himself, everything, must stay still. Sanity depended on total silence, total stillness. Total nothingness.

Still, sounds hadn't obeyed. There was laughter from a guard, the clanging of a door, a curse. Then Khalil heard George's footstep reverberating down the hall. His jailor, coming for more torture. Khalil was going to kill him, with his own bare hands. He wanted to feel the crack of bones and feel warm blood running through his fingers.

"Allah have mercy. Please". He whispered, drawing his limbs into a fetal position – a momentary luxury.

Had he missed her? Did he want her back in his life?

Yes. Jennifer was like nothing else he knew. She made the world right just by breathing. He had never felt that way otherwise – just when he gazed into her glittering blue eyes, like chips of cheap stone in a child's toy. But those azure lights blazed, containing the whole world in them. For one second, an all too brief moment, Khalil had felt alive. Then he sent her away. Did he do that to protect her, or to protect himself? What happened if he allowed himself to fall in love with her again? His whole life would have been a sham, a waste.

But no, he had chosen to protect her. Nothing could touch something so precious as Jennifer. She was a secret treasure that could never be held. She must be released to live. Otherwise, she would just get blown up, or shot. He could face death himself, alone. But not with her by his side. How could you die when you found a reason to live?

Khalil could feel hatred glowing in his face as the door opened. He wasn't ready; he had no choice. He pulled himself to standing and focused his gaze on a mottled spot on the wall.

XXXXX

George saw what looked like hatred flash across Khalil's features. Not so dissimilar from the look Jennifer had shot him as she fled, the coward. At least Khalil couldn't run away from him – at least not physically. George noted the dead look in Khalil's eyes as they fixed on his old familiar spot on the wall. He hadn't needed that spot recently. The urge for security and escape was back.

What a love affair, huh? Put these two back into a room and look at all the explosions. George tried to congratulate himself, sure that Khalil was good and rattled. Tough luck, buddy. You chose a global game where the blood flowed freely. Time to pay up.

Still, being a jerk didn't come naturally. This stunt was different from failing an arrogant or ailing student – those two reasons being the only ones at Stanford that led to failing. The kids he taught thought that grades were real life. But they didn't have a clue. Like right now, playing with the life of a man plotting a deadly bomb blast. This was real. But for the escape of academia…George preferred his games smaller.

"Come off it." George used as harsh a tone as he could muster.

Khalil flashed an even more loaded look. The eyes were black – like the eyes of someone about to be murdered – or so George had read. Indeed, he was trying to murder someone's soul. Perhaps the analogy fit.

Khalil didn't answer. George hadn't expected him to. He let the silence hang for ten more seconds then began to talk.

"You are mad. You feel I'm hitting below the belt." The sullen look, almost too predictable. Poke, and then jab. "She wanted to see you."

"Bastard, she didn't even know that I'm alive, let alone in this country," Khalil said. Another glare. George gave Khalil a lazy smile. Keep poking.

"I think that was the exact word she used to describe me – bastard," George replied. "Great minds think alike, huh?"

"You sadistic pig! What are you doing?" Khalil stood up and knocked the table over, his arm a flash of orange. George tried to congratulate himself for provoking the explosion. He had finally made Khalil lose control. How long had it taken? He would let the man rage, then console him. After a brief interval, he would ask for specific information – the really important stuff – like the forthcoming plot here in the United

States.

None of it felt good. It just was what it was.

"Not doing a thing you couldn't anticipate, Khalil. Should I fly your mother out here too? Has your mother ever been on a plane?" George watched Khalil as he instinctively looked for a way to escape. But there was no escape from a jail cell, and that is where murderers ended up. In a jail cell, or dead. And the walls would just keep closing in. Compassion was for later. Self-hatred for the hours when George wouldn't sleep. Tormenting even the worst of men wasn't emotionally rewarding. But it was necessary.

"Want to see her again?" George asked. As if he could deliver.

"You're sick." Khalil glowered. Still.

"How long do we have to talk tonight?" Daylight had begun to fade. The early evening shadows had softened outside. The room still glared from its unnatural fluorescent lights. No dimmers to soften the realities of jail.

"Give me a piece of paper." Khalil didn't look at George.

George ripped two from his notebook. He handed them across the table along with a bic pen. Khalil grabbed them and began to write. When he was done he handed it back to George. Once the momentum starts to build you must keep pushing.

"A few people I know in Europe. Phone numbers and addresses. You should look them up." His eyes were glued to the floor. George didn't reach for the paper.

"Two more, then I will go." This would do for tonight. If the names were no good Khalil would pay in blood.

Obediently Khalil began to write again. This time he dropped the pen and paper on the table and walked over to the window, his back to George.

"Good night, Khalil. Pleasant dreams." The wound could fester.

XXXXX

George merged onto the freeway. At least it was moving. The 405 sprawled in all directions, visibly clogging up in a mile or so with a thicket of cars, all exhaling fumes. He tried to recall exactly what had prompted him to hop on a plane and fly down to Los Angeles. The crystal clear sunlight did nothing to dispel his confusion. The landscape flashing by had an unnatural appearance, as if in a picture, moving or otherwise. Yet the light did nothing to warm the fog in his head.

The cell phone. Khalil had tried to ditch it in the trash during his London capture. George kept being bothered by the phone. Numbers in Europe were great, but not his focus. Wasn't Homeland Security more important?

George's only physical clue – other than London - was the cell phone. Was Los Angeles about to have its own suicide bomb? It seemed like a logical conclusion, and it didn't stop nagging at him. So, George was going to follow that lead – though how exactly he intended to do so was unclear. He knew nothing about following leads. Was he getting desperate?

He could escape this morning. Washington was following up on the names Khalil had given him last night. Later in the day he would go see

Khalil, back in northern California. By then he would have some indication of whether Khalil had been bullshitting him. The process was slow. Excruciatingly so.

The FBI had traced the London phone number to a cell sold at a store in Westwood. They had already visited the store and, according to the subsequent report, hadn't gotten any information there. Something about a fake driver's license being used to purchase it.

George nimbly navigated the streets. Off the freeway at Wilshire, head east, then right on Westwood Blvd. He tried to follow street numbers, making only one u-turn before finding the shop, nestled between an Iranian market and a Thai restaurant.

Miraculously, George found a parking space. Even more fortuitous, he had quarters with him – not a given on most days.

He stepped out of the car. This street was clearly a mid-rent one. His target was a small rectangle of a place with little decoration. Brown. Splayed across the window-front were signs advertising the best price for different brands of phones. Through the glass, opaque with dirt, George could see cell phones lining the wall. He walked in, questioning himself again as to his next step. But he would have gone anywhere to prevent a bomb blast – this was his world. Indeed, he had gone just about anywhere, to hell and back. Not that it mattered.

A bell jingled as George entered the store, wincing as he stepped on a stained brown carpet. At least the color scheme was consistent. The smell of food assaulted his nostrils. He stood for a minute, alone and unsure what to do. His first instinct was to turn around and leave. Fast.

As if to stop him, a man suddenly appeared from a door tucked behind the center counter. The space itself was cluttered and piled high with papers and phones. George also saw a cup of coffee, half full. At some point George knew he would have to speak.

"Can I help you?" The man's voice squeaked. His accent was Middle Eastern, but George couldn't have placed it more specifically. The mind he could figure out, accents blurred. The man was heavyset, yet he still managed to walk softly. He was wearing a navy suit – odd for the surroundings. The suit was worn and fraying around the collar. George was always amazed at how many immigrants refused to leave behind their identities when they came to the United States, failing to assume a new and perhaps more appropriate one. This man obviously wasn't going to let his reduced circumstances change his self-image.

Suddenly George realized that he hadn't answered the man's question. In fact, he wasn't even sure he had heard it correctly. Instead, he had been standing and gawking, as if watching a movie, not acting in one.

"Well, yes. I mean, I hope so." Was his answer appropriate?

The man stared coldly. His eyes apprised George in an instant, starting from the top of his head and working down.

"Do you want a cell phone?" The tone was clipped.

"No, actually. I want some information." George didn't know why but he felt offended, even angry. The man wanted to make him defensive – his posture was stiff, his lips almost drawn back, his eyes alight. How had that happened so fast, almost as soon as George walked into the shop?

Well, George knew one thing. If something doesn't make sense logically there is a reason. You are missing something. A shop owner or salesperson shouldn't be defensive upon a potential customer's entry. It didn't make sense. George hadn't even identified what sort of information he wanted. Perhaps this trip was a mistake.

"Do you have any ID?" The man stared.

"You mean like a driver's license?"

"No, like a police badge or something." Still, the stare. Then the man grabbed his cup off coffee, sloshing a few drops onto the counter. He took a long gulp but managed to keep his eyes on George even as his head tilted back.

"No, no. I only have a drivers license." Now what?

"Then unless you want rate plans or details on the phones you better leave."

What?

"You don't even know what kind of information I want." George felt a flush creeping up his neck and onto his face. He had never been thrown out of anywhere. Perhaps the FBI had a tougher job than he gave them credit for having.

"I said go. No badge, no information. I am busy."

George's eyes couldn't help but wander around the empty store. Busy doing what? At least the man was openly hostile and unwilling to speak. Not much to deduce. George couldn't do much. The sign on the door had clearly stated that the owner could refuse service to anyone.

George turned to leave. He couldn't help thinking about how many quarters he had put in his meter only moments before. What an optimistic waste. As if he could just fly down here and get what they FBI hadn't. Fool.

George reached for the glass door. A new man was standing just outside, and sprung through the opening without so much as glancing at George, let alone thanking him for holding it open.

The man was young, and like the proprietor of the shop, dark and probably Arab. He was strikingly good looking, and seemed to know it based upon how tightly his flashy clothes clung to his narrow frame. George glimpsed a flash of pubic hair between where the boy's t-shirt ended and his jeans, hanging too low, began. Thank God that style hadn't yet made it to Palo Alto. Then, George gloomily realized that if it had, he wouldn't even know.

As the door closed he heard the two men begin to speak.

"Who was that?" The young man asked.

"An infidel, Omar, my boy. But I chased him out."

XXXXX

"Look at how delicately the head tilts, there. As if the child is both caressing and guiding Venus. Their lips meet, barely. See the lines of their bodies set starkly against the brilliant jewel-like blue in the background."

"Yes," Khalil answered. What other answer could he give? *Pornography, disguised as art?* He smoothed the page, flattening it to minimize the glare from the overhead lights. Disgusting.

Khalil found himself looking back and forth between George and the book – *Art.* A big and heavy tome. Cupids, naked, frolicking around Venus, also naked. An old man floating above them, his arm reaching out, desperate to grasp at a stick of some sort. This room couldn't be real, nor was George. Much as Khalil was the one stuck in mentally destabilizing solitary confinement, it was his captor who had gone over the edge.

"She is lovely, isn't she? Look at the detail, there." George pointed to a spot where the one-dimensional page seemed to gain depth.

"Why are you doing this?" Khalil leaned back. The chair creaked, as if it would come apart with his shifting weight. Perhaps he was wrong; George might have been merely puling one of his tricks.

"I'm trying to show you beauty, Khalil. In hopes that once you see what exists in the world you won't want to die any more." George leaned back, mirroring Khalil's motion. Now that was a trick, but one so obvious Khalil couldn't be sure if it was done for the intended affect. George had to know he would see through it, so how was he supposed to interpret it? The obvious tricks were always a self-perpetuating loop – *if someone knows you know, and you know they know, etc.*

"I don't want to die anymore, George. You know that."

"Tasted a sample too many times, Khalil?" Again, the mirror. Saying his name.

"The painting in your book is a sin." Khalil said. "Mohammed prohibited images of man." Khalil sat up straight, bracing himself for George's response. This was a game; but George's games all seemed to exist without rules.

"Have you read that passage in the Koran yourself, or just heard about it?" George smiled, but no light appeared in his face. "Don't answer. The painting is in London, Khalil. In a museum not far from Piccadilly Circus. You remember Piccadilly Circus."

Khalil nodded. It was too obvious. "Nice shirt, George. I like the stripes." Khalil said. And the shirt *was* nice – lavender button down with ivory stripes. George rarely wore patterns.

"My wife got it for me." George spoke briskly, his tone as crisp as the shirt. "When is the bomb going to blow?"

How did George know? Was it a guess? Khalil floundered. Who knew anything anymore?

"Any day now," Khalil said. George's face was frozen. Cold bastard.

"Really? Do tell." George said. A short response. Never get in your own way.

Khalil now had a headache. The lighting was dull, the room smelled musty.

"George, how would I know?" Khalil answered. "I have been locked up for so long I can't even guess the date. I barely remember my name anymore." Khalil waived his arms. The gesture had probably gone stale but he had run out of new ones.

"Where exactly will it blow?" George demanded. "What is the target date?" He didn't move as he spoke. Neither did anything else in the colorless room.

Khalil forced himself not to sneer. "Chatter picking up? Your spooks getting worried?"

"Increasingly so. And I'm not sleeping anymore. Give me the answers or you won't be either."

"Is that a threat – ignoring the Geneva Convention and sending me back to torture hell?" George knew better than to pull such a cheap trick. Khalil did know the target and the target date. What he didn't know was whether the information had aged out of existence.

"I don't believe in torture." George's voice was firm. "And I will sit here until I get my answers." His eyes were almost the lavender color of his shirt. Khalil had never known someone with grey eyes before. He marveled at how they shifted to match the colors he wore. Blue one day, lavender the next. Could the rest of George assume such varying hues? Did he ever tell the truth?

"Give me a phone and I'll find out for you," Khalil said, knowing it was a dead end.

"You know I can't do that." George picked up the book again, and began to flip through the pages. "Here, look at this one."

XXXXX

George's green and white Nikes hit the rubber belt; it continued its robotic course beneath him. The treadmill was a blessing from his own God and let him run whenever he damned well pleased. Even in the early morning blackness that Karen always slept through. How he yearned to once again enjoy the benefits of tenure. If he didn't get court marshaled for desertion from his real job. A university only had to be so understanding.

He cranked up the speed until running hurt, his legs still stiff from sleep and an inadequate warm-up. The latter was probably the cause of his repeated hamstring injuries. Stupid aching ancient leg.

One more time he increased the speed, struggling to keep up as his feet kept hitting rubber.

The bomb was coming. The feeling was more than a sixth sense. Khalil had admitted it. No one did that – well, perhaps while being tortured they did, but only then – unless a bomb really was imminent. But for a people living on slights thousands of years old, how could imminent mean anything at all? Today, tomorrow, years from now if no one involved blew himself up first?

George tasted certainty, as he felt himself stumble. Probably best to slow down during times of heavy thinking. How could he get the bastard to talk? Anyone who let little slip during torture was always a tough nut. This one had let just enough slip to extend his U.S. government sponsored vacation. How to get the rest out.

George could push. He could trick. He could bargain. He could keep the lights on for a few days (morally, and legally, questionable). He could beg. He could outsmart – which could take months if he had them. He could just hope that God shined a little bit of wisdom down upon him as he tried to make it through one more day.

He cranked the treadmill's speed up once more. Before he went into battle he had to let the pounding empty out his mind. His feet hitting the rubber mingled with the loud whirl of the motor. It was a wonder Karen slept through this racket. Not that he knew for a fact that she did. The less baggage he took in with him, the better he could interpret Khalil's responses. There was a way to get that information. There always was. Somehow he would have to figure it out.

XXXXX

"Kamal Al'Tariq."

"Never heard the name." But, of course, he had. London. Munitions expert. Learned about adding in chlorine last summer in a small farmhouse just west of Baghdad. Or was it Tehran? Born in Pakistan, moved to Britain in 1970, when he was still in diapers. 5'8, heavy-set.

Khalil shrugged.

"Here's a picture of you two." George said, held it out.

"Oh, Yussef. Your informants gave you the wrong name." Khalil shrugged again. The gesture would get annoying eventually. He was bored; it was his diversion.

"You're lying. Tell me about him." George said, expressionless. The room was overcast and gloomy. It took on the mood of the world beyond his small window. Amazing.

"I knew him only casually, at the mosque. We attended the same prayer session on Sunday nights." Khalil decided not to move for a while – another diversion.

"You weren't living in London. How could you attend regularly?" George still looked grim as he spoke.

"Whenever I was in London."

"What mosque?" George said.

"Finsbury." Khalil replied.

"No, he didn't go there," George said. He wasn't blinking now. Perhaps that was *his* diversion.

"Show me the pictures of him not going there," Khalil said, still not moving as the dull light mirrored him.

George laughed. "Look, you asshole, this day isn't getting any shorter because you think the minutes are passing. I have no plans of going home tonight." George said it like it mattered.

"Sleep deprivation isn't allowed. Your prosecutor will refuse to press charges."

"Call your lawyer. Tell me about Yussef." George blinked as the last word came out. Khalil moved. The dank light softened the shadows in George's angular face.

"Don't know much."

George sighed. "Okay. Let's talk about your torture then. Tell me what happened."

No way. Sometimes denial was the best way to cope with a misfortune. Khalil wasn't planning on facing a prior hell to blunt the impact of a more current version. "Yussef is a munitions expert – with a twist in chlorine. He likes very young girls, dark and skinny. He also shoots at small animals."

"Rabbits?" George asked, as if he cared.

"Who can guess? Anything that moves." Khalil let his face reflect his annoyance. Can't always control how you feel; he felt tense.

"Why chlorine in London, Khalil? Is the bomb going to be laced with it?" George said, but he still hadn't perked up. Perhaps the weather directed his moods. Or, he just didn't have moods. At least not in here. Khalil looked for his friendly spider, but could see only webs. Still, he didn't answer.

"Chlorine, Khalil. Why London?" George probed.

"Probably a bomb – that would be my guess. But I can't get you closer. You know how these cells work, George. Information is kept tightly controlled within them. I know Yussef because he gave me a cell phone at his apartment." And, now, that was too much information.

"The one you were caught ditching?" George asked.

"Not mine." Some information was too close to home.

George slid his wire notebook across the cracked table. He left his pen on top. Khalil wouldn't stab him . "Write it out – address, phone number, any friends."

Khalil didn't move.

"Do it." George said. Khalil grabbed the pad and began writing. "When, Khalil? George said. "I need a date. I know it's that damn ice cream shop. When?"

"And no one will believe you, will they George?" Khalil looked up from his writing as he spoke. "Not until you have a name, a date, all sorts of boxes filled in on your forms. Your job is thankless. No one cares until after the bombs explode." Khalil planned to keep pushing, punching, gnawing. He would go until he got George rattled. What option did he have?

"You can try any game you want, Khalil. I will sit here until I get that information." George said.

"It is Friday afternoon. Are you even allowed in here off hours? You will be going home to your wife and your decadent lifestyle. Are you going to fuck her tonight, George?"

George ran his hand across the tabletop, as if examining a new wonder. His white shirtsleeve brushed lightly across the surface and his hand cast a shadow. Khalil watched him, waiting.

"I need the proof on the chlorine training. I need a camp name.

More, Khalil." George paused, certainly not for effect – his tone was too hostile now. Neither cared what the other thought. "You are involved in something with that shop – and you aren't singing. Which means you can't risk any slips. You aren't bothering to protect people outside your cell, only those within. You exposed poor Yussef in an instant." George paused again. Khalil let him.

"It has to be soon, right? We've had you for eight months. What are you looking for, a deal?"

"No deal."

"You are going to rot in here, rather than tell us? That bomb goes off, like I think it will, I can tie you to it." George stared at him, unblinking again.

"George, it's all the same. You kill me, or someone else kills me. What do I get out of telling you anything?" *It has to blow soon. What is the date today?*

"The chance for freedom." George grabbed at the notebook and began to sketch out a calendar. "We can do this. Let's count the days."

"George, I can't answer your question." The words came out in a whisper. Khalil couldn't believe his own weakness – to let so much slip. But he was getting disoriented. He had been in this room for too long. "I don't know. I never knew. That information was kept from me." *Ask me again and I might tell you.*

"What about my guess on the ice cream shop?'

"No, not right." Khalil replied.

"Then where?" George asked.

"The pizza parlor across the street." Which didn't exist. Wait until

George called London and found out it didn't. Next week would be long.

# || CHAPTER FIVE - A CANTO

It was Sunday. Karen was at church, a place George had vowed to never set foot in willingly (other than weddings, funerals and baptisms; and then, willingly wasn't perhaps the most appropriate word). With the kids away at school the house always felt quiet. Over time, George had learned to savor that quiet, sad though its origins were. Sunday morning was his time alone, to read the paper, write, relax or work on a new lecture.

Georgc grabbed his cup of coffee from the brightly lit kitchen and headed to the more somber living room. He sank into the green velvet cushions of the couch. The green was one of the few spots of color in the house. Karen favored natural tones such as ivory and rich chocolate brown. Even the green was a muted version – barely a color at all. George had long ago learned not to have opinions about furniture or color schemes. The keys to a good marriage, he reminded himself.

Settling into the slightly worn, very soft grooves he began to read his newspaper.

"Ring, ring." His serenity was harshly interrupted.

"This better be important!" George's voice didn't hide his annoyance; after all, he was alone, no one to hear. "Who calls on Sunday morning? There should be a law." Still he dutifully picked up the telephone, forgetting to check the caller ID.

"Hello." His unhappy tone hadn't changed.

"George, Tom Campbell." George's tone was no match for Tom's, which clearly reflected an even deeper discontent.

"A bomb went off, in London, less than a block from where your terrorist Khalil was captured, loitering and studying the scenery." Forget the pleasantries.

George could feel the room disappearing. He had been so close to getting that information just days before. And, if he was getting a call about it there must be a concrete tie to Khalil – as he had also predicted.

He felt his mind empty, the normally well-organized thoughts replaced with confusion. Babble erupted from the telephone and he absentmindedly reminded himself to pay attention, to listen. Tom was his boss on this assignment. It was a bomb. Important.

"Suicide bomber, Algerian, like Khalil. Lived in the same apartment building Khalil was staying in while in London. His type of operation, some weird sort of higher-tech bomb involved. Nerve gas is rumored, but not confirmed. I don't have all the specifics yet. Still, according to our friends in London it sounds like a connection. A strong one. Too bad we didn't catch it."

George winced at the not so thinly veiled criticism. London, not Los Angeles, flashed across his mind. He would consider that later.

"How many killed?" George could hear his voice. What was left of his voice.

"Six," Campbell said. "About thirty wounded. Ice cream parlor off Piccadilly Circus, Sunday afternoon."

Then the telephone receiver echoed dead silence. George didn't have anything to say either.

"Thanks for letting me know," George said. "I'll go talk to that bastard tomorrow."

"Go today." Tom's voice made it clear that timing wasn't negotiable.

George hung up the telephone. Could he face Khalil today? Could he keep his emotions out of a meeting without time to process and deal with the bombing? Indeed, could he even organize an approach for getting information without time to calmly reassess the situation, to recover?

At least he had some concrete information to discuss. Perhaps that wasn't the bright side of a silver lining.

George settled back into the forgiving cushions. At least something in life was forgiving. He wished he could sink right into the couch and disappear. George didn't want to face his life. He couldn't bear his responsibilities or his obligations. Someday, death would be a blessing – afterlife or not. Just a complete absence of anything: pain, hurt, responsibilities, lies, deceit. The list was endless, all of it meaningless. Was it this sense of hopelessness that led people to kill themselves and nihilistically take others with them? Escape, and a childish wish to hurt back.

Well, George couldn't just die, could he? Unlike the coward in the London bombing, he wasn't going to kill himself in a fit of petulance.

No, he would face the hell of his life one more day, unless a heart attack or car accident intervened. As if he would get so lucky.

"God doesn't burden us with more than we can handle, my ass!" He spoke to the empty house. Maybe he should get a cat. His wife was never around when he needed her.

No, he was better off alone. This way he could feel the normal emotions that would accompany each stage of his grief. First, he would feel denial. Then anger, which would metamorphosize into desperate bargaining. Later would be deep betrayal, almost a depression in its intensity. He had started to like this man, this killer. Last, he would accept it. Betrayal is endemic.

Still, had he in turn betrayed those who died in London, those children, because he hadn't more effectively done his job? Probably.

So, after some brief self-indulgence, George would reread the file. He had two geographical clues – London and Los Angeles. A bomb had gone off in the first. Khalil had admitted to a potential one in Los Angeles. From now on, no clue could be missed (bargaining). Not again.

XXXXX

The late afternoon sun cast soft shadows, which made the cell look more attractive, muting the harshness that otherwise took over. The room no longer held any secrets, if it ever had. Khalil wondered occasionally who had inhabited it before him, who would follow. Neither mattered. But so often time stretched on endlessly before him as he sat alone.

Khalil's stack of new books lay on the table where he had just eaten lunch. The remains of the meal rested beside them. The smells permeated the air. As always.

He was stretched on his cot, reading a book of poetry from George. Indeed, everything he owned, meager though precious, had been given to him by George. In Khalil's opinion, the book was ridiculous. He deeply disagreed with the author's viewpoints, which were symptomatic of the west's corruption. Khalil eagerly awaited George's arrival tomorrow so he could tell him so.

Khalil heard footsteps echoing down the hallway, getting closer. Always an early warning of a visitor. Since he was expecting no one today he figured it would be a guard.

"No reason to get up for those sons of bitches." He whispered.

The door flung open, typical for the brutish guards. Khalil started to roll his eyes, but then stopped in shock when George walked in. George never came on Sundays.

"This is a surprise. Why are you here?" And Khalil was genuinely puzzled. He was about to mention the book, but sensed a change in the familiar man. His instincts were warning him – watch out. And Khalil always trusted his instincts. They had kept him alive so far, praise Allah.

"Let's sit and talk for a few minutes." George attempted a feeble smile. His voice sounded calm, but it also had a higher pitch, along with a slower pace and clearer enunciation. Had he suffered a shock of some kind?

Khalil followed his lead, and sat down at the table. He said nothing. Wait for the enemy's first move. Sure, they had developed camaraderie. But at times like this, when his body told him to watch out, he remembered his true position – prisoner.

George ran his palm across his forehead, almost as if trying to physically gather his thoughts. His half smile was long gone, replaced by a simmering expression, under control, but still present. Khalil was fascinated.

"You like London?" George asked.

"Not much." Khalil still watched, waiting for a clue. A vague suspicion was brewing. They succeeded?

"Why? The weather, the people, just don't like it? Or, is it because you were caught there?"

"I just don't like it," Khalil said.

George pulled some photographs out of his briefcase. Khalil saw the usual after-effects of a bomb. He saw body pieces, what looked like a dead child, then a screaming woman with no leg. Was the latter the shop girl he had observed just before his arrest? He saw a neighborhood in London, recognizing landmarks from the area of his arrest – when scoping out the ice cream shop.

Khalil felt annoyed at seeing the pictures, impatient even. He expected better from George, had indeed come to respect him. Why would Khalil care about these pictures? He had seen much worse, up close and in person. Was he supposed to get upset? He stared in disbelief at the shell-shocked man. He stopped himself from showing disrespect, such as sneering or shrugging his shoulders. No point in provoking more emotion from George. No one knew Khalil was here. He was a shadow person, and therefore entirely at his captor's mercy.

"Why are you showing me these pictures?" Said Khalil, curious.

Was George so naïve as to think they mattered? Did Khalil want or need to think more highly of him? After all, he had no one else of any intelligence around.

"Look, you bastard, you are behind this. Don't try to bullshit me," George said. Khalil watched George as for the first time during the interrogations he genuinely lost control. Lose control of your emotions; lose control of the situation, Khalil reminded himself.

George paused, almost as if reading Khalil's thoughts.

"Are you proud of yourself?" The voice was back to its normal calm, though it was still slightly slower and higher pitched.

The words hit Khalil with more impact than he could have predicted. Was he proud? The operation was a success. Even without him. He yearned to know if they had used his newer and smaller suicide bomb. Had they inserted sarin? But those questions were only curiosity about his own competence. Still, the plan went off without him. Had his colleagues been so confident that he wouldn't talk, if indeed they even knew of his capture?

Khalil suddenly knew he was utterly alone. No one needed him at all, did they? He should be pleased. His bomb blew up without him. Wasn't that the sign of a good leader? Or was he redundant? Practically, could this bombing be pinned on him? First, some stupid racist bobby nabbed him in London. Now they had come to him after the bombing.

Bad luck. Control, Khalil reminded himself. Could they prove anything, or was it just circumstantial evidence? Did they need to prove it?

George was still sitting there, waiting for an answer.

"I had nothing to do with it," Khalil said. "I don't even know where this happened. Are you implying it was in London?"

"Don't play dumb," George replied coldly. "I have been patient, too patient. I thought I had more time. I was wrong. Now that I have stared into the dead faces of innocent people you have murdered do you think I will help you? Khalil, you better have some damn good information or I am going to recommend a very harsh sentence. The death penalty if I can get it. Is Los Angeles next?" George looked pissed off and unafraid. Was he faking it, another trick?

Khalil sighed. He ignored the questions, and looked down at the pictures. No, George wasn't faking anger.

"You can't execute someone without a fair and public trial. The United States would never live down such an embarrassment – too much against what you stand for. England doesn't have a death penalty, so to get me extradited you probably had to promise not to kill me." Khalil knew his voice was level. What he said had to be right, and he was in no real danger. Or, at the very least he had to believe so. Besides, he did have information. Perhaps now was the time to start bartering it.

George's lip curled. "You're ignoring these pictures. Don't you care? Don't you feel any remorse? Or, at the very least, don't you want to gloat at your successful handy work?"

"I told you, I had nothing to do with it." George had to be crazy, right? Asking him if he cared.

"That isn't good enough," George said. "We have proof – your bomb, a new one. Your tie to the bomber. The location of your arrest. London caught someone else. You have been identified as a participant."

Khalil felt a stab of fear. Was George bluffing? His organization hadn't protected him by changing the location of the bombing – were they aware he had been caught there? Had someone broken?

"You're bluffing," Khalil said. "You have nothing concrete on me"

"Are you willing to take that risk? I am your best chance. We had enough incriminating evidence to put you on a terrorist watch list, didn't we? Do you know the types of sentences terrorists have gotten? They tend to be very long. Sometimes life. Your call."

Khalil stared at him. He needed to think. The idea of rotting in a jail cell forever was horrifying.

George stood up. "Want to keep the pictures?" His voice sounded tired, that much was clear.

Khalil shook his head. They didn't matter.

George started walking to the door. Suddenly he stopped and turned back to face Khalil. "How can you look at those pictures so coldly, even assuming you had nothing to do with this?" Khalil thought he caught disappointment in George's eyes. He exhaled, suddenly feeling the same weariness echoing in George's voice.

"If you knew what I have seen you would understand. It is just more death." He felt obligated to answer this man, though he wasn't sure why. Lying had gotten harder.

"But they were just little children. Children, getting ice cream." George shook his head, his voice soft.

"Those who talk about the loss of innocent people didn't yet taste how it feels when you lose a child, don't know how it feels when you look in your child's eyes and all you see is fear. Are they not afraid that one day they get the same treatment? Osama Bin Laden. Maybe he did it." Khalil kept his voice as soft as he could, mimicking George. Powerful words were more effective when you had to strain to hear them.

George didn't respond. Were his emotions deadened – distracted by the pictures so far outside his normal life? This man had been to Iraq? Khalil waited until George finally spoke, with a harsh voice that wasn't his own. "I can do as I wish, and you have no recourse. If this happens again, and I know it's you, that will be it." George turned back to the door and left, not looking back.

Khalil still felt alone, perhaps more so as he sat in his suddenly empty cell. He also felt confused. What did he really want? That word had lost all meaning. His senses were now deadened. His existence had become unclear.

XXXXX

Omar hadn't turned the television off in days. The bombs, ripping through the crowds of infidels. The masses herded into a sin-filled city. Blood, gore, and the smell of explosives. What could be more exciting. Glorious success.

And a message. This plan had two stages. It wasn't so simple as a few bombs in one city. It was a few bombs in many cities. The success of one stage triggered the next. Now he must be strong, not becoming the weak link in a chain of glorious explosions. It would culminate in an embarrassing failure for the great west and its decrepit, corrupt leaders.

The victims. The ages – ranging from what to what? How could he be expected to care enough to remember? The pregnant woman and her two-year-old daughter. The little boy whose face was ripped off as his mother died painfully just within earshot of his pathetic cries. The employee of the ice cream shop who was left with no legs. Infidels, to the last. All of them condemned, rotting for all eternity as punishment for their crimes.

He, Omar, was part of this. The message released on Al'Jazeera television taking credit and explaining that the bomb was a punishment for western crimes against humanity. The raids through the usual Muslim neighborhoods and mosques. The pictures – bomber, accomplice, suspected accomplice, spiritual leaders – he knew some of them, and recognized others. They were his brothers. They were also martyrs and freedom fighters. Most importantly, they had succeeded. And that was, at the end of the day, what the mission was about. Success.

The west was weak, rotting in on itself, stench invading all around him. Enough bombs, enough screaming and bleeding children, and the pigs crumbled into nothingness. He had told his father so.

The call had come in during the middle of his day. Omar had been jubilant, in a celebratory mood. Until he heard the cold, emotionless voice on the other end of the line.

"How have you been?" A question, yet as articulated by his father nothing could be more likely to end a conversation instead of starting one. Outside his window Omar watched a branch moving softly in the wind. The sun was bright in a crystal clear sky. All was well in his world, and his father was in Saudi Arabia far away. He couldn't touch Omar. Not now, and not ever again. Omar was a mujahideen..

"Dad, did you see the news? One more successful strike against the corrupt west." Omar couldn't keep the pride out of his voice. If only he could admit to his father his own part in the plot, and his larger role in a forthcoming one. He could imagine the bent, but still fearsome, man finally shining with pride at his son's accomplishments. Someday an action would be enough to meet the old man's impossibly high standards. Right? Someday.

"You fool." The irritation was evident. Indeed, the old man sounded furious, as if he took the bombing personally and rested the entire blame for it on Omar's shoulders. That would be nothing new, would it? Omar reflected for a minute, ignoring the rant coming through the phone line all the way from Riyadh.

"Stupid pigs."

"Trouble to pay."

"Always shooting the hand that feeds them."

"Repression will just get worse."

"Hang the lot of them."

Omar lifted his shirt. The pink was a bit feminine, but he liked the fit and the wafer-thin material. Looking carefully enough, the chiseled lines of his stomach were visible through the delicate fabric. He lifted the shirt, careful not to crease it. The muscles were so smooth. Omar marveled at how quickly the definition had increased from his abs class. Low body fat, discipline and genes. It was a good life lesson. Anything could be shaped to fit your desires. All it took was patience and discipline.

The voice at the other end of the line was slowing slightly, becoming less strident. Omar had fulfilled his duty for the day – letting the fool vent his frustrations. He could end the farce now. Right now, actually.

Always best to leave them wanting just a little bit more.

"Dad, forgive me for interrupting. I must leave now, or I will be late for a study session. We have a test tomorrow, and I want to work through some problems with my study partners." Omar kept any trace of respect out of his voice. It wasn't hard to do. Instead his voice was steady and emotionless. As it had been since he was still a young boy and he had vowed to never lose control as his red- faced father did. The man's proclamations were always a curious mix of spit and bravado. They were always much to loud.

"Goodbye, father dear." No, not even irony graced his delicately nuanced and well-trained voice.

The telephone fit nicely into its base. And his shirt draped ever so elegantly over his strong torso, as Omar noticed when he glancing at the mirror on his way out the door. Yet he wasn't headed to a study session. Or at least not the type his father would recognize. He was off to the mosque to glory in his brother's victory overseas against the infidel devil.

XXXXX

George arrived early the next morning. He pulled into the too familiar parking lot. Dew still misted the colorless jail, adding a ghostly pallor. Could the sadness and desperation of the prisoners inside infuse the façade? Was that why the building seemed to have sunk slightly into its foundation? Or was George just finally losing his mind?

Climbing the stairs George stepped into the same entryway, facing the same baby-faced soldier. Soon, he knew too well, the psychotic prison guard would lead him to Khalil's miniature cell.

George was tired. Sleep had eluded him. In his bones a dull ache had settled, reminding him of all that was lacking. Karen had left their bed halfway through the night, probably annoyed by his tossing and turning. At least she had shown compassion, and hadn't complained about the interruptions. But how could he sleep when visions of the victims, dead, injured and in pain, kept creeping into his mind? It was his fault.

Now, Khalil. The bastard. George knew that his success today depended on overcoming his lack of sleep, his personal sense of failure and his emotions.

Entering Khalil's cell George didn't even attempt a smile. He usually ignored standard interrogation techniques; they only worked on low-level morons not on the smart, wily son-of-a-bitch types he got. But today he was going to use intimidation – the most obvious trick. Now he had something concrete on Khalil. And his anger was strong enough to support it. Control your emotions, he reminded himself, channel them. His mantra.

Khalil's body language exhibited no concern for his new, more compromised situation. He probably knew that George could do only so much – the Geneva Convention requirements being the least of it. No, George was only willing to go so far, and Khalil had probably recognized that. Always an Achilles heel in any man. Ethics so often blocked results. But did anything really exist in this shadow world?

Khalil continued displaying no signs of concern as George sat down. That was a mistake. It was a mistake because today George could smell his sweat. The man was scared.

"Sleep well?" George knew his tone was harsh. He saw a question flicker across Khalil's face. A lonely, and isolated, man. Good.

Khalil chose to sneer. An intentional bluff?

"Just fine."

"I expect a lot out of you today."

Khalil shook his head. "You expect too much," he said softly. His orange prison jumpsuit lit the gloomy room like a mutant sun.

Time to go for it.

"You didn't question the pictures," George said. "How do you know the bombing just happened? Maybe I was bluffing, to get information."

Khalil stared, his eyes shifted to his familiar spot of safety, something he had almost stopped doing again with George. George persisted, keeping his voice low.

"I'll tell you why. You knew that ice cream shop. You were checking it out when you were arrested. You also knew that no bomb had detonated there before now."

Khalil stopped. But only for a second. Searching his brain for a new lie? "There have been very few bombs in London since the 80s," he finally said.

"How long have you been in captivity? You have no idea what's going on."

Khalil shook his head. "This isn't going to work. You can't bully or bluff me. I want to talk about a deal."

A deal, the murderous bastard wanted a deal. Momentarily George imagined him torn and quartered, an image from history which had always caught his fancy. Then he felt sad. How had they ended up on opposite sides of this decrepit and peeling table? How much did a smart man like Khalil really know? Probably a lot.

"A deal." George drew out the words. He studied Khalil, obviously, to make a point. His heart was pounding, and he wasn't sure which direction to go. If Khalil had important information – important enough – he would have to try to get a deal for him. That was why George was here, after all. But he had no authority over the resulting agreement, and he hated losing control.

"I need concrete information that I can take to my bosses, to prove that a deal is the best option. After all, we can just keep you here forever – as I'm sure you have realized."

Khalil shook his head, his eyes cold and hard. "I'm not going to incriminate myself without a deal. Especially since you still haven't let me see a lawyer. No concrete information until I se what you are willing to offer in return. I want it in writing and I want a lawyer, my lawyer, to witness it." With that he shrugged his shoulders. "Your call. Otherwise we can both just sit here and rot in this ridiculous jail cell."

"You were part of it?" George probed, still unsure what to do.

"You really want to know?" Khalil just sat .

No, not really, George realized. He wanted to run. The intensity had ratcheted to an uncomfortable level, becoming too personal in the process. Why did he keep throwing himself out there? I do it because it works, he reminded himself. And Khalil needed an answer.

"Yes, Khalil, I do"

"Yes. But you won't be able to prove it." Khalil waved his arm.

George had seen the move hundreds of times by now.

"You just confessed."

"It was coerced. Oh, and George, I can help prevent something bigger." Khalil looked reptilian in his stillness.

So there, George really had no choice. He had to pass the message on. "Okay, I'll do my best." There was nothing left to say. How ridiculous it was, all of it. The jail cell had deteriorated into parody. The whitish paint on the walls had begun to peel, as if the whole place was deciding whether to come down around them both. Probably some crooked painting subcontractor the government had overpaid.

"By the way – the book of poetry you gave me is a farce." Khalil's voice was too large for the room. " The decadence of your society, focusing on twisting words, creating a grotesque facsimile of verse. I will stick with philosophy." Khalil's expression had lightened, perhaps showing even a touch of humor. Was he trying to deflect George's anger and betrayal? Did he not even care? Was he crazy? George had to wonder about this man sitting so passively in front of him. Did he care about anything other than himself? How could he pretend to kill in the name of God? The narcissistic personality.

"Nothing like the great verse in the Koran, right Khalil?" George answered him, though he didn't have to. Khalil rolled his eyes, probably recognizing George's sarcasm. He was westernized enough for that. "Truth be told, I don't like poetry either," George concurred. "I don't have the patience – too much effort for too little gain. But you are becoming a master of patience aren't you?" Just a little dig.

"Anyway," George lightened his tone and continued, "I was just trying to see if you have any appreciation for human emotions."

"Well, now you know." Khalil smiled. George was amazed at how unfazed he was by the bombing – not victorious, not scared. No outward change at all. Meanwhile, George was struggling to keep functioning. He couldn't even figure out whether a potential deal was a victory or not.

"The problem with you is that you don't live for anything." A weak attack that George regretted as soon as it left his mouth.

Khalil's laughter rang out in the tiny room. He shook his head. "No, it is you who don't live for anything. I have found my answer in Allah, in serving my people. Who do you serve, other than your intellect?"

Normally, George tried to be polite. It usually served his purpose. Not now.

"You serve a God who has you kill innocents, children. You haven't furthered your people's cause at all. Rather, you set them back."

"'Slay the unbelievers wherever you find them', as the holy Koran says. There are no innocents among your kind. Besides, you are being a hypocrite. Your country kills people every day, you just couch it as diplomacy. Where is your sympathy for those 'innocents'? Children grow up and wield guns."

"Just because you quote the Koran doesn't make you right." Khalil was playing with him. Baiting him to keep him upset – a great strategy when negotiating. It wasn't going to work. George was too tired so he stood up to leave, removing his burgundy-flecked sports coat from the chair back. Lifting his briefcase from the floor, he opened it and removed the front page from that day's New York Times. He handed it to Khalil. Let the man read about his handy work. George couldn't shame him – that much was obvious. So let him read the damn thing. He thought about leaving without saying goodbye. But, he wasn't one for dramatic gestures. More importantly, he couldn't wreck the relationship he had built with Khalil out of anger. The man was a terrorist; he had been a terrorist when George first walked in the door. What a waste.

"Goodbye, I will get back to you about a deal." Meanwhile you can rot in here, he felt like adding.

"George." Khalil called after him. "You don't have much time."

George slammed the door. What did Khalil mean about not having much time? In that question lay his purpose. George lived for stopping people like Khalil. Asshole.

XXXXX

George dialed Tom Campbell's phone number. He was still in the jail, but had moved to another Lilliputian-sized room – this one a phone booth crammed into what should have been a closet. Probably sound-proof glass on the door, not that he cared.

"Tom Campbell's office." A female voice chirped. Who knew Campbell had a secretary? George only ever called him at night.

"May I speak to him, please. This is George Harris." To George his own voice sounded odd. Not the time to overanalyze.

"Will he know what this is about?" the woman asked.

Let's see. The bomb that went off in London. A potential deal with a terrorist. My resignation. No, he couldn't say any of that.

"Yes."

"One second please."

That quickly, Campbell picked up the line. "What do you need, George?" Campbell sounded tense, his voice clipped. The pressure had seeped through all of them. A rot that would one day collapse in on them all.

"He wants a deal," George said, feeling sick. "Khalil. He basically admitted involvement in London. Something else is up, and he wants a deal." What Khalil had said - if you read between the lines. Too many people didn't trust their instincts even when hidden meanings were made crystal clear.

"Well, fuck him." Campbell's voice boomed through the telephone line.

"Okay, great. Where does that leave us?" George felt irritation growing.

"I don't know. You're the interrogator. Make something up." Ice came through the phone line as Campbell spoke. It would almost be comical to quit at this moment. Except someone would surely track him down with a sniper gun, right?

"We should at least try to work with him," George said.

"Why?" More ice.

"It is quicker. What if another bomb is imminent? He's already stated as much."

"Could be bluffing." Campbell held his ground. George heard the shuffle of papers. The booth-like room on top of George got smaller. Why did everyone always have to give him such a hard time? A far cry from his students who hung on his very words. Who repeated them verbatim to get As on their tests. Even the shelf-like bench he was sitting on hurt. He stayed quiet. Campbell could speak first. That couldn't be his final answer.

"Fuck. Let me think about it, and talk to some people," Campbell said. "Shit. Another fucking bomb." George heard Campbell exhale. "This guy practically admits he is Al Qaeda, and then wants a deal."

"Not practically. He has admitted that much to me."

"One of the names of Khalil's recent list is Maraq A'l Jawri. He has been arrested for helping plan the London bombing." George felt tears welling up in his eyes. Why now? Couldn't he just hold it together a bit longer?

"I'll get back to you." Campbell sounded dismissive. George knew the tone.

"When?"

"When I get back to you."

"What do I tell him until then?" George asked.

"Whatever the fuck you want." And, the phone line went dead. George just sat, and started to pray under his breath. Probably what Khalil was doing then also.

XXXXX

Khalil woke up, his body jerking, his covers askew. Sweat covered him, dampening his prison-issue pajamas. He could see the moon. That window was his only link with the real world, and not the man-made insanity of the prison. The moon was almost full, glowing luminous through the window. Its light turned into real ghosts around him. They whispered, or perhaps that was the rustle of the large tree outside. What sort of tree? That he didn't know, he had never seen it. Khalil only knew the tree existed because of its shadows. His life was nothing more than the whisper of a suggestion.

Except his deal. Hopefully. Perhaps he was now becoming a Don Quixote. Could he trust them to honor any deal? To whom was George relaying his terms? And what choice did he have but to try? The alternative was to continue living here with his ghosts and imaginary characters. Was he ready to rot slowly away?

Allah be praised, hopefully either he or George knew what they were doing. It was all asshole to asshole at this point. And the bombs would keep on going off. The roll of the eyes, a shrug of the shoulder. All of it was a game, trying to outsmart the other guy. Only the bombs were real. How long would this farce take to play itself out?

Sleep wouldn't come again tonight. Khalil was familiar with the feeling, and recognized its manic nuances. His muscles were rigid, his eyes alert. Weariness crept into his bones, impotent in its presence. Better not to fight. He was no longer being sleep deprived by sadistic soldiers. He was in a gentler sort of hell now, and could survive without a full nights sleep. His only option was to start planning. He needed to get out. If he didn't, he would go crazy.

Khalil had been trained not to crack, to hold steady under the enemy's pressure. But he had to get out; waiting was no longer an option. Hopefully, he could control the amount of information necessary to buy his ticket out.

XXXXX

Karen opened the neon pink bakery box. She grabbed a handful of the star cookies inside, dropping them absentmindedly on a plate. The large sugar crystals were densely scattered across the butter-colored cookies. It never ceased to amaze Karen that her otherwise sophisticated husband favored cookies that she associated with kids. Don't children eat elaborately decorated and intensely sweet cookies such as these? Children, and her husband George.

Karen hesitated. Should she get a tray or make George a cup of tea? The tray would be a nice domestic touch. But she had never prided herself on being domestic – after all she was an academic and an expert on Western literature. She had a lot of work to do herself. The cookies were a gesture out of pity for George. He had been in a terrible mood ever since that bomb went off in London. Blamed himself, as if he were responsible for that despicable terrorist he was keeping company with these days

Heading for George's study Karen grabbed a bottle of cold water. It would have to do. She walked through the richly furnished house – feeling pride surge through her as she glanced around. Everything was perfect. Thankfully, George was the sort of man who left decorating up to her.

George sat at his desk, typing away on his computer. Scowling, and his mood had obviously taken a turn for the worse – no small feat considering that it already hadn't been good. Why had he decided to focus on terrorists? He was a psychologist! Couldn't he use his intellect in a less depressing way? Why did her husband have to be the one to save the world? Wasn't tenure enough?

He ran his fingers absentmindedly through his hair – or at least what was left of it – an old habit of his, dating back to when they had first met as young students. It had endeared him to her then just as it did now. He had been so idealistic and, somehow, prosperity and age hadn't taken that out of him. She really should appreciate that part of him more – if only it didn't make him so bearish sometimes.

She looked at the family pictures scattered on the bookshelf behind George. The smiling faces of her children beamed back at her. They were both good kids. At least she and George had done something right. Karen missed them. But, she was also grateful for the quiet. She looked back at George, whose expression hadn't brightened at all with her arrival. It just figured, didn't it?

"I brought you some cookies. You disappeared in here an hour ago and I thought you might need them." Karen's voice was warm as she looked at her diligent husband.

"Can't you see that I'm busy?" He was almost shouting. George was not a shouter.

"Hey, relax. Just cookies, your favorite." Karen tried not to retort in kind. Commitment.

"I can see that," you moron. Karen could almost hear the rest of the sentence. Well, not only wasn't the bomb his fault, it most certainly wasn't hers either. Karen told herself to retreat. This was a conversation they could have later, once he calmed down.

"It wasn't your fault. You couldn't have prevented it," she said. "You are very good at what you do, so please don't blame yourself" or me. That was supportive.

"Who said it was my fault. Do you think the bombing was my fault?" George was definitely yelling now. He was also staring at her, incredulous that she could be standing in his study right now.

"Not your fault!" Karen put the cookies and water down on the corner of his desk and left quickly, closing the door behind her. I love him, she thought, but I don't need to hear this. Behind her, she heard George hurl something onto the floor.

XXXXX

Khalil still wasn't sleeping. For hours, night upon night, he kept thinking about his mother. His poor, weak mother. What a life of death and destruction she had seen. One boy dead, another skating the border between life and death each and every day.

Outside his window the stars were bright. Khalil had immediately known his cell was not located in a heavily urban area – the air was too pure and the nights too intense. He felt so far from home. Yet the vibrant stars sometimes reminded him of the night sky in his childhood desert home.

Before his capture, Khalil had been contemptuous of Americans and their physical squeamishness, especially in their treatment of prisoners. He didn't believe in torture, exactly. Men would say anything to stop pain – even a lie to satisfy their torturer (most of whom were none too smart). Still, a good kick here or there had its place. The Americans were weak – which had benefited Khalil both in the past and in the present. He was living better here than he had while fighting in the beautiful hellholes of Afghanistan.

Now, after spending time with George, Khalil was having doubts about too many things. And he suspected it was because of George. He had developed an affection and respect for his interrogator.

He knew George had used Khalil's isolation against him. Asking philosophical questions. Telling stories. Pretending he existed as an individual, not just a number. Acting like a father. Wasn't that the goal of interrogation, to turn the prisoner into a form of dependent child?

But Khalil didn't get frightened easily. He was seasoned. So they had sent his George, who played not on his physical fears and weaknesses, but on his mental and emotional ones. George knew Khalil would ponder the questions he asked – they played to his weaknesses – questions about life itself. And purpose. Everyone can be manipulated.

Now, Khalil was confused, for the first time since he saw his brother die.

His mind jumped again. He recalled the eyes of the first boy he knew he was sending to die. They died all the time, but Khalil had known this was a suicide mission. The boy had not. He had been barely seventeen, excited to fight the Russians and protect his country. The eyes had been that rich, deep brown of most Afghani men. They had been so trusting. But this boy had not been a complete fool, and a slight question had been visible in them. "Can I trust you?" they asked. The Afghanis were not trusting people, wisely so. Perhaps that had been it.

And, once again, this Afghani had been right to have hesitated. He had been betrayed.

Those deep, rich eyes were closed when Khalil later saw what was left of the battered body, riddled with bullets, a leg blown away. It already had a light coating from the country's impossibly fine dust. Khalil had recognized that having those eyes closed was a blessing he couldn't face them. Nor did he face the boy's parents.

Now such things never bothered him. He was part of a war, as were the men he sent to their death. He had even started recruiting suicide bombers – targeting the young, the poor, and the angry. Khalil had promised them paradise, martyrdom and money for their wretched families.

He thought about the boy in London, dead in the same fiery blast that got George so upset. Another boy, another mother's child, just like all of those who had died in the bombing itself. Khalil felt nothing for any of them. The boy had been a fool, his death no great loss. Hopefully he got some of the paradise for which he had sacrificed his life. One thing Khalil knew was that the boy's life on this earth had contained no aspect of paradise. As for the people getting ice cream, George's point, they, and many others, would have to die, indeed always had died.

Violence begets violence. The world has always been brutal.

Still, was that all there was for him?

Tonight he wondered, had it been a mistake to send that boy to his death? What had Khalil really accomplished – all of it done for Allah? Was his Allah watching? Didn't he understand that these tests were too hard, and the costs too great?

What was the greater purpose? Philosophers had asked that question for thousands of years. Why should he expect to have an answer alone at night in a decrepit and smelly jail cell?

His whole life was now playing out in his mind as he lay stretched out on a lumpy mattress. Wasn't that what you saw during the few seconds before you died – your whole life in slow motion, yet in an instant? Still, his confinement hadn't lasted but a few seconds. Or perhaps he was wrong about that. What was this time in the greater context of history – he was but a speck, that would one day vanish in a puff of smoke.

XXXXX

"Have you seen a child get hit by a missile?"

George willed himself not to wince. He focused on maintaining his calm and controlled expression. Calm and control – key in interrogations, or negotiations. He wasn't yet ready to react, even internally, to Khalil's statement.

"No, Khalil. I have not." A suicide bomb, yes. But not a missile.

Khalil continued on. He had the placid demeanor George wished for. Yet shouldn't this topic be paired with at least a little bit of emotion? George decided he would ponder that later as well. All this repression couldn't be healthy.

"There is a recognition, an expectation. It is coupled with an absolute horror. The children I know have seen death. They have felt it, lived it, breathed it. They desperately don't want to die. Do you want to die, George?"

Khalil rubbed his hands together, as if warding off the cold. Or was he doing it out of glee?

"They also know the familiar whine of a missile. They live daily with the sounds. Bullets, bombs…your pictures mean nothing compared to the death screams of a child, George. The tangled flesh of what was once a person. A child who lost its innocence the moment it left the womb and entered the world of the underprivileged. Have you ever been underprivileged, George? Have you woken up each and every day wondering if you would eat? Worried that perhaps you might die? Enter the rest of the world, George. Step in their shoes, and breathe in the smells. Why is one child's life worth so much more than another's? Because someone was there to take a picture? Because they lived in London and not in Ramallah?"

Khalil paused. His monotone voice was being used to affect, that George recognized. But George was conscious of little else. No, he didn't know. He really didn't know.

Khalil continued. He obviously wasn't expecting a response or he would have let his words linger in the air a bit longer.

"Do you have a deal for me, George?"

George reached into his briefcase, more an attempt to stall for time than for any other purpose. The tangled tiny bodies from the London bombing had once again claimed his conscious mind. The flesh ripped apart, stained with blood. Limbs torn from bodies. A small stuffed bear, still intact but a mottled color of white mixed with bright red. He felt ill.

Regaining his voice, George put some papers on the same familiar table. It was still scratched. As with a person, the deep fissures provided personality. The table showed only one outward scar and hid its internal ones, at least until the pieces eventually came apart at the seams. Or perhaps the scar would no longer hold firm under its weight of books and other knick-knacs. Then the whole thing would just collapse down the middle, hurling its pieces and its burdens into the air.

"Right here. I can give you the basic terms and…." Time to work.

"Get me a lawyer first." Khalil just stared.

"Term number one." George found a firm voice as he kicked into autopilot. This he could do, negotiate. Even if small broken bodies obscured the room around him. He was confident that he could outdo his cellmate in negotiating. Khalil was a fighter, not a diplomat. He spoke in terms of blood. Even if George himself would never exit his own mental cell he would help Khalil escape his physical one.

"…no lawyer." And then George just stared, waiting for a response. He was unnerved, but it didn't matter. Negotiation was a dance, based on strategy and patience.

XXXXX

Khalil could feel a chuckle welling up. His ploy had worked; George was unnerved. No one likes losing control of their emotions. Least of all a trained psychologist. George was above such passions.

Death. Khalil had already dealt with it. He had faced it so many times the shock value was gone. Death was just a part of his life, a constant in Algeria, Afghanistan, the Sudan, so many places he had lived. His brother's murder had opened the door to a world of intolerables. Now he only feared his mother's. Death comes to us all. In George's world it just tended to come later.

"No lawyer, no information," Khalil said.

"No can do." George delivered the words in a staccato style. Certainly not unsure.

"Because?" Khalil drew the word out, elongating each letter.

"Look." George's tone was impatient. He was wearing a pale yellow t-shirt today. It seemed an odd choice for George. "We can't use a government lawyer – conflict of interest. We can't hire you some bastard who will just complain about illegal detention and a list of other things. The U.S. government is in a bind here. You must give in on this issue. Trust me on this if on nothing else. Otherwise you and I will just sit here and stare at each other every day until one of us dies."

Khalil glanced around the small cell. Did he see yet another spider or was it only the ghost of one who had once inhabited his walls?

"Do you have any children?" Khalil asked.

"That's it. I am done for the day." George's tone was emotional, upset. The threat of Khalil's words couldn't have been clearer. Khalil watched him, waiting.

George began to gather his papers, then stopped. He visibly sighed, his long body almost seeming to draw into itself. Resting his elbow on the table, he used his hand to cradle his chin in his left hand. He stared at Khalil, as if seeing him for the first time. Did compassion flash in his eyes? For the first time that day, Khalil felt a bit unbalanced himself.

"It isn't going to work, Khalil. It just isn't. Free yourself. The game is up."

"Okay, stay. Let's work it out."

XXXXX

And so they reached a deal – but skipped the handshake. Khalil was getting four more years of imprisonment, but in a less austere jail. Not so bad, even when factoring in time served. Who could value the chits torture earned you. If this were Algeria, things would be different. But it wasn't.

George was troubled – but, he was no lawyer, so he wasn't confident regarding his concerns. Khalil had admitted involvement in the London bombing. He implied that he was Al Qaeda. Yet he had seen no lawyer, and was being held indefinitely with no charges. He had been tortured. Still, he was an enemy combatant – though his status had been unclear upon his arrest and his torture. He was to be released. Other terrorists with similar backgrounds – and similar rights violations – were getting life sentences. The system made no sense.

"So, you worked as a recruiter and trainer of terrorists – is that right?" George asked.

Khalil shrugged his orange-robed shoulders, a familiar gesture by now. George knew what to expect from Khalil. They had spent so much time together he could also anticipate gestures and intonations – it was like being with your lover, intimate knowledge was so ingrained.

"That word – "terrorist". Can't we use a different word? Someone who fights on the other side of a conflict is not automatically a terrorist."

"Pick a word, Khalil. I don't have time to argue the semantics – though I don't use it like that. I use it for those who deliberately target civilians."

"Freedom fighter." Khalil shot back, causing George to shake his head. Ridiculous. He wasn't going to take the bait. "Go on."

"We don't really have to recruit." Khalil took the cue. At this point he would probably keep talking, so different from when they began. Now each word brought him closer to his ultimate release – the truth really would set him free. George didn't doubt that Khalil would hide important facts nonetheless – most did. You took what you could get. After all, this bird was singing, but for a price. Khalil had never reached that desperate fear necessary for a man to crack open and spill everything. Some never did – inner strength.

"More potential recruits want in than we could possibly accept. Even after we send someone abroad for training in a camp only between ten and twenty percent are actually allowed to join. And that's if our organization even sends them to a camp. First, they need to find us – either through luck or through a contact." Khalil looked triumphant. He ran his finger along the edge of the table, following its outline.

"But wait," George said. "Some of these extremist mosques, like the Finsbury Mosque in London, are famous as recruitment centers for your organizations?"

"Yes, and no," Khalil said. "Sure some members like to hear their preachers. But the mosques each have many members. If you walked in you wouldn't be able to recognize the terrorists, to use your word."

"Sure I could, at the very least the guys with the long beards and the man preaching extremism on the pulpit?"

"Do you think the police haven't tried that?" Khalil said. "Too obvious. How unsophisticated do you think we are? So typical of an American, George. I thought better of you." Khalil shook his head, scolding again. George let the slight go. Khalil continued, his voice devoid of emotion. "We only take someone if he is brought by one of our own, George. We don't take any chances. The potential army size is phenomenal. Countless dissatisfied men want a path back to Allah. Your material, exploitative world doesn't fulfill the spiritual needs of the faithful…."

"Okay, okay. I am not trying to be recruited." George interrupted. This information was so old it crumbled. "Sometimes your proselytizing goes too far." Or did it?

"No man who is truly happy blows himself up, George." Khalil wasn't so easily dissuaded. "Do you know anyone who is not happy? Our young men are discriminated against. They are displaced, dropped into societies based on atheism and sin. They need to find a way to Allah. We provide that."

"Okay, I get your point." George interrupted. Enough! Aren't most people unhappy at least sometimes? George could empathize with the disposed Muslim youth. He wasn't in the best mood himself. So what? Right now, Khalil wasn't spewing the rhetoric of a regional war, but rather that of worldwide destruction. Al Qaeda style. George needed specifics, not a generic rant.

XXXXX

"You are Al Qaeda, Khalil." No more innuendos – establish the fact.

Khalil shifted in his chair. He could feel sweat beading under his arms. Stickiness. Our body always betrays our mind. All those years of evolution and we still shared most traits with the other mammals.

Trust. Could Khalil trust George and the negotiated deal? Would they void it if Khalil's information went beyond their expectations? Mohammed Doha – who had turned government witness was probably dead by now. Hopefully, his death had been planned long before Khalil's capture. A murder in jail was almost too easy. His betrayal couldn't harm Khalil anymore. Could Khalil still hang himself?

For example, by admitting his membership in Al Qaeda. Sure he had implied it – that was different. The room was bugged, so the actual words he spoke mattered. Was such membership a new crime not covered by his deal? Life was one minefield after another.

"George, " Khalil kept his tone soft and controlled. He was educating this man, he reminded himself. "Your question is a very western one. I am not a member of any group, not really. Do I know people in Al Qaeda? Yes, I do. Have I worked with them? Yes."

He paused. Time for all conversation to end – his monologue must begin. Time for his freedom. Would they really let him go? By now just moving to a prison with grass and trees would be enough. He needed to breathe air, not the institutional, bioengineered substitute.

Khalil's sweating had increased, and he could smell his body's pungency. The promise of freedom was so overwhelming his stomach hurt. If George reneged, he would kill him. But he would kill his family first. Allah be praised, the one thing that Muslims had learned over the centuries of humiliation was revenge. Now he had to stop stalling and talk.

"An attack is planned. Five cars will blow up at five different McDonald's drive-throughs. They will release sarin. A lot of sarin." Khalil paused, letting the information hit George, who froze, probably attempting to hide his surprise.

Adrenaline tingled along Khalil's body, stimulating every muscle.

Excitement keeps me alive, he told himself. The sensation mimicked that of drugs, or so he guessed. His brain craved the high of living on the edge. Did sarin provide a similar kick until sucking the breathe out of its victims, crippling their muscles?

I am too important to rot in a jail cell, he reminded himself. He had betrayed his brothers, his cause, and perhaps even Allah himself. What came next? Plunging into the uncertainty of becoming an informer Khalil accepted his choice. He might actually live to fight another day.

His voice continued, strong enough to echo. "It will happen on Thursday, October 18 at 12:30 Eastern time." Just over a week.

"Which McDonald's?" George sounded calm. He even shifted his body as Khalil spoke, twisting his frame in the chair. His worn yellow shirt gaped slightly. A shadow hit the right side of his face. The man in the moon. But no sign of increased emotion.

"Give me a piece of paper and a pen." George did so, and Khalil quickly wrote down five addresses. McDonald's, the maker of Big Macs. A symbol of American imperialism and an affront to true believers everywhere.

Khalil slid the paper back. He had written the target towns and street names, but no street numbers.

"Khalil, I need more details." Patient, modulated. "A plot, date and general location are a great start. I need to know exactly who is involved and how I find them. I need every detail. I need the exact addresses."

"When I will be free?"

"We have a deal, Khalil. But I need more specifics. You know you have four more years to serve."

Khalil ignored the last comment. Was George patient because the bombs wouldn't go off for nine days. Except.

"Sarin. We are using sarin because it's so easy to make." Khalil softened his voice. Could he get a rise out of George? "Chemical warfare is wonderful for us – psychologically. People are always more frightened of a gruesome death. Human beings are comfortable with the likely causes of death — car accidents, for example. They have an irrational paranoia of unknown and uncommon ones. That is how you create mass hysteria. But you should know that, George."

"Why lace the bomb with anything?" Calm. "You won't add many deaths. A little nerve gas won't be enough to create the hysteria you want."

"Well, your government gave the Iraqis sarin to fight the Iranian Shiites. We want to return some of it."

"That is garbage, Khalil," George said. "You couldn't care less about Saddam, the Iranians or the Kurds for that matter. You just want to test it – see how effective it is. You want to frighten people. Sarin exposure is treatable."

"It adds to the calamity. It increases fear," Khalil replied. "Sarin needs to be identified before it can be treated. It's an ugly death. We bring the war to your soil." Enjoy.

XXXXX

Bullshit. Information, leading to bullshit.

George's sixth sense was prickled, alerting him that the interrogation was spiraling out of control. Control was just an illusion anyway, and overrated to boot. But the gut feel, that was real. Khalil would probably be a great subject for the lab – how do you live so dangerously for so long and stay alive?

Nine days. What were the details? What happened in the nine days leading up to the blasts? And why wasn't Khalil telling him?

Khalil stood up. He walked to his bed and lay down with his back to George. George shut his eyes, trying to sense the mood hanging in the air. Once you have spent enough time with someone, especially in desperate circumstances, words often become a hindrance. Non-verbal language spoke louder. Khalil would come to the table when he was ready. George wouldn't hurry him.

The silence was intimate. They were both nuanced enough at reading people to need no more. Why had Khalil stopped?

The room's mood wasn't calm, it wasn't angry. No positive emotion was hanging, limp or otherwise. George kept his eyes closed, listening to the soft rhythm of their breathing as it rose and fell in unison. Not fear, not hope, not desperation. Anticipation, that was it.

George opened his eyes. As he did so he noticed that his sweater had fallen to the floor. Reaching down, he grasped the green wool. Sensing a shadow, he looked up to see Khalil sitting across from him.

"Tomorrow at 11:00 A.M., five bombs filled with sarin will leave Los Angeles bound for different cities around the United States. They will all be transported by car. I don't know who is picking them up, but I do know that they'll be detonated on the 11th. I can take you to the apartment in Los Angeles."

George blinked. Or, rather, he thought he did. A blinding light had hit him in the face, full force. He felt his face react. So much for the illusion of control. Breathe, stop, think, he told himself. This was it, the information he had worked so hard to get. What did he do now?

Breathe, stop, think. Breathe.

Tomorrow. Should George run for the phone now, or should he get further information? Stop.

And, think.

"What is the address?" George asked.

"I don't know it. I have been there, and can take you." Khalil replied.

"Bullshit. You haven't been to the States in years. You said so, and we don't have a record of you entering."

"I lied. Fake passport." Khalil said.

How often? George felt like asking.

"Why are you telling me now?" George asked. Jennifer? Did that stunt really work?

"I'm finally ready." Khalil was calm. Wasn't that how we get, fatalistic, when the whole world is on the line?

"But, I need, in writing, the details of my release. And a lawyer."

"We can't get you a lawyer that fast," George said. "We can't get you a lawyer at all."

"Then I want my terms in writing. Otherwise I won't take you," Khalil replied. Bastard.

"Having them in writing won't help you. You have to trust me on this." George persisted.

"No trust. You are the ones who live in a world of contracts and lawyers. You don't have time, George." Khalil smiled. Campbell was going to love this.

XXXXX

Khalil felt her brushing up next to him. Like a phantom limb, Jennifer was no longer part of his body, yet his nerves kept tingling with the memory of her. Her soft hair always smelled of musk. Her fingernails were always chewed down to the flesh of her fingers. Her stomach curved softly just before hitting the sharpness of her hipbones. He always heard music when he remembered her; she loved music. Every sensation in his long dead body was reawaking, and he couldn't stop himself from visualizing her naked.

This course was destruction. He willed himself to stop. He needed to block her from his mind, otherwise he would meet one of two ends: death or continued imprisonment. George was to blame for this distracting weakness. How had he known that Khalil would have such a strong reaction to seeing her? Had keeping Jennifer's pictures propped up next the one of Hassan alerted George? He should have thrown them back in George's face.

What should he do now? Pray? Perhaps that was his only option. He certainly couldn't ask George to bring Jennifer back for one more look, to run his fingers through her hair, to mold her body into his. She probably wouldn't even come back. How much forgiveness does one person contain?

Khalil knelt down on his floor. He touched his forehead down on the ground. Words flowed from his lips, rote. The game of hardball had started. He needed to regain his internal control. Otherwise, George would annihilate him. The world was coming to an end.

XXXXX

"What do you want now, George?" Campbell's tone was annoyed, curt and perhaps even condescending. Thankless job. In a more rational state George might consider that the tension was getting to Campbell in much the same way it was destroying him. He wasn't in a rational state. He was crammed back into the tight phone closet. His legs were bent unnaturally to accommodate the space.

"Five bombs are going off on the 18th. Tomorrow, they are each to be individually picked up from an apartment in Westwood. Khalil can show us the apartment – he doesn't remember the address. He can tell us the target cities and streets, but not the target addresses. They are all drive-through McDonald's." George drew in his breath. Thankfully, Campbell was professional enough not to interrupt him. Bless God for small favors.

"Less than twenty-four hours." The words erupted, shocking George. "Holy fucking shit, what am I supposed to do? You're all the way on the west coast, and I have less than twenty-four hours? George, I am going to destroy you, you asshole." Campbell was losing control.

Sure, Campbell was upset, George had anticipated that much. He looked around him. Why the hell was he spending so much time in this phone booth? Plywood walls and a bench made out of sponge? With the taxes he paid, the government could have afforded better. Meanwhile,

Campbell stopped his rant.

"You're welcome. I could have given you less than twenty-four hours, not more." George was feeling tense himself.

"A much worse alternative, I agree." Campbell seemed to be recovering. "What the fuck are we going to do?" He paused. George had a moment of hope. Could he offload any involvement in a solution?

"You will be personally responsible for that mission." There we have it. Campbell continued. "You will go. Khalil really says he can't remember the address and needs to personally show us, huh? Interesting."

"Yes. It is interesting; good word," George said. "I wonder if he wants to go, or has to go. But the timing doesn't allow for much analysis."

"Shit. I have a lot of phone calls to make."

"I'm not going. I am…." George said.

"The hell you are not," Campbell replied.

Breathe. "Okay, look, I am a psychologist," George said. "Not FBI, not CIA, not SWAT, not even police. I don't go chasing bombs, I get you information to find them. That is it." Like talking to a child.

"You're going, and so am I now. I need to make some calls, George."

"No, wait!" George cried out. He wasn't done. "Before Khalil will take us he wants his deal terms in writing."

"No can do. He's bluffing. The asshole has no options. After revealing this information he's fucked if he doesn't take us. I have to work this out. Don't you dare turn your cell off or I will personally make sure you fry."

"Great. You're willing to take the risk?" George shifted. His eyes focused on the stripped cushions beneath him. Green, yellow and purple. What discordant colors.

"The deal is shit, George. We can't actually honor a deal with an Al Qaeda."

XXXXX

Khalil remembered how cold the mountain had been that day. The air was crystal clear. Soft lighting lent the jagged edges of the peaks a pink hue. He snaked after Abdi, focused on the man's feet before him, mimicking each step with as much precision as his own tired feet could muster. Mud squished underneath.

The most common form of surgery in Afghanistan during Khalil's time there had been amputations. Most doctors used whatever knife or saw they could grab to perform the surgery on land mine victims. The doctors prayed for anesthesia. The patients prayed they would make it to a primitive medical outpost before they died of shock or blood loss.

Mines had rained from the skies as the Soviets sought to win their grueling battle by extermination or intimidation. The easiest way to clear out a village is to maim its children. Hence the mines in the shape of lighters or pens. Khalil had heard rumors of doll- shaped mines but he had never seen the remains of one.

As Khalil followed Abdi, they walked single file over the tread marks in the grass, avoiding the unknown areas – not sure if an explosive might be hiding there. The system was imperfect. Allah alone could guess whether or not the Soviets had recently rained down a new supply of the mutilating mines.

Mostly the two men were silent. Speech was futile. Both felt weary from the ceaseless demands of a never-ending guerrilla war. Rancid food, when they had food. Nights without sleep. A deep chill that sunk into the very marrow of their bones.

The bonds that grew were intense. Walking through a real valley of death and coming out alive is an experience that can't be approximated outside of the most desperate situations. And they did it daily, together. The majestic mountains, highlighted by the pinks and bluish-purples of an unpolluted sky were their witness. Allah had watched from the heavens and granted them one more day. And the possession of all their limbs.

Suddenly Khalil heard a loud pop and saw a wisp of smoke. He smelled the harshness of a mine's explosives mingled with the sweet rawness of flesh. Blood gushed out of the stump that had been Adbi's leg.

Over time Khalil had developed an innate sense of danger, as if the plastic and metal discs could signal their presence. He learned the hard way that on a primal level the human body recognizes the proximity of death or a threat. The gurgling of the brooks as they slid down steep ravines couldn't drown out the other sounds.

Khalil felt deep inside that something wasn't right, again, now. The recognition had been dawning slowly, his senses dulled by his limited existence – that of a caged animal. He could picture George's face as the man reassured him about their deal. Could George bluff that well? How much was he told?

Why would the U.S. government release Khalil from prison? If they truly recognized his dangerousness – and Khalil knew that George at least did – they couldn't let him out. Or could they?

He wasn't keeping his end of bargain. No, he was playing both sides and revealing enough to try and escape. And if he was cheating, why wouldn't they? The escape plan was crystal in his mind. It'd better work.

XXXXX

No deal? It was mid-day in California. Bombs were to be disbursed in the morning. Khalil wanted assurances on his deal in return for helping stop the pick-ups. And, the deal was a lie.

"No deal?" George's voice shook. He leaned into the wall. It was so close he didn't have to move much.

"No, you'll have to get him to take us without anything in writing. We would just take any such assurances away after the mission anyway."

"So then type it up, and take it away later."

"You're straining my patience," Campbell said. "I have to figure out how to get you to Los Angeles, disarm the bombs' caretaker, disable the bombs and not kill anyone. Those things are more important than typing up a piece of paper." Campbell was clearly exasperated. Jerk.

"We made a deal," George said, conscious of the prayer in his voice. "He is obviously concerned – rightly so – that we may not honor it. We need him now." I am just a functionary, remember, George felt like adding.

"Don't waste your time." Campbell was firm. Uninterested.

"We need his help. We made a deal, we need to honor it." George controlled his voice. This was negotiation, nothing personal. His fists clenched up into tight balls.

"George, look, I won't debate this. I have a lot to do. Thanks for the information; I need to act on it. There is no deal. We can't release an Al Qaeda guy, especially not someone as senior as Khalil. You have to realize that?"

"We made a deal." George repeated. He was right, but he was going to lose.

"No deal. This is my decision, and you must live with it. May I remind you, George, lives are hanging by a thread here – every day – for both of us, though more so for me. I can't let your idealism imperil anyone." Campbell's voice held firm.

"Look, don't preach to me about …."

"We had Hitler," Campbell said. "We had the USSR, now we have the Islamic terrorists. The enemy has shifted over the past seventy years. Now we don't know where they are, nor do we know what weapons they have. If a nuclear bomb drops on the White House — whom do we blame? How do we punish them? We can't even identify our enemy, so how do we deter them?

Campbell continued. "I understand your idealism – so I protected you. I let you negotiate as an honest man. Now I am telling you bluntly – know your enemy. That man you're arguing for is a murderer."

What could George say? This is war, or some other cliché? Campbell was right, wasn't he? But George didn't like lying. Not even for the greater good. If the end doesn't justify the end, what does? Except.

George realized that Campbell's voice had boomed with a new passion. Campbell must be fighting his own little war. Who could even guess at his motivation?

Or perhaps Campbell was just wrong – that by betraying this deal, knowingly, they were lowering themselves. Weren't they reaching the depths of immortality the terrorists inhabited? Their tentative steps had to lead them there eventually.

Unfortunately, George was too tired to care. "So what should I tell him?"

"I don't care."

Another voice, high pitched and immature floated through the telephone, assuming control.

"Daddy, we just got here. I made a fish at school. Look?".

"One minute, Dylan. I'll look in a second." Campbell's voice lost its edge.

"I have to go, George. Figure it out." The words were brisk, but also distracted.

"Okay, Tom." The phone line was dead before George finished speaking.

Children. He had to keep going. Perhaps he could help pass on a better world to them. They certainly couldn't want the screwed up one into which they had been born.

Suddenly, a jolt of fear ran through him. What other decisions had been kept from him? Now what was he going to do?

XXXXX

George's face said no before he finished crossing the threshold. If the expression showed, George wanted to communicate his own disappointment in his results. Otherwise, his face would be as blank as a windswept desert.

"Can't get you anything in writing. Whether or not you help tomorrow is your call. I can promise, however, that if you don't help you will never again see the light of day."

Khalil smiled. Bluff called.

"You don't need to threaten me. I figured it was worth a try." Khalil was gracious in his defeat. The sun shone brightly into the room, it was almost blinding today. Whomever George had called still had time to plan for tomorrow – bare bones, but possible. "What time are you picking me up?"

"How did you know I was coming?" George almost didn't react. Probably had no surprise left in him.

"They couldn't play it any other way." Khalil replied. *So what now?*

"We're on? You'll show us?" George didn't look expectant as he spoke. How real could everything be, anyway? To either of them. George looked like the successful academic he was. He still possessed the same self-assurance Khalil had seen when they first met. Only now, Khalil could see a tightening around his lips, sending small creases down the sides of his mouth. His eyes were rimmed by shadows. The young are incapable of hiding their emotions. Then, when we are older our body betrays our feelings, overruling the control we have developed.

"You're on for tomorrow?" George asked again, betraying no impatience.

Tomorrow. "Yes, of course. I have no choice." Khalil answered.

George's yellow Polo t-shirt had the brand above his chest. Khalil had seen that Polo logo knocked off in every third-world open-air market he had ever visited. Ultimately, those of us looking in do want a little bit of their world, no matter how soulless or godless it is, don't we? He asked himself if he could ever live like George – safe, secure and rich. Not that an Algerian man could drop into a spot on today's map without arousing the suspicion of his neighbors. Could he blend into the scenery tomorrow?

"So what now?" Khalil asked.

George soldiered on. "I need more information. In what part of Los Angeles is the apartment located?"

"Westwood. Will your government really honor the deal, and let me go in four years?" Khalil asked; why play George's game?

George looked back, unblinking. "That is what they said." The lines around his mouth tightened. "Where would you go?"

"Anywhere but here." Khalil gestured around him. The grime was more pervasive; otherwise nothing else had changed over the past months. Only the bookshelf and the numerous books George supplied provided any warmth. Plus, of course, Khalil's collection of pictures, still propped up by his bed.

"Will you go back to fighting?" George was serious, his eyes empty; a look Khalil knew well.

"Will you trust any answer I give you? Will your government?"

Khalil was serious too. These men wouldn't trust him.

"Hell, no. How many years have you been on a terrorist watch list?" George smiled, and Khalil felt a lightening of tension.

"You tell me." He kept his tone friendly in response.

"Touché. I know you well enough not to trust you; my government doesn't trust you – even though you're helping now. Did those people in London a damn bit of good." George didn't falter this time as he referenced the bomb. At least he wasn't being patronizing. "I hope you learn a lesson from all of this – there is another way."

"You're preaching. I expected better from you." Khalil meant it, and made a face to clarify his message. Occasionally George forgot about his own intelligence and education, veering into the self-help culture endemic to the west.

"You have options."

"You know nothing about my world." Khalil couldn't keep bitterness out of his voice.

"Please." George rolled his eyes. "I have lived in your world; I study your world.

"Tip of the iceberg." Now Khalil smiled. He had gotten the better of George on this one. Small consolation that it was.

XXXXX

Could Campbell be any more of an asshole?

George pursed his lips. Keep it all in. Being rude never got you anywhere, did it? Or so said his father. Grimacing was okay when you were on the telephone, even though they could affect your voice. The change was almost imperceptible to most people.

"So, are you going to respond to me or just leave me hanging here on the telephone?" Campbell said. George caught the tone. Definitely rude. And hostile. Still, Campbell had a point – George should answer. About time. Unfortunately, he had nothing to say that he hadn't said fifty times already.

"I'm not going. If I am going, GI Joe isn't." George heard himself shout. Shit – he was turning into Campbell. If I'm going – that means only if you force me through dishonest and manipulative means. Only if you threaten me, my future and my family. Only if….

"You said we had to go to Los Angeles and drag Khalil along." Campbell's tone was harsh. "You said that only by bringing him could we find the guy. You said Khalil has to get him to open the door because if we try a raid he will blow the neighborhood sky high. We are doing what you want, George. So take responsibility for the decisions you've made. I have sold it to all the higher ups I could find – just like you wanted. You must control Khalil. No room for failure here; a lot of lives are at risk."

George felt childhood pressure building up behind his eyes. *Are you really that much of a coward? Be a man.* Playground talk.. He hadn't been physically brave or athletic. Books were his gift. Understanding people. Not guns and war games. Not raids.

"Look, I did help work out the plan – that's true. But I am not qualified to go." *I also didn't lay out the terms of the raid, or the conditions.*

Sitting at home, in his study, George felt safer arguing his release. The lights were dimmed, again, casting soft shadows across his favorite and familiar books, neatly arranged on their shelves. His chair curved into his back, the grooves long worn in. Now he was in his own environment – not crammed into that coffin of a phone booth.

"George, the plan is beautiful." Exasperated, impatient. "It is elegant in its simplicity."

"Yes, and Khalil is between a SWAT team and a bomber with nerve gas. What could be more idyllic?" George's sarcasm again.

"He's a murderer; need I remind you of London?"

"Look, I know that there's no other way – especially with less than twenty-four hours to plan this," George said. "But none of that has anything to do with me. I'm not qualified to go." George kept trying. He could hear Campbell breathing through the telephone. Snorting was more accurate. Tough. They had hired George to interrogate, not go on a mission. He hadn't even wanted the damn job. What would they do if he didn't go? Fire him?

"Moreover, you can't send GI Joe, even if he does speak Arabic." George continued arguing. "Why? You need a better guard. The guy is a kid, and I don't trust him. Khalil could snap him in two in under five seconds. Plus, not to sound paranoid, but something is wrong with that guy."

"That I can do – send a different guard. You are going. End of discussion. This prisoner is yours, and you must complete the job. That was your commitment."

Campbell's voice had turned dismissive. George felt a surge of fury. He wasn't about to be told his 'job', and then politely dismissed.

"I didn't commit to any such thing. I'm an interrogator. Me accompanying Khalil is likely to endanger everyone involved. No agreement to risk my life on SWAT missions."

"Not SWAT." Campbell's voice was annoyed. Tough. "Come off it. What were you doing in Iraq a year ago? If you do your job right you won't be risking your life." *You weak asshole.* George felt the words Campbell hadn't said from his comfortable chair in the nation's capital. All they did in D.C. was move tacks around on a map and decide who else put their neck on the line.

"No, not going to happen," George said. Campbell could use every insult in the book. Still no go. George fingered his water bottle, reading the label, as he evaluated new tactics to try.

"George, we need someone to read Khalil's responses," Campbell spoke up. "The arrest in London wasn't random bad luck. We were tipped off. Mohammed Doha only provided a name. Someone else provided a location." Campbell paused. George sensed he should stay quiet and wait. More information was coming. He fingered his pen, clicking it open then shut.

"Problem is that we don't know if he was set up to provide disinfor mation or whether he was just plain set up." Campbell said. "Whether or not we can trust our informant, or whether he is playing us, is anyone's guess. We don't know how high quality Khalil's information is or if it is a trap. Khalil may not even know."

"But you can't ignore it or you risk five bombs going off on American soil." George finished the thought. Not so hard to do.

"So, you are going." Campbell continued on. "Don't think you have a choice. This is too important. You are the only one who knows Khalil and can evaluate his reactions to the events as they unfold. Goodnight, George."

George could sense Campbell's line go dead before he heard the dial tone. Again.

By now he should be resigned to being treated as a shadow puppet, transparent and barely there. He was a role, no longer being addressed as a real person. He had aged into competent invisibility.

The telephone hung heavy in his hand. He let it drop into the receiver.

# ‖ CHAPTER SIX - LIES

XXXXX

Perhaps he didn't want to die after all. Omar curled into a fetal position. His bedcovers were bunched up around him, more tangled than anything else. The dim light coming through his window told him that Helios's chariot was ending its daily dash across the sky. To be a God must feel divine. Perhaps he was presuming too much by trying to rush his way into paradise.

Omar turned up the volume on his iPod until the music stung his ears. The Arcade Fire's chorus-like melody surged with the increase.

Don't want to fight don't, don't want to die
Just want to hear you cry
Who's is going to throw the very first stone?

Who indeed? When had the first stone been cast? Did it really matter after the passing of so much time? The slights weren't going to stop no matter how many people blew up.

Omar thought he heard the phone ring. The music was so loud he couldn't be sure, so he pulled one of the earpieces out. He heard the beep of his machine and then a voice.

"Omar, this is Stacey. You were supposed to call me two hours ago. Are we still going out tonight?" Her tone was whiny, as girls so quickly got with him. What was the point? First you fucked them, then they clung like leeches.

Omar pulled himself tighter. His knee cracked as he did so.

Fear. Where did it come from? Was he afraid of leaving his body or staying in it? The shifting world around him was leaving no place untouched into which he could escape. Did he even bother to cry any more?

The world had become one sensation after another. Until he had to keep upping the ante, going that extra step to feel alive. Did he have to die to live? Was that the only way he could feel anything again – having his flesh stripped from his body?

The darkening room was the ending of his day. Should he call Stacy back and take her out as he had promised? Could her warm flesh cut the chill in his heart? Or was it too late?

If he disappeared, would it be as if he was never existed?

XXXXX

The morning felt far away, as if Khalil could watch it coming closer yet still see it lingering off in the distance. He glanced at his cell, only half seeing it. Even though he was looking at it for the last time – his purgatory. Today he would either escape or he would die. Slowly he fingered his worn copy of *Don Quixote*. He flirted with the idea of taking it with him. But, his orange coveralls not only made him stand out like a fire engine they also had no pockets to hide personal effects. He went through life without such luxuries. Why should he start worrying about them now? He did slide his three pictures – the one of his brother and the two of Jennifer up his left sleeve. They scratched at the ending of his scar.

It was the pictures that would give him strength to survive the day.

"Allahu Akbar." he repeated many times under his breath.

Khalil's mind wandered. Our days start absent any indication of what they will mean. What types of signs can we read in the early stirrings of life-changing mornings? Most days pass quickly and are soon forgotten. Sometimes we know that important events are on the horizon. But even then Allah seldom grants us a sign to let us know whether things will be all right or not.

Would things be all right today? Would he die?

Khalil thought back to Cairo, as it had been the morning he took a flight to London and his capture. The journey was now about to end. Had there been anything auspicious about that day?

He had awoken to the call of the mezzuen, the morning ritual. As he had pulled himself out of bed he saw the soft peach whisper of dawn creeping into the desert sky. He had spent far too much time in this ancient city to expect a beautiful day. Yet somehow each morning was gentle. Shadows danced among the ancient minarets and mosques as the sun began its climb into the sky. Later it would burn with an intensity that had baked the stone buildings brittle and dry. The mornings held a promise which had teased men since antiquity. Hence the number of dissatisfied men that spent their days sitting in teahouses and dreaming of revolution.

Khalil had prayed, as he had been called to do. He felt the cold stone under his knees as he uttered the familiar words. Later the floor would warm. He would be long gone before that happened on this day.

Walking onto the street he smelt exhaust and rotting garbage. He didn't like this city with its guns and desperation. Khalil's mood was never good during his visits here. The Egyptian sun was beginning to come into its own, early though it still was. He could feel sweat beginning to break out on his back and under his arms.

His taxi was late – of course – he was in Cairo. But the driver was a mujahideen – so at least he was supporting a brother by hiring the tardy dog. Khalil kicked the dust beneath his feet in frustration. Then he watch it soil his already somewhat dirty shoes.

"Good morning, brother." A man pushing a cart. Ali, a Turkish juice seller, who had plopped into Cairo with the grace of a seal over twenty years ago. The neighborhoods were small and gossip flowed freely.

"Ah, Ali. Allah be with you my brother."

"And with you, Allahu Akbar."

"Allahu Akbar."

"You linger this morning."

"I am going to the airport." And now the whole neighborhood will know.

"Ah, where too, my friend?"

Khalil had studied him, trying to keep his mood light. He had no intention of providing a real answer. Spies were another commonality in Cairo.

"Ali is my father's name. Are you an omen, coming here as dawn breaks?" Khalil could feel his sweat now beginning to run down his back and dampening this thin white cotton shirt. Even early in the day the Cairo heat today was oppressive. Or was it the unexpected presence of another that had caused sweat to flow faster?

Ali studied him. His face was simple. He had a broad forehead and his skin was scarred by acne. He walked this street each morning yelling to announce his presence. But why so early today? Khalil now believed that Ali had been a warning sign – he should have turned back from his mission right then. Sent someone else to London.

"Ma'alesh, an omen? I am only a seller of juice." The cracked lips had broken out in a smile. The gap where his two front teeth were missing added a sincerity that his voice could not.

The gap between Ali's teeth was like the gap between the bars in his jail cell window. Yet neither of them would ultimately have any impact on his life. Again, Khalil asked himself – was he ready to die? Not that the answer really mattered. His body would bend to Allah's will.

XXXXX

George felt ill. He felt ill a lot these days. Everything now rubbed him the wrong way. Life was venturing far too close to adventure for his own peace of mind. "Hello", he felt like shouting. "Don't you have people who do this for a living?" But who would listen to him? No one listened to him. So he would have to accompany Khalil on this crazy mission to arrest a bomb maker. And sarin producer.

The nausea in his stomach intensified as he thought about the death sarin caused. Out of control twitching, vomiting, and other things he didn't want to envision. Luckily there was an antidote. But how quickly could the nerve gas kill you again? He would have to look that up on the Internet before he left.

Karen's head rested gently on her pillow. He should wake her to say goodbye. George was confident that everything would go wrong today– because wasn't that currently the direction his life was heading? And once something starts moving in one direction it was hard to break the momentum. Basic physics.

"I could die today, Karen." He spoke to the bathroom mirror a few minutes later. He had decided to spare his wife. Better for her not to remember him this way – morose and fatalistic. Of course, if he did die today she would regret not having had a chance to say good-bye. But truly, what were the odds of something going wrong? George chided himself. Or at least he pretended to.

He was going to be with some commando unit, from God knew what branch of some special service. All was under control. Right? He was part of a perverted video game monitored by someone above; another random piece in the puzzle. Hopefully less a pawn than his overactive imagination let him believe. Life really wasn't like a board game, was it?

He heard a sound and jumped. He really shouldn't be playing special agent. George acknowledged the obvious again and almost laughed at his jitters. Almost.

"George, why didn't you wake me?"

Karen's soft hair cascaded down, messy and full of knots. She looked somehow younger. Normally her appearance was so controlled and predictable. George just stared. His mouth wasn't capable of forming words.

"What's wrong?" He heard softness in her voice, and it made him feel like crying. Everything was all wrong. George felt the gulf between them. As he stared at her he caught a comfort from the iciness of her blue eyes. The light color had always been so distinctive. It was as familiar as his own body, yet it belonged to her alone. He grabbed her, pulling tight. Her thin body yielded into his. Thank God.

"Hey, what has gotten into you?" She spoke, but did not pull away.

"I don't want to do this. I really don't want to go to Los Angeles. It is just too much. Why can't they leave me out of it? Why do they need me?" His voice was strained and he felt weak. Why such trepidation now? He had been to worse places than Los Angeles. Like Baghdad.

"They probably need you to help control Khalil. They certainly can't trust him. You have gotten him this far. They need to make sure nothing goes wrong, right?" Her voice sounded normal, its tones not the least bit strained or uncomfortable.

"Right. Damned right." He answered her, trying to make his voice strong. Yes, he had already heard the explanation. Many times. He had argued extensively, trying to escape the trip. To no avail. Bastards. He suspected that his last minute pleas to God wouldn't help much either.

Still, at least he would be done soon – with this whole interrogation.

George's body strained with the anticipation of resuming his old life. He still hadn't pulled away from Karen. Why couldn't he just hide forever like this – being hugged by his wife in the bathroom?

He caught sight of them both in the mirror. He could only see the side of her face. She seemed patient. For now. He looked like a child. A big and scared child. Taking a deep breath he told himself, "Grow up. You can and will do this." That inevitable moment when we accept that we can't run away any more.

He pulled away and stared into her face – recognizing more things than he cared to admit.

"I'm sorry. I'm sorry for the many ways I have left you over the past few years. I'm sorry for hiding and trying to run. I'm sorry for not being stronger and facing my own choices. I'm trying so hard, but nothing seems to be working. And I know deep inside myself that I don't want to face the truth of what I see." He had surprised himself. Now was not the time to go crazy and pour out his soul. Or, perhaps there was never a better time than whatever moment he found himself in.

Karen, of course, just looked back at him. Her eyes registered surprise but she didn't respond. What else was she supposed to do? Even George couldn't imagine. Perhaps his irrational fear of imminent death had pushed him too far. But was it irrational? How had his life gotten so full of guns, bombs and the people who use them? His life. And hers.

"Oh, George." Finally she spoke. her eyes had gotten misty. The dew of morning. "It's okay. I understand. Really I do."

'Liar.' He thought. Words kept flowing, independent of his mind.

"No, it isn't okay," he said. "None of it has been okay. And I truly do apologize, for all of it. The strain, the stress. Please forgive me. You don't have to understand. I don't understand – this person I have become. Just forgive me." He felt strength returning. Everything was wrong. But it could get better. He would keep reminding himself of that. And the day would end.

He looked at Karen standing before him. Poor woman. She had just woken up and her white cotton nightshirt hung loosely around her shoulders. Her face was pale – after all she had no makeup on. Yet she looked together. She always looked appropriate and it drove him crazy. How did she do it?

"Stone Walls doe not a Prison make, nor Iron bars a Cage;" Karen's voice was strong, and echoed against the stone bathroom tiles. She reached out and brushed his cheek.

"Go free yourself, George. From the prison you have created for yourself. Perhaps after this you will be able to walk away."

"I will try." He whispered the words, and couldn't think of what else to add. He was clumsy, with no poetry to add in return.

"Thank you. I haven't given up yet, George. And I still love you." She kissed him on the cheek. Always appropriate. Some people just had it. "We will fix it. We will get back to where we were."

No, there she was wrong. Even Karen was wrong sometimes.

"It can't be the way it was. We can't go back. Nothing will ever be fully right again. But it will be okay. That I can do." He pulled her tight, and kissed her. Then he turned and headed to the door. He had someplace to be. And he was going to start facing his choices again, much as he didn't want to.

XXXXX

Omar heard the alarm clock. He heard it numerous times – courtesy of the snooze button – until he threw it across the room. Unplugged, it instantly went silent. The night before had been a late one and he wanted nothing more than to remain warm and curled up in bed.

Unfortunately, he was expecting Khalil that morning – presumably to discuss their forthcoming mission. The phone had rung late yesterday afternoon.

"Omar, this is Khalil. I will be at your apartment tomorrow at 9:30. We need to talk."

"Tomorrow? Where are you?"

"We will talk tomorrow. Barak Allahou Fik,"

"Barak Allahou Fik." Omar whispered back, surprised but deferential to orders.

Time was getting short – the plot was to unfold over the next week. Tension over the still unclear last minutes details had been gnawing at him, eating away at his routine and its resulting sanity. The meeting was here, where he lived. A new protocol, strange, and unprecedented. Then, only hours later, more visitors would come to pick up his bombs. His role was almost done.

Omar wanted to call someone, to clarify everything. Not possible. Khalil had been his main contact – a cell phone in Europe. Until it went dead, leaving him with just a silence that ended when the bomb went off in London.

Omar stretched his body, feeling blood seep into in his muscles. The first stretch of the day was so enlivening. What should he do as he waited? His movement must have woken the girl beside him. He felt her stir, and the lumpy comforter, which had rested snuggly around him, was jerked off his leg.

"Omar, what time is it?"

With the clock gone Omar couldn't have answered, even had he wanted to. But didn't she have a watch? Why did she have to bother him when he was still half asleep? He ignored her.

"Omar, why do you pretend you don't hear me. I'm getting sick of this. You can't treat me this way."

He watched, half interested, as Stacey pulled herself into a seated position and spat out her words. Her hair, that fascinating concoction of orange, yellow and burnished gold, tumbled halfway down her back. The sleep had disappeared from her eyes. Just like a woman. Give them a reason to yell and they could forget whatever they were doing only an instant before. So he yawned. How would she react to that?

"Look you chauvinistic son of a bitch, you can treat your women at home however you like. Here, we demand a little respect."

"No, here you get fucked by whichever man can afford to buy you dinner." He smiled, enjoying the game. She always got upset when he gave her a hard time. But she kept coming back.

Her brown eyes flashed in anger. The color was strangely light compared to his own. He thought he saw a small tear forming in the right one. If so, that would be the only weakness she would show. He knew her well enough to predict that much.

"Why do you think you can keep getting away with this crap? Do you think you are special?" The words fell from her lips as if they were the tears she was holding in.

So now what should he do? One thing he knew he couldn't do – under any circumstance – was apologize. He couldn't explain why. He just knew this was true.

"Stacey, my love, your anger excites me. I will never stop provoking it until you stop being so sexy when you are under its spell." He smiled again, this time adding whatever warmth he could muster.

She slapped him, hard, across his cheek.

Omar reached for her and pulled her tightly to his chest. He began to caress her back and softly brushed his lips across her shoulder.

"Asshole." Her voice was less certain now, and Omar felt some of the tension dissipating.

His lips moved to her mouth, and he pushed her down on to the bed, parting her legs as he did so. He heard a soft sigh as her body relaxed into his. Omar congratulated himself for saving what could have been an unpleasant situation. Why did she always touch him in new ways – yielding, yet making him fight so hard to win? Sometime, he would think through how he felt about Stacey, but not now.

XXXXX

The flight felt long. Sitting in the plane, Khalil sensed repressed energy, it filled the air like the chatter of an uninvited guest. Yet the flight itself stayed totally quiet; No one uttered a word during the hour to Los Angeles. When they landed, Khalil stood up gingerly. Much was about to happen. Stepping out of the plane, warm air hit him. It wasn't blistering as in Algeria, but it was warm enough to be familiar. And liberating.

This was it. From this moment on all spare wasted thought wouldn't be allowed. Not until he was safe; if he was ever really safe again. As if he ever had been. Did safety even exist?

George was never close, always keeping a body or a body's worth of space between them. He seemed oddly disengaged. And, indeed, this mission wasn't his normal intellectual pursuit. Khalil had known that George would come. Forced, of course. George's presence was exactly the kind of sloppy planning Khalil was counting on. Anyone with more than twenty-four hours to plan a mission would never send a civilian – even George. Khalil felt like warning George to stand back. But he wasn't going to tip off the enemy. Surprise is one of the most effective tactics in war.

Watching George, especially as he greeted the Los Angeles-based commando team, Khalil knew that George wasn't getting close to the action. And no one could force him – a softy like George would be allowed to fade away. Khalil wouldn't have to decide George's fate. Praise be to Allah.

"Fucking Commie bastard." Khalil felt a nudge in his back. Sean had tripped. Probably drinking too much the night before. It seemed to be a pattern. He could knock Khalil all he liked. Khalil was just glad that Sean's reflexes would be dulled for hours, hung over pig.

"Do you know what a Commie is?" Khalil couldn't resist a jab. He did keep any smirk off his face, trying to temper Sean's reaction. He had to act docile until he didn't anymore. That time would come soon enough. Keep the enemies' guard down.

Sean pushed him into one of the vans on the runway. George was already seated by the window. His eyes were hazy, perhaps opaque, like the eyes of a blind man. Still he gazed at Khalil. Did he see him?

"You look very nice." A faint smile was hinting at the edges of George's mouth. "I hadn't noticed you were wearing real clothes." And indeed he was. A woven ski cap was pulled down almost to his eyebrows. Likewise, his Levi's were rolled up above his ankle. He had shaved his beard however, and the sleeves of his grey t-shirt almost covered his hands. Devout dress may favor his mission with Allah's grace.

"It's been so long. You've never seen me in anything other than an orange jumpsuit, have you?" Khalil felt his pictures, still hidden in his sleeve. He noticed that his voice had turned tender. A strange feeling of addressing an older and respected relative tickled him. Strange. George was probably at least fifteen years his senior, something which had never before registered. Suddenly, George's fragility took him aback. Had this quality always been there, masked by their more adversarial roles? Now, theoretically, they were on the same team, well for a few hours. Of course, things weren't always what they seemed.

"No, and Khalil, I wouldn't notice you if I had. You look so different. Surprisingly so. You could just melt into a crowd right now. I don't think I'd be able to spot you."

Khalil refocused on George's eyes. Was he missing a hidden canniness or strength in George? Was he being manipulated again? Most importantly, did George suspect anything? Khalil, frustratingly, saw nothing, only blankness.

"Old man, I could recognize you anywhere," Khalil whispered. And he watched George smile. For the first time in forever, Khalil felt like a real person, not some shadowy prisoner being carted around the world at the whim of a government he hated.

XXXXX

Khalil wasn't relaxed. George knew it, as he knew the back of his hand and the curve of Karen's back. Khalil was a part of him now. And why should Khalil be relaxed? He was helping the United States government capture a colleague – guns at his back and five bombs facing him. He had to get the door open without triggering an explosion. Any sniff of trouble and the jihadist – on a mission from God — would blow himself and Khalil sky high. Was Khalil afraid to die? He had faced death many times before. Could someone become desensitized to the fear of death, knocking aside centuries of evolution?

But that wasn't it. George sensed something different in Khalil. And he was suspicious. Khalil was falling too easily – a docile lamb as events swirled around him. Why would a trained fighter accept capture? George breathed in deeply. The sun hurt his eyes. This time he wasn't going to let himself care. George was done; this wasn't his gig and he didn't want a part. For once, he was going to absolve himself of all responsibility. The raid wasn't his to lead. Asserting himself into the process would only cause problems anyway. All was off his shoulders. The world would have to stand by itself.

"Old man, huh." He replied to Khalil. "I guess I'm getting up there. Perhaps the worrying is aging me faster than I realize."

"You have no idea what real worry is." Khalil wasn't taking the bait by applying George's comment to the current situation. Which could mean…all sorts of things. Not my problem, George reminded himself.

"I know." George blinked. "Starving kids. Bombs. Death squads. I am very blessed, geographically, by my birthplace."

"How do you feel about death?" George asked. "That sharp look in Khalil's eyes as George continued speaking. One thing he hadn't been able to hide. Not ever. That alertness, the slight tensing of his features. All senses alive. Not so different from how he normally looked. But just different enough.

"I try to avoid it." Khalil answered. Noncommittal.

"And you have done well." George watched Khalil look away from him, toward Sean, then quickly back again. No point getting Sean involved.

"Luck, talent. Allah's will." Khalil sighed. The gesture was oddly modest.

"Luck runs out. Does God's benevolence?"

"You are crazy." Khalil wrinkled his brow, and George noted his control. Dealing with Khalil was like encountering a new animal. You could watch it, and learn about the grace Mother Nature grants certain species. But what happened when you got too close? Wild animals were unpredictable, especially when trapped. And Khalil also had a deadliness that was all too human. Only man kills for sport. George smiled, an effort to deflect the conversation. Now was not the time for debate. Or too much analysis.

"Is your bomb builder going to blow you sky high? Do you want him to? This isn't some sort of suicide mission is it?" George asked.

"I don't do suicide missions. If I did I would be dead long ago."

Khalil looked surprised as he replied.

"As would those you took with you."

"You are trying to antagonize me?" Khalil's eyes blackened. Outside the landscape whizzed by, harmless in its uniformity.

"No." George paused, thinking. What was he trying to do, really? He looked out his window again; Los Angeles rushed by. The too close houses. The hazy air that couldn't cut the sun's brightness. He could see the ocean in the distance. The bomber lived here, built bombs here. He experimented with sarin and who knew what else. Yet the freeway just stretched on, the cars lined up expectantly, as if someday they might move at a more reasonable pace. As if. The world went on oblivious to the murderous groups growing like weeds in its backyards.

George turned back to Khalil, who was now studying his shoes. Okay, fine. He did the same. Brown boat shoes. What an odd choice, like everything else today. The world was off-center.

"I'm not sure, Khalil. Once I thought that by studying people like you, I might be able to understand. But I can't. Antagonizing you won't help. I don't know what motivates you. I can't predict your actions or whether you can change. But my quest for answers, for understanding, never stops burning. Sometimes I even get glimmers of truth. Do you understand?"

Khalil was now watching George, not his shoes. "Don't ask so many questions, George. Don't try to understand. Survive. And don't take the world so personally; it isn't yours to control."

George felt as if he had been punched. Khalil's voice was surprisingly gentle today. Odd. But the message was a good one. What was he fighting for? Why was he always responsible, even when he had no control? Who put the burden on his shoulders? He had, of course. And as a psychologist he knew that doing so wasn't healthy. Emotionally. But perhaps physically, as well. Especially if you factored in things like high blood pressure.

George couldn't walk away, and he knew it. He couldn't stop his interrogations. At the cost of his career, his marriage, his peace of mind and, most of all, his sanity. He was here today, against his better judgment. He couldn't say no. His attempts were feeble, at best. When a burden appeared - he shouldered it. He couldn't stop terrorism, so he hoped to stop one terrorist at a time. But who the hell was he?

What other burdens was he carrying?

George looked at Khalil. Right, of course. But who was Khalil to talk? Look at Khalil's decisions.

"You too, Khalil. You too."

XXXXX

It was too late. Omar found his watch, and it had confirmed the awful truth. He had fallen back asleep; Stacey nestling into him. She, at some point, had disappeared. Judging from the sounds in his kitchen and the smell of coffee she was there. He wanted to blame her – had she not distracted him he would have been up long ago. Unfortunately, his irresponsibility was his own fault. He could recognize that much. Stupid alarm clock.

He pulled himself out of bed, surprised at how heavy and tired his body felt. It was morning, and he had slept well. How could he feel so sleepy, as if he had been drugged? The bitch hadn't slipped him something, had she? Perhaps she was a spy or other such spook. The FBI would be smart to follow him. Or was it the CIA? Omar couldn't remember. "Pigs," he whispered instead.

Well, he had to shower. He had a guest arriving soon and he couldn't greet his visitor without a shower. He could skip the shave. True believers kept their beards long, Allahu Akbar.

And, he hadn't prayed yet either. No one had to know.

A horrifying thought crossed his mind. What if his guest arrived while he was in the shower, and Stacey answered the door? That wouldn't do. She had to go. Now. Omar glanced at his watch. Well, he had a little time. He would send her home after he finished his shower and she finished cooking. The smell of food had subsequently wafted into the bedroom. No point stopping her – he was hungry.

After turning on the shower, Omar faced the mirror. He admired his body while waiting for the water to heat up. His buttocks were so firm, so high. The faint speckling of dark, wiry hair running along his backside accentuated the smooth muscles, drawing attention to their sinewy expanse. Jars of Nivea lined the counter. They held his precious chemicals. From them he could craft nothingness into poison. Stacey knew they held chemicals; she just didn't know which ones. Hiding his wares in plain view and never getting caught was exhilarating. What kind of giant playground did she think she was living in?

Omar stepped into the shower, feeling the warm water spray his body. So soothing. Omar wished he could linger – but today he didn't have that luxury. Work. A meeting. How often did that happen? He quickly shampooed his hair and rinsed it out. Then he used a brown sugar and vanilla body wash to rub the sweat and semen from his body. Turning off the water he grabbed a towel, drying himself as he wandered back into his bedroom.

Today felt like any other, but it was so much more important. What would he learn about his mission? Was his guest coming to provide the final details? Five bombs, simultaneous. What a glorious plan. Soon the United States would know what it felt like to be Israel. They were almost one and the same anyway. Now the Americans would understand the terror of bombs exploding, unrelenting. And everywhere. The damned were finally getting what they deserved. How he loved the drama.

What should he wear?

"Omar, are you coming? Breakfast is ready?" The musky, yet still feminine, voice was like his mother's. As a boy, choosing his clothes in the morning her voice had wafted in through his doorway. He always took so long. The pink shirt, the blue? If his father ever caught him, Omar would be beaten severely. Only girls got enthralled by clothes.

"Hurry, it will get cold." His mother's words, more desperate than he remembered, as he stood in front of his closet. Which shirt? Which was dignified enough for the first day of school? He had felt breathe on his back, frightening him to the core. His dad's breath never radiated warmth. It was the chill that descended before his father's palms began to slap. He could remember the crushing blows as they hit his shoulders. The memories stored in his body would last forever.

"This is for your own good. I'm making you into a man." The

voice, breathy, but eerily excited. Just like the voice his father used when speaking to his good friend Majiid. Majiid of the bazaar, Majiid of the magic, as his father liked to say.

"Omar, please." The female voice. It was soothing sometimes. But not now. Omar braced himself for the beating to follow. Then he realized he was alone. His father was back in Saudi Arabia, as was his mother. The voice was Stacey's. She had probably finished cooking, and was waiting for him. The air conditioner had sent the chilly breath that hit his back and sent him home.

Then, Omar heard the doorbell ring.

XXXXX

Would this ordeal never end? Time couldn't move slower, not even if it tried. Khalil just wanted to know his fate. Allah be merciful, death he could accept. The waiting was a hell unto itself.

Deep inside himself, somewhere in the recesses of his soul, Khalil knew that he wasn't ready to face the bitter sting of death. But his life wasn't in his own hands. That was the foundation of faith, something he had yet to renounce. Still, nothing in the Koran forbade him from fighting for his desired outcome. The Koran was a book of both prayer and war. He had been patient long enough. Too bad timing wasn't his to control. Now he had to sit and wait, his mind a buzz of activity while his body renounced movement.

Dressing that morning. The flight. The drive. His mind kept replaying other trips into the unknown. The fateful one to London. His first trip out of Algeria.

He had headed straight for the hills of Afghanistan, hoping to leave behind the chaos of Algiers. En route he had arrived late one night in Lahore. He was driven to a rundown house for a few day stay, allowed out only after sunset. He remembered the city as a nameless and faceless town, haunted by the deep shadows of a restless night. Banyan tree canopies hugged the wide boulevards. Eventually, he had been taken to a bus. Pulling away from the city's outskirts, Khalil had watched the landscape fade into black. Occasionally they had passed through a candlelit town, smelling faintly of sulfur. The blur of a night that he sometimes doubted even existed.

The driver had been uncooperative.

"Brother, where are you driving us?" Khalil had glanced around the minibus, observing the fear and confusion in his young companions' eyes. Most spoke Arabic, though their accents varied widely. One youth in particular had aroused his curiosity. He was small, wiry and covered in dark hair. Sweat had been pouring out of him, usurping everyone's air. Yet his face was that of a baby, not yet broken by whiskers. He belonged at school, not in a minibus careening toward the Pakistan/Afghanistan border. Twelve, perhaps thirteen. How could his parents let him come? Had they sent him?

"Brother, I asked you, where are you driving us?" Khalil had asked. Not even a grunt in response. No nod or acknowledgement. Just a back and skinny shoulders holding up a tattered blue t-shirt with a picture of Bob Marley on it. But no voice.

Khalil had turned in the other direction, facing the doe-like boy.

"And you, brother, why are you here this evening?" Khalil kept his voice down so as not to disturb two of the men, who had fallen asleep. He was unsure whether his words would frighten the boy or grant him permission to speak.

"Allah be praised, I am here to fight." The voice was in the process of changing and cracked with each syllable.

"How old are you, brother?" The murky landscape, defined only by shadowy rocks highlighted in the moonlight, whizzed by. A sharp turn almost toppled the small vehicle. Still, the moon shone, a perfect crescent. Its presence anchored Khalil.

But the boy didn't speak. He seemed paralyzed. Little did he know that the dangers he was speeding to face far outweighed those of the minivan.

"Brother," Khalil softened his voice, until it was little more that a whisper. "Why are you here?"

The boy moved, as if shaken out of his reverie. "I am here to be a martyr. Like my brother, who died a month ago? My parents sent me." The voice cracked. "I don't want to die. Sir, I don't want to die." Khalil couldn't see his expression because dark was so pervasive.

"Neither do I," Khalil had replied. "No, I don't want to die either. Not as my brother did, his blood staining the hot sand beneath his limp body." The bus once again took a turn – barely – almost sailing over another drop. "So, let us fight. We shall be victorious, for Allah." And he smiled at the boy; mimicking a bravery he hadn't felt. How does one feel brave when hurtling toward a fate unknown?

Khalil saw the boy's body a few months later. He had been castrated; lips cut out and his throat slit. A painful death. Still, he recognized him. A crescent moon-shaped birthmark took up half of the boys face – which he hadn't noticed until the van had reached daylight.

Was he himself ready to die? Why would time change his abhorrence of death? The van he was in kept moving, headed for Westwood.

XXXXX

The day was passing too quickly, much as George wanted it to end. The inevitable dread of something about to happen. Buildings blurred outside his window, their movement briskly matched his heart's pounding. He didn't know Los Angeles well. But he did know the neighborhoods around UCLA, and they had clearly arrived in Westwood, where the bomb maker lived.

Years ago, almost too many to remember, George had interviewed at UCLA. He had almost accepted a teaching position there. Karen had refused to move to Los Angeles. Would his life have turned out differently had his accepted that job? Perhaps he wouldn't have started studying terrorists at all. Would he still be careening toward what felt like a doomed destiny?

Why did he have to be so pessimistic? Perhaps it was from seeing bombs explode – leaving behind mutilated, burning stumps of debris. Or, this attitude could have developed after he became intimate with the men who made bombs in all their nihilistic glory. The raid may not go well. Even if Khalil kept everything above board. But why would Khalil do that – unless he trusted them? And only a fool would trust completely – anyone, ever.

"Hey, Khalil." George spoke up. They had fallen silent a while ago, each lost in his own thoughts. The traffic had stopped, which put them a few minutes behind schedule. Not my problem, George reminded himself. "Have you started making plans for your life after this is all done?" He reached for his seat as the van lunged forward with the breaking traffic.

"Right, there." Khalil ignored the question and instead pointed to a street sign. "Turn right, there." The driver took the turn, and then continued to follow Khalil's direction. George's question evaporated, leaving not even vapors behind.

They drove past an expansive veteran's cemetery, past a row of condominiums mid-construction. Then after a few more turns, and upon passing a row of two-story white apartment buildings, they parked, remarkably. How could fate ordain enough parking spots in Los Angeles now? Were the spot's a sign that God, someone's God, had blessed the raid? Or were they available because the neighborhood mainly housed UCLA students who were in class by 9:00 A.M. on a Wednesday morning?

Pitiful, George chided himself. Searching for signs from God. He had been reduced to a joke. Long ago, George had noticed that divinity's hand seemed passive.

The driver stepped out of the van.

"Stay here." He barked the order before banging the door shut. George watched him walk to the second van and then heard babbling. George observed him in rear view mirror as he talked to another man. Where would be the safest place to wait? His gaze wandered across the nondescript neighborhood, emptied, presumably, by the setup team. Not a barricade nor a person – other than their group – was visible. It felt like a movie set.

The safest place? How about Palo Alto? Why was he really here? A punishment for London? To keep Khalil under control; wouldn't a gun subdue Khalil more effectively? If something went awry George certainly wouldn't have time for analysis. Khalil was motionless. His eyes, in contrast, were darting around, scanning like an eagle looking for a mouse. Great. Hopefully he just wanted to save his own ass, not try something stupid. A grasp of the terrain was probably crucial when your neck was in a noose. A random death in a violent raid could always be justified. Especially when the deceased wasn't even acknowledged as being there.

George should probably follow Khalil's lead. Too bad he couldn't summon the initiative. His own passivity had turned grating. When had he ever accepted his fate before? Khalil seemed to be the only one with any fight in him. Perhaps a reintroduction to sunlight had energized him. Or, something else was going on.

"You okay?" George spoke to Khalil's profile, more to jolt himself out of apathy than for the response. Khalil seemed meditative.

"Are you praying?" George tried again.

Khalil turned to him. Even his speckled brown eyes looked peaceful. For the first time, under the direct sunlight, George saw burnished bronze flecks lighting up the more somber brown.

"I'm fine. Let's just get it over with," Khalil said. The voice was unwavering.

"My sentiments, exactly." George let sarcasm creep into his voice.

What was optimal? Right now he was safe, but overcome by an overpowering dread of the forthcoming events. But, after it happened – whatever 'it' was – he would be stuck with the outcome.

Khalil laughed. Humor overtook his eyes, though they still looked preternaturally calm. "You are just a rookie recruit, aren't you?"

"No, Khalil. I've been all over. We've discussed it before. I'm just not comfortable with these situations." And I am too old to learn.

"That is because you've always been a bystander," Khalil said. "You never had to fight. I have died many times over. But still here I am."

"I've died many times over, as well," George replied. "For me, it is just different. Other people's suffering and misery kill me. I don't detach enough." George stopped. What was the point of turning introspective with a killer?

"Good luck." George let that end his point.

"The worst thing that can happen is death. For me, that means martyrdom. I wish I could offer you more guidance, George." Khalil's face softened. "It is between you and your God." He whispered the words before turning his eyes to the window.

XXXXX

Omar raced out of his bedroom, almost tripping as he tried to pull on a pair of jeans. Tight, the way he liked them, was not an asset when trying to pull them up as you sprinted to stop your girlfriend from opening the front door.

Stacey was still in the kitchen – based on the bangs coming from that direction. Either she hadn't heard the doorbell, or he had been mistaken. Omar went to the door, and peered through his peephole. He would never have rented an apartment without one. No one was visible.

He headed back to the kitchen, almost crashing into a table as he pulled on his shirt. In his hurry, he was manic. But time was the issue; he had an important appointment. Nothing could go wrong.

"Did you hear the doorbell?" Omar watched her dishing scrambled eggs onto a chipped blue plate. She looked so beautiful. Her hair was still damp from the shower, taken while he was still asleep. It hung down her back, brilliant in its simplicity. She was wearing one of his white tank tops, the ones he used for working out. Her russet nipples were faint through the opaque material. She had tied the shirt in a knot around her middle exposing the white expanse of her stomach. How could he ever go back to girls who didn't exercise? The flesh here was so firm, almost taut. Some of his friends considered it too masculine for their tastes. He adored it.

"No, silly." She was standing by the stove, the metal shimmering from longstanding idleness. His kitchen was white. Well, the whole apartment was white. The landlord said the color made turning rentals easier. White was the cheapest color for everything. When one tenant moved out, the whole apartment would be redone in the same color. Of course, the carpets were all somewhat brown, as was the cheap Formica floor under Stacey's feet. Omar never bothered to ask why. He was just glad his chemicals wouldn't stain anything if spilled.

Stacey continued on, her voice husky yet feminine. It sent shivers through Omar. "That was the coffee machine, not the doorbell. You probably didn't even know that you had a coffee maker, did you?" She smiled languidly. He considered acknowledging her words. Instead, he focused on her buoyant mood. She had to go.

"Stacey, you must leave now. I'm expecting a visitor."

"Well, I want to eat first. Why is this visitor such a secret?" She peered at him belligerently. Omar was nervous. She wasn't going to fight him on this, was she? The meeting had to be private; the mission was imminent. He didn't have time for an argument.

"You must go." His voice was firm, and he set his face, trying to look stern.

"In a minute." She turned her back to him, and reached for another plate.

"I mean it." Omar glanced at his watch. Had he read it wrong before? The meeting time had passed ten minutes ago. Had he made a mistake in his haste? Where was Khalil?

"Stacey, are you sure that the doorbell didn't ring? Not even during my shower?"

She turned to face him, still angry. One quality they shared was a short temper. Usually, they both loved the passion their arguments provoked. Omar wasn't enjoying it now.

"It didn't ring. I said it didn't ring, and it didn't ring." Stacey glowered.

Just then, as if to prove her right, the doorbell rang.

"Stay here. You will leave in a minute. First, I'm going to get the door." Omar watched as Stacey, who was closer to the living room, walked towards the door.

"Stop, Stacey, I am warning you."

"You can't treat me this way, Omar. I mean it." She quickened her pace as Omar sprinted to catch her.

XXXXX

Khalil waited for Omar to answer the door. Men were positioned all around him. The layout of their positions was committed to his memory. Perhaps, unbeknownst to him, extra men were hidden in crevices or stashed on a roof, a precaution. Why trust Khalil? American pigs. Imperialists. How many men could it take to capture a rookie bomb builder and a jihadist?

He almost chuckled at his own joke. The answer wasn't simple when the target in question had five bombs. And chemical weapons. All about to be blown sky-high.

Adrenaline was flowing throughout his system, a high the body begins to crave. Fear had run to hide elsewhere. He was ready.

The candle burns. The flames touch the wick, they reach for the sky. Time moves to a rhythm beyond our own, ignoring us, our hopes and desires. We move, doing the best we can. Is there control? Who holds it? Always, we try to beat the flame. When it drowns in the melted wax, our chance expires.

The instant tingled throughout Khalil's body. Only moments before, he had studied the mission commander's eyes. Brad. Bob. Something like that. The man had been barking orders at him, his voice raspy from too many rough blows, not cigarettes. Tough, smart, but fighting to retain control of an ill-conceived and sloppy plan. Khalil had brought them to his own battlefield.

"Okay, Khalil, go up there, and knock," Brad said. "Get the guy to open the door then move aside, fast. You don't want to get knocked over when we storm the door. If you let him shut the door before we get there the building likely blows. You know for sure where he keeps all five bombs?"

Bob, Brad, whatever, had mottled skin and translucent green eyes. He was built like an action hero – a physique rarely seen in any other nation. How much time did it take men to get so burly? Why bother? He was dressed in black, as were his men. It was barely a uniform, really. Mostly just dark blending into darker. Who were they? Khalil knew they wouldn't answer his questions.

"I told you where. An armoire in the living room. He's under strict orders to keep them there – in case something happens to him before pick up." Khalil winked. He hated joking, another American trait, but the man's response would be worth it. "I would personally slit his throat had he not followed orders."

The implied camaraderie of Khalil's wink had to be infuriating. Still, Brad's face didn't change, not a flicker. These men knew about slitting throats. Tough. But flesh and blood nonetheless. Nothing a bomb couldn't rip through in a few seconds.

The two men had been sheltered by one of the vans. No groups larger than three allowed, too obvious. Not that the situation itself wasn't. The surrealism of it – the ordinary neighborhood with a swarm of gun-toting men in black. Khalil looked up at the apartment building standing not twenty feet away. Taupe, the shade of a polluted lake, with two stories housing apartments. Soon this ordinary neighborhood would be famous. Perhaps this would be only the first of many explosions. Hopefully, Khalil would escape and continue the war another day.

"Okay, then." Brad had glanced over Khalil's shoulder, craning his neck toward Omar's apartment. "It all seems simple enough. Remember, Khalil. Fast. I can't guarantee your safety if you don't get out of the way. Sean will be waiting. Go back to him and wait. If you try to escape he will shoot you."

Khalil glanced over at Sean. The guard did indeed have his gun pointed right at Khalil's stomach. A very painful death. Swine.

"Sounds good." Not that I will listen. Khalil then turned and headed for Omar's apartment. Apartment B, on the second floor. He rang the bell.

Standing at the door, he waited. He could hear muffled footsteps approaching. Soon he would start counting.

XXXXX

George just waited. He stood as far away from everyone and everything related to the raid as he dared. They ignored him. Who were these guys anyway? Special forces, SWAT, LAPD? No one had bothered to tell him, even after he asked. Repeatedly. George was the only one present without a gun. Except, of course, for Khalil. George's presence lacked any purpose. Why pretend otherwise? Too bad he didn't have a book to read. Might calm him down. Still, sometimes in life there is no escape.

Why couldn't he shake the sensation of dread? Like a cold hand running up and down his spine it lingered. Was he demonstrating the coward's reaction to danger or did his feelings arise from some long dormant survival instinct?

George watched Khalil ascending the steps to the apartment. The thin body moved with a rhythmic grace. Men didn't move like that in the United States, they lumbered more, their bodies more solid from better nutrition. Khalil's right hand rested on the iron railing, but not for support – the touch was too light. George saw a flash of movement cross in one of the apartment's windows. His stomach lurched. An urge to run shocked him, but he found himself rooted to the ground, his eyes obsessively refusing to turn away.

XXXXX

Omar raced to the door. He tripped, catching his balance by grabbing one of the curtains, ripping them from the rod. Stacey reached the door first. He watched her open it. A man stood there, an Arab. He was of medium height and thin. His eyes shone bright, perhaps from the surprise of Stacey. The face was dramatic, haunted, with a hooked nose and angular cheekbones and jaw.

Was this the great fighter Khalil? Omar's heart sped up as he knocked Stacey aside. He heard her crash to the ground.

"Go to the bedroom now." He tried to use a harsh tone. She went meekly — a surprise.

Omar felt giddy. His surroundings faded as he faced the man at the door. Omar bumped Khalil's shoulder in greeting. He felt proud, the great Khalil was honoring his humble abode. It was Khalil, right? The man was about the right age and exuded authority. Rumors about Khalil's death or capture had been circulating lately. Serpent's tongues speak harshly. The voice on the phone had been Khalil's for sure. The voice he knew. Now he was meeting the man.

"You honor me." Omar lowered his head to show respect.

"I am here to bring greetings from our brother Hamid in Lahore." The voice spoke in Arabic. It was rich, carrying a hint of melody. The sweet sound of memorized code words spoken in a familiar tone.

XXXXX

Time to start counting. Khalil watched the door swing open. It moved too fast – had no one taught this kid that life was about timing? Jerky movements killed the flow. Khalil had but a few seconds to relay his instructions before the door was stormed – all must be orchestrated precisely, not subject to fits and starts.

A young woman opened the door. Had Khalil not spoken to Omar the day before he would have panicked, wondering if the boy had moved. The girl's hair was a bright red. The commandos couldn't miss it. What would they do with their plan now? What would he?

Suddenly, the girl was pushed harshly away. His eyes met those of a young man just as hers vanished from view.

The young man was good looking and cocky. It must be Omar. "Go to the bedroom now." He spoke to the girl, his voice firm. Then he turned back, bumping Khalil's shoulder and part of his chest with his own. The greeting of the mujadeen was both aggressive and respectful. The gesture brought back to Khalil his time in the black rocks of the Afghan mountains. He willed himself to forget.

"You honor me." Omar spoke. Khalil replied with the code words, then proceeded with orders in Arabic. No spare time existed.

"In one and a half minutes exactly, ninety seconds, blow the building up. Can you do that? Answer quickly."

The boy's face registered panic. His eyes swelled in his face as it drained of blood. He began to tremble. Allah be praised. Why didn't they train these people better? Why don't I train recruits better? With all the money we spend, these morons can't replicate real warriors. The battlefield is where the bad are ruthlessly weeded out. This one has no such conditioning. We should have sent him to Iraq first. What now?

XXXXX

George watched the door open. He saw a flash of orangish-red. Was it a woman? A second later a young man was standing at the door, alone. He was dressed in jeans and a red t-shirt. He looked familiar. Had George seen him before somewhere? His brain began to calculate. Then he noticed the SWAT team, those positioned by the door, stop moving.

Suddenly, George could take no more. Why was a girl there? He lunged for a bush. Vomit was already spewing from his lips. His nausea wasn't dispelled, even after he finished. The sour taste polluted his mouth. His eyes went back to the scene unfolding across the street. What had he missed?

The SWAT team was still. Khalil had moved away from the door, which was closed. George heard a pop. Wasn't that the sound just before a bomb exploded? All was still silent. Unearthly silent. George bent over his bush and began to vomit again.

XXXXX

Omar stared at the man before him. The man knew the code, so he must be Khalil. He was telling Omar to blow himself up in one and a half minutes. Why?

"I am Khalil, my brother. We are surrounded. We are martyrs. But you knew that. Allah be praised, shut the door now and do as I say. Do not question the word of Allah. And look at your watch, now! Start to count, and I will meet you momentarily in paradise."

Omar swung the door shut. No, he couldn't question. He had wanted to die a martyr's death, right? Now wasn't the time to wonder if his choice had been wise. Why was the world spinning? The bombs, he had to detonate the bombs. Ninety seconds exactly. How long ago was that? He hadn't looked at his watch immediately, as Khalil had ordered. Had ten seconds passed? Dazed, he tried to focus on the exact time. Watch the second hand, he reminded himself.

Just then he caught a blur of red by the bedroom door. Stacey! She had watched the whole exchange. Luckily, it had been in Arabic. Meanwhile, he had forgotten her presence. What should he do about her? She couldn't stay, and she couldn't go. Well, he didn't have time to decide. He moved to the locked armoire containing the bombs. All five.

Stacey would have to stay. She should thank him for martyring her, too. It promised a rich afterlife for her and her family. Or did that only apply to Muslims? Well, he couldn't bother with remembering. He had told her to convert. It was her own fault if she hadn't listened.

"Allahu Akbar. Allahu Akbar." He muttered under his breath. He had much to do and only forty-five seconds (approximately) left. Complicated prayers didn't fit the timetable. At least he would be praying to Allah when he died.

His fingers slipped off the lock as he tried to open the cabinet. He retried the combination. If you messed it up too many times the lock became impossible to open. He took a deep breath, willing his heart to slow down, even if just a little. He tried again. Mercifully the lock opened, and he swung the cabinet open.

Ah, his babies. The bombs didn't look impressive. Their simple plastic containers had been chosen in honor of bombs long past. Yet inside each was a chamber for holding the deadly concoction of sarin and a high grade explosive – an impressive setup even for a brilliant chemist such as himself. However, his bombs didn't yet contain sarin. He had been planning to put the ingredients in, but hadn't done so. Two tests, Stacey, Khalil dropping by at the last minute. One mistake in filling the chambers would have meant instant death – so he hadn't done it. No matter, the bombs all held explosives. Omar began to fiddle with the cheap wristwatch attached to the detonator. It would trigger the explosion. Just then Omar heard a voice.

"What are you doing?" Stacey was behind him. Her eyes were popping out of her sockets. Why was he fucking a scientist, and a smart one at that? She could probably guess what Omar was doing. It was obvious to someone with her knowledge base. Or was it? Could a soft American, even one like her, raised on cartoons and superheroes, actually recognize a real bomb. Even if it was staring her in the face?

He turned, thinking of the seconds necessary to address her. He needed to conserve the few he had left.

"What are you doing?" She repeated it. Looking back at her eyes, which held a depth of horror he had never seen before, he knew that she understood his movements. Something tugged inside as he studied her. All he really wanted to do was run his fingers through the rivers of still damp, but always-vibrant hair. Did he love her?

"I love you." The words came out as barely more than a whisper.

"Then stop." She pleaded.

He turned his back to her. Their timing was off. Perhaps they would spend eternity together. Certainly that must be the meaning of paradise. But he couldn't touch her now. That would defile him in Allah's eyes. Not a good move. Besides, he had so little time, and a lot to do. He must not question the call from Allah.

XXXXX

"Get out of the way. We're storming the door."

Brad's face was red and seething. Count. Remember to count.

"Hey, stop. Don't do it," Khalil said. "Omar didn't trust me. He is calling to check and see if I am really who I say I am. I disappeared for quite a while. He was right to be suspicious." A blatant bluff. Even if Omar had wanted confirmation he had no one to call. The beauty of a decentralized network. Catch a functionary, and follow him to nowhere. Not that Brad could figure that out in 120 seconds. "In a minute he'll be back to open the door. But not if he sees you on the doorstep. His door has a peephole." Khalil gestured, slowly easing himself back down the stairs. Hopefully, Brad wouldn't follow. He had to storm the door; he couldn't risk Omar detonating the bombs. What a terrible job.

"No way, Khalil. We tried it your way. We are going in. I'm not giving the asshole time to do anything – not even check up on you." Rage smoldered in Brad's face.

"You don't get it. This guy isn't expendable. He's an expert chemist – a bomb builder and chemical weapons expert. He's not allowed to blow himself up for no reason. You're overreacting. Give me a few more minutes." Thirty-five seconds left. Khalil had to get down the stairs.

"Get away from the door, Khalil, or I'll shoot you myself. We are going in. No more taking chances." A swarm of men, big necked and mean-faced, stood behind Brad. There was barely room for Khalil to pass them by. He leaned into the iron railing,

Khalil shrugged his shoulders. "You're making a big mistake." See you in hell.

"Get your ass over to Sean, now."

Khalil nimbly navigated the cement steps. They would hurt if an explosion propelled chunks at him. Sean was waiting. His gun was still pointed straight at Khalil. The plan couldn't be going any better. Twenty seconds left. The sound of the door being rammed filtered down as Khalil leisurely strolled the last few steps toward Sean. Fifteen seconds. Khalil felt a flash of uneasiness. What if Omar messed up his timing? Was the door beginning to give? What if he didn't follow instructions?

Recruits had been known to back out. Suicide isn't so easy. Hence recruiting people that accept the inevitability of orders. Omar was an chemist – he better listen.

Khalil decided to ignore Sean, and headed to George instead. Poor George, he didn't belong here. Khalil smelled vomit in the air. George? Time to be tested. Funny how fate could control life. Well, if George were smart and stayed back, he might live. If not, Allah be praised, what can you do for an infidel?

Out of the corner of his eye Khalil saw Sean's face register surprise and then rage. Who walked away from a man waiting for you with a gun? Only the most foolish, deranged or deadly.

XXXXX

George watched Khalil in disbelief as he argued with the team leader. What was the man's name again? Then his eyes followed Khalil as he sauntered down the stairs after apparently losing the argument. Khalil walked toward George though they both knew he was supposed to go to Sean, the guard in charge. What was Khalil doing?

The men at the apartment door had put tape around it. Was that to protect fingerprints? One of them was aiming a gun at the door handle. Or was it pointed at the lock? George couldn't be sure. Their attempts to force it open by ramming hadn't worked. His stomach was empty; otherwise he would probably be vomiting again. Still, Khalil kept calmly heading in his direction.

George remembered leaving Karen that morning – the one thing that day which had happened as it should. Khalil kept getting closer.

XXXXX

Horror. Stacey's face registered horror. Omar ignored her and continued jiggling with his wires, forcing himself to do Allah's will. Events weren't supposed to be like this. He should be recording a goodbye message. The film would have declared his intentions and shown him as a hero. Then the world would see his supreme devotion to Allah. Instead, he was being given ninety seconds to explode a bomb. No sarin, no message. Would he still get the glory that is a martyr's due?

Omar registered noise. Stacey was talking. She lunged at him, coming out of nowhere. Who did the bitch think she was? Didn't she realize the importance of his mission? Omar raised his arm and knocked her away. She cried out, but he just continued fiddling with his wires.

The bomb's artistry was sublime. It was simple, compact, but powerful. Omar had always been a good student, and this bomb was the culmination of so much time perfecting his craft. He looked down. The delicate wires weaved carefully through the device. Overriding the timer was simple, and the next thing to do. Slowly, watching Stacey out of the corner of his eye, he began to move the watch's hands. He stopped for a moment, transferring his right fingers to delicately maneuver a wire. It had to fit right in there. It did.

"Stop, you must stop." Stacey was crying now. Tears were streaming down her face. She was staring at him. Horror or perhaps betrayal had commandeered her features. How many seconds did he have left? Then Omar felt Stacey's hand grasping his finger, the one holding the wire. She better not try to stop him physically. He would quickly disable her – they weren't even a close match; he could crush her. Suddenly, surprising him, she pulled back.

He sensed her presence just above him. Then she began to move, running for the door. If he tried to stop her he wouldn't be able to detonate the bomb on time. He let her go. She didn't have enough time to get help. Her time was up.

Stacey was a smart girl. Dating him had obviously been a lapse of judgment – no doubt about it. Did she have a chance of surviving? Could she run fast enough to escape the bombs deadly fingers, Omar wondered? Not likely.

XXXXX

Five more seconds. Five more steps. Khalil sensed Sean's gun. It had followed him as he walked down the stairs. It continued to trail him as he walked to George. Of course he'd ignored Brad's instructions. They weren't for his benefit. Sean wouldn't shoot him because he went to George. He would threaten, but so what. Sean would be too scared of George – who would complain if Khalil was shot doing no harm. Moreover, Sean actually seemed to respect George.

George eyes were round as he watched Khalil getting closer. His face was troubled, yet accepting. The faint smell of vomit still lingered in the air.

"Hey, Khalil, you fucker…get over here." Sean was moving now, pistol cocked. It would take him between two and three seconds to join them.

"I'd rather wait with my buddy, George," Khalil said. Get a dialogue going. Distract them. The element of surprise should never be underestimated. Omar had eleven seconds – then his own work would begin.

Sean was sweating. He wasn't holding up well. Overweight, out of shape, hung over again. And bulky. Bulk — physical or mental – always got in the way. The symptoms of the decadent west showcased in one man.

"Relax, Sean. Let him be. You're the one with the gun – join us here, in the shade. Forget the histrionics for now." A delicate voice had spoken. Calm, in a volatile situation. Shocked, Khalil turned to George, who always managed to surprise him. Khalil had already discounted him, vomiting in the bushes. Yet, now, the man was alert. George wasn't a seasoned fighter, but he hadn't broken when plans went awry. Good to know. Never underestimate the enemy. Six seconds.

Sweat seethed across Khalil's body. It framed his face, ran down his neck, and to the underside of his arms. The body doesn't forget what danger feels like.

XXXXX

What the hell was going on? Things weren't going as planned. The door was shut, Khalil was by his side and the commando team was still busy at the apartment door. The lock hadn't given; was it reinforced? George heard Brad's voice. "Everybody pull back – this has taken too long. Pull back to positions."

The men began moving down the stairs, guns cocked. Plan A had shifted to plan B after plan A went haywire. In the same stoic manner they were now presumably beginning to execute plan C. Impressively, they had predicted that events could go so askew. How efficient. Now if they could only control the bomber.

Sean had sidled up to Khalil. His gun was level with Khalil's gut. His caution seemed melodramatic. George protested, but diplomatically. "Sean, you make me feel secure. I'm glad to have you. But, please, be careful with that thing." George's attempt to lighten the mood fell like an anchor. Neither Sean nor Khalil moved a muscle.

Then, the guard blinked. His red eyelashes brushed the bone under his eye socket. George noticed sweat on his face. Shifting his glance to Khalil he saw the same wetness. They were all nervous. Sean's shoulders settled into his backbone, and George caught a waft of body odor. The man was an oaf. But, his eyes had brightened with the compliment. He probably didn't hear them much – poor bastard. Never the quickest, he finally responded.

"Thank you, doc. That means a lot to me." George was touched that he actually seemed genuine. Sean was probably the only man present who actually ever meant what he said. Turning to Khalil, George put Sean out of his mind – didn't matter, did he? Well, not at this moment.

"Why did you leave?" George asked Khalil.

The man shrugged. "They told me to."

George was about to follow up with a more specific question. So typical of the asshole, being cagey. If the mood weren't so tense George would have anticipated it – Khalil liked to play games. Before he could articulate his concern his eyes caught a movement. The apartment door was opening. He saw a flash of red? What was it? A woman's hair.

A loud roar pierced George's ears, deafening him for an instant. The earth jumped, almost knocking George over. A rush of heat followed. A blue light illuminated the apartment building before it disappeared into a flaming swirl of red and orange. Time no longer moved forward as his body stiffened. He heard a gasp as it escaped his lips. Was it really his?

Before his body sensed it coming, debris hurled toward him. Body parts, wood, stucco, and other unidentifiable chunks spewed through the air as the building hid behind a cloud of black smoke. One beautiful orange flame leapt up into the air, clearing a path for itself. George's body refused to respond to the chaos around him.

For what seemed like minutes, but could only have been a second, the neighborhood fell silent. Then, the wail of a car alarm filled the murky air. The streets should have been cordoned off fifteen minutes ago. Hopefully that part of the plan had succeeded.

A harsh chemical smell, mixed with smoke, assaulted George's nostrils and stung his eyes making them water. The devilish perfume awoke him from his stupor. What was mixed into that bomb? Please let it not contain sarin, he prayed.

George heard choking next to him. Were Sean and Khalil all right? Had either been hit by random projectiles? As George turned he was horrified by what he saw.

Khalil had Sean in a headlock, his right arm crushing the larger man's windpipe. The guard's gun was nowhere to be seen. Sean's face was red. His tongue jutted out of his mouth and his eyes bulged like those of a Halloween ghoul. The man's breath was coming in chortling gulps.

"Don't do it." George heard his voice, surprisingly strong. He had expected it to crack or come out in a whisper.

Khalil looked confident. No, he looked triumphant. His brown eyes glowed, lit by adrenaline and perhaps the comfort of familiarity. This was what he did – wasn't it? Fighting, detonating bombs, crushing a man's neck. Khalil had come home, right back to where he started. And, Khalil had won.

"Don't do it. You don't have to do it. Run, I won't try to stop you. Just go." It was a plea to save Sean's life. George had been the one who insisted that Sean, not GI Joe, come today. If Sean died, then George would be guilty forever. Please, Khalil, please. His eyes begged. "He doesn't deserve to die." None of them did.

Khalil just smiled.

XXXXX

Pulling his arm tighter, Khalil felt the crack as he crushed Sean's windpipe. It wasn't a question, whether or not to spare the guard. Keeping him alive was too dangerous. That was all that mattered at this point. Safety, and freedom. Sean, however, was being paid to resist.

And, quite frankly, it was payback time. Kufr, infidel. Khalil had never liked Sean.

Khalil let the body fall with a thud. Sean's head crashed onto the ground. Limp, but not yet lifeless. The flesh was still hot.

"Goodbye, George." Khalil held Sean's gun in his hand. He fired, a bullet straight to the chest.

Then, Khalil turned to run. A bullet flashed by him, missing him by an inch. A sniper had obviously survived the bomb. What an unpleasant surprise. Khalil heard the familiar hum of another bullet. He jumped quickly. No one had mentioned snipers so Khalil had no idea where they were positioned. Khalil fled, zigzagging away. Hitting a well-trained man wasn't easy. Khalil could outwit one sniper. Allah be praised, let there only be one.

He weaved between the parked cars. The sniper's bullets chased him. Everyone else was most likely dead. Omar – rookie that he was – had succeeded. He heard a dull plunk when a bullet sank into metal. Move quickly, but not stupidly, he reminded himself. In moments the police would arrive. Praise be to Allah for his civilian clothes not his normal neon orange jumpsuit. Khalil looked ahead, noticing some cars stopped at a traffic light. He should steal one; but it was complicated in Los Angeles, where most people locked their car doors.

He wanted to risk a glance back at the mutilated apartment building. He couldn't afford such a luxury. Each second must be channeled into survival. The odds weren't exactly on his side. Still he felt confident. He had survived so much worse.

XXXXX

Khalil held Sean's gun and pointed it straight at George's chest. The guard was a limp mess on the grey concrete. Tears blurred the smoky flames raging just past Khalil's shoulder. George's nose tingled as he stifled a sneeze. The buildings around him sharpened in their definition as their surroundings faded behind them. George heard a roar and saw red spatter across Khalil's shirt. Of course Khalil had shot him.

Weightless, George felt his body being flung back, moving beyond his control. He struggled to retain hold of something physical but instead found himself staring up at a lone cloud in the sky. Hadn't the crystal blue expanse been clear earlier?

Yes, the sky had been empty before, the blue a stunning robin's egg color. The cloud continued its flight, now that it had been released to run free. No, George himself was the one in motion, his arms outstretched though he didn't remember why.

George felt his head hit the pavement. Only at that instant did pain flash through his body before the cloud disappeared.

Everything had to end this way, didn't it? The day had been wrong before it even started; never accept one last assignment. Never meet an enemy on his own terms. The list of nevers would go on forever, without him. Whose God had spoken, words crushing in their clarity, empty in their meaning?

XXXXX

Khalil pondered his options. If he stole a car he would eventually have to abandon it. The authorities – upon finding it —would then know which direction he had headed. How long would that take? Something could be said for just getting out, fast. Too bad he wasn't in a city where people walked. Pedestrians stood out like lone trees on a prairie in west Los Angeles. If only he had time to rip his clothes and smear dirt across his body. Then he would look homeless and no one would see him. How long before the streets were being combed in pursuit?

So much easier to disappear in the countryside with its nooks, caves and bushes. Here there would be no peace until he reached a safe house. Luckily, there were many of those nearby – his brothers were everywhere. So many young men willing to fight the great United States.

The closest one was in Brentwood; if it was still there. Could he make it? The house was a mile or two at most. Not far, but who could guess about the marauders pursuing him. What competence level was he fighting? Escapes were always risky, and his options almost non-existent. "War is such that the supreme consideration is speed." He took Sun-Tzu's advice, and moved.

Khalil changed direction, and headed toward Wilshire Boulevard. Allah be praised, he would be an easy target on that huge expanse of open road. First, pass the freeway entrance and exit, then eventually he would reach some shops. Well, Allah had blessed him with success thus far today. Perhaps his luck would hold.

Khalil saw a woman in front of him. She had long, flowing blonde hair and was pushing a baby stroller.

"The itsy bitsy spider...." He heard her gentle voice filling a small bit of air.

Wasn't that George's song? Poor George. He should have stayed far away from the men with guns.

She moved gracefully, ambling along the sidewalk in the heat. Did Jennifer walk that slowly now, her hair blowing behind her? This woman wasn't so different from Jennifer with her blue jeans and lean legs. Why was he risking even one passing thought about Jennifer?

As he got closer her head whipped around. He saw a glimmer of fear in her round, brown eyes. They were alone on this stretch of the sidewalk.

He smiled at her – extending the normal American courtesy. He had no reason to scare her. She couldn't have been safer. His only business was to hurry. Her eyes registered his friendliness and she smiled back. Her smile was lopsided and her lips were thin. She continued to shield the baby stroller with her body as he passed her. Later, would she see a picture of him on the television news and recognize him - a terrorist walking within arms' length of her baby?

"Good afternoon."

"Same to you." And he was gone.

How would the news describe today's events? They couldn't report the truth. For so many reasons. He turned a corner, and picked up his pace. He was going to make it.

Many years ago, he hadn't felt so confident.

# || CHAPTER SEVEN - FREEDOM

Khalil had arrived, back to where his life began. Algeria. He had escaped again, leaving behind only his captor's mangled bodies. Omar, Brad, the girl. Had any of them reached the heaven promised by their chosen God? And George. What about George?

He wiped sweat from his eyes. It pooled like tears and misted his eyelashes.

The sun felt hot. It cast a brilliant glare across the landscape, obscuring things beyond recognition. Dust flew with each of Khalil's footsteps. The air smelled of rotten fruit, spices and exhaust. Khalil could almost make out the familiar hut as it came closer. A starved and rat-like dog ran toward, him then scampered away.

A jumble of memories replayed in his mind, as always happens to people approaching a long absent childhood home. Some of the memories were happy, many not. He had walked this same path when he carried Hassan in his arms to rest at the door ahead. The oppressive heat now was exactly as it was then.

How long it had been since his last visit to his mother and Algeria? Ten years at least. No one had been able to force her out of her hut. Nor would they dare while he lived. Justice was swift and absolute here.

The broader neighborhood surrounding the hut was unfamiliar. His childhood shops and houses were gone, replaced with larger buildings. Wasn't that happening everywhere – tearing down the old to make way for the new? The new was always so much larger. And louder in all senses of the word. Globalization.

Dust had already claimed the new buildings, as the desert always will. Specks of sand filled crevices and lightly frosted the rest. The street was crowded, particularly near a busy fruit stand. Yellow mangos dominated the stand, leaving room for only a few green oranges. The fruit was un-dyed, and looked completely unlike the fruit he had left behind in the west.

This world seemed unreal, with its smells, noises, heat and throngs of people. His home, so long abandoned, had become mythical.

Everything had started here so long ago. The streets had been washed clean by blood, his trails fading into nothingness. What sort of trail would he leave today? Hopefully, none.

Many of his mother's neighbors would happily turn him over to the police – to torture, perhaps even execution. The community was sharply divided. Some would hide him. He could trust no one - too much blood had been spilt on both sides. Vengeance still held sway over village life.

Yet he had decided to come home – for a very quick visit – in spite of the risk. Life was dangerous after all, wasn't it? A bomb could explode anytime, anywhere. And did. But home was a haven, when he allowed himself one. Khalil wanted to feel his mother as she held him. Part of him wanted to cry on her shoulder. He wouldn't. But he would hold her – for as long as she would permit it. He would joke with his sisters, and laugh with their children. And he would share his stories of adventure and intrigue. What a life he led. They had never left Algeria.

Then he would leave. And that would be that. Or would he decide to visit Jennifer next?

XXXXX

The sunlight woke him up, piercing his eyelids as it came through the diaphanous white curtains. George studied Karen, still asleep. Her chest rose with each breath. She was like a child, really. Her body small and slight.

They had been spending a lot of time together. Finally. The bullet lodged in his gut had meant long hospital days for her and a lot of pain for him. Even with the morphine and whatever other painkillers they had dripped into him, his life hovered.

Had Khalil meant to kill him? Surely he was a better shot than to miss the major organs. Well, that dilemma was best forgotten: George would never know for sure. He certainly wouldn't conveniently run into Khalil in the supermarket.

Karen opened her eyes.

"What time is it?" Her voice was husky, but it wasn't angry or dismissive anymore. Nothing like a brush with death to rekindle old bonds.

"Around 5:30. A little after." George winced as he turned to look at her. The wound hadn't scarred over yet, and it bothered him every time he moved. At least he was alive to complain.

"You couldn't sleep?" she asked. If only she knew that the light had woken him – she would probably buy new curtains. Karen's face was creased from the pillow and it had an early morning puffiness.

"No, my dear. I woke to the sound of birds." A flash of confusion crossed her features.

"You're right, George. I hear them." She replied excitedly. Amazing that he could now get enthusiasm out of her. Indeed, there really were singing birds outside their window. "Are you okay? Do you need more medication?" Concern crossed her features.

"Maybe I'll take a pill later, but I'm fine," he said. "You know, I think people get weeded out in their 40s. If we make through that time period, there isn't much the world can do to us." He said.

"George, I didn't mean fine at that level. I meant the bullet hole." She paused. "Still, you do have a point. But, you're ignoring what we do to ourselves. That never stops." She lifted her head and rested it on her elbow. "You know what I mean?" The sun shone across her, lighting her like an angel. His angel. The ecru walls provided a serene backdrop. Sometimes an absence of color is just right.

"I'm going back." He had to tell her. Sooner was better than later, if he was going to leave her again.

"I figured as much." Karen said. Still she leaned on her arm, not moving. The white sheets holding her in an embrace. He wanted to touch her, but felt too much the betrayer, yet again.

"Come with me." He still had a chance didn't he? Why couldn't he take her with him this time? Why should he fight his war alone? "Write a book about what you see. Start paying attention to what men say while they are alive, not reading them after they have died. Haven't you always wanted to write a book, not just academic papers?"

Karen smiled and shifted higher. George saw the gentle freckles that dotted her arm. "I have never wanted to write a book. I don't want more than what I have. I am not an idealist the way you are. But perhaps I will try it. The university owes me a sabbatical. Where should we go?"

"Wherever they need us the most." George reached out, and brushed her cheek.

To information or to sign-up to receive information about the sequel, please visit www.meganlisajones.com

www.ingramcontent.com/pod-product-compliance
Lightning Source LLC
LaVergne TN
LVHW010557100826
845148LV00014B/2741
*9780976861768*